Mover

By: Christopher Alan Griffin

Table of Contents

Prologue:

"Speak," said one of the soldier's stepping closer to their captives..

A sea of armor circled two kneeling men. Several spears hovered mere inches away.

The two men knelt at the center of the circle of warriors, uncertain of their fate. The soldiers' golden armor glistened in the noon sun. Their helmets obscured the faces within.

"Him...He made me bring him here," said one of the captives, raising his weak arm to point toward his fellow prisoner.

His words brought the spears closer.

"You are not the one who came before?" A voice pierced the air from behind the spears. A few of the soldiers parted to allow through a soldier wearing armor with intricate engravings. The soldier observed the two intruders before him. The frail, older prisoner, his long hair unkempt, wore ragged robes. A meticulously groomed young man knelt next to him, eyes closed, with a small smile on his face. The young man wore a ridged black bodysuit that responded to his smallest movements. The old man was shivering, while the young man was in a world all his own.

The officer advanced closer to the men as the captive's bodysuit reacted further. Now, the skin of the suit appeared like shifting sand, swirling with chaotic intensity.

"Of what is that suit made?" asked the soldier, his voice growling from behind his faceplate.

"It is made of the earth," the young captive replied.

"I know of nothing on earth that moves like that. Of what is it made?" repeated the soldier. His growl grew louder.

"Based on your limited knowledge, that would be difficult to explain."

The officer towered over the two. "A spear may seem limited to a gun, but they can end life all the same." The officer raised a hand to the army at his back.

5

"I have come for Atlas!" said the young man.

"Adam, please," interrupted the old man, who struggled to face him. The spears inched ever closer.

The name caught the soldier's attention.

"Adam? I know that name."

"Yes, that is my name. The time has come for Atlas to be passed on."

"Passed on? You mean stolen," stammered the soldier. "Our people fought for this island, for ourselves. We knew one day someone would come for Atlas as we came for our predecessors, and someone before us. Should you win, the time will also come when someone will take it from you, Adam," said the soldier.

"Life is fleeting; why should this be any different? Yet we still make the most of the time we have," replied Adam.

"Will anything be left of us?" said the soldier.

"Did you leave anything of the ones who came before me?" asked Adam.

"No." The officer took a step back. The soldiers around him started to fill back in. "How did you find this city?"

"Him," said Adam, gesturing to the old man at his side.

The officer studied the old man closely. "You are not the one who came before? Who are you?"

The old man looked to Adam, who said nothing. "I...I...am Crantor. A disciple of Plato."

"He passed the knowledge to another?"

"Plato is dead," snapped Adam.

"I will not see this place end!" The officer began retreating amid the horde of soldiers.

"Everything ends," replied Adam.

"Our army numbers in the thousands. How many more have you brought?" quipped the soldier.

"None."

"Goodbye then, Adam," cracked the soldier as he disappeared into the sea of golden armor. The path closed behind him.

Adam raised his hands in front of him, palms down. A tremor surged below the feet of the army. The quietness of the air was deafening

"With all your infinite power, why is genocide the only way?" asked Crantor.

"Once my goal is complete, this genocide will never have taken place. All this will be a faint memory of a past that never was."

His suit generated thousands of ripples across its surface. Tears filled Adam's eyes as he flipped his palms face up. All the rocks and stones of the earth emerged from the ground and launched into the sky. The air cracked like thunder. Crantor clung his hands to his ears, desperately trying to stifle the sound. The stones ripped through the soldiers, killing them instantly. The bodies of the soldiers fell to the ground around them. The moment seemed to end before it began. Silence returned once more. Crantor curled up tighter on the ground, trembling.

Adam stood up amid the endless number of soldiers' bodies as his emotions took hold. He had known for years what he must do. The thought of the moment to come filled his mind with doubt. The tremor in his right hand was returning, and he clenched his fist to hide his vulnerability. The image of her face flashed across his mind as he tried to focus on the task at hand. As he looked ahead at the brilliant city before him, knowing what he must do, her name brushed across his lips .... *Eve.*

Chapter One:

The Telegram

"Seven forward, three to the right."

Counting the heads on the sidewalk in front of him, Kori spotted his target. He had to wait for the opportune moment, and he would have him. Three weeks had passed since Myles had stolen the canister. Three weeks of waiting. *What was the goal, the purpose?* He could intercept Myles at the cafe four blocks up and one avenue over at 11:17 a.m. At that moment, no one on street level would be looking. That would be his opportunity to use Atlas to get Myles to a secure location for questioning. *About as straightforward as a day ever gets,* he thought.

Myles was a predictable runner. He had tried several times to use the device at the same location. They say the definition of insanity is repeating the same action and expecting a different outcome. Myles is the personification of that concept. *A typical corporate job.*

This place was chaotic enough to keep Kori's mind distracted from most of his own thoughts. He needed the escape from the voice in his head telling him to leave and never return. A voice screaming at him to act on his anger, to seek revenge on the one who set him down this path. The name of the man responsible was on the tip of his tongue, but he refused to say it. The name was poison in his mouth so he glanced around him to buy a few more seconds of distraction.

The lady about to pass him caught his eye. Every time he redid the day she would bump into him. He had examined her past once on another job. As Kori was mid-thought, she peeked up to meet his stare. As their eyes met for a moment, she gave a quick smile. It was amazing how simple someone's life could look from the outside. Had he been anyone else, all they would ever know of her was that smile.

His thoughts drifted to Serena, and the anger returned. His attention strained to get back to the task at hand. Myles was still in sight. He was still on time.

The next person Kori observed was a little boy standing by the newspaper stand. The boy stood with his eyes closed, signing with pride atop a small egg crate while his father sat on the ground playing guitar. Was he really on this avenue already? He smiled and stopped for a moment to relish the experience. He was on schedule with Myles and could spare a few moments. This boy was a legend in the country music world. In seven months a record executive would be walking right by here and witness the boy singing. He would go on to win many awards and go down as one of the top country artists in history. It was a touching sight, a glimpse of bright things to come in that boy's future.

Kori was lost in the moment until he realized he had only ninety seconds until contact with Myles. He fished a few coins out of his pocket. All he had were several coins from 2130, a dime from 2047, a gold piece from 1732, and finally a few quarters from 2003. Kori took the quarters and tossed them into the open guitar case. As he went to put the rest back into his pocket he paused. He turned and took the 1732 gold piece out. This should help things out a bit, he thought as he tossed that in the case too. He didn't know the exact value of the coin, but he knew it would be enough to help them out for a while, a kind gesture from a stranger in time.

As Myles turned the final corner heading toward the cafe Kori began to close the gap between them. Up until now he had stayed thirty paces back. Moving to within fifteen paces, Kori turned the last corner. He could see Myles constantly checking each face that passed him, not sure if any one of them was a mover. He was checking either side of him, waiting for a strike. Off in the distance the cafe sign could be seen, growing larger and larger as they approached.

Kori reached into his pocket and pulled out Atlas, anticipating its imminent use. As he closed to within ten paces a sudden chill came down Kori's back; something was off. His paced slowed to a stop at the sensation. Kori kept his glance at Myles, still looking around at each person who passed. Something was different. He was being watched.

He looked up to the windows to see if maybe he had miscounted the number of people looking out the window at that moment. It wasn't up there, but something was definitely not right. Kori checked across the traffic-filled street, looking at each window to see if anyone was taking notice of him. Then he saw him.

A stranger in a white hoodie was keeping pace with Myles from across the street. Kori couldn't see his face, but he knew the man was watching Myles. *Runners don't work in pairs,* he thought, returning Atlas back to his pocket for the time being.

As they got a few doors down from the café, the hooded man turned to cross the street. He was a young man, maybe late twenties, possibly thirty; he was clean-shaven, although his hoodie looked very dirty. *Maybe he'd stolen it to conceal himself.* Kori studied what he could of the man. His anger crept back into him momentarily as he strained to keep his composure.

The hooded man closed on his target and grabbed Myles. He spun him around at the exact point where Kori had originally planned. Kori quickly scanned the street to see everyone had turned away for that briefest of moments. He thought for sure the man was going to snag Myles and take him away, but he didn't.

The hooded man was saying something to Myles, but with his back to Kori he couldn't see what. Myles looked shocked to see him, so they probably didn't know each other. Myles didn't say a word as the hooded man spoke to him. This couldn't be good.

Kori ducked behind a nearby cart to keep himself out of view. As he talked to Myles, the hooded man pulled an old-looking, battered and worn, envelope out of his pocket. Myles carefully opened it and start to read what was inside. Whatever it was, Myles turned white the more he read. When Myles was done he folded it up and gave the envelope back to the man, then the two started walking again in the same direction down the street. Kori couldn't let this go on any longer. It was time to move things along.

Kori walked much faster, gaining ground to catch up to the two. When he was about twenty paces behind them, the hooded man looked over his shoulder right at Kori, no expression on his face, then casually turned his head forward again. *Did he recognize me?* Kori searched his own memories for a similar face, but didn't come up with an answer.

They approached a large glass office building that reached high into the sky. The hooded man leaned over to Myles and gestured toward it, and, immediately, the two of them darted towards the entrance. Kori knew that this meant trouble, and things could get out of hand quickly.

As they reached the front of the entrance, suddenly the hooded man grabbed Myles and pushed him toward the doorway, both looking directly at Kori as they disappeared inside. Kori stood in front of the door for a moment to brace himself for a prolonged fight. He heard screaming and several gunshots from the inside. He took one breath and launched himself through the door.

Kori came through the door and immediately had to stop. Both the hooded man and Myles stood there with guns in hand, and the hooded man had a hostage. The rest of the lobby patrons were on the floor. Some were wounded, others quietly lay face down, looking frightened

"I told you there was a mover on your tail," said the hooded man, readjusting his grip on the handgun he had pressed into a teenager's head.

"What the hell is a mover? What is going on here?" asked Myles, looking visibly shaken and nervous. "What does he want?"

"Shut up, Myles." The hooded man moved his hostage back a few steps so he could keep both Kori and Myles in his field of vision. "Movers are slick bastards. They remember everything you do or say, so shut up."

"No, I need you both to leave me alone. There is somewhere I need to be, so I am going to leave now. Jonis—"

"Jonis Harper?" said Kori immediately, cutting Myles off, instantly assessing everything behind the name of the hooded man. "This is different for you. I thought you got out of this line of work?"

"AAAAGH....You're lucky I need you alive, Myles," said Jonis, squeezing the trigger on his gun tighter.

"I don't need you looking over my shoulder. I'm sure a mover or whatever the hell he is isn't so bad," stumbled Myles.

"You don't remember, Myles. It's something they do to you. They can make you forget—" said Jonis cutting off the last bit of his sentence again.

"You know we don't do that, Jonis. It's difficult to remember a life you haven't lived yet," said Kori starting to take a step forward, but Jonis matched his step, thrusting the hostage forward with him.

"Don't do it, mover. I will kill her."

"What do I care?" Kori could feel the old rage filling him up. Part of him wanted to kill everyone in the room. The name of the man responsible for his pain appeared in his mind again. His fists clenched at the thought.

The response surprised Jonis. "Movers are supposed to protect people. You have to save everyone, right?" said Jonis, tempting Kori to take another step. Yet Kori remained still.

"What is a mover, exactly?" asked Myles, still trying to put together what was going on. "You're not a cop?"

"No, I am not."

"It's useless to talk to them, Myles. They don't care about anything except the job at hand. It's pointless to ask them about anything else," said Jonis, trying to get a handle back on the conversation. "Except there is one thing I need from you, mover."

"From me? Original."

"Which mover you are? I want to know who I'm dealing with."

My name is Kori."

"Kori? I know that name," said Myles with a sudden look of fright. "They warned me about you. They were specific about it. Get me out of here, Jonis. Right now!"

"We will get out of here, don't you worry. So, Kori?" Jonis stared back to him. "I've heard of you. I heard you went rogue or something after your wife was killed."

He said it. A pit built in Kori's stomach, and every fiber of his being wanted to scream in pain. Kori's blood was about to boil.

Jonis cracked a smile. "That was you. You see, Myles, I have been watching these movers for quite some time. No one ever watches the movers, so they didn't know I was following. I learned their secrets and their weaknesses."

"And you think you have it, do you?" said Kori, gritting his teeth, forcing the words out.

"I got it figured, I said. Now give me the book?"

Kori narrowed his eyes at the statement. A peculiar thing for a runner to ask. Very few times had anyone gotten as far as the book, a closely guarded secret of the movers that had never been fully cracked. Simply knowing of its existence does not pose much of a threat, however. *I will let this play out. I will not redo this day.*

"What book?" asked Kori.

"Don't play with me!" yelled Jonis, twitching the gun in his hand. His hostage struggled against his grasp, but Jonis held them tight. "I know you have it, that it's here. All of you carry it. If I have it, I will know all of your locations. Give it to me!"

He even figured out that much more. Too bad he didn't get the rest. Pity.

"You wanted to ask me about a book, Jonis? You don't have anything else beyond that—you want me to give you a book? There is a bookstore around the corner; would you like me to pick up something for you?"

"I've watched movers enough to know—"

"Yes, but you do not understand, Jonis. You are not the first to notice that sometimes people carry books."

"But it's always the same book," snapped Jonis, pointing the gun at Kori and tightening his grip on the hostage.

"You don't know anything else about it, so why would I indulge you any further? You're wasting time," said Kori, taking a deep breath.

"You will give it to me, or I end everything," said Jonis, clicking the hammer back on the gun.

"End what? You're holding a hostage in the middle of a lobby. All these witnesses know your face as well as mine. You got nowhere to go. Shooting me won't change anything. A telegram has already been sent. It's a matter of time, Jonis. You and I both know time is all that matters."

"But the game has changed, Kori. Wondering what the letter was I showed Myles before coming in here? Why he turned white, and why he would much rather be somewhere else? Something I know you didn't put in that telegram."

"And what would that be, Jonis?" said Kori indifferently, knowing there was not much he could come up with to postpone this much longer.

"That the antimatter device... is here."

Kori, who had been mostly apathetic up to this point, snapped his attention to Jonis's eyes. He studied every twitch in his face, looking for a reason to prove he was lying but was not seeing it. His anger made him slip again. He couldn't afford more mistakes.

"What? What do you mean here? Myles is scouting the location today, then retrieving the device from out of town tomorrow. He was set for detonation on Thursday of next week. What do you mean here? Now?" asked Kori.

"In this very building, in fact," said Jonis, the smile coming back to his face.

"This isn't the target building. You wouldn't achieve your goal."

"Who says what our goal was anyway?" said Jonis. "The plan was to execute that goal, as you say, but after watching you all so much I proposed a new plan. To find you. If we knew where you all were, it would easier for us to achieve our objectives. Which is why you will hand over the book now."

"I don't have it on me," said Kori, his eyes still locked with Jonis's.

"Where is it?"

"Close," Kori said, realizing what building was across the street.

"Well then, let's go," said Jonis, cracking a smile. Kori could see the amusement in Jonis's face.

"But before we go there is something you must give me."

"I'm not going to give you anything—ever, mover," said Jonis.

"Then I'm afraid there is no book, and you will have to take your chances with the gun." The gambit made Kori's skin crawl. A hint of doubt flashed across his mind.

Jonis tense. He looked confused. "Fine. What do you want?"

"The word you use when you have lost control. What is the runner name for it, your trigger?"

Jonis burst out laughing almost letting go of the hostage in the process. "Me, give you my trigger word?"

"Yes. That is my price. You want the book. I want your trigger word. With that, I will even explain the book. The part you don't know."

Jonis stopped laughing. Kori sensed Jonis may have a plan. . "Chaos!"

Kori smiled. "Then wrap this up and follow me." Kori turned toward the door, eyeing the clock on the wall as he left.

"What—why did you do that?" chimed in Myles, who was at a loss through most of this. "But the letter said..." he whispered to Jonis.

"Shhh," Jonis whispered back, as Kori had already turned and was waiting outside.

"Can't he use the trigger word against us?"

"Movers don't do anything without their telegrams. It's the pitfall of their whole operation. They can't make a move unless they have a backup plan in play. We can't let him out of our sight. Now let's go."

Myles let go of his hostage, who went running for cover behind a nearby counter.

"Are you kidding me?" said Jonis, who let his hostage go in the same direction. "You have to mean business." He shot his hostage in the leg as she ran. The rest of the people kept their heads down in fear of also getting shot. "Now they know," said Jonis.

The two men put their guns away and headed outside to meet Kori, who was glancing over the newspaper on a nearby stand. He noticed Jonis and Myles from the corner of his eye.

"Is the hostage dead?"

"No sense in killing them when the big show is on its way."

"You could say that," said Kori, turning toward the street, his apathy consuming him once again. *What am I turning into?* "The book is in that building." Myles and Jonis looked across the street to a hotel that reached high into the sky.

"Let me guess..."

"Top floor," said Kori finishing the sentence for him.

Kori crossed the street with no regard as to what cars were coming and never looked up despite nearly being hit. *Please hit me,* he thought, partially hoping one car would end his suffering.

The commotion Kori caused had brought the cars on the street to a standstill as Jonis and Myles crossed.

"You're bringing too much attention to us, mover," whispered Jonis as they reached Kori on the opposite sidewalk.

"It doesn't matter. None of this ever truly matters anymore," said Kori, looking to the sky momentarily.

Jonis and Myles looked at each other, feeling as though their grip on the situation was slipping.

They made their way into the elevator, hitting the top floor button, number seventy one. Kori appeared quite alert, and there was an eagerness about him that would lead one to believe he was enjoying himself. Jonis looked a man on a mission. He had an almost military air to him, like a soldier heading into the field. Myles looked nervous. He was out of his element, trying to maintain a handle on the situation. He clutched the letter in his pocket like his life depended on it.

They hit the top floor. Jonis cringed when the doors opened, expecting there to be a team ready to arrest him, but there was nothing. It was an empty hallway of an upscale hotel.

They walked down the corridor until they reached the door with the number 717 stamped on it. Kori reached into his jacket pocket. Jonis put his hand over where his gun was, anticipating an attack.

"Relax, Jonis."

Kori pulled his hand out, revealing the hotel keycard. He slid the card in, and the light turned green. Jonis reached over and slammed his hand down on the handle and shoved the door open. He cut past Kori to be the first one in the room. Kori casually stood by the door, gesturing Myles to go in next. Myles went carefully past Kori, giving him a wide berth.

Jonis was looking around at the hotel room. There was no luggage, no clothes—no evidence that anyone was staying in this room. The beds were perfectly made, and nothing in the bathroom had been used.

"What is this, Kori? Where is the book?"

Kori, still with his hands in his pockets, casually walked over to the nightstand in between the beds. He opened the drawer and pulled out the book. He held it up without saying a word and lightly dropped it on the bed.

"That's the book all movers use?"

"Yes. A rather elegant solution. The Bible."

"But why?"

"What's the one book you can find in nearly any time period?" Kori said lightly, amused at his question. He down on the edge of the bed.

Jonis picked up the book and began rifling through it. Myles dropped into a chair in the corner, his mind reeling in confusion.

"Where are the markings, notes, anything—there's nothing written in here. How does it work?" asked Jonis.

"I told you there was a part you didn't know. The secret?" said Kori.

"Tell me."

"Then have a seat, and I will tell you."

Jonis sat directly across from Kori so they were no more than few feet apart. He knew if Kori made a move, he would only have seconds to stop him.

"It's a book code, isn't it?" asked Jonis.

"Yes, it is," said Kori.

"For every book code you need a set of numbers. What's the set of numbers?" asked Jonis.

"Simple. Let me ask you a question. What is a number that all citizens of this country have to memorize for the entirety of their natural lives?

"A phone number?"

"Phone numbers can change; it's a number that is assigned to you and you have to remember. Your social security number."

"I'll be damned. Right in front of us the whole time," said Jonis.

"Yes. Again...elegant," said Kori.

"How does it break down, then?"

Myles was watching the two of them with a look of complete bewilderment. His mind was trying hopelessly to wrap his head around the conversation transpiring in front of him.

"What is your social security number, Jonis? We will start there."

"782-57-2539."

"Now you want to look at the first set of three digits. This is the reason your social is written with the hyphens in those spots. They are a clue to the breakdown of the numbers in the code. The first three numbers correspond to the book, the section, and the paragraph. So apply that to the number 782."

"Okay," said Jonis, flipping through the book. "Seven puts me in the book of Judges, and there is a section eight. Now I am looking at paragraph two. It says what have I accomplished compared to you'?" said Jonis.

"It is rather fitting, isn't it?" Kori asked again, smiling.

"Very funny; what's next?"

"The next bit is looking at the second set of numbers, the fifty-seven. They, of course, correspond to the line and word. When you go to the fifth line and locate the seventh word, what do you get?" asked Kori.

"I get the word 'your,' " said Jonis.

"Exactly, indicating this is the location of your checkpoint," said Kori.

"This is too wild for me," said Myles in the corner, slumping back in his chair.

"The next bit focuses on the last set of four numbers, the 2539. The number two signifies the first two letters of that word are important. The way it goes is the second letter of the word gives you the state, and the first letter gives you the town or city. So in that word the second letter is an O, which would mean your state would be Oregon. The first letter in the word being a Y which would put you in a nice little town of Yamhill," said Kori.

Jonis was scribbling notes in the pages as not to miss a single detail. He would need all the notes to relay them back to his superiors.

"The next two numbers can get a little tricky. The five and three signify how many spaces to the left and right of the letter O, and these letters will give you the street name. Five spaces to the left you get the letter N, and three spaces to the right you get a H. In the town of Yamhill, the only street to match those letters is North Hemlock. The last part is the last three numbers, 539. This gives you the street number. So if you were a mover, the checkpoint where you would designate what time to be there every week, would be 539 North Hemlock in Yamhill, Oregon. "

"Sounds like a fascinating place for a checkpoint," said Jonis.

"Ingenious, really," said Kori.

"Who created this code?" asked Jonis.

"A man I hope never to see again," said Kori with the tremor in his hand returning to him. "It was his solution to bring order to ...disorder." His body tensed from the thought.

"Well, I need to thank you, Kori, I really do. It's a very clever system you all have going on here, and you have my sincerest gratitude for showing me what it all means, but I am afraid our business together is nearing a close," said Jonis.

Jonis reached for his gun and raised it to Kori's face. In the same moment Myles launched off his seat to raise his gun to Jonis's head, dropping the letter he was clutching. Kori was lost in thought. *Serena... I could have saved you. Damn you, Roark.* His mind betrayed him to think the name. The shock brought him back to the moment.

Kori slipped his hand out of his pocket and held it out to his side. "Quite the situation we have here," Kori said, staring into the barrel that was inches in front of his face.

"What's in your hand?" said Jonis, clicking the hammer on his gun.

Kori slowly opened his hand to reveal Atlas, in the open position. Kori's thumb was already on the dial, the rings had already been moved.

"What are you doing? What are you gonna do?" asked Jonis.

"My job. What was the word? Chaos." With the tiniest motion of his finger the room was filled with a brilliant blue light. Jonis and Myles covered their faces as the light burned through their eyelids. As quickly as it happened, Kori was gone.

,,,,,,,,,,,,,,,,,,,,,,,,,,,

Seventeen forward, three to the right,

Kori walked down the street, counting the heads in front of him. He could see Myles back to his nervous self. That had been close. There must have been something else written on that letter they didn't mention. Thankfully, Jonis never asked if he should look at the new or old testament. Some people just didn't learn.

Kori passed the couple holding hands he'd seen earlier, and he could see the young singer on the sidewalk. All the familiar memories swept over him.

He crossed the street to where Jonis would be coming up to intercept Myles, and he could see Jonis come out of an alleyway, constantly looking over his shoulder. *May as well get the letter now,* he thought as he came up in front of Jonis and yanked him into another alley.

"Hi there," said Kori.

"Oh shit!" said Jonis, surprised. "What do you... what do you want from me?"

"The letter in your pocket. That's all I want."

Jonis took the letter, shaking, and passed it to Kori, who immediately stuffed it in his pocket. Jonis staggered a few feet away. "Which are you?"

"Chaos."

Jonis immediately turned and ran as fast as he could. Kori, right after him, broke into a sprint. Jonis ran into the couple, forcing them apart.

Kori needed to stop Jonis before he could return to dealing with Myles. Jonis was frantically running, fumbling with a messenger bag Kori had not paid any attention to the last time. Jonis got out something small and then darted into the street.

Kori raced into the oncoming traffic about twenty feet behind him. As the runner cut across lanes in front of cars, he was leaping over their hoods much easier than Kori had seen the last time around. Jonis had been covering up some abilities. They raced into an intersection, and Jonis tossed a small object

21

into a set of cars to his right. One of the cars exploded in a haze of fire. The explosion drew Kori's attention to the right, but as this was happening, an eighteen-wheeler was coming from the left.

Everything slowed down. The truck slammed on its brakes, but Kori knew it couldn't stop in time. As the truck began to pass in front of him, he saw his path. He took a leap up between the trailer and the cab, narrowly clipping the back of the cabin. The opening was just wide enough for him to slip through without losing sight of Jonis. Grinding metal could be heard behind him as the truck crashed into the debris of the exploded car.

Kori looked up; Jonis had gained some ground and was now farther down the street. The runner was frantically tossing to either side of him what Kori knew were grenades. The street became a war zone as Kori made his way after Jonis. As each grenade went off the air filled with smoke and pieces of metal. Jonis was throwing grenades into oncoming traffic, turning vehicles into weapons against Kori. People all around him were injured, screaming out for help, but Kori couldn't stop. He couldn't be deterred from his plan.

Up ahead, he saw Jonis duck into the same hotel as before. Through all the commotion, he hadn't realized they had been running to the same street where he had intercepted Myles before. *Curious*.

Kori got to the entrance and found everyone making their way outside to see the commotion on the street. Sirens wailed in the distance. Screams could still be heard from outside as Kori made his way across the lobby of the hotel. Jonis was nowhere in sight. He looked over to the elevators and saw one was on its way up to the top floor. *Even more curious*.

He again got the feeling something was off. He ducked inside the next elevator, and as he hit the button for the top floor, he tried to think about the possibilities. He reached into his pocket and pulled out the letter Jonis had given Myles. It was certainly battered as if had been on some battlefield for some time. He unfolded it and started to read:

Due to unforeseen circumstances it has been determined that the mission entrusted to Myles Tiegue will yield an unsatisfactory result. Your mission to intervene and acquire the necessary book from Kori is a go. Myles has been deemed expendable, and his services are no longer required. If, however, you advise his participation in your plan you may utilize him to your needs. The contents of the box you received contains all items requested. Designated trigger word for this mission is Chaos. Should Kori intercept you before you contact Myles regarding this matter, retreat to site J.

Kori read the letter several times, wrapping his head around it as he re-read each sentence carefully. No way could a runner get that organized.

He was so lost in thought he hadn't realized he had reached the top floor until the doors opened to the same empty hallway he'd been in only moments earlier. The sounds of chaos could be heard outside as he approached the room. As Kori grabbed the door handle, he felt a hint of uncertainty. He opened the door to see Jonis standing in the center of the room, waiting for him.

"That was clever, Jonis. I'm almost impressed," said Kori.

"Thank you," replied Jonis.

"You put a lot of effort into this one."

Jonis held a tight grin, staring at Kori as he surveyed the room. It was just as empty as before—nothing moved, nothing used.

"So, Site J then?"

Jonis's smile slid from his face.

"Yes it is. What do you think? You approve?"

"It's a decent-enough spot."

"How far did I make it the first time?"

"You had it in your hands. I even explained it to you. You sat right there."

"I was supposed to have killed you before you could reach for Atlas. What went wrong?"

"Well, you thought Atlas was in a different pocket. Simple deception sometimes gets lost in this line of work," said Kori.

"Has anyone else come closer than me?"

"Nope. You get that title, for what it's worth."

"Well, good. At least I can say that," said Jonis.

"Well assuming you can talk later is another thing entirely," Kori said as he sat on the same edge of the bed where he had sat earlier.

"So where is the book in here?"

"In the nightstand drawer. The Bible."

Jonis ripped the drawer from the stand, grabbed the Bible, and stuffed it into his backpack. "Is it that complicated?" Jonis said as he zipped up his bag.

"Yep, very," Kori said, slouching a bit and looking more exhausted by the second.

"You know I wasn't lying earlier," said Jonis.

"About what?" asked Kori.

"About the bomb here in New York."

"It's across the street, isn't it?" asked Kori.

"No, actually, this time it's in this building, Site J."

Jonis pulled out his gun, but instead of aiming it at Kori he spun around and fired several shots into the window, bursting it open. The room filled with a swirl of wind. Everything was being blown around. Jonis turned back toward Kori as he tightened his jacket and backpack to his body. Kori remained slouched on the side of the bed.

"Hey, mover?" said Jonis, yelling over the wind.

Kori barely lifted his head to look up. A pit formed in his throat as his mind betrayed him once again. *Roark*.

"Thanks for the second chance," said Jonis.

Jonis pulled out a box from behind the bed, about the size of a shoebox. It looked heavy by the way Jonis carried it. With one final smile, Jonis lifted the box and threw it out the window.

"Later, mover."

Jonis threw himself out the window after the box. Immediately, Kori was on his feet as he took off at a sprint and stared straight out the window. Without hesitation, he sailed over the windowsill out into the open sky. Silence was all he heard passing through the window, and he turned his gaze downward as he fell. He could see the box falling in front of Jonis. It was slowing his descent, which meant it had to be a gravity well. As Kori's body fell, he could feel the shifts in gravity from the device. As he fell faster, his feet met up with the glass walls of the building. He took off in a sprint down the side, trying to gain ground on Jonis.

Jonis looked over his shoulder to see his pursuer. As the box tumbled, they fell in and out of freefall. Jonis began to fire blindly behind him. Bullets flew past Kori, but he never took any steps to evade them. Part of him wished to be hit. He heard the sounds of bullets hitting glass behind him, and pieces of windows caught up to Kori as they fell.

He was getting close to Jonis, but he knew he would only have mere seconds to act. With a few final steps, he launched himself down as hard as he could. The glass of the building cracked with the effort as he cast himself off. Jonis saw this act and slammed his fist into his chest as hard as he could.

From within the building a rumble could be heard as, above them, the top part of the building split open. A deafening sound filled the air and shattered all the glass on the building. Kori surged past Jonis just enough to kick the device away so now there was nothing stopping the both of them from meeting their demise.

In the last seconds before they hit the ground Kori held out Atlas far enough for Jonis to see. All Kori could hear was Jonis screaming as he hit the dial and all went blue again.

\\\\\\\\\\\\\\\\\\\\\\\\\\\\\\\\

Seventeen forward, three to the right.
Kori thought as he walked down the street, counting the heads in front of him. Surges of adrenaline filled him up. His

steps were uneasy, readjusting from the effects of the gravity well. He could see Myles walking along nervously, as always.

He passed the same familiar faces. There was Jennifer passing him to the left, bumping into him once again. He could see the couple walking in front of him, and there was the little boy singing away on the sidewalk. For tradition's sake, he took out his old coin and tossed it to the boy. Old habits die hard.

Now, Kori knew Jonis's game. This time he would get a handle on it.

He cut across the street, keeping an eye on Myles as he went. This time, he would need to keep tabs on him to try and sort all this out. He had other things to attend to, and he walked quickly to catch up to Jonis sooner.

As he approached the alley he had seen Jonis come out of last time, Kori checked his watch. He was approximately two minutes earlier than before. He had these precious seconds to try and get the upper hand on Jonis. Kori started down the alley slowly, scanning every inch of every corner. As he passed a large dumpster, he saw it. Tucked in the corner of the ground at the back of the dumpster was the backpack he had seen Jonis with both times before. Kori reached down and grabbed it, pulling it over his own shoulders. He pulled the straps tight so no one would be able to take it away from him.

He continued down the alley to a small opening at the back of a restaurant. As he approached, suddenly a wind kicked up and a slight electricity ran through the air as a white light flashed, revealing Jonis lying on the ground. Kori paused a moment while Jonis stirred and got to his feet, unaware that Kori was right there.

"Hi there," said Kori.

"WHAT?" snapped Jonis as he spun around to see Kori. His eyes flicked over Kori, pausing on the straps of his backpack, then back to Kori's eyes. "What? How?"

"It took a few tries—trust me on that."

"But how did you get here," asked Jonis.

"It was a good plan, Jonis, I applaud the effort; I really do. That was a level of ingenuity I haven't seen in a while. Be proud of that—you made a good plan," said Kori.

"It should have worked. It has to."

"Not everything happens the way you think it should," said Kori.

"Who said that?"

"A man I knew once; I don't see him anymore. Doesn't matter."

"So what now?"

Kori shot forward and punched Jonis, with his whole body weight crushing into Jonis's head. The force knocked Jonis back into the brick wall, rendering him instantly unconscious. Kori reached down and searched Jonis's pockets and found the gun. He pulled out the gun and slowly looked down on the runner.

"It was a good plan, Jonis, I'll give you that, but it was destined to fail."

Kori held up the gun and fired two shots into Jonis's body. The shots echoed through the alley. A moment passed before Kori tossed the gun near the body. He looked at his watch to note the time of the shot. He knew he had only four minutes before Myles would be in front of the cafe where he was originally supposed to intercept him before all this mess began. He started running to make up for lost time.

He sprinted back, glimpsing the boy still singing back on the sidewalk while his mentor examined the coin he had dropped earlier. He turned his focus forward and darted in and out of the crowd, racing to his target. He checked his watch every few steps, knowing he needed to be precise.

He rounded the corner and knew he would have only one chance at this. He could see Myles approaching the cafe ahead. As Kori raced, he pulled out Atlas and begun turning the dials with his right thumb. He ran as fast as he could to get the timing right. Myles reached the spot and slowly started panning around like before, but Jonis was not there to intervene. For round number three, Myles was alone like he was originally supposed to be.

Myles turned his gaze finally toward Kori when they were only a few feet apart. Kori lunged forward as the clock on the building across the street clicked to 11:17 a.m. He hit the dials of Atlas as he tackled Myles in a brilliant blaze of blue light. In a flash, they tumbled to the ground of the empty hallway on the top floor of the hotel across the street. The timing was perfect.

Kori composed himself and got to his feet first. Myles had been thrown into the wall during the tackle and was reeling on the ground. Kori reached down, searched Myles, and found the revolver he had been carrying. He found the gun and aimed it straight at Myles, right in the middle of the forehead. Myles was starting to sweat in his fright.

"Wh... what is this?" asked Myles, his voice trembling.

"The backpack you gave Jonis and left for him in the alley. When did you put it there?"

Myles stared at Kori in disbelief. The odds were incalculable. A moment passed where Myles couldn't find the words.

Kori clicked the lever back on the gun and pressed it lightly on Myles's forehead. Myles looked up to Kori's eyes in desperation.

"I'm waiting."

"It... it was yesterday."

"WHEN?" Kori barely flinched while his voice resounded down the hall.

"At noon, around noon."

"Thanks," said Kori, swiftly pulling the gun away from Myles's head. A ring was still apparent on his skin from where the gun had been pressed. Kori took a few steps back and again pulled Atlas from his pocket. He set the dials and stopped for a second, looking back at Myles.

"Screw it," he said as he raised the gun at Myles.

"No please!"

"You'll be fine," said Kori as he pulled the trigger. The hallway fell silent after the gunshot. Kori stared at Myles on the floor as he clicked the dials into place and was gone in a flash of blue.

\\\\\\\\\\\\\\\\\\\\\\\\\\\\\\\\

"Eight forward and two to the right."

Kori mumbled as he walked through the crowd one day in the past. It was nice to see different people. Kori didn't have much time to get to the alley. He passed the usual newsstand and found a nice corner to wait at while Myles approached. He could see his target hunched over slightly, carrying the backpack, which appeared larger than when he had seen it on the ground earlier. The gravity well! Another piece of the puzzle clicked into place. He would have it this time. He saw Myles duck down the corner and checked his watch briefly to see that it was 11:57 a.m. *Just enough time,* he thought as he too slipped into the alley.

As Kori came up behind Myles, an old feeling hit Kori. Myles spun around as Kori quickly grabbed Atlas and furiously hit the dials. He grabbed Myles before he could drop the bag at the spot. In a flash of blue both of them were gone.

With a crash, the two dropped onto a narrow piece of floor. The place they landed was moving. Myles snapped up first and immediately had to grab around for something to help him balance. As he looked around he saw that they were on a small jet. There were no other passengers, just an empty private jet. Kori slowly got himself to his feet to face Myles.

"Confused?" asked Kori. Kori rose to his feet. He wiped his forehead and saw blood smeared on his hand.

"Chaos," said Myles, gesturing a mean grin at Kori.

"You hired Jonis, not the other way around. Very good. I didn't get that. Outsmarted a mover; I guess a congratulations is in order," said Kori.

Myles took a slight bow as he looked around for a way off the plane.

"How high are we?" asked Myles.

"Around fifteen thousand feet."

"Perfect," said Myles checking compartments for a parachute. "I'll land, and we will be back on schedule."

"Unfortunately not," said Kori.

"You didn't stop Jonis. He is still a go and you don't have him, do you?"

"I don't need to stop him. The detonator is here with us. I destroy it, and the bomb can't be armed manually. It needs this detonator. All I have to do is make sure you don't hit the button," said Kori.

"All you have to do..."

Myles turned and leaped at Kori, knocking him to the floor. Myles landed a punch on Kori and reached for the bag. Kori twisted Myles's arm up to the nearest chair and hit a few rib shots into Myles, who curled over from the pain. Myles managed to get up on one knee. Kori twisted his own body, kicking Myles's knee out from under him. They continued to struggle until Kori saw the revolver stuck in Myles's waistband. As Kori reached for it, Myles could see what was happening and grabbed it himself. When Myles swung it around to fire, Kori hit his hand, causing him to waste a shot.

The bullet hit a window, blowing it open. A rush of air filled the cabin. The pilot could be heard yelling into his radio for a mayday. Kori held Myles's wrist keeping him from pointing the gun at him, forcing Myles's arm around so the gun was almost pointed back at Myles. As the gun got almost in line with his nose Myles fired off the remaining rounds, tearing more holes in the hull.

The plane had started to point down now as the pilot tried to get to a lower altitude. Myles threw the gun at Kori as the two jumped to their feet. Kori grabbed the gun.

"It's empty!" yelled Myles.

Kori calmly reached into a small inside jacket pocket and pulled out a .45 caliber bullet.

"What... how?"

"I really wasn't prepared for Jonis, but I was ready for you all along," said Kori as he loaded the one bullet in and set the barrel. He raised the gun, but not at Myles. He raised it in the direction of the pilot.

"You were right," said Kori.

"About what?"

"It is chaos," he said as he fired. The bullet ripped across the plane, hitting the pilot in the back of the head and causing him to slump forward against the handle. The plane shot into a steep dive, throwing Myles forward toward the cockpit. Everything in the room went with him as the cabin went vertical. Kori grabbed the nearest chair and caught the bag as it fell. He supported himself against the back of the next row.

Myles landed against the door and turned himself around to look back up at Kori.

"What are you doing?" He screamed to be heard over the rushing air.

"I'm ending this loop now. It's done, runner. You lost," said Kori.

"There is no plane crash today. People will notice."

"We will land in water. There won't be any evidence to be found. You don't even know where we are, do you?"

"I don't recognize anything. There aren't any buildings. Where are we?" asked Myles.

"Alaska," stated Kori.

"What?"

"Goodbye, runner. It was a pleasure working with you. See you around, maybe," said Kori.

"Wait. You can't leave me like this."

"It was all your choice. I'm sorry."

Kori pulled out Atlas and set the dials. He took one last look out the window at the scenery rushing up to meet them. With one last look at the fright on Myles's face, he left in a flash of blue.

\\\\\\\\\\\\\\\\\\\\\\\\\\\\\\\\\\\

"There is the man of the hour now," Kori thought as he leaned against a wall with the strap of the heavy bag digging into his shoulder. Jonis was just coming out of the alley, looking around for his bag.

"Hey, Jonis!" Kori yelled, causing Jonis to spin around in his direction. His face was a mix of sudden horror and confusion.

"Chaos!" Kori yelled without moving in any direction. He kept his hands in his pockets and stared at Jonis. His target immediately went white and ran back into the alley. A small flash of white could barely be seen just after Jonis disappeared. *All done with,* Kori thought as he crossed the street to the cafe. He grabbed a paper from the newsstand as he approached and sat down at one of the tables. He lifted the heavy bag and placed it at his feet so he could relax for a bit.

A waitress came over, and he ordered his usual drink. He flipped the paper over and began reading the day's headlines. He flipped to the second page and found what he was looking for:

Big news in Alaska yesterday, June 24, when at 10:30 a.m. local time, a 7.0 earthquake struck the barren land 100 miles east of the city of Barrow. After a twelve hour search for casualties, the efforts were discontinued due to the difficult terrain and lack of known population.

Perfect. Crowd goes wild. Kori continued reading as he sipped on his espresso. The sounds of the city slowly started to become noticeable to him again. Cars starting and stopping, the sound of brakes being stomped on, sirens wailing in the distance. Kori had his face so buried in the paper he was blind to it all, so the sounds became his awareness.

As he was reading a car pulled up to the curb just in front of him. Kori dropped the paper to reveal a Rolls Royce limousine.

Kori sat silently as the driver got out and moved around the car without so much as even glancing in his direction. He opened the back door to reveal a man, maybe in his mid-fifties, smoking a cigar. The man stood and looked directly at Kori.

"Well, good morning to you," said the man with a pleasant smile. Kori sat still, partly stunned that someone was actually approaching him. "May I sit down to join you?"

"I suppose," was all Kori could put together to say to the man.

"Well, frankly, I am surprised to see you here," said the man, putting out his cigar.

Kori readjusted himself in the chair to better face the man. He folded the newspaper and laid it down on the table. He shot a glance to see the driver standing by the back door. He quickly scanned all around the intersection to see two cars, one at either end of the street parked with men standing around them. *A trap?*

"And why is that?" asked Kori.

"Well, I just certainly can't believe it. I mean, I was told you were certain to be here, and I had nothing more than someone's word that you would be, and yet here you are." The man cracked a small laugh. "It's just something."

"What are you talking about?" said Kori bewildered by the conversation.

"Let me introduce myself. I am Secretary of State Stanley Murdock. I was appointed to this matter, and I believe I need you to shed some light on this for me."

"I will certainly try," he said, tossing a light smile at the secretary.

"Well many years ago a situation was brought to my attention. It was brought to me by the postmaster general himself. He handed me a letter ...or well, a telegram as a matter of fact, and said I would be interested in it. As you know, telegrams went out of existence some time ago, but it was the delivery date that he said I would be interested in."

The secretary paused a moment, anticipating a reply, but none came. Thoughts raced through Kori's head about what could have gone wrong, and when? *I haven't noticed anything. He said years; that would have been noticeable by now. We don't send telegrams over that much time. Doesn't make sense.*

"Go on, sir," said Kori.

"The telegram was sent from the island of Hawaii, in the year 1941."

Kori's eyes widened at the statement. *Can't be,* he thought unable to say anything. He simply nodded to keep the secretary talking.

"The morning of December 7th, to be precise. It was a small post office just outside the harbor. Our government has been trying to understand the message written on it for decades. Finally, when telegrams were being phased out, the post office was unsure how to ensure delivery since the message had become quite famous by that time. The instructions were that it be delivered on this day, at precisely twelve noon, on this corner, to a man in a tan suit, and it even mentioned that he would be reading a paper and sipping coffee. You are the only one here fitting that description."

"Pretty vague," Kori interjected quickly.

"Yes, well, that message specified the man's named to be Kori Mover. Would that be your name, son?"

"Mover is not my last name."

"But you are Kori, right?"

"Yes, I am."

The secretary looked up and down the street, waving at the men waiting on either side. They each nodded in recognition, and the secretary returned to his normal position.

"Glad that's established. Now about the message written on the telegram. We should talk in my car about it."

"We'll talk here," Kori said.

"This is a matter of national security!"

"It's about a lot more than that, Mr. Secretary. We will talk here. This spot is secure. I'm sure of it."

Mr. Murdoch looked around at the men waiting and finally sighed and looked back at Kori.

"Fine. The message referred to the attack on the harbor."

"There were a lot of messages about the harbor on that day, sir," said Kori.

"This one was sent out before even the White House knew of the attack. It predates every message by hours. The message indicates that whoever sent it knew of the attack before it happened. It also indicated that a soldier was the catalyst for the attack, a man named Andrew."

Kori sat up straight, running the name through his thoughts.

"I don't know that name," said Kori.

"You are sure?"

"Positive."

"The message went on to talk about something called an Atlas."

"WHAT!" Kori snapped.

"Excuse me?"

"The message actually used the word Atlas, not just a reference to the world?" asked Kori. *My god...what has happened? No way has something of that magnitude gone unchecked for decades. What if Adam found out?*

"No, the message was specific; the suspect has whatever Atlas is."

"The sender would know better than to bring this matter to me."

"What does it mean?" asked the secretary, leaning over the table.

"It means... that someone has made a very grave mistake by contacting me rather than someone else."

"Well, that's why we need your help, son. You may not like that it came to you, but it did."

"What else did the message say?" asked Kori.

"Rendezvous instructions, but those are not any use to us," said Murdoch.

"What were they? Let me see the message."

"George, would you get the telegram out of the car, please?" The driver ducked inside the backseat, searching for the envelope.

"The instructions were to meet outside the post office at two p.m. that afternoon." The secretary chuckled as he said, "Clearly not possible."

The driver came back out and handed the envelope to Kori.

"Well, perhaps you know the man who sent it; his name was at the end of the telegram."

"Was it?" said Kori, cutting himself off and starting to take out the message.

"A man named Roark," said the secretary.

Immediately, Kori slammed his fist so hard on the table his cup jumped up and spilt all over. *No No No. It can't be. How many years has it been since I heard that name aloud?*

Blood appeared on his knuckles. "That man ruined my life. I refuse to help you or him."

Mr. Murdoch nearly stood up from the shock.

"What's the matter? I came out here to personally ask you for help."

"HOW DARE HE SEND ME A TELEGRAM?" Kori crumpled up the telegram and stuffed it in his pocket. "He has some nerve to even speak to me again!"

What if Adam finds out? Why bring me into this? What has he done?

"What happened?" asked Murdoch.

Kori struggled to contain himself.

"Will you help?"

"If I don't kill him," said Kori.

"What?"

"Nothing. Thank you for the message. You can go," said Kori, trying to take another sip of coffee from the now-empty cup.

"We are not done here."

"Oh, yes we are." Kori stood up, turned, and walked away without even so much as acknowledging the secretary's presence.

"Where are you going?"

Kori stopped and turned back to Mr. Murdoch. "Someone was once taken from me, and I intend on getting her back." As he spoke, tears came to his eyes. "I have waited so long. It's been so many years. I won't let him torture me with it anymore."

The secretary stood there stunned, unable to make sense of what was happening.

"It's time to reclaim my history." Kori took out the telegram and Atlas, quickly read the last instructions, and set the dials to the proper time. He looked up once more to the onlook of everyone on the sidewalk. "God help me..." All the people saw was a flash of blue, and he was gone.

Chapter Two:

December 6th, 1941

"I remember where I was," said the young lieutenant James Pilon, looking over the rails out to sea. The night was quiet. No different than most, as one might suspect, but there was a feeling of deliberateness about it. It would be a night history would remember.

The lieutenant was a young man in his twenties, dark hair with a jock build. His hair was slicked back, one of the few men who didn't have a shaved head. Only a few more hours until the mission got underway, and a fate would be decided. The thought hung heavy in his mind like a weight he just couldn't let go of. This would be a fate that history would either come to regret or hold up as a moment of victory. It would not disappear into time as a lost memory or a forgotten dream. This would be a night to define a century.

"Where?" asked the man to his right, casually leaning on the railing. A typical man, most would think. *A mysterious man,* thought James.

The man was a quiet individual, plainly dressed in an ordinary tan suit. The jacket looked as if it had seen a few summers, but the white shirt beneath it was crisp and clean. The stark blackness of the tie stood out, as equally worn as the jacket. His shoes looked like they had been polished some days ago. He did not look like a man anyone would raise an eyebrow toward or give a second look to. He had barely said a word to anyone up until this point. *Not from the Navy,* were the words Cap used to describe him when he came aboard yesterday. No rank, no uniform, and no ID. He just had a gold pocket watch James had seen him with right before they came aboard.

He does not seem like a man that can be trusted, thought James. Any man that appeared to have gone out of his way to come across as plain couldn't be up to any good. All he had were orders, written on a telegram, of all things, from the President of the United States. All James heard was that his name was Roark; he didn't catch a last name. *Probably doesn't even have one,* he thought to himself glancing over at him. He was just a man in a tan suit with orders from the president. A very mysterious man.

"I was with Adele at Hula Joe's when we first got the word," said James, fixing his eyes on the horizon under the moonlight. "I couldn't believe it. I couldn't tell her what was happening; how could I? How could you tell the love of your life that the world would be a different place tomorrow? How could I tell her that we may not live to see tomorrow? How could I tell her that? It was only moments earlier when I asked her to come back to the ship with me to spend the night." He paused, letting the moment hit him again. The thought quieted his voice. "If she had stayed the night and we hadn't known the Japanese were coming, we both would be dead."

Roark saw James pause for a second out of the corner of his eye. "I was stationed on the *Arizona*," James continued. "I had a concert set for tomorrow, and I play with the ship's band. We both would have gone down. I don't know what's worse— the notion that we both could have died tomorrow or the fact that she couldn't stay over tonight." James turned to Roark and it was clear the lieutenant's eyes had turned red. "She turned me down. She turned me down ...so it would have just been me. It's a fact that this could have been my last night on earth if that had happened."

Roark maintained his silence. He could tell James was keeping most of his feelings under tight watch. Due to the circumstance he felt it appropriate.

"Scary thought," whispered James. "Cap said if the Japs made it here, based on where the *Arizona* is in the harbor, it would have been hit the hardest, possibly even have been sunk. Thoughts like that haven't let me sleep since I left that bar; they will keep me up most nights from now on I expect." James forced a smirk. "What ifs, you know?"

"They are the two most terrible words—what if," Roark finally said with a quick smirk, and then it was gone. "They can push us to do terrible things, or they can haunt us till the end of time." Roark turned to face James, trying to lighten the mood, "The important thing to note is everything you told me won't happen now, and that's what you should focus on." Roark put a hand on James's shoulder, feeling his trembling nerves.

James gave a small smile. "I guess."

"Where did you meet this girl?" Roark said brightly, changing the subject. "She must be special. Most girls spend their whole lives looking for a man that will worry as much about their well-being as you do for Adele's."

James returned to his position, leaning on the railing, and his eyes wandered back out to the horizon. A slight resemblance of calm returned to the lieutenant.

"It was a normal day." Roark could see the shift in James's demeanor. The thought brought a bit of warmth back to his calm. "I had to be on detail at ten a.m., and usually I have coffee at my place then head out." James paused to take a deep breath, releasing a lump of stress his body didn't want. "That day I slept late and didn't have the time, so I went to this little coffee shop. I saw her there." He paused for another moment, letting the memory take over. Roark glanced at him to see the thought was bringing the man back to normal. "You know when you look at a girl, maybe only a few seconds go by, but you... I don't even know what you call it. It's like this feeling that this girl will be in your life for more than those few seconds. That feeling you will see her again. That kind of feeling, you know?"

James's smile grew bigger. The lieutenant's confidence had been restored with a strength he had forgotten he had.

That's more like it, thought Roark.

"It's a good feeling," said Roark, letting his own memories come to him from another time.

He liked these talks with James. Roark was not as mysterious as James thought. He was a mystery to everyone else, but everything was not a mystery to Roark. His station was somewhere else, another time, but he would often come back here to talk to James. After all, Pilon had a very strong connection to Roark. It was Roark's escape from his own troubles. *Everyone needs an outlet.*

"So why are you here?" asked James, cutting the silence. Roark had known this question would come up eventually.

"I'm here under orders, like you, and that's all you need to know." Roark's response was flat, a matter-of-fact tone he had gotten use to speaking in.

"I'd argue that is not an answer," said James, smiling at him.

"I am simply here to watch over things." He could see James was still expecting a more complete answer. "We meet up with the Japanese fleet in an hour. We hope we can turn them around without a shot fired, and then go home and have a drink," he said, smiling right back at James. "It's that simple."

"Without a shot fired, huh? That would be nice," said James sarcastically. He broke into a quick chuckle at Roark's summation of what was to come. "It's not a drink I'm looking forward to getting back to," said James, looking back out at the sea. "It's Adele."

"That girl's got your heart, doesn't she?" said Roark in admiration. *Specific reasoning like that is something to be envied.*

"I'm going to ask her to marry me." James had his full confidence back now. His eyes gave a hope to the night now, and Roark could sense that. "Once we get back, the concert is set for tomorrow night. After the last song I'm going to call her up on stage and propose to her right there in front of the ship. I got it all figured," said James, lost in thought.

"No pressure doing it that way, I guess. Congratulations are in order, I feel," said Roark patting him on the back. This was the only moment Roark felt he could cling to for hope. He couldn't remember how many times this conversation had been played out with James, but each time he was filled with the same warmth.

James reached into his pocket and pulled out a small blue velvet box. "This is what I'm going to give her." He opened the box, and inside was the most brilliant sapphire. Even in the moonlight it shined.

That's the ring, Roark thought to himself. *The ring that will be passed down for eight generations until it will be lost during....* The sudden thought of the ring's eventual fate darkened the moment. He quickly brought his mind back to the present.

"And thanks, but the congratulations will be in order after she says yes," said James, chuckling to himself. His laugh had an awkwardness. "Well, I got to go do a last check on munitions before we get underway. I'll catch up with you after," said James, shaking Roark's hand.

"I'll see you after, and there will be an after—you can be sure of that," said Roark smiling and giving a wink back to him.

James started to turn, but something made him pause to face Roark once again. "Roark, I wish I had your confidence that tonight would be a success."

"It will be a success, lieutenant, but only if you accept the possibility of failure will you have the courage to ensure you are victorious"

"Who said that?" said James with his eyebrows clenching in a perplexed surprise.

"A very wise man," said Roark with a reassuring look and a calm smile that still seemed out of place for him.

"Well let's hope he turns out to be right." James shrugged, letting it go without another thought.

"Indeed."

James returned to the look of a man with a mission and disappeared through a doorway, leaving Roark alone looking off the starboard side of the ship. If only he could tell Pilon that those had been, in fact, his own words some twenty years from now. They would be words said to his son as he retired from the Navy. It was a phrase that would be passed down through the generations of his family.

A perfect end to his favorite conversation, he thought. Roark knew already how things would unfold. He knew the mission would be a success. He knew there would be no shots fired.

He remembered every detail of all the events to come. He remembered the next night, when James would propose to Adele once tonight's mission was declared a success. He pictured the event unfolding in his mind.

It would happen back at Hula Joe's. The band had just finished playing a rendition of "Chattanooga Choo Choo." The conductor turned to the crowd still quieting down from the cheering of the popular tune and said, "Well I hope you all enjoyed that little number, but now we have a special surprise for you, and especially for one young lady out there tonight. James, take it away." James put down his instrument and approached the microphone, still with a bead of sweat on his forehead.

"Hello everyone," James said into the mic. "Hi back," said a voice in the semi-drunk crowd. A few people burst out laughing, and James gave a nervous chuckle.

"I, I have something prepared here," he said as he pulled out a small, crumpled piece of paper from his jacket. "It's a poem I wrote for someone out in the crowd tonight. Adele, could you come up on stage for a minute?" James looked out into the crowd through the bright lights and could see the beautiful woman he was talking about stand from her table. Adele stood with a shocked look on her face. She was a short brunette with shoulder-length brown hair. She had on a simple, midnight-blue dress, his favorite color. In her hair she had a butterfly beret he had given her when they went on a trip to Maine together.

She made her way through the tables cautiously as James stood frozen, watching her. She reached the steps and tripped on the second step, but James had come over and caught her by the arm just in time before she fell. Their eyes met, and they both instantly smiled. They laughed to themselves, Adele turning a little pink as they made their way back to the mic.

"The poem is called 'When I look at you.' When I look at you, I wonder how you made me a part of you, the look in your eyes, and the feel of your touch; in my heart it is true. When I look at you, you fulfill everything I lack, a sweetness, a purity; you keep my mind my body, on track. When I look at you, the world falls into place, one smile, one kiss, and my heart can't keep its pace. When I look at you, I know how to make you a part of me; I hope that when you look out, you look at me. "

"That's beautiful," said Adele, putting her hand on James's face. The crowd went silent at the touching moment that was unfolding onstage. A few sniffles could be heard out in the room.

"You mean more than anything in the world, Adele, and there isn't a single place I would rather be than by your side. Being with you has made me the happiest person alive, and I know the single best decision I will ever make in this world will be to spend the rest of my life with you."

The audience gasped as he said the words. A few people rose to their feet as James got down on one knee. Adele put one hand to her face as tears began to roll down her cheeks.

"Addy-Delphine Blackwood, will you marry me?"

"Yes," she said, leaning down to kiss him. "Of course, yes, I will."

"Yeeaaa!" A man in the crowd screamed as the whole place erupted in cheers. The crowd was louder than any other moment in the concert. People everywhere could be seen wiping tears away, and they clapped as loud as possible. It was one of Roark's fondest memories of James.

He looked up and down the deck of the *Hornet*. The air was very still. It was 11:11 p.m., December 6, 1941. By the time the Japanese turned around it would be Sunday, a day Roosevelt would declare to be a day to remember. A day where diplomacy would persevere, he would say. At the thought, Roark took a deep breath. *A good night,* he thought to himself.

He walked along the railing; the air was crisp. The stars were bright, and Roark thought the sight would make quite the postcard. The first few visits to this time he'd made sure to stay out of the way and not interfere with anything, but recently he had taken to seeing some of the moments that went into this historic night. The mission was so secret, and since no one was allowed to talk about the mission he was able to talk to multiple people without having to worry about potential ripples that he would later have to tie up.

He then made his way up to the bridge, which was busy with activity. Captain Marshall was there, with his first officer hovering over him, explaining the latest report about their current speed and ETA to interception. Next to him was Colonel Doolittle looking, of course, worried.

"Okay we are doing eighteen knots. Reduce speed; we don't want to seem too intimidating and ready to fight," said the captain to the rest of the bridge. It was clear he was the only man in the room who seemed ready to handle the evening ahead.

"We should get the planes ready to fly," said Doolittle, taking a step in front of the captain.

"No, we don't want to give the Japanese the impression that we are going to attack. The point is to talk them down, not blow them out of the water."

"Our planes should be already in the air. If things go south, which they will, all we have are P-40s. If I had gotten time to prepare the bombers to take off from the ship, we would be much more prepared." Doolittle's voice rose through the sentence, ending in almost a yell.

"I understand your concern, I do. Look, everyone is on a hair trigger here, but we can't go looking for a fight in a situation like this," said Marshall.

"My training is to be ready for any contingency. We have to be ready to take off at a moment's notice," said Doolittle, noticeably nervous. He walked around the bridge, circling as if standing still was not an efficient-enough action.

"The last thing we need is to give them a better reason to attack. I will not be responsible for a Second World War here," said the captain, dropping the words on the floor as if they were anchors to his thoughts.

"Well you may very well be," said Doolittle in as calm a voice as he could. The words were so calm they filled everyone in the room with more fear than any the captain could produce.

"Well go down by the planes, then, but you do not fire up a single engine without my say-so," said the captain with the utmost sincerity. "If even so much as one plane starts up, I will have you arrested."

This scene that unfolded before him always impressed Roark. It was a mission that would go almost smoothly, yet there was so much tension in the room. All he wanted was to announce how everything would be all right, but he was sworn to silence. It was the first rule of his profession, to protect history as it is. Do not change it or manipulate it. Besides, there were not many would dare change such an event as this. So much rode on what transpired here tonight that it would be foolish to attempt something so brash.

"We are to talk them into turning around. Do not fire— do you understand me?" continued the captain with a look of almost fright. The words cut through the room like lashings.

"Well, you can't trust these Jap bastards. They traveled across the Pacific specifically to destroy Pearl Harbor. They are already poised to draw first blood. We are in the snake pit now. We have to be ready to defend ourselves," said Doolittle, stopping his pace and facing the captain with a look of stern, morbid confidence.

"WE will be, but we talk first," said the captain, gaining some composure and matching Doolittle's glare.

They held each other's look for a moment, then Doolittle left the room without a word. Roark then went toward the captain; no one even knew he was there. "That guy always made me feel a little jumpy."

"Roark, didn't see you there. Come in," said Captain Marshall in an immediately brighter tone.

"How are things looking up here, Cap?"

"Good, I hope, as long as Doolittle doesn't make any sudden moves on me," said Marshall, returning to his normal duties.

"Yeah, well, that guy's career was built on making sudden moves," said Roark, almost amused at the memories that came with that thought. Doolittle was a brave man, one with guts, the kind of guts that makes a man a little crazy. *It's always good to have a man like that on a mission like this.*

"They must know we are here by now"

"I don't doubt it, but that is a good thing, is it not?" asked Roark, leaning against the open window. He found reassuring that all the crew members reduced the chances of anyone acting on nerves and potentially doing something stupid. He felt any amount of comfort would be useful.

"And how is that a good thing exactly, Roark?"

"Take into account the state of mind of the Japanese. They are coming all this way to pick a fight with a Superpower. Essentially walking up to a dragon with a knife, meaning to prick its finger. You don't do a thing like that without some hesitation. It is that hesitation that will work in our favor. They are just as nervous as we are." The words rolled out of his mouth effortlessly.

"I will believe that when we are on our way home," said the captain disconcertingly.

"I suppose I can live with that," said Roark.

"Well we are coming up on final preparations. Stations everyone, Roark, if you please."

"Of course. I'll be out of the way."

This was usually the time Roark would take his leave and let history go its way. He left the bridge to head back down the side of the ship. Off on the horizon, lights were just becoming visible in the dark. They were the lights of the Japanese. A proud moment in history, *too bad not more people could be here to see it,* thought Roark.

As he casually strolled the deck, he passed the spot where he and James had spoken earlier. A flash of the wedding to come gave him a momentary smile. *Perhaps I will stop in on that sometime. Give them some anonymous flowers or something.*

As he thought, he turned down a corridor to head back to the cargo hold. He reached into his pocket and felt the cold watch in his hand. It was the only room on the ship big enough to use Atlas without anyone noticing.

As he turned a corner, he could see a sailor racing toward him.

"What is it, sailor?" asked Roark.

"Sir, a dead body, sir. I was heading down to the engine room and right in the corridor was a body."

"Any idea how he died?"

"Sir, a gunshot wound to the back of the head." A moment of panic came over Roark. He suddenly felt his body start to sweat.

"Show me," said Roark.

The hallways all looked the same. Corridor after corridor, endless, like a maze. He had never been down this part of the ship. He had never needed to until now. Suddenly, they reach the one.

The hallway was already buzzing with activity. It was frantic commotion among a stressed environment, a bad combination. Everyone was crowding to see the body that lay in the open doorway.

"Move, everyone. I need to see the body," cried Roark, trying to push his way through the mass of uniforms.

A sailor reached to turn over the body to show Roark.

"No, don't touch him. Don't touch anything. Everyone back away—I need some space," said Roark. His mind raced through what could have caused this. *It couldn't have been anything I did. I spoke with James, and then I went to the bridge. None of it had any ripple beyond those moments. There was nothing I said that would have provoked this. There isn't time to evaluate this.* Roark checked his watch. *Thirty-five minutes and this is out of my hands and beyond anything I can do on my own.*

"Do you think it was a saboteur of some kind?" asked a seaman recruit somewhere in the crowd. The crowd murmured with the idea.

"One must have somehow gotten aboard," said another, adding to the momentum.

"Maybe there is more than one; there could be more roaming the ship as we speak."

"That's enough!" said Roark, getting to his feet and facing the crowd. "Who knew this man? Did you know him?" He pointed to the nearest sailor. "How about you?" He pointed at another.

"I knew him, sir. He is Seaman Recruit Roberts, sir," said a scared sailor, making his way out of the crowd, tears apparent in his eyes.

"Everyone on this boat was in final checks; what was recruit Roberts tasking?"

"He was to make final checks on the engines, sir," said the recruit, trying to wipe the tears to maintain his composure.

"So he had access to the engine room, did he?" Roark leaned down to check the pockets of the body. "It's gone; the key is gone."

The crowd broke out into murmurs once more.

"It must be the Japanese; they had to have sent a spy," cried a voice in the crowd again.

This is getting out of hand. Thirty minutes left, then I am in serious trouble, Roark thought to himself. "Who could have done this? It's not the Japanese." The murmurs of the crowd drifted back in his mind as he relived every second of his trip here. *If it was a runner, then what was the endgame? No one in his right mind would try to change something on this ship, especially now. Think—what does everyone on the ship go on to do after the mission is over? James gets married. Marshall goes on to captain this ship for a few more missions until it gets sunk off the Cayman Islands, and he goes down with it. The entire crew serves their various times, then go home. Less than ten go on to die in service. So it cannot be to save a life.*

"We should search the decks and find the spy," a voice said. The crowd stirred to go, but Roark's voice rose above it.

"Shut up, the lot of you. The Japanese fleet is still miles off; there's no way they sent over a small ship from that far away without us noticing, end of story. Now, we do have a murder on our hands here. What I need now is everyone to search the decks for someone not wearing a uniform. My guess is this person would not have any kind of ID you would recognize. Start with the engine room. I want two men at every entrance to the engine room, and do not let anyone through without my express permission, understood?"

"Sir, yes, sir."

"Then move," said Roark with the greatest sense of urgency he could possibly muster. *If it is a runner, and God help me if it is, then he could only be out to sabotage the ship.*

"Sailor! Come here." Roark motioned over the sailor who was tearing up over Roberts. "I'm sorry for your loss; I take it he was a good friend?"

"He was, sir."

"What's your name?"

"I'm Petty Officer Third Class Bowman, sir."

"Well Petty Officer Third Class Bowman, what do you say we honor Roberts by finding the person responsible for his death and strike more fear into them than we will the Japanese, huh?"

"Sounds good, sir," he said, still trying to regain his composure.

"Then let's move the body to a better spot than the hallway, all right?" *If everything gets put back the way it's supposed to be, he may get his friend back,* thought Roark.

"Thank you, sir."

"I'll help him move the body, sir," said another sailor who was listening in from behind Roark. "Roberts was my friend too. I owe him my life."

"Thank you, sailor," said Roark, now free to get back to something he had been worried about. His mind went immediately back to James. He had to make sure he was all right. If there is any kind of history he wants to make sure is intact, it's his own history, thought Roark. Never has a mover's family line come into jeopardy before. There is no telling what would happen if his ancestor met a premature demise. It was a notion he did not want to think about. Entropy is a funny thing sometimes, but the possibility existed that if James died, then he might go along with him. *I must find him,* Roark thought. *If James goes, then I might not be able to fix any of this.*

As Roark turned to go find James, a crushing explosion resounded down the halls of the ship. The entire hallway dropped to the left. A force knocked into Roark that took all the air out of his lungs. He dropped to one knee from the pressure. His mind went blank for what felt like an eternity. He wasn't sure how much time went by. He couldn't be sure if it was an hour or a second. His ears were ringing. Everything was black and out of focus.

He tried opening his eyes, but even open, everything around him was a blur. The hallway was a haze of smoke and dust. Roark struggled to his feet to try and get some bearing on what happened. Over the ringing, cries and yells for help could be heard near and far.

He turned back to the two sailors who were picking up Roberts. He saw the three men on the ground by the doorway where Roberts had been found. They had burn marks all over their bodies. He tried to take a step back toward them, but he was so disoriented he fell on the first step. He reached out for the wall as a guide. When he put his hand on the wall, he could feel the tremors from the explosion still moving through the walls.

My god, what happened? he thought as he stared at the two men he had spoken to moments before. They now lay motionless on the floor. He reached Bowman first. He turned Bowman over to find only more burn marks. A flash must have come through the door right at that moment. He put his fingers on Bowman's throat. There was no pulse.

"No," said Roark, closing Bowman's eyes and gently placing him back on the floor. Next, he moved to the other sailor. *I never got his name*, thought Roark to himself. A man died helping a friend and I never got his name. A regret he shouldn't have to have. Three lives changed, and who knows how many more.

I don't know if I can handle this. He looked at the three lying on the floor. *This is something I may not be able to undo.*

"JAMES!"

At that thought, Roark carefully laid the unknown sailor back down, being careful to treat him with as much respect as possible. He leapt to his feet and threw himself down the corridor as fast as his legs could carry him.

For the first time since the start of this profession he had a sense of panic. His clothes felt sticky from sweat. On a long-enough timeline, everything could be righted, but the added element of his ancestry threw a complication beyond measure into the mix. He was the only mover to know something went wrong. No other mover would notice the change until tomorrow. By then it would be too unclear to sort out the details. There would be no start point, no telegrams received...or sent. *I must survive this night with James, for everyone's sake.*

As Roark turned each corner, trying to get back up to the crew quarters, the damage was becoming clearer and clearer. The explosion was larger than he anticipated.

"The Japs fired on us!" yelled an officer racing in the opposite direction. As the moments passed more and more sailors chimed in to that theory. *It's impossible*, he thought, climbing over more debris and bodies. *Could the same runner that came aboard here have gone over there and set off a torpedo?* The odds of such an event raced through Roark's mind. *After I find James I must get to the bridge to see what's going on.*

"You there, sailor—Lieutenant James Pilon's quarters?"

"I don't know, I don't know, sir. Everyone is giving different orders, sir. I'm not quite sure where I'm suppose to go," said the very frightened ensign. He must have just joined the Navy, and this was the first crisis he had run into. The fear was causing his hands to shake.

"Take a deep breath ...we are to stations. Go there now and wait for further orders from the captain. Did you see anyone around who might be able to point me to the lieutenant's quarters?"

"Officer Eames is down that way, sir. He could help you."

"Thank you... What's your name, son?"

"Kenson, sir."

"Thank you, Kenson."

As Roark turned to go, Kenson grabbed Roark's shoulder. The look in Kenson's eyes, no word could describe. He had the look of a man who has accepted his fate, but was too terrified to believe it.

"Are we going to make it through the night, sir?"

"We will, Kenson. I can promise you that. You will see the sun again. Just keep focused on that and you will be fine."

"Okay, sir, I will try." And with that Kenson took a long, deep breath and disappeared around a corner. Roark thought about the very real chance he might never see Kenson or anyone survive this night. It was more about fixing the situation now as opposed to rescuing it.

Roark headed down the hallway Kenson designated, unsure of what lay ahead of him. As he got to the end of the hall, he found a mess of activity. Sailors moving in every direction, panic starting to take its toll. As he made his way farther he could see the focal point of the mess of people.

There, in the middle of the main hallway, was Eames. He stood fixed, an anchor in the sea of hysteria. Every sailor that passed him, he stopped him, shouted an order, and shoved him along. Roark got the impression that if this man were on some battlefield back in medieval times, while everyone was running for retreat, this would be the man turning them all around, one at a time if need be. The sight was almost a relief for Roark. Someone he could finally rely on beside himself in this craziness.

Eames was built like a heavy-hitting boxer. He looked like a person who could fight a whole war without ever lifting a gun. He had an intimidation factor about him. It was no wonder that people listened to his orders even though he wasn't the captain. He had that authority about him.

"Officer Eames, I need your help."

"You're alive? We figured since you were from Washington you must be a pushover sissy like the rest of those politicians," said Eames with a hint of disappointment.

"As flattered as I am to hear you say that, I need your help locating a Lieutenant James Pilon."

"You know I lost a hundred bucks on you."

"What?"

"A hundred bucks that at the first sign of trouble we would find you dead or on a lifeboat a hundred yards out. Yet here you are... alive."

A tremor rippled through the floor and walls again, causing the lights to blink a few times. Eames acted as if it was just another day. His calmness was almost irritating.

"I appreciate your honesty, Eames, I really do. Now, about James?"

"All right, all right— James's quarters are on B Deck, but with everyone to stations he is most likely up by the starboard guns. With so many men not where they are supposed to be, who knows where he may have wound up."

"Thanks, Eames, I'll try to not make you lose another hundred next time."

"Well, the current bet is if you make it till morning," said Eames with a slight smirk, yelling to Roark as he was heading down the corridor.

On B Deck his thoughts became more and more desperate thinking about what fate had in store for James. He thought about the consequences of James not surviving the night. What would happen to him should James die? If James were to die would he not vanish himself as his descendant? The concept alone made his headache only worse. It occurred to him that he might also not last the night himself. Even though they were not that far away from the shores of Hawaii, there was no certainty he would be able to make it there alive. Even using Atlas at this point seemed like a useless notion. Sure, he could go forward in time, but where would that put him? With his fate uncertain, what certainty would be gained in going forward? The same was true with going back, without knowing how and when everything went wrong, he would simply be doomed to the same fate again. He had the power of time travel at his disposal and yet as powerful a tool as it was, it offered no aide.

Roark arrived at James's door only to see it standing ajar. Roark hesitated a moment, bracing himself for whatever lay on the other side of the door. He slowly pushed the door open and stepped in. James was not there. A mix of relief and panic spread back over him again. There was relief that he did not find him dead, but James's fate was still undetermined.

He gazed around the room for the first time in his life. The first thing that caught his eye was the picture by his bed. He knew the face in the picture; it was Adele. He had seen this picture before. He had seen it once at his grandfather's place. It was kept in an old locker up in the attic with other family relics. The picture he had once seen as a child, so battered and old, looked pristine and new now in his hands.

It was a strict rule to not take any item forward or backward in time. As simple an action as someone recognizing the picture where it was not supposed to be could cause unseen ripples that would go years without being noticed. The thought that this picture could wind up on the bottom of the ocean, lost in the change of time, caused a flinch in Roark's character. *This is not where this picture is destined to be,* he thought as he slipped the photo out of its frame. *This belongs with James.* As he slipped the picture into his jacket pocket, he moved to the other end of the room to James's desk. He knew that somewhere in its drawers lay the ring that would one day go on Adele's finger.

The piling up of emotions was causing an unfamiliar stir in Roark. He felt he had a personal duty to uphold. *There is so much we take for granted in time. It is there always in the backs of our minds. We take comfort in the knowledge that the past cannot be changed, that it is forever engraved in time. If people only knew how fragile it is, like life. It's there in front of us, in the people we love. Then one day it's gone, forever changed. A cruel, hard truth we must accept. That's when we rely on the past to remind us of the life, the love, the kindness that can exist. It's when people come along like here, and go further and try to rob us of even that memory. To leave the world without that warmth.*

Roark realized his hands had turned into fists. He smashed his fists down onto the desk. The rush of reality washed over him, and suddenly the sounds all around were crystal clear. The sense of calm a mover should have came back to him. He walked back out of the room armed with knowledge, his memory he would use to save this one.

As he moved through the running bodies a familiar voice was yelling out orders about something; it was not clear. He recognized the harshness of the voice. "Where am I on the ship, B Deck? Where is this near? The exit to the runway...Doolittle!" He raced down the hall toward the voice. *He cannot let loose any planes, that would doom things further*, he thought as he rounded the last corner to see the man, blood running down his face, throwing out orders to pilots to suit up and literally throwing one pilot at a plane.

"What the hell do you think you're doing?" Roark screamed into Doolittle's face. He could see the sweat and the blood and the terror locked in Doolittle's eyes, but a fierce conviction behind it all.

"We are going to get back at those Jap bastards for what they did here. I am going to make sure none of those Jap ships make it back to Japan," he said, staring out at the night sky beyond the runway.

"We are not even sure they did it. We cannot take action before we know what's going on. You can't let a single one of those planes get off the deck; you have no idea what is at stake here."

"Oh, I do know what is at stake. No prick from the capitol is going to tell me what I can and cannot do with my planes. They are taking off as ordered by me! The first planes are about to leave now," said Doolittle, poking Roark in the chest. It was clear that talking was not going to do anything to sway his mind.

"Now you listen to me," said Roark, grabbing Doolittle's jacket and bringing his face close enough so that Roark's eyes were all he could see. He lifted him so his toes were the only part of him touching the ground. "I am above you on the chain of command. I order you to stand down those planes. You will shut them down and wait for a command from either the captain or myself. Absolutely nothing happens until then. Do you understand me? Do you understand that?" Roark was screaming into the man's face now. He could feel his own hands starting to shake under Doolittle's weight. Making a man like Doolittle understand required something dramatic. After a moment passed, however, he knew he couldn't change his mind. The look in his eyes did not falter.

"Those planes are taking off. They are, and God help me, I will take out as many of them as I can before they take us down."

"No they won't." Roark dropped Doolittle, but before he could regain his stance Roark landed a heavy punch across Doolittle's face. He could feel the pain in his hand as he landed a second strike across the other side of his face. *This man cannot continue to give orders, so I have to make sure he can't.* He grabbed Doolittle and swung him into the nearest wall, knocking him out. A small crowd had formed.

"Colonel Doolittle is acting out of fear and is unfit to perform his duties. No planes are to take off. Shut down all engines immediately," said Roark, making eye contact with each and every sailor before him. Each one knew the sincerity that came with his statements.

"But, sir?" said a pilot coming over, putting on the last of his gear. "A few planes have already started to get underway."

"What? We have to stop them." Roark began to sprint down the deck toward the planes. He could hear the engines getting louder and louder. He reached the first plane, which was still stationary. He gave the kill engine signal. The pilot immediately obeyed, and within seconds the propellers began to slow. As he raced to the next plane, which was just starting to leave its spot Roark grabbed a flare from one of the techs and lit it. As he ran, he waved his arms in the air as fast as he could. After a few agonizing seconds the pilot finally turned his head to see what was happening. The pilot brought his plane to a stop and cut the engine. He had done it.

"Sir, a plane is at the start of the runway!" said a sailor coming up behind Roark.

Roark began sprinting as fast as his legs could carry him. He raced, but as fast as he was running he couldn't get even with the plane to see the pilot. He broke off toward a pile of materials that were stripped from the plane for weight earlier in the night.

As the thought of what he must do entered the back of his mind a very cold chill went up his spine. He reached into the pile and picked up one of the machine guns that usually hung out the side of the bombers. He brought it around and aimed toward the end of the runway. As the plane began to enter his line of vision, cries began behind him. Several men were running toward him now, but as the plane got in his sights, Roark took a single breath and squeezed the trigger.

A rage of bullets streamed out of the gun. The first few bullets went off into nothing, but then a few hit the right wing of the plane. As the plane moved across, the bullets went farther up the wing and started hitting the fuselage. As the bullets began tearing up the plane a sight that burned into Roark's mind occurred. He could see the pilot turning to look right at him, a look of pure horror that the bullets hitting him were coming from his own ship.

In the second he saw the pilot's face, the plane went up in a burst of flames. For a moment the bullets continued; he was unable to release his finger from the trigger. He could feel the sensation of tears welling up inside, but none surfaced.

A necessary evil, he thought to himself. *It will all be righted in the end.*

He let the moment hit him. As he turned to drop the gun, a sailor tackled it from his hands. He now had several sailors landing on top of him. As he struggled to get to his feet, he could see some sailors were filled with rage, others with pure shock.

"Why did you do that? Why?" said one of the pilots getting out of his plane.

"No one can take off. You cannot leave the ship."

The pilot walked up to Roark and threw a mean punch right into his jaw. He took the punch; he knew he deserved it. *They can never understand.*

"I'm sorry" was the only thing Roark could manage to say as he turned to go back inside the ship to head up to the bridge.

"You're sorry!" said many voices behind him as he left, each one louder than the last. "How could you just be sorry?" *I must keep my focus forward. I cannot regret what can be fixed. I can fix it,* he thought as he wiped his nose of the blood from the pilot's punches. The wreckage of the plane would prevent any others from taking off. As he turned the corner up to the bridge he braced himself for the next wave.

The bridge was a far cry from when he was here earlier. It was a state of pure, confused chaos. Some sailors looked out the window at the plane wreckage, trying to make sense of it. Others had binoculars trained out the starboard windows. Several men were hunched over radars and technical blueprints for the ship. In the middle of it all was the captain. Earlier, he had a look of calm, a sense that he commanded the room. Now, he had a shade of concern, which made Roark all the more unsettled.

"Captain, what's happened to us?" asked Roark, moving away from the door. Captain Marshall rose and turned to Roark with a look of morbid fright in his eyes.

"I don't know. There was an explosion down by the engine room, that's all I know," said the captain, swiftly turning back to his charts.

"Was it the Japanese? Did they attack?"

"I don't know, I can't be certain. All I know is that we are going down. I am trying to pump her out as best we can, but more water is coming in than going out. I have orders for us to turn around, and we are moving back toward Hawaii," said Marshall without looking up at Roark again.

"But the mission, sir?" asked Roark, knowing what a moot point it was to ask.

"We can't damn well show our strength to the Japanese with a sinking ship that's on fire," said Marshall, slamming his fist on the table. The action silenced the room. "I know how important this mission is. I know what it means to turn around, but we can still make a stand at dawn just off the shore. I just know we can't go up against their fleet in this condition. It won't work. It just won't," said the captain, lowering his head as he spoke. He had a look of defeat in his eyes.

"Um, sir?" said a sailor bent over the radar.

"I wanted so much for tonight to be a success. A great moment for this country, and now it's gone, Roark," said the captain, lifting his head slightly.

"It can still happen, Cap, at dawn like you said. The most important thing is the mission and if heading back in to save the ship and try again is the best option, then that is what we must do. We just have to make it till morning, right?" said Roark moving to the captain's side.

"Um, sir?" said the sailor once again with a nervousness in his voice.

"I know, Roark. It's just making it there I'm not sure about."

"Um, sir?" said the sailor, rising from his seat.

"What is it, sailor? There is enough going on—what is it?" said Marshall, snapping at the young man.

"Sir, I have been checking the radar..."

"And?" said the captain, frustrated.

"There was no torpedo or missile launched from the Japanese," said the sailor, hesitating again.

"So the explosion was from some sort of engine failure then?" asked the captain with relief that war was averted for now.

"No sir, reports from our search teams say that it may have been sabotage, sir," said the sailor, immediately sitting down.

"What?" said the captain. The room had fallen silent again. Roark moved with the captain closer to the sailor.

"Sabotage, how?" said Roark staring through the sailor. *It IS a runner,* thought Roark. *But who in their right mind would do this, set the world down this path? What could be gained?*

"I'm not sure, but one team reports pieces, well fragments of some kind of device attached to one of the engines. It's nothing like we have ever seen before. It's nothing the Japanese have is what I mean, so it couldn't have been them," said the sailor choosing his words as carefully as possible.

"Thank you, sailor," said Roark. *It is a runner, and he or she may still be on the ship.* It was his worst fear confirmed. He did not have enough information to go on to fix this mess. He needed to get down and see the device. "Tell the team to gather up all the pieces and wait for me to come down there."

"Aye, sir," said the sailor, turning back to his post.

"Wait, what is going on here? What does that mean, Roark?" asked the captain, grabbing Roark's arm.

"This is what I am here for captain, in case of a saboteur. Allow me to do my job," said Roark, carefully removing the captain's hand from his arm.

The captain had a mixed look on his face of profound anger, shock, and utter bewilderment. "Did Washington know there would be a saboteur? Why I was not informed of this? Who is this man that thinks he can stop it?" So many questions ran through his mind, but with so much going on already he didn't have time to question Roark further. "You better fill me in once you know more, Roark. We will have words later," was the final word from the captain.

"Yes, sir," said Roark, turning to go when something caught his eye. A figure out the window, a person standing by the bow of the ship past the wreckage of the plane. He squinted his eyes further; there were two figures. He let a moment pass to see that they were both standing completely still. If it were not from the light of the downed plane, he would not have seen them, but it was still too dark to make out who they were.

Roark started out of the bridge, going down the stairs as fast as he could. *Was this the man he was looking for? Are there two runners? I must choose my words carefully to get as much information as possible from them.* He was moving down the corridors almost in a daze now. All the sailors waiting for orders went by in a blur. When he reached the deck where he had shot down the plane, the deck was now empty. All the pilots had heeded his order to abandon the planes. As he approached the still-burning plane he could see the body of the pilot in the cockpit. His heart dropped a beat at the recognition of what he had done. Once he passed the wreckage the figures were now in front of him. *Now I can put this right,* he thought to himself, approaching the two figures who stood side by side. *Now I will protect history.*

"I was waiting for one of you to show up" were the first words that came from the first shadowy figure. "I figure I would have seen you some time ago. Isn't that what you people do, show up before I do something? You're late then." The man said spoke in a solemn tone. There was sincere disappointment in his voice.

"That's not exactly how it works, stranger," said Roark, making sure he composed himself to his usual concealed demeanor. "What's this about? Kind of a random spot to turn up in, the middle of the ocean."

"It's a beautiful night, you know." The figure paused and looked up to the sky in an unusual sense of wonder given the moment. "I was just thinking it right before you walked over."

The ship listed to the starboard side, just enough so that they had to lean to stay upright.

"It is a beautiful night," said Roark, never even considering looking up. He remained fixed on the figure. "It's a beautiful night save one thing, though." Roark held up his index finger, staring at the dark figure before him. The explanation was obvious on his face. Roark's face cringed a bit as a flash of the crowd cheering in his mind flashed across his memory, the thought catching him off guard for a moment

"No, I like it like this. The way it is supposed to be. Something needs to be fixed tonight," said the figure, looking down. Roark couldn't see what the figure's face looked like, whether he was crying or not. "An evil was done to me!" the figure said in a raised voice with a hint of desperation.

"Evils are done to us all," chimed Roark in quickly.

"No, not like this. Not like what was done to me." Roark could hear the crack in the man's voice.

"What was done to you?"

"In time." He could hear the figure catching himself. "This must be done first. I wouldn't expect someone like you to understand ...or care. None of your kind cares." The figure trailed off as he spoke. "*The Hornet* won't last the night," said the figure. The statement had a sense of finality to it.

"*The Hornet* is not supposed to sink for another year and a few months. That's the goal?" said Roark holding his stance. *What is this?*

"You are starting to live up to your reputation. It is impressive—you know your history. I did my own research as well, you know. I know what this evening is. I know what was supposed to happen here. I also know that there are not supposed to be any movers here," said the figure, whose eyes Roark could now see through the dark.

How would he know that? thought Roark. Checkpoints are contained in book code known only to movers. No other person in the world would have access to that information.

"I am impressed you managed to use a jib so accurately. It's always tricky to use a knockoff. The time may be right, but you could wind up anywhere in the world. Unless you traffickers came up with a new design, you managed to land on a ship in the ocean. One stroke of bad luck and you would have had quite a swim," said Roark hoping to get something out of the figure.

"Well, we all have our little secrets, don't we—our little mementos of the past. I met a man once, a truly remarkable man. He told me to write my own history, to take my life and my future and do what I wanted to do with it. So I had a chance to do something extraordinary, and I'm taking it. Something was taken from me, and I intend on getting it back," said the figure.

The figure paused for a moment then went searching for something in his jacket. His hand must have landed in the right pocket, for a slow smile came across his face as he slowly pulled out a small object.

Roark's face froze at the sight. In the figure's hand was a small gold pocket watch identical to his own. *Impossible,* he thought to himself. "No other person in the world can get one of those."

"Yes.....it's Atlas," said the figure with his smile growing ever bigger.

"Who did you take that from?" asked Roark, the gravity of the situation filling him up.

"It was given to me. It's an impressive trinket. One could do a lot of damage with this little thing. All you should be concerned with is that I have one and I'm not sure I want to be done with it yet," said the figure, returning the shiny gold watch to his jacket. "Where are my manners? I saw you earlier talking to a man by the railing. I thought before the night is out, you two should get reacquainted."

The figure threw the second figure forward into the light; it was James. His hands were bound, and a rag was tied in his mouth.

Roark stepped forward to grab him. "JAMES!" As Roark moved forward the figure grabbed him once again and dragged him back into the darkness.

"You son of a bitch," cried Roark. "He is just a man..."

".....Whom you obviously care for," said the figure, who stepped into the light himself. "What is he to you? What would happen if he were to die tonight? I'm sorry this has to happen, but it must. He promised me so much. I have to remove you from the equation. He told me I have to do this. No one can know what I am doing."

The figure turned back to James. The figure reached into his jacket again and pulled out a dark object.

"You have my sympathies," said the figure aiming the object at James.

"NOO!" yelled Roark reaching for the object.

A gunshot echoed across the deck of the ship. The moment seemed frozen in time. James's eyes glazed over as he fell back. His body fell and disappeared over the edge of the ship.

Roark turned to the figure and lunged forward.

"Stay right there," said the figure, aiming the gun at him. Roark felt frozen as a searing pain spread through his body. The figure stared at Roark, surprised. "You are still here? I was told he was your ancestor." *Why didn't that work the way he said it would*? the figure thought, panicked. "Apparently, manipulating the past is far more convoluted a thing than I anticipated."

"You're a dead man. Mark my words," said Roark. "Once I set things right, my attention will be set on you. You do not want a mover to focus his attention on you. There is no place or time you can go where I won't find you."

"Oh I think I'll be all right. Never has someone like me acquired an Atlas. Never has anyone tried to change this much history. I will expose the movers for what they are, and I will put control of history back into the hands of man. I will return history to what it really is," said the figure, grabbing another small, dark object from his pocket.

"One man cannot dictate how history is written. You have no idea what road you have set us down after tonight. You think you're better than anyone else?" said Roark.

"Do you? I am returning control to the people, to chance, but I am needed to take it away from the movers first. By noon tomorrow Pearl Harbor will lie in ruins and America will be forced to wage world war with Japan. By doing so World War three will have been averted. Hundreds of millions of lives will have been saved. I will expose the movers for what they are. How everyone has been lied to about you. History will know," said the figure.

"You can't know that. There is no way to judge the future. You witnessed yourself changing one thing in the past does not guarantee a change in the future. I am a direct descendant of James. You shooting him should have killed me, but it didn't. You have no idea what will result of your actions here," said Roark.

"I will make sure it happens the way I need it to, mover. I will be there to ensure our future."

"It won't work, runner. You don't know what you're doing. Things will only get harder from here," said Roark, raising his voice to a point of desperation.

"Well what happens, happens, and isn't going to happen any other way. Isn't that right, mover?" The figure winked after saying the line. He tucked his hands in his pockets, satisfied with himself.

"That's right." Roark had known that phrase for some time. Where had he heard it before? *Is the figure really giving me a clue?* "You are telling me your next target then?"

"A game like this requires a skilled opponent."

"This is a game now?"

"No, but I still need you to play. Perhaps this will give you some time to think it over," said the figure, raising the small object in his other hand. "By the way, you can call me Andrew," said the figure, pressing the small object.

A thunderous explosion ripped open the back of the ship. Suddenly, the deck dropped, and Roark fell backward, catching himself on a tie-down on the deck. The figure put his gun away and pulled Atlas out once again.

"I bid you farewell, my friend. I'm sure we will meet again in time. I did the world a favor tonight."

"I will find you," said Roark, still trying to hold on as the ship pitched farther and farther back.

"Of that I have no doubt," said Andrew as he opened the watch and set the dials. As he flipped it closed a bright blue light enveloped him and he was gone.

The ship was sinking fast now, leaning back and to starboard. The planes were starting to slide across the deck. The metal beneath his feet buckled as the ship twisted itself from the weight. Cries for help could be heard all around. It all had happened too fast for anyone to get lifeboats in order. The ship listed sharply as each deck flooded in seconds. He frantically looked around for anything that would float once he got into the water. The pile of cargo that was on deck had wooden boxes mixed in. They would be what he would go for. As the ship tipped, he pushed himself away and dove into the freezing water. The cold stung his whole body as he entered.

He surfaced to a mess of debris and burning pieces of metal and planes. He could see the ship continuing to submerge into the depths. The explosion must have ripped the whole back half of the ship apart at the speed she was sinking. Roark looked around and saw the floating boxes and made his way to them. Around him, he could see several other survivors scrambling together. A few sailors managed to get a small motorboat free as the ship was sinking, but only a few men got aboard in time.

As Roark swam toward the small boat a hand reached out to him. It was Kenson.

"You made it, sir."

"You too, Kenson, you made it," said Roark as he pulled himself up into the boat.

"We got to get back at the Japs for this, sir, no matter what it takes."

"We will have to get back at them in time, but this was the work of someone else," said Roark, looking back over the debris.

As the ship foundered, the array of damage began to sink in. Thousands of souls aboard and less than a hundred made it out in time. He could feel the responsibility of tonight on his shoulders. It was the single most massive change any runner had ever attempted before. *How had he known where our checkpoints were? How did he get an Atlas, one of the most strictly guarded pieces of technology in history? Who did he get it from?* All these questions burned into his mind as they raced the boat to round up survivors and make their way back to shore.

It was dawn when they saw the shore. As they went, a low rumble could be heard from behind them. As they strained to hear over the waves, out of the mist came a plane, then another and another. They were Japanese zeros.

"What are they doing?" asked a sailor, shaking from his injuries.

"The attack on Pearl Harbor has begun," said Roark in the most somber tone a person could speak in.

"What can we do?" asked the sailor, looking at anyone who would look back at him.

"We live to tell what happened. That is what we do," said Roark.

By the time they made it to shore the sounds of distant explosions could be heard. The beach was barren, and people in the streets were running to their houses or any building they could duck inside. Once their boat hit sand all the sailors disbursed in every direction. Some were just running for cover; others were running to find a vehicle to get to Pearl Harbor.

"Where are you going, sir? The harbor is this way."

"There is something I have to do first. Can you tell me where the nearest post office is?"

"Wait what? The post office? World War Two just started—we need to fight and you want to go there?"

"Look, goddamn it, I need to get a message out, and it's more important than any of us. Now tell me where it is."

"Fine. It's at the end of Hanover Street. That's if anyone is even there to help you."

"Thank you. Godspeed to you, sailor."

"You too."

He raced down the street with smoke now appearing on the horizon from the direction of Pearl. As he reached Hanover Street there were cars abandoned all over. Houses had their doors left open. Everyone had just dropped what they were doing and ran. It was a scene no man should ever have to see. He reached the end and saw the little building that was the post office.

He crashed through the front door, and found an old man there, frightened out of his mind.

"I need to send a telegram," said Roark, stepping up to the counter.

"Now?" said the old man. "We are being attacked. I don't think we should be here."

"It's a matter of life and death. I need to send a message," said Roark staring right into the man's eyes.

"Ah.......Okay. All right, I'll do it," said the man, grabbing a telegram form from the shelf. "What do you want it to say?" A look of surprise was stuck on the old man's face.

The old man watched as Roark began scribbling as fast as possible. The man was straining to read what was being written that was so important. He could only make out single words, something about December 6th, a Andrew, something about an Atlas, meet at 2nd and Main, bring the book, at 2:00 p.m. today.

"What, today? You want to send a message out for someone to arrive out here by this afternoon? I don't understand," said the man, trying to make sense of the message.

"Don't worry about it, just send it."

"Where to?"

"Send that to 42nd and 7th Avenue, New York, at that date there" said Roark writing down the date as he was saying the message. "At 12 noon."

The man stared at the address for a minute, "Now a man from New York is going to make it out here," said the man, looking confused as another explosion sounded in the distance.

"Yes," said Roark. "Now, sir, point me in the direction where I can get a rifle and help get back at these Jap bastards."

"Your head isn't right, son, but why not," said the man as a smile came across his face. "As soon as I send your message I'll join you."

Roark immediately began making his way to the door. The man looked down at the message once more and read the date it was to be sent. Suddenly, a look of even more confusion came across the man's face. "Sir?"

"What is it?" said Roark, turning back to the man.

"The date on this... of when to deliver the message?"

"I made no mistake—that is the time I want the message delivered. Exactly at that time, no sooner," said Roark. I will wait outside for you."

"But this is eighty years from now," said the man to Roark as he was going out the door.

"I know that," said Roark, disappearing into the morning light as another explosion sounded overhead. "And so does the man who will receive that message. I owe him vastly more than my life."

Chapter Three:

Futures Past

"You look beautiful," he said, watching her come out of the apartment building. She was the love of his life. The one thing that brought him out of his world at the base. As she came down the steps she smiled at his words.

"You're biased, that doesn't count."

"Sure it does."

"Noo, but it is sweet. Thank you." She leaned over and kissed him on the cheek. He took her hand and walked her to the car. "So where are we going, James? Don't keep me in suspense."

"Well, first we are going to Hula's."

"Ah okay, the 'go to' place."

"Yes, I know you saw that one coming. Then I wanted to head down to the beach afterward, actually."

"Romantic. I guess we can do that." She smiled at him again as they reached the car.

"Hold on a sec," said James as he got in front of her to open the passenger door. "Can't break old habits. Got to maintain the good track record on this."

"Why thank you!"

"It's no problem." James carefully closed the door and quickly headed around the back of the car and hopped in the driver's seat. He put the key in the ignition, and the car revved to life. He put his hand on the shifter and suddenly he could feel a warm hand on top of his. The feeling made him pause, and he turned and saw Adele smiling at him. No words were spoken, only a moment where the two of them smiled. He leaned over and gave her a small kiss.

"Hi," she said softly while the two of their faces were still inches apart.

"Hi," was all James could say back, his smile matching hers. "We don't have to go out tonight, you know. We could sit here."

Adele smiled and thought about it for a second. "If we didn't have people waiting for us I'd love to do that. Maybe after the concert tomorrow we could do this."

He could never say no to her. "Sounds like a plan. It's going to be hard to drive now, you know."

"Why?" she said with a small giggle.

"Cause I want to look at you," said James, sitting back upright in the driver's seat, still looking at her.

He put the car into gear and turned his attention back to the road.

She folded his hand between her own as she stole looks at him while he drove. Each look was accompanied by a smirk that washed over her face each time.

"Gene and Karla going to be there?"

"Yup the whole crew, everyone from rehearsal. They let us out early so we could get a good night's sleep before the performance."

"And to you all, that meant going out and getting drunk."

"Something like that," said James trailing off into a chuckle. "We're not alcoholics, I swear. Only on the weekends."

"It's Saturday, hun."

"Right. I meant during the week."

"Picture of the modern Navy you all are."

"Hey now, we have been known to be serious on occasion."

"The key being 'on occasion,' dear."

James just smiled and gave her a quick look. "That's why I love you, always keeping me in check."

"If it wasn't for me you would have been kicked off the *Arizona* months ago."

"OOH, now the truth comes out. You think you're the reason I'm where I am?"

The two were laughing now. "Yes, I absolutely am."

James lifted the hand she was holding and kissed the back of hers. "I know you are. I like you, you know. I guess I want you to hang around for a while longer," he said, grinning the whole time.

"I suppose I can bear to stand you for a few more minutes," she said, grinning out the window.

It was a perfect night in Hawaii. The moon illuminated everything in sight, making all the trees and houses glow. As they turned down a little path, a small building came into view with very elaborately strung-up Christmas-style lights. Around the front was a huge porch, where a band was already playing assorted music. A large crowd grew out front. They could already see Gene and Karla leaning by the railing on the porch. When they saw James's car they both waved and immediately started making their way down to the car.

James pulled in at the end of the row and before he could even kill the engine Karla reached Adele's door. She shot a quick look at James, then opened the door to the very excited Karla.

"Hey Addy, I was wondering when you were going to get here."

"Hi Karla," she said as Karla nearly squeezed her to the point of suffocation. She could smell the gin on her breath;

clearly, she was several drinks deep already. "How's your long weekend?"

"Oh, it's fantastic—we went snorkeling yesterday off Maui."

"It made me reach lobster status though," said Gene as he came over a little sluggishly.

"Yeah, you look a little red there, buddy," said James, coming around the car to shake his hand.

"How are you, Karla? You look like the one who was smart enough to use suntan lotion," he said as he hugged Karla and kissed her on the cheek.

"I know, right? I kept telling my Geney to use some."

James shot a look at Gene as he gave an embarrassed grimace. As Karla was talking James mouthed the word "Geney?" to him. Gene shook his head slowly. He was probably turning red, but with the sunburn it was barely noticeable.

"Shall we take it inside so I can buy Gene a drink?" asked James, putting an arm around Gene.

"I like that idea," said Adele, picking up on the cue.

"Thank you for that," said Gene quietly to James as they made their way back up to the porch.

"No trouble at all. I think a shot might be in order for us guys, though."

"Heard that, dear," said Adele, trying to look over both her shoulder and Karla's

"Us guys got to have something—I mean, just look at him," James said, gesturing toward Gene.

"Yes, for that, that's all you two," she said, grabbing Karla as she tried to make her way to the bar. "Oh noo, you need to take a break there, missy."

Adele led her toward the back deck near the ocean. "We will be over this way," she said back to the guys as they made their way to the bar.

"Karla looks like she is having fun," said James, leaning on the bar and settling into the atmosphere of the place. Some music started, and the room was perfect. No wonder this was the place to be on a Saturday night.

"Ha, yeah, she is a lightweight for sure," he said with the girls off in the distance laughing about something.

"Oh, I wholeheartedly agree with you there."

Gene turned to look at the girls in their element over by the back porch. He had the look of a man in love.

"Just look at them."

"I am," said James, smiling as he looked in the same direction.

"It's perfect, isn't it?"

"Almost."

Gene turned and sat on the stool. "So when are you going to ask her, the whole ship is waiting for it, you know," he asked seeing if he would get an answer this time.

"How about that drink?"

James signaled the bartender and held up two fingers. The bartender nodded and rummaged for two shot glasses.

"I'll take a Jack, James."

"Who said I'm buying?" asked James.

"Look at me," said Gene, pointing to his own face.

"I suppose. It would be too sad to make you pay for yourself."

"You're too sweet; what Adele sees in you is a mystery."

"Keep talking, see how long my generosity lasts," said James, offering up the first shot glass as a toast. Gene matched his movements and threw back the first drink.

"You're still avoiding the question."

"I have thought about it."

"Oh wow, hallelujah, people—we got progress. You going to ask her tonight? Good a night as any."

"The concert tomorrow," said James.

Gene stopped for a second to take in the statement.

"Really?"

"Yep, I'm going to ask her tomorrow. Right after the Chattanooga."

"That's awesome."

Gene sprung forward and hugged James. James was taken aback at the sudden outburst of emotion. As the moment passed where Gene embraced his longtime friend, reality slowly sunk in what was happening. Gene immediately shot back to where he was sitting.

"Sorry."

"Didn't know you had that in you."

"You're finally going to ask. It's a big night."

"I got it all planned. Picnic on the beach after this. See if she will stay on the ship tonight. Spend the day with her tomorrow and ask her at the concert. Could you come up with a better weekend?"

As Gene was listening to the plan being laid out, he could see Karla pushing her way back toward them.

"Hey James, put that thought on hold for a minute—here come the girls."

James turned just to see Adele grabbing his hand and pulling him in for a kiss.

"What's the conversation over here?"

"Oh, you know, boring Navy band stuff," said Gene, turning red again under his sunburn.

"And how are you feeling, darling?"

"I was feeling great until they showed up."

"Who showed up?'

"Those damn military police ruining the evening. They are just standing over there," said Karla.

"What?" said James, putting his glass down, trying to search the crowd. Searching from face to face, hoping Karla was just going on with nonsense.

"You sure you saw MPs, dear?"

"Yeah, they are right there," she said, pointing back toward the porch the girls were at earlier."

"Did you see them, Adele?"

"I thought she was making it up, so I never looked. They never come out here, that's why we come here," she said with a chuckle. Hula Joe's was beyond the harbor limits. It was outside the patrol lines, so they never came out this far.

"James," Gene said, grabbing his shirt and spinning him around. Two military police officers in full uniform stood in the doorway as the bar went on without even noticing them. They didn't talk to anyone going by them; they just stood there searching the crowd, looking for someone.

"Gene, we may need to check this out."

"Aye, Lieutenant."

"James, is something wrong?" asked Adele, still holding his hand.

"I'm sure everything is fine, honey, I'm probably the only officer in here so it's probably me they are looking for. I'll be right back," he said, kissing her hand. "I'll bring Geney back too," he said, smiling at Karla, who was still drunk and holding onto the bar.

The two started off toward the MPs. "What do you think they are here for?" said Gene, straightening himself up as they walked.

"Don't know, but they wouldn't come out here dressed like that for nothing."

As they approached the men, the MPs locked on to them and started over to meet them.

"Lieutenant Pilon, Petty Officer Gorman, I'm sorry to interrupt your evening."

"No worries, guys—what brings you to the party?"

"It's a matter of national security, gentleman. You both will have to come with us now; we are launching in two hours."

"Whoa, whoa, hold on. Let's back up a few steps here. What's going on?"

"I'm afraid I can't go into that here."

James looked over his shoulder to see Adele looking on with a worried look on her face.

"Sir, I'm proposing to my girlfriend tomorrow, and you're asking me to leave before that. You better give me something if you expect me to actually go with you right now," he said, sobering up with each second.

"I'm very sorry, lieutenant, but it's extremely important."

"How important?" said Gene, folding his arms, looking like a bouncer.

"We are launching a mission, and if unsuccessful it could result in the single largest attack against the United Sates in history. We have one shot, tonight, to prevent that."

"Who would do something like that?" asked Gene, still standing tall.

"Japan. The entire Japanese fleet is mobilized and on its way here. If we don't stop them they will be here by morning and the Harbor is their target. Less than one hundred people know about this, so it's advisable you don't tell anyone. You have five minutes to get ready. We will be outside. Gentleman."

"Oh God," said Gene.

\\\\\\\\\\\\\\\\\\\\\\\\\\\\\\\\\\\\\\

The words hung in his mind as Roark emerged through the door out into the sunlight. The light hit his face, and he looked up into the sky and closed his eyes. He took a deep breath and tried to let the moment hit him. He knew what road he was heading down by what he did. It was an action that couldn't be undone. He wished there was anyone else he could have contacted. Kori was the last person he ever wanted to ask for help from. They were connected by a past he wished he could forget. *I have done such wrong to him,* thought Roark.

He cringed as the thoughts came over him. He had been the cause of so much pain in Kori's life. "If there were any other way. If I could take it all back I would. You are the last person I would ever ask this from after what I did"—he mouthed the last line under his breath as he let the air out. He kept his eyes closed as muffled sounds all around him barely registered to his ears. He reached into his jacket pocket and pulled out the picture he had taken from James's room aboard the *Hornet*. It was too much.

He dropped to the ground as the tears came over him. He pressed the picture to his face, trying to deny what had happened. He imagined the look on his face as Andrew pulled the trigger. He screamed in his head over and over for it to stop. His knuckles turned white as he pressed his fists against his forehead. He prayed for any sort of way he could undo everything right now. "I failed," he continued to scream out at the image of the lifeless body of James in front of him. "I failed you," he screamed. He screamed it over and over, unable to control the emotion flowing through him.

As he screamed he felt hands on his shoulders and the sensation of someone kneeling next to him slowly. He tried to open his eyes, but everything was still blurry from the tears. It was the old man from inside the post office.

"It's okay, son. You're okay. Who did you fail? It's okay, tell me—who did you fail?"

"Everyone."

"No you didn't, no you didn't, we haven't lost yet, son. Pull yourself together; we need everyone today. What's your name?"

"James....ehh....Roark, my name is Roark."

"Roark what son?"

"Just Roark," he said, getting ahold of himself. He took the picture and held it, looking at it once more. The old man stared curiously at him as he straightened the crinkled edges of the picture. *It looks almost the way I used to remember it,* he thought as a sense of déjà vu came over him. He looked up at the man as he put the picture back in his jacket pocket. "Did you send the telegram like I asked?"

"I did. I'm sure the boys in New York are going to have a field day with that one. You might set a record with that. Who do you expect to get the message that long from now?"

"Someone I did a horrible thing to once, but he is the only one I can trust with this. I still don't know if everything will be all right between me and him, but there is no one else."

The old man helped Roark up from the ground, dusting off sand from his jacket. "You are a mess. I didn't really notice earlier—you caught me off guard with everything—but what happened to you?"

"You ask a lot of questions."

"Someone like you, I'm sure everyone asks you a lot of questions."

"I can't tell you. It's something that will be addressed later. Once my colleague arrives," said Roark.

"I almost forgot you are out of your mind for a minute there. Where's my head?" The man laughed, gesturing for him to follow him to his car. The old man put his key in the trunk of the car and lifted the lid. Inside were a few rifles and some boxes of ammo. "We better get to the harbor; those boys need our help. Pick your poison."

Roark picked up the M1 and stuffed his pockets with ammo. "Time to bring some hurt."

"Now you're making some sense. Get in—I'll drive."

The two jumped in the small car and started toward the harbor. In the distance a swarm of planes could be seen making dive passes below the trees and out of sight.

"Those must be high-altitude bomb drops. They are targeting the battleships."

The old man stepped on the gas. His knuckles turned white on the wheel. As they drove, the sounds of planes got louder and machine gun fire could be heard. The planes were spraying the harbor with bullets. Stray bullets landed closer to them as they drove to the gate. Roark rolled down the window and hung out with the rifle.

"Keep her steady; the planes are low enough I might be able to clip one."

"Got it."

Roark aimed up at a zero turning to make another pass. He slowed his breathing and focused on the pilot's cabin. A thought of James flashed in his mind as he pulled the trigger. He could see he missed off to the left. The plane was barely out of range. He knew with each second the plane was getting closer. He inhaled a big gulp of air once more. He narrowed his eyesight and slowly began to exhale. He squeezed the trigger, and it was as if silence suddenly engulfed the harbor. A second passed, then it happened. The plane made a sudden jerk to the side then began to slowly barrel-roll downward.

"Yaaaaaaa!"

"That's how it's done!"

"One down!"

"They ain't taking us without a fight."

As the plane spun down in the distance, another zero suddenly flew into a sharp bank, circling around on them. It became apparent they were the only car moving, and the plane must have spotted the plane crash and then the car.

"Get us off the road, now," said Roark.

"Why—we're nearly in?"

"Get us off the road!"

The plane opened fire on the whole street as bullets ripped holes in the pavement and tore through a house next to them."

"Holy......"

"MOVE!" cried Roark, gripping the rim of the door. The plane whipped past low and began to bank around again. The old man stopped the car on the front lawn of the next house and clamored to get out. Roark hopped out of the window and moved around to the driver's door. The plane opened fire again, and more bullets hit everything around them. Roark dropped to the ground as the car got blasted with a wall of fire. The barrage lasted a few seconds as the plane roared overhead. A moment passed as his mind went blank.

"All right, he passed—let's go."

Roark was holding the man's hand through the last blast and stood up to help the man out when he realized the man's arm had gone limp.

"Hey, c'mon, no, no, no, c'mon."

Roark frantically searched for a pulse. He shook him desperate to get any semblance of life out of him, but it was too late. He reached up and closed the lids of the man's eyes. He looked down to see the man wore a name tag from the post office. It read *Stanley Guertin.*

"You're a brave man, Stanley. I will never forget what you did for me, and what you did today."

He put his arms around the man, pulled him from the car, and brought him over to the tree in the lawn. He sat the man up against the tree in the shade and folded his arms.

"I'll fight for you. You're at peace now."

He put his hand on the man's crossed hands as he said it and rose to keep heading toward the harbor. He was only a few hundred yards from battleship row, and he could see the mass hysteria that had been going on already for some time. He ran with his rifle to cover the last of the distance without being seen by any other planes. Men were scattered all over the dock setting up .50 caliber gun nests made from whatever they could get. Bodies were strewn all over the place. It seemed like everything was on fire in the harbor. Every ship was covered in smoke and flames. All through the harbor, men were frantically swimming in every direction, trying to get clear of the planes' attacks. The sound was comparable to having a stick of dynamite being set of in your ear every second. It was a sight no man, woman, or child should ever have to see in their lifetime. The scene could make any man, no matter how tough, stop in his tracks. Roark felt a sense of hopelessness creep up his back. He lifted the rifle to his chest and headed toward the nearest gun nest.

He made it a few steps forward and then he spotted in the distance a name on the side of a nearby ship. It was the *Arizona*. He knew then he had to try and help however he could. Roark turned to run down the dock when suddenly everything went quiet for a few seconds.

"BOMBER!" a man yelled. Everyone ducked behind the nest as the brightest flash engulfed every inch of his sight. An earth-shattering blast knocked him clean off his feet. He thought his ears exploded as he was blinded, lying on the ground. He felt as if all the life that he had in his body had been blown away. He opened his eyes, but all that was visible was the most brilliant of white lights.

Moments passed without time to measure them against. He wasn't sure how many seconds or minutes were going by; there was only white and silence. As he lay there trying to recover whatever was left of himself he recalled a quote he heard once when he was a kid. *When you hear the sounds of devils....all else is quiet.* The phrase repeated in his mind over and over.

As he was repeating the phrase he could hear himself saying the words. He couldn't tell if he was saying them aloud or not; everything was muffled to his ears. As the world began to catch back up to his body the distant sounds of reality began to creep back in as well. He could hear muffled cracks and snaps of gunfire. He could hear distant yells and stomps of boots. The screams of pain were overcome by the roar of planes flying low overhead. *These kinds of sounds, these kinds of devils, all else is not quiet,* he thought, trying to move.

Through the fog of sounds one sound was beginning to stand out over the rest. It was a voice. The sharpness of the voice was a source of strength that seemed unfamiliar to him at a time like this. As Roark tried to look around for who the voice belonged to, figures began to emerge from the white. Shadow upon shadow began to rush past him as if he were dead. Each one seemed to stop at this voice for an order, then it would dart off in another direction.

There was a break in the shadows where the source of the voice seemed to notice a man on the ground listening. The figure moved toward Roark and began yelling at him. Everything was still unintelligible, but it seemed like he was yelling for him to get up and move. Roark squinted to get a better look at the figure slowly coming into view. The figure reached out a hand to Roark, and his arm was close enough to focus in on. The figure's arm was covered in a single tattoo. It was a dragon breathing fire that stretched all the way up to his sleeve and probably continued up onto his shoulder. Roark reached out and felt the sudden jerk, pulling him to his feet.

Once on his feet the image around him came into focus. The *Arizona* was rolling on her side, with countless soldiers running to rescue as many as they could. All around him guns were still firing and planes were still dropping bombs. What Roark had hoped was a figment of his imagination came back to striking reality.

The man in front of him was still yelling but was now in sharp focus.

"Are you okay!!"

"I don't know," was all he could say. There was no clear answer he could give. He knew what had to happen to fix everything, but he was completely helpless to the present.

"Well get okay; we got a job to do. Now get over to the *Missouri*. Their guns are operational, but they are getting hammered. Only a matter of time before that gets hit too. Get over there and get to it. We are not letting them have this harbor easy—you got me, soldier?"

"I'm not a soldier sir. I'm a civilian. I won't be of much use."

"This is not the day for that, son. Everyone is a soldier today."

Roark fished out the battered telegram with Roosevelt's orders on it and handed it to the man.

"What the hell is this?"

"That is my order, sir."

"Will you stop calling me sir," he said reading the note, remaining completely still amid the chaos. No inch of the man was out of control.

"Everyone is not in uniform, sir, apologies. I can't tell."

The man shoved the order back to Roark. "I'm Master Chief Warren Griffin. You can have that back, I get it. I still could use you on the *Missouri*."

"I need to find the hospital," said Roark, taking the photo out of his jacket and showing it to the chief. "There is someone there I need to find."

\\\\\\\\\\\\\\\\\\\\\\\\\\\\\\\\\\\

James took a deep breath, watching the MP head back outside to wait by the jeep.

"Whoa."

"Yea."

"Whoa," said Gene again, putting his hands over his face, wiping the sweat off his forehead. "I can't believe it. Did that just happen?"

James kept looking at the MP, now in the distance. Every thought about the rest of the night and what could happen raced through his head. The image of him proposing to Adele slipped back into his mind. The thought that it might not happen crept in. *It will happen. I will see us married*, he thought, but even his optimism seemed lost in the moment.

"I don't know," he said, almost in a whisper.

"What?" said Gene, leaning in quickly, missing what was said.

"I don't know. I need to think."

"What are we going to tell the girls?"

"We can't," said James looking over Gene's shoulder at Adele and Karla. "We can't tell them the truth."

"What do you mean we can't tell them? The world could end tomorrow. This could be the last... "

"Hey. None of that."

Gene stopped before the end of his sentence. "We have to tell them something, James."

"We can't, Gene. We tell them...it's a training exercise."

"You think they are going to believe that?"

"We had a night exercise a few weeks back. It will work."

"I don't know, James."

"Look, I know you want to say something. So do I." He took out the ring and flipped it in his fingers. "I was going to propose to her. You're right, there's a chance I may not ever get to do that, but we can't go into this thinking that way. We have to believe tomorrow will come and we will still be here."

"I hope so. Get me to tomorrow morning, and then I'll believe you. That sobered me up quick."

"Let's go tell them. Follow my lead."

"Heh, I can barely speak to you right now. I can't focus."

"I need you, Gene. This is why we're here."

Gene took a big breath, blowing out loudly. He was sweating pretty hard now and did not look well. James forced a smile back onto his own face and took the deep breath in his head. As they turned to head back to the girls, James picked up as if they were mid conversation about the MP. They made their way over to the girls who greeted them with another round.

"What was that about?"

"You wouldn't believe that guy." As he spoke, a cold sweat began to creep over him.

"What did he want?"

She handed him the drink, and he felt that somehow Adele looked different than before his talk with the MP. He noticed every detail of her more clearly. He noticed the curve of her smile as she looked at him. Her eyes studied him, waiting for an answer. He wanted to tell her she was beautiful. He wanted to tell her everything. He had never lied to her; he'd never had to. He wanted to say that everything would be all right. He wanted to tell her the truth, but his lips betrayed him.

"There's..."

Gene looked up from his glass with a nervous look. No one else noticed, but Gene's hands were shaking. He had a look on his face that he might never make it back to this place. James stayed, looking at Gene as he spoke.

"... a training exercise. Tonight."

Gene swallowed hard, hearing the lie. He quickly choked down the rest of his drink.

"A training .... exercise?" Karla snapped before Adele could say anything. "That's so mean."

"They decided to do a training exercise tonight. Just like that?" Adele looked more skeptical.

"Yes, well, honey, they can do that. It's the Navy." He watched her, wishing he could tell her the truth. He could hear the words he wanted to say in his head. He could hear her reaction. He could hear her wanting him to stay and be safe. He couldn't have her worried about him.

"What kind of exercise? When will you be back?"

"Later tonight," said James without really thinking. In his head he was explaining about the mission to her like he wanted to so desperately but realized he'd said that part out loud. The words came out in a somber tone. Gene stared at him in disbelief.

"Later tonight?" said Gene in an awkward voice.

"Yes. Come by the ship later on. I'll call when I get back, then I'll let you on. "

Gene looked at him, more scared than nervous. He could see Gene starting to mouth the words "What are you doing?" through his pursed lips.

"It would be too late then," she said sadly.

"You sure?" he asked as some sweat built on his forehead. He could feel himself getting chills up his back.

"You okay, babe?" Adele put her hand on his forehead. "You're sweating."

"Yeah just a bit warm. I'm fine."

"If you're coming down with something maybe you should get out of this exercise and go lie down. Your concert is tomorrow."

"I'll try, dear. So is that a no on seeing you later?"

"I'm not boarding the *Arizona* after midnight on a weekend," she said with some sarcasm and smiling at him again.

"Well, okay. But we got to go. Ready, Gene?"

"I guess." His voice was higher than before.

"Have fun," said Karla, not fully realizing what was going on. She leaned forward and gave Gene a hug. He kissed her hard, and James could see he was whispering that he loved her. His heart sank, rethinking what was about to happen.

"You do look beautiful tonight," he said softly.

"Why thank you. You're biased."

"I know."

"I'll see you tomorrow then?"

"Of course." He kissed her softly and whispered that he loved her. She whispered it back. He pulled back, and she smiled, staring into his eyes.

"I'll see you tomorrow," she said again putting her hand on the side of his face gently.

"Good night, my lady," he said, smiling.

"Good night, good sir," she said, knowing the meaning.

"Let's go, Gene."

They turned to go, and the girls went back to their drinks. James looked back over his shoulder before they went through the door.

"We going to see them again?"

"Yes. We have to."

`````````````````````````````````

"The hospital? There's nothing wrong with you. You scared to fight?" said Warren, stepping up to Roark. "You listen to me, whoever you are. We are at war. Now I don't care who put you here, you get over there and fight back. Japs are going to shoot at you no matter what you're looking for."

"I'm going there with or without your help. This goes beyond even this. I hear you, but I have to do this."

"Fine, but know you're a coward and I have no respect for cowards. The hospital is that way." Warren pointed down the dock without looking. He was staring at Roark unflinching while everything was going on all around them. The guilt in Roark grew worse as he turned toward the hospital. He knew he was turning his back on the fight. He kept focusing on the goal of all this; he couldn't let the guilt in. He took some steps down the dock and turned to look back at Warren, but the man had already walked away. He walked defiantly, pulling other men off the ground or out of the water. He was the man Roark wanted to be. The one that could be relied on to get the job done.

*Maybe I am a coward*, Roark thought, still watching him move without hesitation, still performing despite the chaos. It was something to be admired. As he gained more and more respect for the master chief, the more that word hung heavy within him.

"Coward."

He put his hand on his heart. A pain rang through him at the touch. It was a mixture of guilt, regret, and envy that overtook him. As the pain grew sharper, he clenched at his chest but immediately stopped. He could feel the outline of the photo
`````````````````````````````````

in his inside pocket. He knew he had to press on, but how? What could he say? How do you tell the news that a loved one is gone, murdered by a man in time? A murderer who is still out there, escaped, having gotten away. How did you say that it was his failure that he was gone?

He realized his feet were carrying him forward without thought. It was no reason that drove him forward, only guilt. The events on the Hornet from the night before seemed like some distant memory that blurred away into white. All of it appeared as flashes in his mind as he walked—the dead sailors in the hallway, the chaos on the bridge, the face of the pilot before he shot the plane, seeing James right before he was shot.

He noticed some sailors crouched behind a jeep as he walked. He wanted to be like Warren.

"Get up and fight," Roark said, but the words that came out were not of a strong man. The words that escaped were hoarse and weak. The sailors just stared at him, frightened. The drive in him was gone. Earlier today he had such purpose, but now, looking around at the attack on the harbor, all he felt was defeat. Now he couldn't even get a few men hiding to stand. All he could do was turn his head and let his feet continue forward.

As he reached the path to the hospital, he realized he was not alone walking in the same direction. At first he noticed a few, then more and more. It was all the injured of the attack moving in droves toward the hospital. Some men were crying, most looked confused, and some could barely stand. Many were carrying their dead brothers, or what was left of them. One man that was walking was burned over most of his body. He screamed with each step, using all his remaining strength to make it to help. A man came up behind him, almost running. He was carrying what was left of his severed arm. As the horde moved, bombs could still be heard in the distance, causing everyone to react and duck. The only thought that materialized with every passing soldier was, "It's my fault." The words slipped out in a whisper, but in his head he was screaming it at the top of his lungs. The pain returned in his chest as he looked up to see the hospital approaching.

The scene before him was a flood of bodies. Hundreds were rushing to fit through the tiny doors to the few that could help them. As the surge got closer to the door the injured mass had to squeeze together. All the bloodied bodies were pushed against him. He did what he could to try not to hit them but managed to fit through the door, only to find the horror get worse.

Inside, everyone was screaming, grasping, and pulling at the nearest person that could help them. The floor was a mix of blood, sand, dirt, and debris. As bombs continued to be heard outside, each one sent a shudder through the building, shaking all the windows and cabinets. Above the roar of the wounded, louder still was the yell of the doctors to each other and the nurses struggling to communicate amid the confusion.

Roark scanned every face to try and look for her, but every nurse he saw looked the same. A simple truth had escaped him until this moment. He had never met Adele before. He had talked with James numerous times at the railing and he had seen her picture, but he never had seen her up close. How could he find her in this and know for certain it was her, and once he found her, what would he say?

"Doctor, I need a tourniquet over here stat," a female voice said, cutting through a crowd of soldiers ahead of him.

That's her, he thought, not really knowing why, but a jolt went up his spine as she spoke. But where was she?

"Needle and thread here," the voice cried out again. Roark pushed forward, climbing his way through the mess until he got near enough to see her. She looked just like the picture. The first thing he noticed was the butterfly clip in her hair.

Before he could even take in the thought that he finally had met her, reality reared its head. She turned, looked right at him, and then looked past him to the doctor.

"Morphine!"

She looked back to the man on the table who was shaking almost uncontrollably from a neck injury.

"You there, put your fingers here," she said without looking up. Roark was lost in the moment watching her work, seemingly detached from the situation.

She looked up quickly, right at him. "You, two fingers, on his neck and put pressure on the wound." He reacted slower than normal, in disbelief of what was happening, and quickly tried to focus and follow the command. He pressed his fingers down on the man's neck and could feel the man's quickened pulse.

"Ma'am?"

She continued right on working not even flinching when he started to speak. She worked with such speed, stitching up the man's leg wound.

"Ma'am."

"Is he bleeding a lot from his neck?" she asked looking to where Roark had his fingers.

"No, but I... um."

She kept working but looked up at him with an expression of pure exhaustion yet a remaining sense of purpose.

"What is it?" she asked softly.

``````````````````````````````

"Good evening, gentleman. I'm sorry to pull you all away from a well-deserved leave, but I'm afraid we have an event that demands immediate action," said Colonel Doolittle, standing at the front of the briefing room staring back at all the men still in civilian dress.

"Earlier today we received word that the Japanese fleet not only mobilized but left port and was on its way here to Hawaii. Just a few hours ago it was confirmed that they could in fact have planes here by morning. You do not need me to tell you how devastating that would be because, as you know, we are not at battle-ready status. Your job tonight is to go out there tonight, meet them head-on, and ... dissuade them from launch. Now my superiors believe we can talk the Japanese down without a shot fired. I was not raised that way. I believe we have

91
``````````````````````````````

to not only dissuade them but make an example of them to show that no one can ever get this close ever again. Between you and me, men, if things go south—and they will—sink the bastards. You all have your orders; you all have your posts. Be aboard in fifteen. That's all."

"Aye, sir," the crowd said in unison.

They all stood up and made their way outside onto the dock toward the *Hornet*.

"Whoa," said Gene, catching up to James. "You think Doolittle is right?"

"About what, Gene?"

"That World War Two is going to start tonight."

"I don't think so. We already had one; I doubt too many people are after a second. It's fine to be a little cautious, though," he said, putting a hand on Gene's shoulder. "I'll look after you, no worries."

"I just want it to be over."

"You can say that again."

As they made their way to the ship, a car pulled around from down the road, coming toward the ship.

"Well, that's an awfully nice car." The two turned to watch the car pull up close to the ramp. The driver scurried out and ran around to the back door. Doolittle made his way over the car to greet its passenger. The back door opened, and a younger man came out. He was dressed in a clean tan suit, black tie, and black shoes. As the man got out of the car, he checked his pocket watch that looked to be made of gold.

Doolittle immediately started talking in the man's face, almost yelling at him. The man calmly took out a small piece of paper and handed it to Doolittle. The colonel gave him one final look and said something to him in a low voice. All James could make out was that his name must be Roark.

\\\\\\\\\\\\\\\\\\\\\\\\\\\\\\\

"What is it?" she asked again, looking right at him.

Roark just looked at her, frozen, not knowing what to do. All he could do was stare.

"I'm sorry....... I mistook you for someone else."

"Well I'm busy; go help Doctor Mills over there. I can finish this."

He turned and walked away; he couldn't bring himself to look back. He came all that way and he couldn't do it. He couldn't tell her that James was gone. She was going to think he was on the *Arizona*. There would be no good-byes.

He slumped out a side door between buildings. He had failed in every sense.

"So you see now," said a voice once he felt the quietness of the alley.

Roark turned his head slowly toward the voice. A young man was crouched up against the wall. He wore an expensive-looking grey suit with a silver tie. His hair was slicked, and his shoes had a high shine. He sat on the ground, hugging his knees, staring up at Roark.

"What?" was all Roark could muster.

"I'm sorry I didn't introduce myself fully earlier," said Andrew. The man stayed tucked on the ground as everything whirled back to Roark. He hadn't expected to see this man so soon. A mixture of hate, jealousy, revenge, and envy all hit him at once. His body became rigid from it all.

"You!" he said, clenching every muscle in him.

"You had to see, Roark, you had to see what would happen, had to see the cost that had to be paid." Andrew was staring hard at the wall across from where he was crouched. Roark wasn't sure if he was looking up out of fear or concentration

"How could you do all of this?"

"You needed to see where I was coming from, where my motivation was." Andrew suddenly shot a direct look up to Roark. "You remember the third world war, Roark?" The question startled Roark. No one had brought up those events in some time. A forgotten moment in history. "Do you remember the invasion, do you remember what they did?" The images raced through Roark' mind as Andrew spoke. He remembered the faces of people lying on the street. He remembered the silence in the cities, the emptiness. "They walked into people's homes. People watching television, making coffee. They were obliterated...just for being there." Roark remembered it was the war no one saw coming. "I was returning from Afghanistan. I Skyped my family days before, telling them I loved them and finding out as I landed in Boston that the invasion had begun, and they were slaughtered." Tears could be seen in Andrews's eyes. "My wife was killed and my son, one year old. How do you think I felt on that day? It's what you feel now." It was as if Roark were struck in the face with the feeling of guilt. "Between the bombs and the genocide, ten million people were killed in one day—one day. The whole country was torn apart. I vowed I would do everything I could to fix that."

"There was nothing anyone could have done, Andrew. We weren't invaded; they were already here. The troops were living among us as cab drivers, postmen, and police. They were living as ordinary citizens. Nothing anyone could have done would have changed anything. We were unprepared."

Andrew was not fazed by Roark words. "A man showed up at my house some months later." Roark's face contorted at the admission. "The man explained how I could get my family back. He gave me this gold watch. He helped me make the decision to change history. To save them, to save all those people, to save my family. I knew sacrifices would have to be made to ensure it didn't happen. Now you see what has to be done to save so many more. To save that life, that love, that belief, that future, to achieve all that, they first must be broken. Now you see that here."

"Changing the past does not guarantee anything in the future will be different. It's a gamble." Roark was pleading with him now. "So this was just a statement." Pointing behind him. "Blowing up a base in the middle of the ocean just to stop an invasion that hasn't happened yet."

"Then there's you, mover. It's your job to protect history. It's your job to ensure that invasion happens, to ensure my family gets killed. Only once you know what you are, you can move forward. I know what I am, but the only way forward for me is to go back. Try again."

"What else do you plan to do?" Roark knew this would go on and on until this man got what he wanted.

"Our country was invaded by Japan and destroyed, so for this war we need to win, and if changing just one thing in the past isn't enough to guarantee the future then I will make this war so grand it will forever change how wars are fought, and then, maybe, it will be enough. I need to involve America in the greatest war the world has ever seen. It will show America's strength and dissuade anyone from attacking us. I have other nations ready to play their part."

"Why are you telling me this?" Roark was growing more concerned with the complexity of what he was going to have to overcome.

"I need you to see that sometimes changing history is the correct path. You can witness all the things that you are keeping from everyone. That is my purpose. I know you were once tempted by the idea too, Roark."

"What?" His mind went blank at the phrase. Only two people in the world knew about that. "Who was the one who came to you?"

Andrew looked up to Roark with almost a half-smile and in a flash of blue, he was gone.

He barely could make sense of what had been said. What has been started here? So many questions buzzed around his head, it only made the pain in his chest worse.

Before he could even regain his stance, he fell against the same wall Andrew was against. He needed a moment to breathe, to think. The weight of it all made him land hard on the ground. He closed his eyes for a second to catch his breath.

As his eyes closed, he thought he saw another flash of blue. Suddenly, he felt himself being pulled up and shoved against the wall. *He's back*, he thought as he slowly opened his eyes. He squinted to focus on the face in front of him, which had more rage in it than he had ever seen.

"How dare you bring me into this," said the voice as he let go of Roark. Roark slumped back down on the ground, too weak to stand.

"I'm...I'm so sorry, Kori."

Chapter Four:

Fate's Dream

"Don't hurt me," said Crantor, doubled over on the ground. The old man clutched at his sides through his robes. He had long grey hair and a scraggly beard. He looked as if he hadn't bathed in some time. He wore the robes of a monk or cleric. "I did what you asked."

The old man pleadingly looked up to Adam, coming closer to his despair. The man that approached seemed out of place. He was a tall, handsome man in his early twenties. He had blond hair, blue eyes, and carried himself with an authoritative poise. He was dressed in an outfit made of black stone. It clung to his body like a second skin but was covered in strange lights. The old man didn't know what to make of it.

"Are they all secure?" Adam asked, looking at something on his forearm. As the old man watched, the blond man started touching one finger to whatever was on his forearm, each touch making a noise.

"They are."

"All one hundred of them?" Adam snapped to look at the mess on the ground below him. "It is essential there are none left behind."

As he spoke, an explosion could be heard in the distance, and distant sounds of screams started to ring out.

"What's that?" asked Crantor, cringing on the ground, struggling to look toward the sound he heard.

Adam looked in the direction of the sound, but he had no reaction and turned back to what he was doing on his forearm.

"You needn't worry about that. Just loose ends. There are none left behind, correct?"

"There are none. There were only one hundred. They said that was all there was. Why do you want to take them from these people?" Crantor asked, begging the man for an answer.

"For the greater good, my friend."

Adam checked his watch and saw 11:45 a.m. on the face. "Ok, last loose end," he said, squatting down to eye level with the old man on the ground. "There is one last thing, old man. The journal."

"What?"

"I know you have been keeping a record. A journal of our journey, how we got here, what I have been doing. I can't let you take that back to the world."

"I haven't kept any such thing," said Crantor, pleading with him. The old man was sweating, trying to hold himself together enough to speak. "I swear I haven't."

"I'm not much for interrogations." A revolver materialized in Adam's hand, and he let it hang in front of the old man's face. "Do you have the journal on you?"

Crantor dropped his head, and tears trickled to the ground. "Why? Why do this? Why do this to these people? What did they do? I never should have brought you here."

"This is not the time to blame yourself. These people are the victims of their own devices. If it weren't you it would have been someone else. It's as simple as that. Now do you have it on you?" asked Adam.

Crantor, with trembling hands, reached behind his robes and pulled out a broken leather book. He held it out to Adam.

Adam walked away a few steps. "Toss the book over there."

"Please."

"Toss it over there, now."

Crantor tossed the book a few feet away onto the open ground and immediately went back to clutching his side. The exertion stretched his stomach, and his pain returned.

Adam turned to face the journal on the ground and studied it from afar for a moment. He reached into a small pocket on his left sleeve and pulled out a small capsule. He walked over to the book and broke the capsule over it. A few drops fell over the journal. He pulled a few matches from the same pocket and struck one. He watched the flame and let it go.

As it fell the old man closed his eyes and turned away from the sight. The match hit the cover, and the book burst into flames. Within seconds the book started to crinkle up, causing the book to open, partially revealing pages and pages of dated entries, each written almost in a frantic scribble. As fast as he had lit it on fire the book was nothing more than ash.

"And now it's done."

"What's left now?" asked Crantor.

"Everything. A new era is about to begin. You helped me achieve the first step," said Adam.

"I mean, what's left now for me?"

"In ancient Egypt, servants were buried with their pharaohs. Essentially, they were immortalized with the greatness of their past. You will be remembered for what you have done. Immortalized with the greatness you brought here."

The old man put his forehead on the ground, reaching under his robes where the book had been, and pulled out something clenched in his fist but hidden from Adam.

"No loose ends," he said as Adam turned around and raised the revolver. He squeezed the trigger, and the old man slumped to the ground. Another explosion rang out in the distance as Adam checked his watch one more time. The time read 11:55 a.m., and he walked off into the woods away from the explosion.

A moment of silence passed around the body, until a few steps could be heard. With his last breath Crantor saw feet approach him. Covered in tattoos and strange designs, the feet stopped right next to him. The old man reached up and gave the person what was in his hands. As he let go of the item he fell back to the earth; the last bit of life had left him.

The person held the item, a crumpled piece of parchment. He unfolded it to see a map with a location circled on it. On the bottom it read, "To undo this lie, find me and send to this address." A set of explosions started in the distance. They got louder and louder, so the person clenched the piece of parchment and disappeared into the trees.

She snapped awake, screaming "NOOO!" She awoke covered in sweat, breathing heavily. She sat up, frantically looking in all directions. The room was dark. Everything there was still.

It was raining outside, and the soft drops could be heard against the window. The room was almost barren, with only the bed and her desk against the opposite wall. The walls were painted all white. It had a very institutional feel to it. The other bed in the room was empty since she had no roommate. She hated this room. She hated this place, but it was out of her control. All she could do was make the best of it.

Through the silence she could hear the door lock. Swiftly, a figure swung open the door and flipped on the light. Instantly, the room became blinded by brilliance. Her eyes hurt while they adjusted. It was the head nurse, Susan. Her uniform was immaculate. She came over to the bed, sternly staring at her in the bed.

"Mary-Ellen, are you all right?" asked the nurse, sitting on the edge of the bed. She had a look of concern on her face as she waited for a response.

"I'm fine," she said, sounding annoyed and tugging at the covers from under the nurse.

"I heard you yelling."

"Yeah, it's nothing," she said, looking out the window.

The nurse studied her as if trying to discern a diagnosis from simply looking at her.

"Well, what was it?"

"It's nothing, I said."

The nurse sat there as if Mary had not responded that way. She folded her arms. That's what Mary hated about this place. She was sixteen years old, but she was treated as if she was five. She couldn't have any privacy. Everything that happened needed to be explained away as if there were something wrong with her. She felt like she had no freedom.

"It was a dream."

"Was it the same one?"

Are you serious? she thought, but she answered, "Yes."

"Do you know who the two people are in the dream?"

"No."

"Did it go past the old man being shot?"

"Not by much."

"How much further did it go?"

"God, this is so embarrassing." Mary adjusted to face more away from the nurse.

"It's good to talk about it. It's part of the process."

"I hate the process, Can't it wait till morning? Why does it always have to be right after?"

"It's fresher this way," said the nurse, inching closer on the bed to put a hand on Mary's back. "Keep going. What happened after the shot?"

"The guy dies, okay? I see feet coming toward me. It's as if I'm the dying man. He gives a piece of paper to someone, like a map or something. It says something on the bottom."

"What did it say?"

"I don't remember."

"Try."

"I don't know, okay? Maybe later. Sometimes it takes a while for all of it to register. It's nice to not remember something for once. It's nice to not remember something for once. Let me have that, please."

"It must be hard," said the nurse, sounding sympathetic.

Mary could feel her eyes watering, but no tears fell.

"It's a nightmare."

"It concerns us that you are having nightmares. That it's getting to you. That's why you're here. No one has ever had your condition. They only recently named it because of you."

"Oh yeah, what do they say I have?"

"Let's talk about that later. Do you want to talk more about the dream?"

"It feels so real when it happens," said Mary-Ellen, turning back to the nurse. "I don't want them."

"I know, dear, but that's why we are here to help you."

Mary curled up under the blankets facing the window. *I don't want anyone's help,* she thought, closing her eyes as hard as she could.

The nurse gently patted Mary's back and stood up from the bed. "We'll talk about this more in the morning."

Mary could still see the tattoos on the foot in front of her. It was as if that image were floating in her mind. She tried desperately to look up to see what the person looked like, but as she strained to see, sleep finally got the better of her.

"Mary-Ellen it's time to get up, dear."

"What?" snapped Mary. She flicked open her eyes, but immediately had to close them. She felt like she had only slept for a second. It was brighter in the room now than the night before. She let her eyes focus and saw the nurse standing at the edge of the bed. As soon as Mary readjusted to speak, the first nurse snapped her attention to another immaculately dressed nurse standing at the door.

"And with that we have Mary-Ellen Hammond in room 717. All accounted for, so I'm off."

"Thank you. All set. See you tonight."

Mary's nurse made her way for the door with a small smile. She winked at Mary as she left. It was her normal morning routine. It had been that way since she could remember. Her parents had left her here when she was very young as a last option because they did not know what else to do. She couldn't focus on anything, not her schoolwork, not her friends; she was forgetful and couldn't even retain enough information to do chores around the house. She would wake up with the same violent dream over and over about an old man being killed in cold blood. The confounding part was that she could remember absolutely everything about her life. She could tell anyone about the minute details about anything that had ever happened to her; it was only learning new information that was the problem. The orphanage had tried everything—hospitals, psychologists, even hypnotherapy. None of it worked. This place was their most desperate option.

As Mary looked out through the barred windows, she could see the blue sky but not the sun. Her room faced west, so she couldn't see the morning sun. She heard the morning breakfast cart squeak into the room.

"The usual today, mademoiselle?"

Mary knew they voice. Ian, the boy who worked the food cart, was a volunteer from the local high school. She had a crush on him and seeing him was the one bright spot of the day.

"Of course, kind sir."

The boy took the tray off the cart and put it on the bed table. "Got you some bacon in there too. Figured you would want some."

All Mary could do was smile and wink at him. The day nurse was standing in the doorway watching them and made sort of a coughing noise.

"See you tomorrow."

"Bye."

The boy headed out with the cart, and the nurse closed the door behind him, leaving her once again by herself. She took off the lid of the tray to reveal the usual. A cup of yogurt and a banana. Tucked under the banana were two strips of bacon, taken from the staff kitchen, no doubt. *Thank you,* she thought to herself, crunching down on the tasty bacon.

As she finished the second piece she heard the door unlock again. The day nurse stepped in, looking rather surprised.

"Mary-Ellen, when you are finished I need you to get dressed quickly and come with me."

"I'm done," she said quickly. She hated the yogurt here and leaped at the opportunity to get away from it. She threw on some jeans and a zip-up hoodie and headed for the door. She knocked twice to signal she was ready, and the door opened to the day nurse.

"Right this way."

"What's up?"

"You have a visitor."

"My foster parents haven't come here yet."

"No, I'm afraid it's not them, Mary-Ellen. It's two other visitors, actually."

"Well, who are they?"

"They said it was absolutely urgent they speak with you. They are policeman—detectives."

"What did I do?" she asked, sounding annoyed.

"Do as they ask, young lady."

"Fine."

They approached the visitor's entrance to the building, which looked nothing like where her room was. Everything up here was carpeted and smelled like flowers. It looked like the lobby of a rich hotel. Mary drudgingly followed the nurse to a double set of wood doors.

"They are right through there, now—in you go."

"You're not coming in?" asked Mary, slightly shocked. No patient was allowed to go anywhere unattended. It was a primary rule of the building.

"In you go. I'll be waiting right here."

Mary suddenly had a very nervous feeling about all this. She swallowed hard and pressed on the doors, and they opened without a sound.

Inside looked like a very nice office for royalty or something. There was a big fireplace and three large individual leather chairs arranged by it. The other end of the room contained a massive desk that looked like it weighed a ton.

As the door closed behind Mary-Ellen, a moment passed of silence, but as the door clicked shut two very well-dressed men in tan suits stood up and walked around the chairs toward her. They both smiled warmly and approached her.

"Ah yes, Mary-Ellen, good of you to come. Welcome, I'm Roark," said the first man, stretching out his hand. She cautiously reached out her hand and shook it briefly. He had a sort of charming desperation about him.

"I'm Kori. Nice to finally meet you," said the second man, who was dressed exactly the same as Roark. She immediately had a feeling about the second man that he had a more quiet intensity about him, as if he were a severe storm bottled up into a form of perfect subtlety.

"Hi," she said. "Shop at the same stores, you two?" she said, straining to ease the mood. The two men chuckled as they headed back to their seats by the fire. "She's funny," said Kori without looking back as he plunged back into his seat.

As she and Roark made their way to their seats, Mary studied the two men. They both wore identical tan suits. Their ties were stark black, which matched their black shoes. They both wore the same watch on the same wrist. Apart from their appearance she noticed subtle differences between the men. The one called Kori appeared much more relaxed and uninterested than Roark. Roark appeared much more on edge, as if he was holding back something. There also seemed to be a tension between them.

"So, who are you?" asked Mary, carefully sitting down in her armchair. She shot looks to both of them, unsure who would answer her question.

"More on that later," said Roark after a moment. She noticed he didn't look her in the eye as he spoke.

"I don't know you. We haven't met before."

"No, we haven't. Though it is my aim and goal to change that fact," said Roark, now looking her in the eye.

"I have a very good memory," she said, staring right back.

"Yes, that's part of the reason we are here. You have a very unique case, Mary-Ellen. Word travels quite fast."

"Are you two doctors?"

"No!" said Kori in a blunt, loud tone. Kori was fixed on the fire. He looked as if he had no choice but to sit there and couldn't have cared less about the conversation. The smile he had when he first greeted her seemed like a distant memory.

"Forgive my colleague. He is not very delicate sometimes."

"So what do you want if you're not doctors?"

"You could say we specialize in your condition. Well, it's not even a condition—more of a gift."

"It's not a gift. I hate remembering everything. It's tough to concentrate. Anyway, do I have to be here? I'd like to go back to my room now. I don't know who you are, and I'm uncomfortable sitting here," said Mary, starting to get up.

"No, please stay. We are consultants. Please, we will explain. We just need a few minutes of your time," said Roark rising toward Mary.

Kori barely flinched, still staring at the fire.

"Your memory, which your doctor's say is a condition, does have a name."

Mary stopped on her way to the door.

"It's called hyper-themystic memory," he said, moving around her chair toward the door where she was.

Mary turned to face him. Her face crunched up, trying to understand the term. "You're making that up, I've never heard of it."

"It means you remember absolutely everything," chimed in Kori, rising from his position. He stood up but did not move in any direction; he was still fixed on the fire, but his words carried through the room. "Another name for it is total recall. It means your memory is, for lack of a better word, perfect." As he spoke the final word, he turned to look at Mary for the first time since she walked in. "Right now you could tell me everything you did today down to the smallest detail, and about yesterday and the day before that. You could tell me everything about your seventh birthday party, who came, what they all had to drink, and even what clothes they all wore. You can remember the minutest details about everything you have ever experienced or read about."

Roark darted a quick glance at Kori without moving his head.

Kori continued approaching Mary. "You could even tell me about the day of your birth if you wanted to. No one else in the world could be capable of telling me that, but you can. You are unique, Mary-Ellen, one of a kind," said Kori arriving right in front of her.

"You make it sound... beautiful. You make it sound like something anyone would want, but I don't. I don't want it. I don't want to remember it all. I remember my dad giving me up for adoption. I tried to forget that day, but it keeps replaying in every detail, my father leaving me here," she said in a shaky voice.

"There is no discipline to your mind," said Roark, standing by her chair. "There is no control to it, so memories overcome you. It keeps you from managing it all. It keeps you from moving forward. That is where we can help. "

"How do you know about all of this?"

"We have it too," said Roark, putting his hands in his pockets. "Now, can you please sit down and join us again?" Roark gestured to the chairs.

A few moments passed while Mary stood by the door. Kori was fixed on her now. He looked at her as if he were trying to look through her. Slowly, she moved away from the door and passed Kori. As she passed him he remained looking at the door. His glance then dropped to the floor before returning back to his chair. His expression once he sat back in his chair resembled that of guilt.

"So you have it too."

"Yes," said Kori before Roark could say it. It came out almost in a whisper.

"Yes," answered Roark more directly. "We learned to control it. Not let it cloud our lives. To use it as a tool, if you will."

"Oh. That must be nice. Whatever you call it, it's caused me nothing but trouble. My foster parents considered me a burden. I can't make friends. No boy will date me 'cause they all think I'm crazy. I have nightmares. I want it all to stop."

Roark had a statement on his mind but couldn't say it. He had never had to counsel someone before. Not in this way. He had no experience with situations like this. He didn't know how to respond.

"I'm sorry about all that. I am."

"What can you do to make it go away?" she asked, sinking into the chair. She felt heavy thinking about all of it. She didn't care to be sitting there, but she didn't care to be in her room, either.

"What's your favorite subject, Mary?"

The question entered her mind and caused her to stop. "What?"

She noticed that both Roark and Kori were staring at her now. Both seemed intent to hear her answer.

"History, why?"

"Tell us about it, which part?"

"What does that have to do with anything? Is this something to help me control my memory or something?"

Roark gave a small smile at the answer. "Yes."

"American history. I like World War Two the most."

"Great. Tell us how we got involved. I'm a fan of history myself," said Roark.

She shot looks to both men and found Kori had lost some of the color in his face. He sat looking at her as if a weight were resting on his shoulders.

"Well, it was Pearl Harbor, as everyone knows."

Roark re-adjusted in his seat. Kori shot a look at Roark, then immediately shot back to Mary.

"The attack," said Roark with a strained jaw. "And what of the *Hornet*?"

"Well, yeah, that's the ship used for the retaliation."

Roark cleared his throat and leaned forward a little in his chair. "The...the what?"

"Don't you know your history? The response to Pearl Harbor was a mission launched from the *Hornet* to Tokyo. The mission led by Doolittle."

"Ah, he lived," said Kori under his breath.

Roark lifted a hand to his chest. The pain had returned for a moment. Neither Kori nor Mary noticed the action.

"Of course, he lived through the harbor attack," said Mary without missing a beat.

"No I meant the…" said Kori. Roark shot a look to him, causing Kori to end his sentence. "Right, yeah, the harbor."

"You didn't know that?" said Mary, looking between the two of them.

"Well this is a lesson for you; don't worry about us," said Roark, returning to his normal appearance. The pain still lingered behind his forced poise.

"You still might want to visit a library, catch up on a few things. They do still exist, you know," said Mary looking at Roark.

"That might not be a bad idea, considering," said Roark.

The two men exchanged glares, each then looking off in a different direction.

"Purely hypothetical question for you, Mary," said Kori, leaning forward in his chair abruptly.

"Kori, don't," said Roark calmly.

Kori continued on without listening to the attempt. "What if I were to tell you it was the opposite?"

"Tell me what is the opposite?" said Mary, sitting back in her chair.

"Everything you just said." Kori calmly sat back and crossed his legs.

"Now you're talking fiction. I know what happened. You can read it in any textbook."

"Well therein lies the problem. What if what is in those history textbooks is incorrect?"

"So what if every textbook ever written in the last 71 years about the Pearl Harbor attack and whatever else is incorrect? That's what you're asking me?" said Mary, starting to raise her voice. "What the hell kind of conversation is this?"

"It's just a question. What would you think?" said Kori, still calm.

"I'd say it's impossible, for one. I know what I know," said Mary sternly.

"So there's no way you could be convinced otherwise? Hypothetically, of course," said Kori, studying her.

"You would need a lot of evidence, which you don't have."

"Of course," said Kori, leaning his head on his hand.

Several moments passed where no one spoke. Kori sat staring at Mary. Mary kept switching from the floor to Kori. Roark was looking at the fire when he suddenly turned.

"Could you entertain and indulge me a notion then?" said Roark, relaxed.

"This ought to be good," said Mary, rolling her eyes.

"What if the attack on Pearl Harbor were the direct result ...of.. a failed attempt at peace?"

Mary's face twisted in surprise and bewilderment. "Okay, I'll play along. What attempt?"

"The *USS Hornet*."

"What do you mean?" said Mary, even more confused.

"The *USS Hornet* went out the night of December 6th and attempted to intercept the Japanese before they could launch to talk them into a peaceable resolution."

"What would be the failed part?"

"The ship never made it there. It was sunk before it arrived," said Roark, looking back to the fire.

"Well, right there your notion can't make sense. The one part your story hinges on is purely wrong."

"Which part is that?" said Roark, leaning forward a little.

"*The Hornet* doesn't sink until two years after the attack. If you say it sunk the night before, then what was the ship that continued on for two years carrying out missions?"

"Simple, another ship was re-named to cover the truth. Not many knew of the December 6th mission, it wouldn't be that difficult," said Roark, leaning back again.

"Oh sure, yeah, sounds just like any other conspiracy theory. An answer for everything," said Mary, rolling her eyes at the two men again. Neither Kori nor Roark reacted to her statement.

Suddenly, Kori leaned off the edge of his chair. "So if we were to show you our evidence, make our case, could you discern if what we are saying is truly incorrect? If we showed you the facts, could you tell us the difference between fact and fiction?"

Roark watched Kori, then calmly waited for her response.

"I could tell you in a heartbeat what was wrong with it." Mary's opinion of the two men was dwindling by the minute. *This whole thing is a waste of my time, but what else am I going to do today?* She liked the momentary power she was getting from these men, and it would be fun to pull one over on them.

"Great, let's go beyond the attack now to the rest of World War Two. Could you settle other conspiracy theories for us?" said Roark, folding his hands.

"I know them all, yes," she said, smiling.

The two men cracked such subtle smirks they could barely be noticed.

"Good, I think now would be an appropriate moment, Kori," said Roark, staring at the floor toward Kori.

"We will be taking you out of here now, Mary," said Kori.

"What do you mean? I'm not allowed to leave, and I still don't know you. This has been fun, don't get me wrong, guys, but I think I'll take my chances here."

"He didn't really phrase it as a question, Mary," said Roark again flatly, with his hands still crossed. He looked up to Mary with a straight face.

"We need your help, and, well, what we need your help with cannot really be explained here and now. It has to be shown to you," said Kori rising from his seat and walking to the desk at the back of the room.

"What has to be shown?" said Mary, getting a cold chill up her spine. Suddenly, she wanted out of this room. She didn't want to be near these two men anymore.

"I packed you a bag of clothes; you will need them. We can get more if need be," said Kori, pulling a stuffed backpack out from behind the desk and walking over to her with it.

"I'm not leaving here with you. If you touch me, I'll...I'll scream. The head nurse is right outside," said Mary, getting up and getting behind her chair.

"I thought you said she wouldn't be this difficult, Roark," said Kori, turning to him.

"Now listen, Mary, we said we were not going to hurt you, and we are not going to. We need your help, your knowledge of history. What we need to achieve, we cannot do without you. I promise that as soon as we are done you will be safely brought back here, unharmed. I don't need you to trust me—given the circumstances I can understand why you wouldn't—but this is an opportunity to use your skill, your gift and do something extraordinary." Roark walked closer as he spoke. Mary backed up to match his pace. He reached out his hand in the gentlest fashion. Kori put his hands in his pockets and studied her.

"I don't know what's going on here," she said shakily.

"I know, but take my hand. Please," said Roark warmly. Behind his back Roark took out Atlas and held it tightly to him. Kori was holding his Atlas in his pocket, ready.

Mary lifted her hand. It was visibly shaking. *What am I doing?* She placed it on his hand, and as soon as she felt the coldness of his skin, all she saw was a flash of blue.

She opened her eyes and saw Roark, but everything around them was different. She felt extremely dizzy and her whole body felt hot. She immediately collapsed to the ground; her legs felt like jelly. Suddenly, she felt sick to her stomach.

"Breathe, just breathe, it will pass," said Roark calmly.

"This is dangerous," said Kori, sounding angrier than he had back at the hospital.

"I know, but it's done now. She has the intel we need for this past. It might be the only advantage we get. We need her," said Roark, looking out the window.

As the sickness subsided, she started to take in her surroundings. They were in some sort of warehouse. The large room was completely empty. Everything looked old. The floor creaked when the two men walked around. The place smelled old. Everything was silent, but outside the muffled sounds of trucks and voices could be heard. It sounded like it was very busy outside these walls.

She tried to speak, but nothing came out at first. She could see the men continue talking, but she couldn't hear what was said.

"You risk her life with all this. If you misstep even once her life is in jeopardy," said Kori, making his case.

"I know."

"You don't care about putting other people's lives in jeopardy anymore."

Roark just stared at Kori. He knew exactly what he was talking about. "We have been over that, Kori. You know how I feel about it."

"I'm not letting you forget it," said Kori, walking away from him.

"What did you do to me?" said Mary, finally able to get words out.

The two men moved closer to her and stood looking down at her. Roark crouched down to be at eye level.

"This will be difficult to explain, but this was really the only way to make you believe us and not just think we were crazy. We did not do anything to you. What you are experiencing are the after-effects of the manner in which you traveled here. You are no longer in the hospital where we were," said Roark, gesturing around them.

"Where am I?" said Mary in a scratched voice.

"Hawaii," said Kori. Roark snapped a look of concern up to him. Kori just shrugged and walked away.

"What?" she said, confused.

"We are on one of the islands of Hawaii. The Pearl Harbor base, to be more precise," said Roark, trying to smile warmly, but the pain grew in his chest again. Flashes of Adele, James, and Warren ran through his mind quickly. *Coward,* sounded in his mind.

"How is that possible? Did you drug me? Then carry me out. We got here so fast, I can't remember."

"No, we didn't drug you." Roark took out his Atlas and raised it in his hand to show her. "I used this."

"A watch. A pocket watch?" she said, squinting at the gold piece of jewelry.

"This is no ordinary watch," said Roark with a hint of a smirk. "This watch has the ability to take you anywhere. I can set the dials inside to whatever point I wish and once I close it. You're off. Just like that."

"That's impossible. Nothing exists like that."

"And yet, you're here," said Roark, placing the watch back in his jacket pocket.

Mary put her hand on her head. A headache had immediately sprung up.

"It will pass. Traveling this way is a shock to the system. The first couple of times always feel that way. After a while it subsides and you get used to it," said Roark, rising to a stance.

"Why did you take me to...Hawaii?"

"I told you before we left, we needed your help with something. Remember?"

"You said it was about conspiracy theories. Separating history from fiction," said Mary, still holding her head.

"That's right. We need you to help us track where things deviate from the actual version of history. Where these conspiracy theories come from, and how to protect the truth."

"I don't understand."

"What if I told you that the mission the night before the Pearl Harbor attack actually did happen, and due to a saboteur the mission was a failure." Mary winced through the pain, trying to understand it all. "The mission was lost because of one man. That one man is still out there, and he has the same resources we have. This watch. He has the ability to seriously damage the course of history, and that's where you come in."

Her head was reeling, trying to get a handle on all of this. "So, if I were to believe you, he did that all those years ago, and you're talking as if he is still out there now. He would be dead by now."

"Well, not if we went back to that time to do something about it," said Kori from where he was standing off by the window. "Not if we went back to that time all those years ago."

Mary chuckled to herself. The idea was absurd. *Time travel?* "You expect me to believe you two can time travel." Her laugh grew louder. "So not only are we in Hawaii, we are in the past too?" She got the strength to get to her feet and staggered away from the two men. "This just must be some part of the hospital that I've never been in before."

"Come outside with me," said Roark, gesturing toward a door on the opposite end of the warehouse.

"Why?" she said, turning to face him.

"Proof," said Kori. "You don't believe us, then go see for yourself."

She looked at the door and suddenly the weakness in her legs came back, but she remained standing. She slowly walked across the warehouse floor. The boards creaked under her feet as she moved. She passed Roark, who just stared at her as she passed. She reached the door, and the sounds she heard earlier were louder now. She turned the knob and swung the door open.

A blast of hot air was the first thing to hit her, and she was almost blinded by the brilliant sunlight. Her eyes focused, and the sight in front of her was a shock the likes of which she had never known. It was the Pearl Harbor base, destroyed. Ships bellowed smoke from their burning decks. Everywhere there were men picking up their fallen brothers. Everyone was covered in grime, soot, and blood. Boats were picking up men still swimming to shore. Bodies were being pulled from the water. Screams for help could be heard all around. Tears came to her eyes, and all she could do was put her hands to her face. The image of that sight would stick with her for the rest of her life. Roark and Kori came up behind her. She could feel Roark's hand on her back.

"Is this...?"

"December 7th, 1941. Yes. The attack ended thirty-five minutes ago here," said Roark. He couldn't look up to the sight. He looked at the ground only. Kori looked around at the destruction and could only look to Roark to see the effect it had on him. The only expression Kori could muster was anger.

"How is this possible? This can't be real. It has to be a nightmare."

"It's real. The gold watch I showed you doesn't just allow travel across the world, but into the past as well."

"I can't believe this. I don't know... what to think."

"This is happening, right now. A man with the same watch as we have came back and sunk the *Hornet* last night. What you see here is the result of that failure. You know the future of this time. We need you to tell us when history gets altered again from here forward. There is no textbook to tell us what will happen next, but to you, it's all stored up there." Kori gestured to Mary's head.

All Mary could do was look back out over the harbor at the scene before her. She couldn't say anymore. The weakness returned to her legs, and she began to fall. The image of the burning harbor all turned to black before her. Roark was quick to catch her and picked her up to bring her back inside the warehouse. He laid her down on the floor in the corner.

"That was too much to throw at her, Kori. We agreed to not let too much out too early," said Roark, rising to look back at Kori.

"She had to know; we don't have time to waste here. It could be hours before she wakes up. We should have learned more information from her before we brought her here," said Kori, firing back at him.

"She had to see it."

"She had to see what *you* did, you mean," said Kori, advancing.

The pain resurged through Roark, causing him to grab his chest quickly.

"It's happening again, is it?" said Kori, circling around to the front of Roark.

"It's under control," said Roark, straightening up.

"Who knows what the price of that may be?"

"You don't need to remind me of that, Kori."

"Maybe I do," was all he could reply. Kori returned to the window he was at before. Now all they could do was wait until she woke up. Wait to put their faith in a sixteen-year-old girl.

Chapter Five:

The Plan

"How dare you bring me into this?" said Kori as he let go of Roark. The man slumped back down on the ground, too weak to stand.

"I'm so...sorry, Kori. I'm just so sorry," said Roark, trailing off into a whisper. He sat slumped in a mess on the ground. He was a wreck of what he used to be. He had only been here once before, but this was different. *This was personal.* He wanted to take out Adele's picture, but he couldn't gather the strength to lift his arm. He could imagine the feeling of the paper, running his finger over the image. The image in his pocket felt more real to him than standing physically in front of her. His heart felt a shock of pain at the idea. *Have I become so detached I can't even face reality anymore?* he thought, hoping all of it would go away, but there was no escape. *Even if I can undo all of this, I would still have the memory. That will never go away,* he thought, letting another pain shoot through him.

"I'M TALKING TO YOU, ROARK!" screamed Kori as he kicked Roark in the side, knocking him over slightly. Roark barely flinched, doubling over onto his side in the alley. Roark was searching the ground, looking as if he had dropped something but there was nothing to find.

"ROARK!"

The alley came into view for him finally. Kori was towering over him, screaming his name. All of it washed over him like waves. He could sense everything around him, yet none of it mattered.

"I...I, hear you," said Roark barely in a whisper.

"No, you do not! Not yet," said Kori as he crouched down to be at eye level with him.

"How could you bring me here, Roark? How could you bring me into, this?" he said, leaning in, staring into the seemingly lifeless eyes of his fallen former friend.

"I know....I know, I've caused nothing but pain," said Roark, closing his eyes hard at the thought. If he could sink any farther into the ground from his guilt he would. "All I have ever caused anyone is pain." As he spoke he opened his eyes again to look up at the sky. Above him was a haze of smoke from the burning harbor. Through it he could see bits of blue sky here and there. He felt that's how his past looked to him, nothing but a haze of black with only brief glimpses of light showing through. *It's all fallen apart.*

"But how could you do it, Roark? She was my wife. My own love, My, own, wife." The words cut through Roark. He couldn't withstand the torment anymore. All the blue was gone from the sky, and only black remained.

"All she ever wanted was to be like me, to do what I do." Kori stood as he spoke and walked to the edge of the alley to look out on the harbor. The image barely fazed the man. The view he saw was not his burden to bear. "She wanted so badly to do anything I could. So I trained her. And then right when she was in the middle of it, I find out about YOU. How could you keep something like that from me? How could you keep something like THAT from me? And now she's dead. Then you tell me I can't get her back no matter what I do, and even if I fix the moment she's dead anyway. Now there is no way I can get her back. I'll never have another moment with her, see her smile again, or have my life back—because of you."

Roark clutched his chest as he heard the words. He tried to upright himself against the wall, but the pain wasn't going away. He looked to see Kori staring at him. The man Roark saw was not the old friend he remembered. What he saw now in Kori was a cold, hardened man. Anger and regret had taken over and left him nothing but empty. All the joy that once was, had gone.

"I damned you to hell, and told you never to find me, never to contact me, and to not interfere with anything I did ever again. For ten years, you stayed away. Ten years I was able to push back all that hate I had for you. Then one day I get a telegram with your name on it." Kori advanced on the fallen man. Roark could see Kori's hands turn into fists as he approached.

"Give me one reason why I shouldn't kill you now? Or give me one reason why I shouldn't leave you in this alley in this...hell you created for yourself?" He stood now, towering over Roark, who was now sitting upright against the wall. Roark couldn't look up at him. He was staring at the wall opposite, thinking. Everything raced through his mind as he tried to get a handle on anything that made sense. "You deserve no better. If I could doom you to live forever, I would, but I can't. I hope you rot in Tartarus with the rest of them."

"He killed James. James was killed last night." The words escaped Roark almost in a whisper. The words felt like defeat. His voice was hoarse still, and Roark choked after the sentence.

"Why is that of any importance to me? That doesn't make us even. I lose a loved one, and now you lost one." Roark pushed himself up the wall, trying to stand. Kori took a step back, watching him, making no effort to help him whatsoever. Roark managed to get to his feet but still was leaning on the wall. He didn't have the strength to stand on his own.

"He sunk the *Hornet*." Roark managed to look Kori in the eye for the first time since he arrived. A cold chill went through

Roark. The two of them had not looked directly at each other in a very long time. They were not what they used to be.

Kori broke his blank stare for a moment. The statement's meaning eluded him for a second. He tried to wrap his head around what it meant. "What do you mean, the *Hornet*?" Kori was so quick to set Atlas and come back to confront Roark he hadn't really absorbed what date and year he was coming back to. Kori turned to look out over the harbor. "This is Pearl Harbor, isn't it? What the hell have you done, Roark?" He turned around to the man against the wall. "What in god's name would make you come to this time?"

"James." The name was all he could muster to say. He was still trying to get his voice back. He forced himself up to a straighter stance to be more even with Kori.

Kori stepped forward toward Roark as his face crunched. "Who is James to you that you would risk coming here? You know the risk of even being here. The rules were very clear, Roark. That list was created specifically to prevent something like this, and you had the audacity to break it." Kori drew closer until he was right in Roark's face. The two of them locked eyes for a moment until Roark looked off and stumbled away from the wall.

"I'm his descendant," said Roark, staggering off down the alley to look out at the harbor, leaving Kori by the wall.

"You're his descendant? Are you telling me that not only did you break protocol to come here, to this time, but you actually contacted someone in your lineage?" Kori grew frantic with his words as he spoke, realizing the gravity of it all as he thought more about it.

"I did," said Roark, placing a hand on the edge of the alley wall, staring out at the insanity. "Ten years wears you down, Kori. Living with that kind of regret eating away at you." Roark turned to look at Kori dead on. He pushed off from the wall so he could stand on his own. He straightened himself up as he spoke. "Everyday I see your wife. I hear her name on the street constantly. I remember that night. I remember getting out of the car and seeing what I did." Roark turned away from

Kori, once again staring off in all directions. Kori stood frozen in place. His face was as rigid as ice. There was no sympathy or emotion present in his eyes.

"But you didn't take it back, did you? You let me bring her into this world of ours, bring her into the world that killed her. And after all this you expect me to help you in your time of need." Kori turned away from Roark and started walking toward the other end of the alley. "You clean up your own messes, Roark. You will not receive any aid from me." His voice trailed off as he got farther away.

"This runner is different!" Roark did his best to raise his voice as loud as he could, but it still came out flat.

"I do not care, Roark. It's your problem, not mine," he said, his voice growing softer.

"He has an Atlas!" said Roark in one last desperate plea. He moved back over to the wall and put a hand on it to steady himself.

Down the alley he could see that Kori had slowed his pace and stopped. He didn't turn around; he just stopped. He couldn't tell what was going through Kori's mind, but he knew the chance was great that he would still be left to deal with all this on his own.

Kori turned just enough to look back at Roark over his shoulder. He didn't speak; he just studied Roark. He then looked back toward the direction he was going, then at the ground. "Are you sure?" He continued to look at the ground as he spoke, but his words carried throughout the alley.

Roark was leaning on the wall, still with his back to the harbor. He pushed himself off the wall to face Kori. "I am," he managed to say with a little more power than he had before.

"You should have sent that telegram to someone else. You should not have sent it to me," said Kori, continuing to look down.

"I can't fix this between us. Maybe it will stay broken for the rest of our lives, but with this, you are the only one I could have sent it to. I'm sorry for that."

The look Kori gave him had an expression Roark couldn't place. It had every emotion from hatred to curiosity to isolation. He recognized the last expression as remorse. "Who is the runner?" The words were said as Kori looked down to the ground. The words offered no hope of assistance, just the mindless words of their business, nothing more. Sadness overtook him as he said it, knowing the momentary surrender it took to say it.

"He's a soldier. A motivated one." Roark sounded out of breath as he spoke. He was squinting as if trying to speak through some kind of pain.

A group of soldiers began to pass the alley and some men looked in at them as they passed. They looked at each other as if deciding whether to call on the two men for aid. Roark contorted himself around to face the men but grimaced with the motion. Kori stood firm, staring at each man who made eye contact. As the soldiers met eyes with Kori they immediately looked away.

"We shouldn't keep talking here." Kori remained steadfast, staring out into the open. "People will start asking questions soon about us. We will finish this elsewhere." Kori reached in his pocket and pulled out his Atlas. "Let's go."

"Go where?" said Roark, pushing himself away from the wall.

"The checkpoint at the hotel." Kori was staring at the dials, moving them slowly under his fingers as he spoke. "I'll see you there."

In an instant he was gone. Roark winced at the blue flash. He found himself alone once again in the alley. He spun himself around, expecting to see Andrew on the ground once again, but he saw no figure around. He took out his Atlas, which now felt odd in his hands. He looked down at it and felt a sudden disconnect from the situation. Everything else before last night felt so long ago. He thought about the last time he had seen Kori and how their friendship was. He knew the first time they spoke would be like this, and where he was going there would be more of the same. He braced himself for what was to come when he reached the hotel.

He opened the watch and slowly spun the dials to the familiar setting. He looked one last time out toward the harbor, and without breaking his stare closed the lid and the scene washed away into a field of blue.

The flash of blue subsided, and the scene that was right in front of him was vastly different. Around him now was an all-too-familiar hotel room. It was room 717, just like he remembered.

"This was hers. Her checkpoint," said Kori. He always spoke in the same tone and fashion. Kori was sitting slumped on the edge of one of the beds. He sat as if he were a ragdoll placed carefully there. He barely moved as he spoke. "Do you remember?"

Roark was on the floor when he arrived. He pushed himself over to sit up against the side of the opposite bed. A mixed sense of relief and weight came over him.

"She was good," said Roark, looking off.

"She was better than you," snapped Kori, his eyes noticeably redder. "She was better than me. She..." He cut himself off. His mind was overcome with memory. It was too much for him. He strained to maintain the composure he spent ten years putting up to brace himself for this day. He held his finger up as if it were holding that thought on the end of his finger. "She...was better than me."

A silence fell over the two of them, each lost in his own guilt. Neither was sure how much time had gone by. Roark let his mind go blank for a moment, trying to cling to any thought he could for more than a second. He felt his eyes close. He couldn't remember the last time he had slept, not that he could sleep anytime soon. He wasn't even sure how long he had been awake. Whether it was hours or days.

He opened his eyes to see that Kori's eyes had gotten redder since they were in the alley. He looked as if it was all he could do to keep it together. He saw him gather in a deep breath and hold it for a moment before letting it out. He never broke his gaze at the wall, as if there were some picture placed there at one point. "What happened to you, Roark?"

The question brought him back into the room. It rang through his blank mind again as he struggled to listen to it. He closed his eyes again, trying to focus on the question. His past seemed so foreign to him now. "I'm not who I was." He realized he said it aloud. The words fell out of him, lifeless, like he was on the floor now.

"No, you are not." Kori pushed himself to his feet and dragged himself to the window. He leaned his body weight on the sill. The creaking of the wood could be heard as he pressed onto the frame. "People looked up to you as an example. To be envied." A brief smirk barely became visible on Kori's lips, then immediately vanished. "You helped to start all of this."

"Stop...please." Roark raised a weak hand, gesturing to stop. He pulled himself off the floor. He got to his feet and turned away from Kori. It was getting darker in the room as the sun set outside. Roark slugged off into a darker corner of the room. Memories of the early days came into his mind. A flash of the crowd cheering flickered across his mind. The image startled him as he lurched forward from the corner back into the light.

"Maybe your demons have caught up with you," said Kori, who was watching him from the window. How pathetic Roark looked to him. All he could think of was that to some degree Roark deserved what was happening.

"There's so many demons though, aren't there? So many," said Roark, trailing off. His lips continued forming words, but no sound escaped across the room.

"You ask for my help, then you crash like this. Pull it TOGETHER," said Kori, raising his voice on the last words. Coldness came to him as he took a step toward Roark.

"I remember Eric Ledger," said Roark abruptly, staring straight ahead. Kori stopped mid-step in the middle of the room. The name struck him unexpectedly. Roark's eyes were red in the light. Kori stared at Roark with a perplexity that couldn't be placed. The name was familiar to him.

"What did you say?" asked Kori, stumbling at the question. Roark's red eyes lifted to meet Kori's probing gaze. Roark took a step forward. His clothes were disheveled now. His appearance matched Kori's opinion of his old colleague. How pathetic Roark looked. He almost had a shred of pity for the once-great man. "Why would you bring up him?"

""We should talk about Eric," said Roark, trying to stand up straight. "Let's get that out of the way." Kori continued to stare at Roark, shocked. It had been nearly ten years since anyone else had brought that name up to him. It was a name he had tried so very hard to bury, but now Roark had chosen to resurrect it.

"You promised me to never mention that name again." Kori sounded a cry of desperation as he raised a pointed finger at Roark, but it fell on deaf ears. His mind suddenly was filled with all the memories of that name, that night.

"In the alley before, there was a chance someone could have been listening, but in here it's isolated. We need to talk about that night. We need to talk about Serena... your wife." Kori dropped his arm, and Roark stood up straighter. The two switched places as Roark now advanced and Kori shrank down into a corner. "The story of Eric Ledger and his wife was in fact you. You hid the truth to save your own skin, so you could then try and save her without interference from any of us."

"Not without interference," said Kori in a low voice. "There was you." Kori drifted against the wall, staring toward the ground. His hands went to his pockets.

"I have to live with that night just as much as you do. I'm haunted by what happened just as much as you." Roark's voice was growing louder now, filling with more guilt every second.

"You took my wife away, Roark. You were driving the other car. You had been drinking, and you veered into my lane. It was you who caused the accident, and it was you who kept me from changing that night and getting my WIFE back." Kori's voice spiked with rage before quietly dropping back to where he was.

"I couldn't change it either, Kori. I tried so many times. Her fate couldn't be changed. I tried to explain that to you. It's something I have to live with just as much as you." Roark sat down on the corner of the bed, leaning toward Kori, trying to make eye contact with the man. He placed his hand over his jacket where Adele's picture was as he pulled himself up to sit upright.

"I was so mad at you, Roark. So mad at you," Kori said, keeping his head low. "It's a cruel joke that we live in, Roark. The power to change the past, yet the one thing we want to change, we can't." Kori lifted his head and looked at Roark. For the first time Kori gave him a look of almost a sort of understanding at what Roark had been living through. That perhaps he was telling the truth of his guilt. It was easier for him to think Roark was remorseless, but now he could see the state the pain had left him in.

"But now I need your help to change this, Kori. This soldier has the power to change a lot more than anyone else. He doesn't hold the same one-way ticket as the others, and his pain runs deeper than ours. I need your help."

Kori still sat on the floor as he peered out the window. "How could his pain run deeper than ours? Every person has their own demons, just as we do. Deeper than ours; all pain runs deep in the hearts of man. What dark corner of history did he come from?" said Kori. Roark stood and walked to the window to look out as well. A moment passed while they both scanned the horizon for an answer.

"He is from the third world war," Roark said, still staring outside.

Kori's face went white. He immediately pulled himself to his feet, staring intently at Roark. "My god, where was he during that? I was never tasked for that time." Kori's eyes dropped to the floor, his mind scanning his thoughts for any information on that event, but very little surfaced.

"I was only tasked there for a very short time. From what I gather he was abroad in the service, and his family was killed during the first massacre that started the war," said Roark.

"Yes, I remember that part. Everyone remembers it. A hundred-thousand or more were killed in their homes. I can't imagine. If his family was in that, then it would be a soldier's worst nightmare. His family that he was trying to protect by being so far from home, and they get killed in the one place he wasn't. Now he is trying to change history to prevent that war?" Kori gained a small strength as he finally could make sense of a thought for the first time since he got the telegram from Roark.

"He means to start a war today to prevent another tomorrow. The problem is that he doesn't know how his actions affect this history. He can't see past his own cause. He knows about us, though, and for now that's dangerous enough." Roark took off his jacket and laid it out on the bed. "Are there clothes in the closet?" He felt some composure return to him for the moment.

"This thing between you and I isn't over, Roark. I can't just drop it and move on," Kori said, stepping forward. He had too much anger still within him to just let it go. Flashes of his wife on the ground came back to him. An image of Roark stumbling out of his car clouded his thoughts. One second was all it took to shatter two sets of lives. He knew their friendship would never return to what it was. *But what can I say to him now that it was so long ago?* he thought to himself. "There are supplies in the bathroom as well.

"I'm going to pull myself together. I'll be right out," said Roark, disappearing into the bathroom. Kori could hear the shower turn on as he sat on the bed facing the window. The flashes continued in his mind as the feelings of that night hit him as if they just happened moments ago.

\\\\\\\\\\\\\\\\\\\\\\\\\\\\\\\\\\

"We're going to be late," said Serena, texting her friend Kim in the passenger seat of the sports car.

"We will be more than fine. Just fashionably late. It's my vacation; I can be a little late to my own birthday party. No worries, love," said Kori throwing the Porsche into the next gear. A smile came to his face as they cruised down the oceanside drive. It was a calm night where the stars glowed bright in the night sky. The hum of the motor could barely be heard over the radio quietly playing some pop song he had heard a hundred times before. He had the window cracked just a bit so he could smell the ocean coming through the opening. He couldn't remember the last time he had been here.

"How's Roark coping?" asked Serena, turning off her phone finally and putting it in her purse. She adjusted herself in the seat, fixing a wrinkle in her dress. She turned to look at Kori. She liked staring at him while they drove. It always made her crack a small smile, which Kori could always see out of the corner of his eye.

"He's been drinking a lot more. He was forced into a leave of absence the other day," said Kori flatly, rolling the window the rest of the way up so it was a bit quieter in the car.

"You didn't mention that earlier—why didn't you tell me that?" asked Serena, concerned. "I would have gone over there and visited him or at least have given him a call. Don't keep stuff like that from me. He's going through such a hard time right now. I feel so bad for him." Serena trailed off, looking out into the night sky. "Did you invite him to the party at least?"

"I left a message, but he didn't pick up." Kori turned up the music a bit on the radio. "I tried, honey. We should just let him be for now." Kori returned his hands to the wheel and focused his attention to the winding road along the coast.

The beach point was coming up with a sharp turn around a rocky ledge of the beach. Kori slowed the car a bit to round the curve. As he rounded the corner no one was in sight, which came as a relief, for Kori knew of all the accidents caused by this particular stretch of road.

As Kori reached a straightaway along a small drop-off to the beach below, something caught his eye up ahead. It appeared something was coming down the road from the other direction. At first he thought it was some kind of animal in the road, maybe a deer or something. As it drew nearer, he realized it was traveling too fast to be anything like that. It was a car racing down the road with no headlights on.

"Hey, honey, fasten your seatbelt. Somebody is coming at us with no lights." Serena straightened up in her seat to grab the seatbelt. The car raced closer, and Kori saw a brief glimpse of the driver. The dark car was drifting back and forth in the lane as it approached. Out of the corner of his eye Kori could see Serena hadn't yet put on her seatbelt and was fumbling with it in panic.

Kori saw the driver snap his head up as he finally noticed there was another car on the road. The driver reacted by swerving the car left, right into Kori's lane. "Hang on to something!" was all Kori could say as he, too, had to swerve to the left to dodge the car. The road on that stretch was so narrow Kori knew he would go over the edge. The Porsche crashed through the guardrail and pitched sideways, passenger-side first, over the twenty-foot cliff. The jolt of the guardrail rocked the passenger side door open, and Serena was pulled out. Kori could only look on in horror as the seat next to him emptied. He turned to see the sand racing at him and closed his eyes as the car hit straight on into the sandy beach. The crash launched him forward into the airbag, but the car hit with such force the seat came loose and pinned him against the steering wheel.

\\\\\\\\\\\\\\\\\\\\\\\\\\\\\\\\\\\\

"So how will we proceed?" asked Roark, coming out of the bathroom in a new crisp tan suit. He was now dressed as any normal mover would be dressed. His white shirt was once again perfect. His black tie stood out sharply against the white, and he wore a fresh new khaki suit jacket. He at least looked the way he once did long ago.

"First thing we will need is a failsafe. If this soldier knows how we work, then no more telegrams. We will need to do things the old-fashioned way, through a teller," said Kori. Roark gave a look of concern. He had not heard that term since he first started as a mover. *Ages ago,* he thought. He knew a teller was a person who everything was told to so they could keep a sort of mental record of all the events that had and would happen. Nothing would ever be written down, and the record would be impossible to steal. The most important part would be that the teller would be unknown to the enemy so he or she could be easily disguised.

"When was the last time a teller was used? I have never used one. I just know of the monk." Roark remembered hearing stories of the monk. He was a brave man.

"That's because that was the one and only time one was ever used. That was Adam's doing. It requires someone with a perfect memory, like us." Kori had been looking out the window since Roark emerged from the bathroom. His mind was still on fragments of memories, each haunting and comforting him as they flashed by. "Whoever we get cannot be told of the risks. They must not know the danger they face."

"Or what they could be used for. It's too much to ask of one person." Roark threw down the towel he was holding. He put a hand to his face. The shower had let him forget about the things of the past day temporarily, but now as he emerged back into the room things crept back into his consciousness. "For you to suggest such a person, I would guess you do not expect either of us to live through this." Roark had his back to Kori as he spoke.

Kori turned solemnly toward his former colleague. "Roark, your lineage was broken. You don't have much time left anyway, which would leave only me to deal with the soldier. The possibility has to exist that I may not be enough. I'm merely trying to be cautious." Kori looked blankly at Roark. Roark raised his eyes to meet Kori's for an instant, then he darted his glance away. Roark raised a hand to his heart; the pain had returned for a moment. The pain felt like ever-increasing, brief heart attacks. He felt as if someone had punched him in the chest.

"There's only one around that we could talk to—her," said Roark, holding his chest until the pain started to subside.

"Your approval, then?" asked Kori, staring at Roark. "Unless you have another way." Roark still faced away from Kori and pulled Adele's picture from the jacket lying on the bed near him. Kori saw it briefly as Roark lifted it.

"You have it," said Roark feeling the photograph under his fingers. "I'd rather her not know of this between us. It will be difficult getting her to go along without it. We can't tell her everything and then have her turn on us." Roark placed the picture in his jacket pocket as he turned to face Kori.

"Fine. She will be all we have if this doesn't work. You know where she is?" asked Kori, starting to pull Atlas from his pocket.

"I do. A hospital in Massachusetts." Roark pulled his Atlas and set the dials.

"I remember the place. Roark?" His colleague looked up one last time before he shut the lid on Atlas. "Don't mess this up again."

"I won't," said Roark as the flash of blue consumed him.

"Damn you," whispered Kori as he thought of the picture Roark had picked up. He looked at the gold pocket watch in his hand. How he hated this thing. A curse and a gift concealed in gold. One last deep breath and he, too, was gone in blue.

``````````````````````````````````````

An eternity seemed to go by before Kori opened his eyes, still trapped between the seat and the steering wheel, facing the empty passenger seat. He couldn't see Serena anywhere. He could hear the ocean off in the distance, and the wind blowing sand around the inside of the car. He felt panic growing in him as he struggled to search for any sign of Serena. "Serena!" he yelled frantically over and over, hoping for any sign she was okay.

He braced himself to slide free. He started to slowly slide himself over to the opening in the passenger seat. He made it a few inches when a sharp pain went up his body. His leg was broken, and with it wedged between the edge of the seat and
``````````````````````````````````````

the bottom of the steering wheel, every move made the pain worse. His desperation made him pull himself one last time toward the opening. With the one great effort he reached freedom, but he heard several cracks in this leg from the move that caused a pain that made him scream out.

When he opened his eyes he could now see around the wrecked car. There was no sign of Serena. He called out her name again and again to no response. He tried to get himself up on one leg so he could search. His left leg was covered in blood, and he couldn't look at it long enough to assess what damage was done. He searched, looking all around for Serena as he made his way crawling, using his good leg to get back up to the road. Just when he was almost up the hill, he saw her. Her body lay motionless just off the road near the top of the hill. He called her name louder, tears streaming down his face.

He crawled faster and faster toward where she was, then reached out and placed his hand on her face. She was noticeably cooler to the touch. He refused to think the worst and started whispering her name in her ear. Every time he said her name, he looked for any sign of movement, but each time nothing happened. As he leaned in closer, he put his hand on her side and immediately lifted it. Her dress was soaked in blood. The impact of the fall had punctured her side. His cries grew more frantic as he started to break down at the fear she may be gone. He wrapped his arms around her tighter and tighter, sobbing into her shoulder. He wanted so badly to undo this moment.

Through the cries he heard movement from the street. He desperately tried to turn his head to see what it was. He could see the other driver stumbling out of the car, a bottle dropping to the ground.

"Oh my god, no, no, oh my god," the driver kept saying. The driver tried to limp over to Kori, but Kori cried out against him.

"Stay back—don't come any closer. Get away, you son of a bitch. You did this. You did this, you son of a bitch. You did this. I'll kill you I swear if you come any closer." Kori didn't know how many times he said it. The driver collapsed in the street. Headlights could be seen coming; help was on the way. As the car drew closer it illuminated the road for the first time, and both Kori and the other driver could see the carnage that was done that night. Kori tried to raise a hand for the approaching driver. He swung one arm desperately while holding Serena with the other. As he yelled for help, he turned and saw the face of the other driver. The sight drove all the pain deeper. The pain was so great Kori screamed out again, louder than he had before. He held Serena tighter as he cried. The face of the other driver was his friend Roark.

\\\\\\\\\\\\\\\\\\\\\\\\\\\\\\\

Everything was still spinning. *It was a dream,* she thought. It had to have been a dream. Even when her eyes opened, everything was still blurry. She did not want to get up. If she got up, she would have to face the day and everything that came with it. She wished to recede back into sleep. Things seemed to make more sense there. She opened her eyes again. The two men in tan were sitting in chairs talking. They seemed disinterested in each other as they spoke. She couldn't make out what was being said. One of them glanced in her direction and reacted by gesturing to the other. They both stood, and she immediately regretted staring at them. She pulled herself up to a seated position, realizing she was back in the warehouse again. She had prayed it was a dream.

"Afternoon," said Roark with a stiff smile. "I apologize for putting you in this position. Sometimes it's simpler to show rather than to tell, but you had to believe us and we didn't have all day to explain." The two men gestured for her to come over to where they were sitting. "Come join us. We will answer any questions you have. You must have quite a few by now." The other man, Kori she remembered his name, suddenly had a warm smile, which seemed stranger on him than on Roark, who held out a hand to help her up. As she followed them over to the chairs, it was clear she wasn't dreaming.

As she collected herself, she heard another voice echoing through the large room. It was coming from a radio playing on a small table neatly set up alongside where Roark had been sitting. A familiar voice came on the radio, suddenly piercing the silence. "Yesterday, December 7th, 1941. A day that will live in infamy, the United States was suddenly and deliberately attacked by naval and air forces of the empire of Japan..." The voice trailed off as Roark turned the volume down on the small radio. An embarrassed smile came and went across his face. He had meant for her to hear that bit of the speech.

"I need a glass of water. I have such a headache," said Mary, sinking into one of the chairs. A pressure was behind her eyes from all that was happening. The voice from the radio repeated in her mind. She remembered reading about it before in class. It sounded strange to hear it now. The headache pulsed behind her eyes as she shut them, seeking relief.

"Remnants from the trip. It will pass with time," said Kori, returning to his chair. "Take my water. I hadn't taken a sip yet." Kori handed his glass over. As she took it from him, she noticed a kind of sadness cross his face. It only lasted a moment, *but it was definitely there,* she thought. As she sipped, her headache subsided slightly. She had barely been awake a minute and she felt as though she had been awake for several hours at least.

"Is this real?" she asked after taking another sip of the water. Her eyes were searching back and forth between the two men for an answer. Her voice was tired.

"It's real," answered Roark, lifting his gaze to match her look. "And right outside is Pearl Harbor, just as it was in 1941. As it is now. Bringing you here, to now, was the only way to convince you that we are for real." Roark held her look before trailing off to look down at the floor. His words carried the same kind of sadness as Kori's eyes.

"It's just hard to believe. It still doesn't feel real," said Mary, placing the glass down on the table, shaking. "So you two are suppose to be what, from the future? Who are you?"

"Yes we are from the future, but as to who we are, that might take some time to explain," said Roark, folding his hands onto one another. Both men attempted to maintain an air of sincerity. "But we haven't been back to that time since we began doing what we do, and that was quite a long time ago."

"I obviously couldn't go home if I wanted to. I'm stuck here," she said, frustrated. "You basically kidnapped me." Her headache was increasing again. "And I don't suppose you're going to take me back until I do what you want, so I have time."

Her voice was hard now. The two men shot looks at one another. She hadn't meant to sound so angry about all of this. She was just as intrigued as she was upset about being brought here. *I'm in the actual past*, she thought. *It's unbelievable.* She couldn't get a handle on what to feel. Her anger struggled against the intrigue and the fear she felt. It all only made her exhaustion worse.

"We are sorry to have dragged you into this, but we are desperate for your help. There really is no one else we could have asked. Period," said Roark sincerely. He swallowed hard, showing a momentary nervousness that led her to believe he was telling the truth. "What we are trying to do is unprecedented. It has never happened before, and to deal with this matter required desperate acts. I am sorry. If you can allow us to explain certain things, perhaps you will agree to help us." He paused for a moment, waiting for a reply. She stared back at Roark, mixed emotions coming and going across her face. He waited a few more moments before continuing. "You asked who we were. You must understand that is an extremely difficult question to answer without knowing some things about the future, or to put it better, my past."

"Our past," Kori interrupted.

"The future takes a lot longer to get to than you might think," continued Kori. "Humanity does achieve greatness eventually, as you would expect it to. The technology that one might expect the future to hold, as evident in any science fiction book or film, does eventually come out, but again much further along than you can imagine. The more immediate future is not all that different from today, just more time has elapsed." Kori kept on as if he were continuing to speak, yet no words left his mouth. He gave a look of awkwardness to the two of them, acknowledging his poor choice of words.

Mary was hoping for a more extravagant answer than what Kori had described. Usually, the precept of the future was met with a more idealized version of hope than what was given. Her thoughts showed on her face, which Roark picked up on.

"It was that hope I think you're looking for that initially drew us to the job," said Roark, forcing a smile. "The chance to see something beyond our days. It was the chance-of-a-lifetime opportunity." He paused, swallowing hard. He quickly pressed his hand to his chest pocket and pulled it away immediately. The action was so quick Kori didn't notice. "Obviously, that hope is lost on us now." Roark held a smile. The kind of pleasant smile she knew her parents gave her all the time. It was the sort of smile that hides the truth. She didn't what truth he was hiding, but she knew it was there. "And maybe with your help. We might get a little piece of it back."

"What the future holds, you can probably guess most of it," said Roark, returning his hands to his pockets, a somber tone coming back to his voice. "As life became easier people expected more—more from others, from the government—and this led to problems. The less fortunate expected to be taken care of by the wealthy and after a while it reached a breaking point in the social divide. The same thing happened in other countries as well. Things broke down as they do. The United States was undone not by any war with terrorists or a foreign power, but it was undone by its own people and government. It's obvious now where it all started, but seeing it now you can see where the hope was." Roark spoke so blankly of the future as if it already happened. He spoke of what could be as if were merely a chapter in the history of us.

Mary was growing discomforted by these two men. There was a carelessness about the way they described things. They spoke as if the future couldn't be changed, as if it was set in stone already.

"The future isn't set though," said Mary, cutting Roark off. Roark stared at Mary blankly. Kori looked away from the window toward the girl. Kori expected the statement.

"What is the future but someone else's past, and you must not change the past," said Kori. Her statement had snapped him out of his daze. "It's that sort of thinking that put us here."

Kori adjusted himself in the seat more toward her direction. "What started everything was a paper that was published, hinting that time travel may be possible. It would be well over a thousand years before the discovery would be made, but it was a notion that drew increasing interest in the idea."

The words "a thousand years" stuck with Mary. It was the first measure of time either one had given as to when they were from.

"Fast-forward to a world where everything in society was all about the latest gadget, the newest trend, and popularity was determined by the latest tech. Really, the future isn't really all that different from today. You can swap out the material things, but the mind-set is the same. The problem was that the government didn't know what they had when they went public with the discovery. It was decided by the government to not let the general public have access to the tech because it was deemed too dangerous. Traveling through time comes with the highest of price tags."

Mary-Ellen's mind began racing more now. Images of her parents came to her. Home resounded through her head. She wished she could go home as Kori continued to speak.

"The devices themselves, which years later and several models later, would come to be known as jumper boxes, or jibs for short, resembled that of modern day smartphones. They were small and could be easily concealed. Mainly, they looked like phones so they could be openly carried and not raise suspicion." Kori spoke with a pride about the devices. He felt remnants of how he used to talk long ago.

Mary couldn't help but feel an uneasiness. She remembered Ian. She remembered how he visited her room each morning to bring breakfast. She looked forward to each meal, hoping he would be the one to come. *It feels so long ago,* she thought to herself. The gold watches came to mind suddenly. *He said that time travel devices looked like smartphones,* she thought. *Then what are those watches if they aren't what he's talking about?* She realized Kori had been talking for some time as her thoughts drifted off. Kori was deep into a technical explanation of time travel in general.

"...who eventually discovers antimatter, and quite separately, dark matter," continued Kori as if deep in some lecture her teachers used to give.

"I'm really not that good at science," said Mary, interrupting Kori. He stopped speaking, surprised at the interjection. "I don't know what any of that means. I have no idea what antimatter or dark matter is." For the first time, Mary showed her actual age was.

"Yet you followed everything else he said prior to that?" Roark chimed in from a few feet away. Mary hadn't noticed that Roark had moved off to sit by himself. She noticed him putting something in his jacket pocket. She made out the distinct backing of an old photograph. She saw that he took great care to place it in his pocket rather than stuff in his jacket. "Has your undivided attention been on what Kori is saying?" asked Roark casually, standing up and joining them.

All she saw in Roark in that moment was her father. Only her dad spoke in that tone. "Well, I'm curious about the watches. Those gold watches you two carry." She turned her stare to Kori. "You said they were jumper boxes."

"Jibs," cut in Kori.

"Whatever, jibs, looked like phones. Your watches don't look anything like phones. They look like something out of the 1800s. What are they?" Her words came out rushed and frustrated. She realized she was rambling and silenced herself, biting the inside of her lip to try and stifle her inner feelings.

"I was getting to that," Kori said, sounding short. A frustration had been building in him this whole time from explaining so much to a young girl. He forced himself to see his wife as she was when they first met. The hope of seeing her again outweighed his now steadily increasing anger. *How stupid Roark was to bring her,* he so desperately wanted to say to him, *but she will have her uses.* The afterthought eased him as he continued to speak.

"Then get to it, please." The words resembled that of a tantrum thrown by a naïve girl. So young, thought Roark, drifting into the moment and out again. Only one person was on his mind, and he needed to remain focused on it.

"As I was saying," Kori continued as if he was never interrupted. He started up a casual stride back and forth across a small space as if lecturing to a small crowd. "The devices were small, but the price tag for one of these jibs was about a hundred-thousand dollars." Kori paused, anticipating another outburst, which came immediately.

"That's it!" she replied, shocked by the number. Kori smiled briefly, amused by her response. "I figured it would have been more. At least a few million. I mean, we discover the greatest scientific anything ever, and it's only that much?"

"Well that's not the extreme price tag I was talking about. Not all price tags relate to money, in this case." Suddenly, Mary got a chill, fearing her journey home now seemed a lot longer than she had hoped. "Where the price comes has to do with the strings, if you will, or rather the stipulations that come with the greatest discovery of the age."

Mary was a little more scared now, worried about what the strings were and how she was now involved against her will with whatever they were. She had the sudden urge to run as the thought and the feeling filled her up, but immediately she realized how pointless that would be. Her apprehension kept her locked in the chair. She shot a look at Roark, seeing he was still dazed and of no help.

"One such rule, or string, was that such a device was only good for one trip. One day in the past, and that's it." A hard pit formed in her stomach. Suddenly, all her hatred toward her parents seemed so in vain. She wanted nothing more than to meet her birth parents.

"One..." her voice cracked out, whispering. She almost couldn't breathe, the anxiety was so great. A crushing weight of utter hopelessness was setting in that these two men, these two horrible people, had taken away all that she had loved. And they were just standing there—didn't they know what they were doing? She was screaming at them in her head, but all she could do was sit there in silence. Her eyes started to water. "I wanted my future. I wanted so much." Her last words were barely audible. Kori continued without having heard the last bit.

"Well, that's the second rule, in fact. One can only travel into the past." He studied Mary, expecting another outburst, but this time none came. He saw she was no longer looking at him as he spoke. She had the same look Roark had on his face. He was losing her attention, but he continued still. "Like any travel—walking, automobiles, trains, or aircraft—you must know your destination. You would never get in a plane if you were unsure when or if the plane would ever land. When it comes to the past, we know what has already happened. You can research your destination thoroughly; memory can be useful at times if need be, but with the future, it's all an unknown, so travel into it is impossible."

Mary remained motionless, staring blankly out into nothing. She looked limp in the chair. One tap, and she appeared as if she would tip over and topple onto the ground.

"It is the third piece that is the most dangerous. It's the piece that keeps everyone from traveling by this means."

Mary broke her daze to bring her eyes up to meet his, still unable to bring words to her lips.

"Entropy. If you change something in your past on a significant level, you may not be able to come back to the present."

"How would you know?" Her words sounded of defeated terror.

"You wouldn't. Your day would end and upon waking the next morning you wouldn't be back in the present. You would still be in the past. Forced to relive your entire life. Wherever you were in the present would all be lost."

"Why would anyone do that to themselves?"

"Desperation," said Roark. She hadn't noticed that he had gotten up and was standing between Kori and her. He was almost standing over her with his hands coolly in his pockets. "You put anyone in THAT desperate place, with nothing left to lose. When going through all that is the only way to change your past, you will turn to any solution, no matter the cost.

Mary suddenly thought of the time. *How long have I been here?* A sudden rush of panic whirled through her. She leapt to her feet, breathing heavily. She frantically looked back and forth between Kori and Roark. "How long have I been here? What's going to happen to me? Why did you bring me here? Why are you going to kill me?" She was hysterically screaming right at the two men, who did not move. They just stared back icily, waiting for it to end.

Mary stopped screaming; she was hyperventilating from the anxiety, and she collapsed back on the chair. Kori took a step forward, only to have Roark gesture that it was close enough. "Remember, we are talking about past events. Just like any technology, improvements were made, not that anyone else got the benefit of it. Future generations were kept out of reach of the public. You are not subject to the conditions of the jibs."

Mary was trying desperately to calm her breathing. She looked up to the two men, shaking. It took all her strength to keep herself upright. "I'm not going to die?" was all she could manage.

"No, of course not," said Roark, smiling warmly. "The last generation of devices is what brought you here today. Roark took out his gold watch and delicately held it out to her. "Open your hand." Mary raised a weary arm and held out her open hand. "This is what brought you here, we call them Atlas." Roark placed the watch in her hand. It was warm to the touch and light as a feather. The cover had an extremely intricate design carved into the lid. The latch to open it stretched all the way around the lid. She couldn't imagine how it opened. She felt some bumps on her hand as if there were something on the bottom of the watch, but as she began to turn it over to inspect the other side, Roark whisked it away from her again. He had a concerned look, noticing her curiosity. "And now you have your answer about the watches."

Roark returned the watch to his pocket. He crouched down in front of her with a very stern expression. He had a look she hadn't seen before: rage.

"Now listen to me very carefully." His words were heavy. Kori was moving around behind Mary. She was trapped. Her sense of fear was returning. "Now is where we need your help. You know the history of this place better than we do, and we do not have enough time to research everything. You are to be a guide and help us figure out how things go. Understand?" Mary was terrified. She feared what they were going to do. A small nod was all she could do.

"Why don't you know the past?" she squeaked out finally.

"This is an altered past," said Roark, raising his voice slightly. "You are from the future result of an alteration of the past by a certain individual that we need to find. That's all you need to know about him for now. To you and everyone else, this past is the way of the world—but it isn't."

Mary swallowed hard. All she could do was hang on to the hope of home, even if that hope seemed impossible.

"Help us, and I promise you will see everything you know again. It will be as if you never left, not even for a minute."

There is no hint of truth in his face, she thought. She had sent that look before. *I need that watch; it's my only chance.*

"Okay," she said meekly.

"The first thing I need from you is a name," said Roark, inching closer to the girl.

She was shocked by the sudden simplicity of the question. "A...a name? Nothing else?" Her shock was matched by her confusion. All she got as a response was a hard, blank look from the two of them. There was nothing but anger in them.

"Whose name?" she asked, almost whispering. She was afraid of the response.

"I need a name of someone who was behind the scenes around this time. Someone who had a hand in everything and knew how to find information on anyone and anything. A man with secrets, who knew how to use them against others. Can you tell me a name of someone like that?"

He paused while she thought. She tried to swallow the fear to stay focused on what she needed to do. These men were her captors and her saviors. She needed them to get home, and they needed her for who knew what. She feared where she would be the next time she woke up. Only one name met the criteria set by the two men.

"There's J. Edgar Hoover. He had secrets," she said timidly.

Roark smiled as she spoke and then grew even bigger right after. He looked up and nodded at Kori. She saw that he had his gold watch in one hand and reached his other out toward Mary. Kori stood up to look down at Mary, grinning. "Time to go."

After he spoke his face went stone straight. Mary wished she would wake up back in her bed, but she knew she would not. Home was so far away. As she closed her eyes, she started to scream out a word, but it was lost in a wave of blue.

Roark took out his Atlas and immediately the pain that he had been suppressing the whole meeting doubled him over on the ground. He let out a loud gasp. He grabbed his chest and felt the stiffness of the picture in his pocket. Staying on the ground he took a long, deep breath and spun the dial on Atlas. All that remained was the empty warehouse. A moment lost in time.

Chapter Six:

Andrew

"Look at Daddy. Look. There he is. C'mon, honey, look at Daddy." Her voice lightly went through the air, trying to get little Chloe to look at the screen. Chloe was looking sharply off to her right and left, trying to look behind her. She was always more interested in whatever was behind her than in front.

"C'mon, honey, look here," said the voice on the screen. "Honey, this isn't going to work if she doesn't see me."

"She is still more interested in what is behind her than anything. She knows she is missing out on the cool nothing going on behind me," she said, smiling at her husband on the screen. The baby briefly turned and saw the face on the screen.

"She's looking. Hi, baby. Hi, honey. You look so beautiful. You have your mother's eyes."

"That's your daddy, Andrew. Do you see Daddy?"

The baby reached her tiny hands toward the screen with her fingers outstretched. Her mom kept her from touching the screen. "Oh no, baby, don't touch that. She likes to push things. Anything she can touch she pushes, especially anything on the table during feeding time."

Andrew laughed, leaning closer to his screen. "She is adorable, love. I'm sorry I haven't been able to call sooner; they have us out on rounds all the time."

"It's okay, honey. She's here now. We're a family. Let's just enjoy the time we have. You can make up for lost time when you come home."

A moment passed between them and when she opened her mouth to speak again, suddenly she went silent. She sat there watching Chloe happily playing with a wrapper she had just found on the edge of the desk, and immediately he knew something was wrong.

"Hey, honey," he said softly, leaning in closer to the screen. He pulled his chair forward to be closer to the table. "It's okay. It's going to be okay, love."

She swiftly looked up directly at him, and he could see she was on the verge of tears.

"No it's not okay. I miss you." Her voice was starting to squeak.

He loved her, but he knew how delicate and fragile she could be. It had only been getting worse as the months went on. Chloe had not even been born when he left for Afghanistan, and now she was almost a year old. *I know I've been gone for so long,* he thought to himself. "I miss you too, love. Two more months, and I'm back for good. Back in your arms. Then I'm done."

"You don't understand, you don't; You think you do, you keep saying that, but you don't, okay?" She was struggling to wipe the tears with one hand while balancing Chloe with the other.

"Hannah, love. It's almost ..."

"Can you come home now, please?" she said suddenly, pleading into the screen. "Please!"

They'd had this same discussion two months ago. She would always do so well the first few months, being strong for the both of them. It was toward the end of each tour that she would start to fall apart on him. It was difficult for him to focus on what he was doing because he knew how lonely she was at home.

Andrew let out a sigh. He loved talking to his wife but hated how this point was always where this conversation would wind up. He looked away from the screen for a moment and had to fight the tears that wanted to come out. He had to keep the strength for both of them. He wanted to say yes, to tell her he was on his way home, but that moment was still so far away.

"I promise that when I'm home, which will be soon, love, that I will never leave your side again. Wherever I go, we will go together. Okay, love?" He fought the tremble in his voice.

"I know. I'm just sad." The tears were starting to subside. She just had an occasional sniffle she was trying to suppress. Her eyes were a little red now, looking at the screen.

"I'll sing to you when I get home," said Andrew, smiling at her. She let out a sudden laugh, wiping her eyes again.

"No," she said after another laugh. She shook her head as if to shake off the last memory of his attempted singing.

"You don't like my singing, love?" he said sarcastically. "I'll sing a bit for you now." He sat himself upright in his chair and made a throat-clearing sound, ready to belt out a note.

"No, let's not subject Chloe to your, um, super singing skills just yet, honey." Chloe made a squeak, playing with an envelope she just found.

"See even she wants to hear me sing, but if you insist." He turned and looked at Chloe. "Maybe I'll sing you something later, when Mommy isn't around." He winked at her even though she wasn't paying attention to her daddy.

Hannah sighed a little with a small smile, but at least hiding it better than a few minutes earlier. The two were at a loss for words all of a sudden, staring at each other.

Suddenly Chloe made a sudden screech of laughter as she threw her arms up and down, almost knocking herself off the table. Hannah reached behind the baby, steadying her. "What got into you all of the sudden?" she said as she noticed Chloe looking at Andrew.

"Oh, now you see me, do you?" he said, smiling at the little face looking at him. "I love you." He leaned closer to the screen, smiling.

\\\\\\\\\\\\\\\\\\\\\\\\\\\\\\\\\\

"That about does it for what I have for you," said Claire, playing with the pieces of paper laid out in front of her on the large conference table. It was the conference room at the front of the building. It was usually free this time of day, so she thought it would be perfect to house her monthly check-in meetings with each of the employees.

Kaito was her last employee to check in with. The room had ten chairs in it, and Kaito sat a few seats down from her, which was the perfect distance so she wasn't yelling across the room at him. He knew that was the seat he should sit in, as it was the only other chair in the room pulled away from the table from the previous one-on-one meetings.

"Unless you have anything else to add? Questions, concerns, complaints?" She laughed to herself, thinking of something else. It was always obvious what she was thinking.

"No, I don't think I have anything besides the whole promotion thing we talked about earlier. Otherwise, no complaints here. I heard about the meltdown last night with, well, you know." Kaito laughed in the same way Claire did. A short burst of laughter that was quickly stifled.

"Yeah, I got out of here not long after that started. I try not to get too close around her. Once Donna got involved, I was like, I'm outta here."

Kaito smiled and let out a sigh as he shook his head jokingly. "I'm glad she doesn't sit near me anymore. Well, I do miss it a little. She was entertaining at least."

"Yeah, she is. So congrats on the promotion again," Claire said brightly, switching subjects. "But the pay increase won't kick in until July, unfortunately, so you have a few more months to go. It's not public yet, so keep it to yourself. Probably, we won't let everyone know until around June. You are the only one to get a promotion. All promotions were supposed to be frozen, but we fought for you 'cause, you know, you deserved it. So, I hope you're happy with us. I think we have a great group, and everyone gets along, and..."

"No, I'm definitely happy here," said Kaito, cutting her off. "I love this group. Everyone is so great, definitely the best co-workers I've ever had. I'm glad I can move up and still stay with the group and this client. I feel I have a really good grasp on processing. To move to another group now would be starting back at square one. Thank you again—really."

"Well, you're welcome." Claire stood up, starting to collect all her papers. "How are the queues out there?" she asked, standing up straight with a back-to-business expression.

"Um, there were around forty or so when I came in, which is a little weird just starting into May. We still have plenty of time; it shouldn't be a problem." He always spoke so calmly, another reason he was so well liked by management. His reviews always said he was one of the most pleasant employees to work with.

The two turned to the door, and Claire got there first. The door opened, letting in all the sounds of the office. The familiar clicking of the keyboards being hit by the numerous employees in that part of the building came flooding into the small meeting room.

As he made his way back to his desk, Kaito didn't like making the awkward eye contact with the temps that were always standing up in their cubicles. He pulled out his phone to pretend to be busy. Turning on the screen he saw a message from Kim. *Kisses for your review, you will be great,* it said. *Thanks love, I think I'm in a pretty good spot here...I love you,* he typed back, smiling to himself. He hit send and saw the little delivered appear under the message. Turning up his aisle, he put his phone back into its loose sunglass bag case and placed it in the corner of his cube. It slipped back into his pocket as he slumped down back at his computer. His fingers knew what to do to log back into everything and resume his work. The voices in the distance reminded him that he still had a long work afternoon ahead as he heard some coworkers on the phone and others telling each other about the weather. *Two more months until the pay raise kicks in,* he thought to himself, pulling up another image to process.

As he pulled up the account number on his left computer screen, his phone buzzed in his pocket. A smile came to his face, knowing it was the return *I love you* from Kim. He continued pulling up the history when he noticed it was 11:59 a.m. on the bottom corner of his screen. *I'll take lunch at 1, I can make it,* he thought with his stomach grumbling.

He took his phone out of his pocket, thinking if he didn't turn the screen on it would keep buzzing every so many minutes, indicating a new message. Through the sunglass case he used as a phone case he could see the screen was still lit. Undoing the string holding the bag closed he pulled out the phone, casually sliding his finger to unlock it.

At first he scanned the text, expecting to see the three familiar words he had being saying back and forth with Kim for the last few months, but what he saw was something else. He held the phone, staring at the screen, devoid of any thoughts registering what he was reading. He put his finger on the screen as if to feel the symbols shown on it, trying to feel the texture of the words. Suddenly the room went quiet. He felt so isolated sitting in his chair. His right hand was trembling, and he could feel himself starting to sweat.

"You forgot this." The voice pierced the stillness as he looked up to see Claire staring at him blankly. She was holding out his pay raise information. She held it out to him, frowning t the startled look on his face. "You okay? You look like you're hot?"

"I'm fine." The words started out chokingly. "I'm fine," he finally said, sounding more normal. "Thank you." He took the page and swung around to his computer as she walked away with her usual squeaky shoes.

He put the phone down on the desk with the display still on. The message was still there. He reached down to the bottom drawer of his desk and found the key to it in his pocket.

Shakily, he pushed the key into the lock, knowing that after this there would be no going back; it was all or nothing.

He pulled open the drawer and reached inside. He pulled out the pistol and placed it on his lap. Next, he pulled out the small messenger bag. Inside the bag numerous clangs could be heard as its contents shifted. He swung the strap over his shoulder with his grip on the gun growing tighter. He stood to peer down the aisles. Everyone continued clicking away on their keyboards. It was the final breath before the storm.

Suddenly, a gunshot rang out in the distance. Screams could be heard as a second shot rang out, then a third. More shots rang out from another direction. People started standing up around him. A moment of eerie calm remained on his co-workers' faces; they were unsure of what was transpiring. Some stood frozen, staring blankly in the gunshots' direction; others scanned around the room as if an answer would present itself if they only looked for it. Claire came down the aisle, frantically repeating, "What's going on?" She stopped in the middle of the aisle and noticed Kaito holding the gun. She had a look of sheer panic.

"Now I have become death, the destroyer of worlds," was all he said, whispering to himself as he gripped the gun so tightly his fingers grew numb. He kept repeating the phrase inaudibly as he raised the gun up and pointed it at her. She stepped back and turned to run, and all he saw was the flash of the shot. As he moved down the aisle, he moved his gun from right to left, hitting every coworker in the aisle; others were running down the hall. More and more shots could be heard from every direction. He figured there had to be dozens of people like him moving about the building. His phone still on his desk, lit up with a vibration a second time. The words that were now displayed were the three words he had hoped to see before: *I love you*.

\`\`\`\`\`\`\`\`\`\`\`\`\`\`\`\`\`\`\`\`\`\`\`\`\`\`\`\`\`\`\`

"So what day will you be actually back here, at home with us, Andrew?" It was the question Hannah had been wanting to ask every day since their last video chat. She asked the question every single time they spoke as if she had never asked it before. She liked hearing the answer, because each time he answered with the date it was always that much closer. It would be that much closer to him returning back into her arms.

"In May, May 3rd, love. Probably sometime around noon." He always smiled every time he said the date. He could tell when she was going to ask that usual question. Hannah smiled back at the man on the screen.

"This year, right?" she brightly quipped in response. "Not the next one?" *She had a way of popping up with cute questions,* he thought.

"Yes love, this year, 2014. Not the next one," he said, chuckling. "Then I'm done with active service completely. Then I can get a normal job, not one that puts me on a battlefield a million miles away. I can stay right where I need to be, with my loves." The two smiled at each other. The warm thoughts of how life would be a few short months away filled the two with the hope that had been absent from Hannah for an eternity.

\\\\\\\\\\\\\\\\\\\\\\\\\\\\\\\

Yuen gripped his tickets closely with his left hand as he moved through the crowd with his son in tow, clamped onto his right. "Come, come quickly. The game will start soon—we must get to our seats."

They reached the ticket booth, and Yuen slid the tickets under the window. *Finally here,* he thought to himself. It was the father and son trip he had been planning for weeks. He had always wanted to take his son to his first Red Sox game. He was so excited when he had bought the tickets for the May 3rd game. It was nearly noon, and he didn't want his son to miss the first pitch. The event staff checked the tickets and let them in.

"Where are our seats?" squeaked his son from under his Red Sox hat that was too big for him. He had the strap pulled as tight as it could go for it to stay on his head, but even then it kept slipping down over his forehead. His son wore all Red Sox apparel. His large hat had fallen off at least four times already this morning in the car, but he loved wearing it and refused to leave it behind. *It will be a miracle if he doesn't lose it,* he thought, checking once more that it was still on his head.

As they scurried through the mass of people heading into the park, Yuen suddenly felt his son stop walking, which jolted him to a stop too.

Before he could turn to ask why his son stopped short, the boy asked, "Dad can I get a pretzel?"

His first thought was to say no, but then he noticed the three-dollar drafts the vendor also served.

"Sure, let's get some pretzels, sounds like a good idea. It's after eleven—why not, right?"

The two managed to get over to the vendor, and they each got a large pretzel with salt. It was the beginning of a perfect day, he thought, giving his pretzel to his son to hold while he led them into the park. Most people were already in their seats as they made their way down the steps. Farther down he could see the two empty seats approaching.

"Here we are, now you take the inside seat, go ahead." His son walked into the row and climbed up on the seat. Yuen put his beer down and took off his jacket. It was hotter than he thought it would be.

"I can't see over people's heads, Dad."

"Okay, try this." He folded up his coat and placed it on his son's seat, acting as a cushion. His son sat on it and suddenly had a big smile as he was just tall enough now to see the game that was about to start. Yuen took his bag that had been in the aisle and tossed it under his seat and sat down himself, finally able to relax and enjoy. After the two-hour trip into Boston he could now breathe easy.

The beer felt cold in his hand, making him enjoy the sensation all the more. A gentle buzzing could be felt in his pocket. *She is probably checking to see we got here all right,* he thought, reaching for his phone. "Whoops, forgot to tell Mom we're okay."

"Uh-oh," was all his son said, about to take a big bite out of his pretzel with a giggle.

He got his phone out and flipped it open. Immediately, he froze. "No, not today," slipped out of his mouth in a whisper. He noticed dozens of people all around suddenly were pulling out their phones as well. A sense of panic came over him as he looked around more and checked his watch to see it was exactly noon.

"Son. Look at me," he said frantically, turning in his chair and grabbing his son by the shoulders. His son dropped his pretzel, it was so abrupt. "My pretzel."

"Listen to me," Yuen said shakily. "I need you to cover your ears and close your eyes. It's going to get very loud and people will be yelling. I need you to stay put right here, and I'll protect you, okay? Just stay here."

"What do you mean, Daddy? Is this a game?"

"Yes, yes, it's a game. Everyone here is going to play too, okay? So whatever you hear, just stay put and close your eyes." He lifted his son's hands and placed them over his ears. His son looked at him, and Yuen nodded in approval. His son closed his eyes and tucked up on the seat.

He pulled out his bag and placed it on his lap. Around him people were doing the same and checking around them as well. One man made eye contact with him from a few seats in front. The man nodded at Yuen as Yuen nodded back. He felt tears come to his eyes as he and the numerous others all slowly stood from their seats. He looked around to notice that there were not just dozens, but hundreds, maybe more, all doing the same as him. *There are so many,* he thought as they all stood silently in place.

"The regret of December 7th, 1941, will never be forgotten," a man suddenly screamed out, reciting it with his eyes closed.

"Today we finish what our forefathers meant to do that day," said another man. Other people in the audience, still sitting, looked confused, and some yelled for them to sit back down. Yuen could see in the distance others that were standing were speaking as well, causing commotion he couldn't hear.

He cleared his throat and took one last look at his son before saying, "Now I have become death, the destroyer of worlds." Some of the others turned to look at him, and they nodded once more.

Suddenly, all the men standing pulled out guns and quickly began opening fire all around them. It immediately became chaos as people everywhere started running and climbing over seats. Yuen moved to stand in front of his son as he too pointed the gun he'd pulled from his bag and started firing. He had tears running down his face now as he quickly searched for the nearest people to him. With each pull he whispered, "I'm sorry." There was no turning back now. Across Fenway he could see the flashes of the hundreds of guns being fired. People tried desperately to take cover behind seats and even other people to use as shields, but there were too many ready to fire. *We are everywhere,* he thought.

He realized that each shot he had fired had missed. He frantically checked the nearby gunmen to see if they noticed, but all were caught up in their own rampage. It had been so long since his forced training that he was no longer as skilled as he once was.

"Quick, son, take my hand. We are leaving, now!" He grabbed his son's hand as tears went down the boy's face. The hat fell off his head, lost in the crowd. One of the gunmen noticed and yelled after them.

"The job isn't done yet, Yuen!" snapped the gunman. The man had splatters of blood all over his face and shirt.

"My son is not part of this. I'm taking him home." Yuen looked rattled, but it was clear he could be convinced otherwise.

"But then you will come back?" asked the man starkly. The words sounded like more of an order than a question.

"Then I'll come back," Yuen called as he returned to taking his son up the steps of the stadium. The look of panic never left his face as he spoke. As he went back and forth in his mind over whether he would return, he stepped carefully over the fallen victims, moving up the rows passing other gunmen. He swallowed hard as they reached the top of the section. Looking ahead, he thought most of the death was behind him, but out the window he could see the city ahead was burning.

\\\\\\\\\\\\\\\\\\\\\\\\\\\\\\\

"So how is Chloe getting along with your sister's baby? They become fast friends?" Andrew said quickly, moving to the next thought on his mind. Their conversations usually didn't last too long. He was only allotted so much time, so he knew he had to cover as much ground as possible.

"Yeah, they're buds. You like your playpen, huh?" she said to Chloe, who was busy drooling, biting her pacifier hard. "Oh, and she has two more teeth coming down on the top. I think they are either the canines or the set right in front of those. There's more swelling on the top teeth than when the bottom ones started to come in."

"Hopefully they come in quick so the both of you will feel better," he said, smiling.

"You have to go now, huh?" she said, looking off at the clock.

"Yeah, love, I do. I'll call again in a few days when I get back from patrol. I love you, love. So, so much." Andrew blew a kiss at Hannah and then blew a second to Chloe, who was still giggling, hanging on to a piece of crumpled paper.

"I love you too!" Hannah said, making a scrunched-up face, blowing back a kiss with her free hand, her other hand still holding up the baby. "I wish it was a few days from now already. I miss you."

"I miss you too. Gotta go, love. Bye Bye."

"Bye, love."

He still saw her smiling face resonating on the screen as it went black. He held the picture in his mind like a freeze-frame. He knew he was so close to going home, and yet three months still seemed like a long way away. The happiness he felt now seemed like a sadness he couldn't shake. For a moment he hated being where he was. The heat from the Afghan desert blew under the door behind him. He sat for another moment, hoping to delay his return to reality for a second longer. He smiled at the screen once more as if she were still sitting there looking at him. All that flowed through him was love for the girl of his dreams back home. With a deep breath he stood, straightened his shirt, replaced his cover, and turned to step back into the world that he knew. The only thing hanging in his mind was the day he would hold her in his arms again, May third.

\\\\\\\\\\\\\\\\\\\\\\\\\\\\\\

"Let's go, Yakata, it's your bet!" snapped Roger, the cigarette loosely hanging out of his mouth.

"Call," said Yakata with a devious smile.

"He's bluffing, Rog, don't play into his game. It's bullshit, trust me," barked Collins, chomping on his gum loudly from another seat.

The sun beat down on the players as they sat at a makeshift table near the barracks. Suddenly, a gust came by and blew a few of the cards off the table while Collins and Bradley ran to pick up the strays, both repeating obscenities as they raced to pick them all up.

"You didn't by chance catch a peek at my cards, did ya?" asked Roger suspiciously.

"No, I didn't look at your damn cards. It's your show; let's see 'em," said Yakata, leaning back in his chair and crossing his arms with a big smile.

Roger flipped his cards to reveal his hand. "Boo-ya, check that shit out, three of a kind," he said, cackling with his New

York accent. Several onlookers grunted their amusement, looking to Yakata for his next move.

Yakata was known around the base for being a good poker player. He was the best player at Devens. He had entered a tournament in Boston once and made it through several rounds before being eliminated. As far as the other guys were concerned, he was an all-star player.

"Good hand. You know, I'm really sorry, Roger. I have to confess I severely underestimated you. I truly didn't think you had it in you, but you surprised me after all," he said calmly, placing his cards face-down on the table.

"I knew it, I had you." Roger smashed his fist on the table. "I did it." He burst out laughing so hard the veins in his neck could be seen. "I DID IT!" he yelled right in the face of Yakata, who continued to sit there calmly.

"Hey, Barnes, you know what today is, don't you?" asked Yakata, leaning back in his chair, still smiling.

"May 3rd. Cleaning day."

"That's right. Cleaning day, and in about five minutes it will be noon, which means you now have to clean every bathroom this side of the base." He smashed his fist on the table in the same fashion as Roger and leapt up to his feet, cheering. He reached down and flipped over his cards. "Full house! Put that in your pipe and smoke."

He turned to the guys and started high-fiving them as they all still looked a little stunned. Roger still had one hand raised as if to cheer, but now the expression had left his face as he scanned all the cards in disbelief of the results.

"Hey, hey, that can't be right. I had you. I HAD you!" said Roger over and over, hoping if he said it enough it would become true.

"Well, really, I should say thank you, because if you hadn't bet cleaning detail we would all be on the floors scrubbing away. Now, it's just you." The guys erupted in laughter again, patting Yakata on the back. "That's what you get," he said, putting his arms up.

"Shit," was all Roger said, looking at the first bathroom he would have to clean.

"Yep, all day," said Barnes, looking drunk-happy.

Slowly, the guys started wandering off to the barracks. Yakata went over to Roger and extended a hand.

"Getting one more jab in?" said Roger, looking at him skeptically.

"No, my father always taught me to show respect to your opponents in any game—after a few jabs, of course."

Roger quickly shook his hand, then immediately let go. "Get out of here, got a lot of work to do, ya know," he said with a smirk. "Next time I won't let you win."

"Sure thing." The two nodded, and Yakata turned to head back to the barracks.

As Yakata turned he saw a gathering outside the barracks. Soldiers from all over were running toward the crowd. "Hey, Roger, something's up." Roger looked up from the card table and saw the crowd. "Let's check it out! Looks important, whatever it is."

The two made their way to the ever-increasing crowd as mumbles of something serious could be heard growing among the group. He felt his phone vibrating in his pocket. He felt that it could wait until after he found out what the crowd was for.

"Hey, what's going on?" Yakata asked the closest soldier. "Shh."

"Is that the base commander up there talking?"

"Shhhh!" was all the soldier said. Several others gestured for him to be silent as well. Suddenly he felt that something very serious was happening. It was a struggle to hear what was being said.

"I repeat, we have just received word that there is a situation going on inside the 95 Beltway. There are live reports from every town that sleeper cells are attacking all over the eastern part of the state. So far, there appears to be heavy casualties, as there are believed to be large numbers of sleeper cells. We do not know what brought on this attack or who is doing this as of yet. I need everyone ready by 1230 to move out.

Danger close and immediate. More information to follow upon move-out. Now, get to it." The commander immediately turned and began moving away while the crowd began frantically shouting orders among itself.

Yakata and Roger joined the other guys and made their way back to the barracks. Once inside, the scene was ordered chaos. The base had never had a danger close, immediate muster before. Preparations for a situation like this had not been done for some since basic training.

Yakata began grabbing gear and prepping his backpack when he remembered his phone had rung. He quickly pulled out his phone and threw it on the bed. He swung on his backpack, put on his helmet, and then picked up the phone again.

He clicked on the screen as he was turning for the door. Immediately, he froze, reading the message. Suddenly, all the momentum he had, his training, froze him completely. He looked up and around him at all the men getting ready to go, and his eyes gazed from person to person. Everything felt cold. He had not thought it was going to be today. He had put it out of his mind for so long he was starting to believe the day would not come.

The seconds ticked by as Roger stopped in front of him on his way out the door.

"What's up, man—you look white. Don't feel guilty, man, It was only a poker game. I'll get you back next time." He hit Yakata on the side of the arm and headed out the door. Yakata was still frozen, standing by his bed.

Slowly, he walked over to the door and closed it gently, locking himself and the other dozen or so soldiers left inside. He turned slowly to see that some soldiers noticed what he was doing and had stopped as well.

"Hey, man, what are you doing? We need to leave. You heard the commander."

Silence was the only thing he could manage. He just stared back at the other men as he felt sweat go down the back of his neck. He saw up on the wall that the calendar read May

3rd, 2014. This was the day he would regret for the rest of his life.

"Now I have become death, the destroyer of worlds. The regrets of December Seven will not be forgotten, but they will be repaid."

As he spoke, gunshots could be heard faintly all around through the walls. Multiple outbursts of shots broke out. Yelling could be heard in between the exchanges.

Yakata pulled out his rifle from under the bed.

"Hey man, you can't bring your rifle into the barracks. What are you doing? Put it down"

As if possessed, Yakata raised the rifle and began pulling the trigger. He felt the shocks with each pull as he looked from target to target. Each shock brought a pain in his chest. Every shock was a part of him that was dying.

\`\`\`\`\`\`\`\`\`\`\`\`\`\`\`\`\`\`\`\`\`\`\`\`\`\`\`\`\`\`\`\`\`

"Hold," said Andrew as the men were rounding the corner near the outskirts of Kabul.

He raised his rifle as he covered a nearby alley to his left. It was hot out, and what was worse was that there was no wind. There was no relief from the dry, hundred-degree weather. There were no clouds in the sky either to provide shade or to ease the heat. His clothes were stuck to him from the sweat. They had been walking for hours, since they had taken fire from the two civilians. Andrew knew they were close to a safe house for the insurgent group.

Ahead of them down the street was a small red building. All the windows were covered with cloth, and he could tell there was some movement inside. His gut told him this was the place. He checked his watch; sundown was getting closer. He checked around to see the whole area must have been deserted.

He pressed the radio to his throat: "Red structure, my 11 o'clock, two teams, front and back." He turned and gestured for three men to follow him and waved the other four down the alley to the rear.

"You think these are the guys, cap?" asked the soldier right behind him, whispering.

"Been tracking these guys for days. They can lead us to Al-Shazar. Then bingo, all she wrote for that." He lined up his three men opposite the red building's front door.

"All right, listen up. Stevens and I, we got the door. You two are in first." He pressed the radio to his neck again. "Second team, two and two, same pattern. We go." He checked his watch on his wrist. "Sixty seconds. Let's go."

The men silently moved into position. Andrew and Stevens crept along under the windows, sliding up to either side of the door. The other two soldiers quickly and quietly raced up to the front of the door. Andrew and Stevens aimed their guns at their respective targets. Andrew aimed for the lock on the door. Stevens aimed for the hinge keeping the flimsy door on the wall. Once they all were ready, he got the nod from Stevens.

"Execute."

The shots echoed simultaneously. The shots filled the doorway with light. Through the flash and smoke the two soldiers kicked through the door and into the compound. Dual shots were immediately heard from the back of the building with the two soldiers from the second team entering from the back. Nothing but yells could he heard by the soldiers moving through the one-story building, room by room. Each yelled 'Clear' as they moved with raw precision until they all converged on the back corner room. Sitting on crates with their guns and a radio were two extremely dumbfounded teenage boys.

Several of the soldiers began cries of, "Don't move, hands in the air. Do it, do it now." One soldier began repeating it in the Pashto language, to which they both began shaking in fear and stood up with hands raised.

"How did you know these two would be in this shithole, in the middle of all these other shitholes?" asked Stevens again. The other men seemed equally surprised at how they all appeared to have arrived at a needle-in-the-haystack location.

"Well, it definitely took patience, I'll tell you that much. I mean, these guys are good, let's make no mistake about that, but you got to know how people think, what their reactions will be. It's just moves and countermoves. You know, guys..." Andrew turned to address the two boys being tied up on the floor. "If terrorism didn't involve hurting anybody, the wonders I could do for your organization." Andrew smiled as he spoke. He felt the moment of pride come over him as he knew his multi-year search finally was paying off. He knew he was that much closer to Al-Shazar. *But that is the next guy's problem*, he thought, walking back out the door into the sun.

"I'm sorry you can't finish out the hunt there, Andrew," said Stevens, coming out behind him and taking off his helmet. "You could always stay another round, finish the job."

"Is that what you're doing?" said Andrew quickly, unstrapping his helmet. Even with the still-stagnant heat, he felt cooler with his helmet off. He could feel the faint wind coming through the buildings.

"Well, I got nobody worrying about me back home just yet. What's another year? I wish you could hang around."

"Once I'm done, I'm gone, Stevens. I've been out here way too long as it is. It changes when you have a wife and kid. Suddenly all the danger, all this, stops being, you know, adventure and excitement. Now it... what if something happens to me? Who would take care of them, you know? It's time for me to go home."

"How long until you're done, then?"

"Four days. I'm home on Friday, May 3rd, in four days. I say that out loud whenever I can. That's the only way it feels real is when I do that. Then it's nothing but my family and the Sox at Fenway."

"Red Sox suck, man," said Stevens, smiling wide.

"They are still better than the Yankees." Andrew lightly punched Stevens in the arm. Stevens went to hit him back, but Andrew stepped out of the way. "It's sad they let someone as slow as you into the military."

"You going to call in the helo, or be a smartass all day," said Stevens, putting his helmet back on his head and going back into the building.

"Relax. It's all good," said Andrew, raising his radio and staring off into the blue of the sky.

\\\\\\\\\\\\\\\\\\\\\\\\\\\\\\

The man shut the door of the cab so hard the car rocked. His fare was a fat, sweaty businessman of some kind. His shirt appeared a few sizes too tight, and small sweat stains were starting to show through. His fares generally disgusted him every day; it was the main amusement of his day. The businessman shifted to the middle of the backseat. He was breathing hard when he leaned forward, squinting to read the I.D. card of the driver.

"Good morning, Mr. Hayato. I need to get to the North End, please, and I have a lunch reservation, so please hurry. Thank you." He spoke so slowly, Hayato was almost offended by the man.

"Hayato is my first name," he said flatly. He tried to contain his muted anger. He felt contempt for his fare. He lost count of how many times he would have loved to kick his fares out of the car. A couple of weeks ago he had done just that, and his boss put him on suspension for the commotion. Today was only his second day back, and he already felt he was on the verge of another incident.

As he weaved in and out of lanes heading through Newton, he could see in the rear view his fare almost drifting side to side with the turns. The man almost looked a little carsick.

"Could you please take it easy, sir? Please. It's a little... much. Please, thank you." The words fell on deaf ears as Hayato just grinned to himself and kept on driving the same.

"We have long way to go to get to North End quickly." He deliberately chopped up his words to sound more foreign than he really was. He also figured this would give him a good excuse should the man yell at him for the erratic driving later. The language barrier was always a good defense as a cab driver.

He realized he had taken off so quickly that he forgot to start the meter. He checked his watch and figured they had been driving for three minutes. The time showed 11:57 a.m. May 3rd, 2014. *Fare started at 11:54,* he thought to himself. Right as he made another sharp merge to the left lane on Route 9, he hit the meter so the action would go unnoticed.

Suddenly, the businessman was staring at his phone intently, holding it up close to his face.

"Excuse me, could you please turn on the radio? Please, something's happened in the city. Facebook is going crazy that there were shots fired at Fenway or something." The man had a panicked look on his face.

"Okay." He carefully tuned on the radio, becoming just as concerned as the man. *There was a game today, I think,* was all that ran through his mind. He turned up the volume, and, sure enough, there was a special bulletin:

"For those of you just joining us, I don't know how else to put this. The city of Boston and the surrounding areas are under attack. It appears that only moments ago, an unknown number of attackers began firing at dozens of locations throughout the area. All the assailants are plainly dressed, and their numbers are continuing to grow. There is no known motive except to cause mass casualties. All residents are urged to get out of the city if they can, or to stay inside and lock all doors and windows. I repeat, this is an ongoing crisis, as new groups of attackers are popping up as the minutes go by. Initial reports indicate the majority of the shooters appear Japanese. These reports have not been corroborated. For those of you just..."

As the message was broadcasting he realized his phone had been vibrating the whole time. His fare now appeared more panicked than ever, staring at him. Slowly, he brought the car to a halt. They were in Brookline from the looks of the townhouses surrounding them.

"Could you please let me out, sir?" The man was starting to sweat as he spoke.

"Look, if you think I'm involved with this, you're wrong," answered Hayato angrily.

"I'm not saying that, but please let me out." The man was already holding onto his jacket and bag, waiting for the doors to be unlocked.

"We can turn around and leave the city if you..."

"No, no, no....look, please, I'm sorry, please. I'm fine; just let me out. Thank you." The man was stammering to get the words out.

Hayato clicked the unlock button and waited for the man to start to inch his way out of the car when he reached for his phone from his pocket to catch who was trying to reach him. He figured it had to be his neighbor. They always got along, and no doubt she was checking up on him due to the radio message.

He flipped open the phone, only to freeze at the message displayed. Suddenly, he looked around outside and everything made sense. *It couldn't be today, could it?* he thought, turning the radio up louder. The man speaking on the radio was repeating a similar message to the one he had said earlier, only now it seemed more and more reports were saying all assailants seem to be Japanese.

He reached under the passenger seat to grab his bag. The businessman was just getting out of the car as he pulled his gun and silencer out of the bag. Quickly, he screwed on the attachment and hastily grabbed the handle to get out of the car.

He launched out of the car and raced around toward his fare.

"Hey, you!" he said, catching up to the man. The gun was drawn as he gripped the handle so tight the gun shook in his hand. He stopped right in front of the man, with the gun inches from the businessman's face.

The man froze solid, dropping his bag and jacket. His hands stretched up in the air as he began pleading with the cab driver.

"Don't shoot, don't shoot, please. I didn't do anything. Don't hurt me, please, don't. I have a family. Please, don't. I'll give you whatever you want. Anything, please."

"Stop it!" Hayato screamed. He looked around to see the street was empty. Everyone must be in their houses. "Listen,

The regrets of December 6th will not be forgotten. You Americans stopped the attack on Pearl Harbor before it could happen. You shamed my country, but now we will shame America."

The businessman was crying, trying to listen to what Hayato was saying. His knees were wobbling, on the brink of collapsing.

"Go now, go and tell your police, your government, what is happening here. Today is the start of a new country, a new Japan. The disgrace of America ends today. Go, GO!" Hayato waved the gun for the businessman to run. A moment passed where nothing happened. The businessman was still in shock as to what to do. He was certain his life was mere moments from ending.

The sudden realization that he could go struck the man as he left his bag and jacket and started to run down the road. The man never looked back; he felt that if he had, all that would meet him was a bullet. Hayato watched for a few moments, still with his gun raised, before finally letting it fall back to his side.

Everyone's in their houses, he thought once again, letting the decision he had to make come over him once again.

"For Japan," he said whispering to himself as he picked the nearest house in front of him. He felt the wind against his side as the quietness of the street enveloped him. As he crossed into the shadow of the building he felt the coolness against his neck. Sweat was forming between his hand and the gun, but he didn't release his grip at all.

He reached the front door of the townhouse and pressed his ear to the door. Inside, he heard footsteps moving up a staircase and the cries of an infant. His hand reached to the doorknob, only to find it locked. He checked the street once more to still see the coast was clear and knelt down to pick the lock like he had practiced dozens of times before.

A few shots rang out in the distance. The wave was getting closer, and now was the time for him to do his part. The lock clicked, and he knew he was successful. Again, he tried the knob, and this time it effortlessly turned, and slowly he pushed the door open.

Inside, he felt at home. *This is cozy,* he thought, looking into the living room. A jacket and a card were near the door. The card had the name Andrew written on it as it lay unopened. Over the arch to the living room were strung up letter reading *Welcome Home*. He looked to his left into the kitchen area, where there were glasses all lined up; two bottles of champagne sat unopened as well. Must be a party here later on tonight, he thought, walking carefully to the stairs.

"Not so much anymore," he mouthed as he leaned to peer upstairs. He smiled as he saw the steps were carpeted. He knew these would cover the sounds of him going up, and he wouldn't be noticed.

Step by step, he crept up the steps. Once at the top the first room was empty with the door open, so he ducked into it quietly. Inside was some kind of office. There was a large computer with a webcam mounted on it. Next to it on the desk was a calendar marking Skype dates, the most recent one being two days ago. There was a big outline around the current date of May 3rd, stating 'Andrew comes home today at noon.'

Suddenly, he stood up straight. Someone was expecting this guy any minute. He peered down the stairs to see he had left the front door open. Quickly, he stepped out of the room and continued down the hall toward the sounds of the footsteps. The sounds were coming from what appeared to be the same place the baby cries were coming from.

He took one last, deep breath and kicked the door all the way in. Hannah spun around, screaming as she quickly grabbed the baby bottle and threw it at Hayato. The bottle hit his hand, forcing the gun down as he squeezed the trigger, firing a shot into the floor.

"Stop!" yelled Hayato, pointing the gun at her. Chloe began screaming. The sound pierced the air. The reality of the situation sunk in as he knew he had reached the point of no return.

"Please don't hurt my baby," pleaded Hannah. She quickly lunged for the gun, but Hayato was too quick and fired the gun at her twice. He caught her as she fell toward him. He frantically laid her down on the ground, only to see his arms were covered in blood. He couldn't think or speak as he couldn't believe what was happening. *Why did this house have to have a baby and a mother?* he thought to himself over and over. He had hoped that every person he would meet on this day when it finally came would be like his cab fare. He thought everyone would be the typical American, easy to hate. Now that he was faced with a mother and her child, he couldn't help but feel like the very monsters he was out to eliminate.

The room was quiet now. Moments ago, he could barely hear his own thoughts, but now everything was silent. Frantically, he searched as he stood up, looking for the baby. He saw the changing table where the baby was, but all that was on it was blood. He slowly took a step, then another, walking around the changing table until he saw what he had feared was on the other side.

Tears began rolling down his cheeks as he looked down again at his arms, at all the blood. *What have I done?* ran through his mind as he felt his face drain of blood. The gun was still shaking as he gripped it, so he tucked it in his pants, only to see that he had gotten even more blood on his shirt. He started wiping each arm with his hands trying desperately to wipe away the blood, but it just smeared it all over his clothes more. The confidence that had been building up inside of him for so many years preparing for this day seemed so lost now. His whole body wished and pleaded to undo the last five minutes of his life. He thought about his fare, and how he wished to take back everything he had said to him. *The only memories that man will ever have of me is cruelty,* he thought, staggering out of the room back into the hallway. He felt it took all his might to take a step now, as if all motivation he previously had was already released and all he felt now was exhaustion. He was overcome with hatred for himself. *The lowest of the low is to kill a child so small*, he thought as he tripped his way down the stairs. As he made his way to the door he looked up to see the *Welcome Home* sign hanging there. How he wished could apologize to that man flashed in his mind. *Andrew could walk in at any moment now and find me here,* he thought as he reached the front door and stepped outside. *I deserve everything he would do to me.*

Outside, everything was still quiet. The gun had the silencer, so it was unlikely that anyone had heard the shots. He walked out into the empty street, hoping a car would race by and hit him so he wouldn't have to live with this guilt anymore. He had known what this day was going to be, but he knew now that he didn't have it in him anymore. *Maybe I never did,* he thought, staring blankly ahead of him. As he turned to look up the street he thought he heard a noise. The movement of his body pressed the gun handle into his stomach. He looked down, realizing he still had the gun. Slowly he gripped the handle again pulling it out of his waistband. Staring at it now, he suddenly felt a sense of acceptance as he knew what would have to be done.

An eye for an eye, he thought, gripping the handle tighter. He raised the gun and placed the barrel against the right side of his head. For a moment he heard a bird chirping up in a little tree across the street. Looking up to the bird he let the sunshine hit his face once more.

Today would have been a nice day, he thought as he closed his eyes, whispered the words *I'm sorry for my sins,* and pushed the barrel into his head as he squeezed the trigger and all disappeared in a flash of black.

\\\\\\\\\\\\\\\\\\\\\\\\\\\\\

Andrew raced the car between the abandoned cars. Everything had happened as he was in the airport terminal. He had called Hannah, warning her not to come pick him up and that he would get home however possible. All the rental counters in the airport were abandoned within a minute. He hopped the counter and grabbed the first set of keys he could get his hands on.

Looking out the window he could see smoke rising from various places all around. Along the side of the streets people were strewn out along the sidewalk, gunned down. The speedometer read seventy miles an hour. He was almost home.

Turning onto his street he immediately slowed down, as his street was eerily empty and quiet. He glanced in every direction; the situation read as an ambush to him, yet there were no signs to confirm his suspicions. *Everyone must be locked inside, the radio did give those directions,* he thought as he suddenly noticed the sight immediately in front of him.

He hit the brakes as soon as it registered what it was in front of him. He put the car in park and slowly stepped out of the car. *My gun's inside,* he thought as he stepped toward the scene. Before him lay what looked like a man in his late twenties, lying on his side. Suicide immediately came to mind as he quickly examined the scene below him. The man still held a gun in his hand.

"Interesting he would use a silencer to commit suicide in the middle of the street," he said to himself, squatting down, deciding what to do about the body. His first instinct was to get him off the road so no one else would hit him. Right as he was about to grab the man's hands something caught his eye. *That's a lot of blood on his shirt,* he thought, circling the body. *Definitely not from his attempt, but something else,* he thought standing up. "Oh no," he said out loud before he quickly glanced around him from door to door, searching for where this apparent murderer came from.

Every door around him was shut until he stopped on the one door he had hoped not to trace it to. Immediately, he launched into a sprint toward his home. "HANNAH!" he yelled, racing through the open front door. "Hannah?" he said, stopping in the entrance. The words 'Welcome Home' swayed with the breeze he had brought into the house. The silence in the house was deafening. Every cry out for Hannah went unanswered, and there was no baby's cry. All he could do was hope that they had left somewhere and he'd just missed them.

As he was about to turn back toward the front door an odor caught his attention. It was a metallic smell. It was a smell he was used to, but usually it was in the field. Sensing such a smell in his home was out of place. Worry began to fill him up as he made his way up the steps, the smell growing stronger and stronger as he reached the top.

"Hannah?" echoed down the hall. Still there was no response from any direction. He walked quickly, opening each door and flipping the lights on. His hopes rose and fell as each room was a disappointment.

Finally, he reached the door that was open a crack and knew the origin of the smell was coming from here. As he put his hand on the door to push it open a crushing feeling overcame him; he feared the worst was in this room. He hesitated to open the door all the way as he couldn't contain his emotions anymore.

He stepped into the room and saw the bloodied remains of his beautiful wife and his one-year-old daughter. Immediately, he fell to his knees and let out an inaudible scream in pain. All the feelings of love fled out of him as he crouched over, screaming even harder into the blood-soaked floor. He reached over for Hannah and felt her cold arm in his hand. A gasp escaped him as he gently tried to pull her closer. He wished to say something, but it was as if his face and expression were frozen. Slowly he could feel himself getting weaker as all his motivation for living drained out of him. His body wanted to pass out, but he didn't want to close his eyes. "God, why?" he kept repeating over and over in his mind.

His eyes rested on the changing table, which he could barely even see through the tears. Where, where was she? He was screaming even harder out in his head desperately panning the room for his beloved daughter, whom he had never met. He knew he couldn't check the room without letting go of his wife. The pain of the loss was too great for him to handle. He was gasping for more air as he collected himself and carefully laid his wife back down on the floor, gently folding her arms. *I'll be right back with our baby,* he said to her in a thought. Looking around again he found he could only bring himself to a crawl as he made his way around the table, but once he saw what was on the other side he collapsed on the floor again with an unimaginable shooting pain coursing through his whole body. He let out another scream, but this time he heard it echo through the house. He crawled over to the baby and didn't know whether to leave little Chloe on the ground or pick her up. He had never held a baby before, and he couldn't bring himself to pick her up now. He picked up the blanket that was lying nearby and carefully placed it over his daughter. He managed to say out loud for the first and last time to his daughter in person, "I love you."

\\\\\\\\\\\\\\\\\\\\\\\\\\\\

Andrew sat in his living room, alone in the dark. The attacks had left so many dead that funerals for the victims would be delayed for weeks. His wife and daughter remained in the hospital morgue, where they had been for three days. He realized he had been in the same clothes for two days. He sat in his chair, unable to speak. He blankly stared out into the room. *What do I do now?* he thought solemnly. *What's the point?*

The knock on the door startled him. A deep sigh came out of him as reality snapped back into place. Next to him, he saw the glass of scotch he had poured for himself yesterday. He hadn't taken a sip of it yet. *Nothing matters*, he thought, staring at it for a moment longer.

A second knock could be heard right as he got to the front door. He opened it to see one man standing with an awkward sort of half smile. The man extended his hand stiffly.

"Hello, my name is David. I'm the detective you spoke to the other day on the phone. You said I could come over. Is this a good time?" After a few moments the man put his hand back down to his side, realizing the gesture wasn't going to be returned.

Andrew simply turned away from the door, leaving it open, and went back to his chair.

"Ah, thank you." David stepped inside and moved to sit opposite him on the couch.

As the man came over to sit, Andrew finally took in the appearance of his visitor. The man was dressed in a slightly tattered-looking tan suit. The shirt looked brand new, but everything else seemed as if that suit had been worn every day of this man's life. He was clean shaven with brown hair, maybe in his late twenties. His hair was combed like something straight out of the early sixties.

"I spoke to you yesterday? I don't remember speaking to anyone yesterday," said Andrew flatly. He was trying to think of anything he had done in the last few days, but everything seemed far away and blurry.

"Well, first I wanted to say how sorry I am for your loss. That whole day was a tragedy, and I sincerely will do my best to do whatever I can during this difficult, difficult time." The man was leaning forward as he spoke. *There is a stiffness to him,* thought Andrew, as if he were on edge. *He must be going door to door of the victims.* Andrew felt something was off, but he didn't care to put any stock into it.

"We spoke yesterday morning. It was a short phone call, mainly to set up this meeting. Yours was the first case across my desk that day and I always try to treat every case personally." It sounded like a sales pitch. Andrew remained motionless, watching the man as he spoke.

Andrew abruptly lifted his hand to stop the man from speaking anymore. "Did you catch him?" he asked with his eyes watering a bit. "Tell me you got him." His hand was still raised slightly off the couch. David could see it was shaking.

"That's what I'm here to discuss with you. If I can ask, we need to journey back to that day, and I know that will be difficult for you, but that's the main reason I wished to do this in person. I understand the gravity of this and how hard it must be on you." David put his briefcase on the coffee table. Andrew had not even seen him come in with one. He lifted the top of the case and removed some papers. He kept them all face-down, closed the lid, and readjusted himself in his seat. The man

174

looked uncomfortable on the couch, as if he couldn't wait to leave.

"Do you remember what you saw when you turned down this street?" There was deliberateness to his words. Andrew sensed that every question that he would be asked, this man already knew all the answers to. *Rookie cop,* popped into Andrew's mind.

"Yeah, there was a dead guy in the road. Then I found my family murdered. Which would you care to discuss further!" He realized he yelled the last words to David. The man remained stoic on the couch, barely even flinching as Andrew strained to be as loud as possible.

"Did you recognize the man in the road?" asked David calmly.

"Are you kidding me?" asked Andrew, leaning forward. "Get out of my house; I'm not doing this now. My family is gone, and you're asking me for help on another case. Who do you think you are, you insensitive jerk?" Andrew snapped to his feet and pointed at the door. David looked small on the couch. This time he flinched as Andrew berated him.

Shakily, David rose from the couch, then suddenly straightened up and looked as confident as Andrew did. "That man in the road killed your family, Andrew." The words hit the floor like cement blocks.

"Don't you say that!" snapped Andrew. "You don't get to say that to me. I have been wishing every second since I lost my family that I could have come home earlier that day. I wished I could redo those last hours. How if I came home I could of stopped whoever it was. How I could have saved them."

David swallowed hard, placing a hand on his chest pocket. Hints of sweat were forming on his forehead.

"I would give anything to fix what happened, but I can't change the past," screamed Andrew breaking into a sob. "I can't change it," he repeated. He kept repeating the sentence, but each time he grew quieter and quieter, hunching over and turning to go back to his chair.

Suddenly, David lurched forward and tripped Andrew, who hit the floor with a loud thump. David lunged forward to land on top of Andrew, raising a knife he had pulled from his waist high in his right hand, ready to strike.

Andrew lifted up and spun, throwing David off to the side. An elbow caught David in the jaw, jolting his body enough to knock the knife from his hand. The moment gave Andrew enough time to get to his feet and make his way to the nightstand by the end of the couch. Opening the drawer, he grabbed the revolver inside and whipped it around, pointing it shakily toward the now-bloody face of David.

The two men were breathing hard, staring at one another. Andrew struggled to comprehend what was happening. David had a look of scared desperation on his face. He had the look that Andrew had seen on countless faces before. The look of deep fear was all over the man.

"Who are you?" asked Andrew. The gun was shaking more now as his finger gripped the trigger. David flinched slightly over and over, expecting the shot any second.

"That's complicated," stated David in a calm voice that seemed disjointed from his physical appearance. Andrew's face appeared stone straight. "Try," was all he could say through his teeth at the man. "You actually a cop?" he said trying to steady his hands.

David wiped his nose clean and gestured that he was returning to the couch. "No," was all he said as he sat back down where he was before. He looked infinitely calmer now than when Andrew first pulled the gun on him. David managed to compose himself in that fraction of a moment. Andrew almost had the fleeting feeling that the man knew he would wind up in this position. *Almost like he wanted it to,* thought Andrew, sitting back in his own chair and keeping the gun pointed at David.

"Then who are you?" asked Andrew again in a hoarser voice. He swallowed hard, waiting for a reply. A mix of anger, confusion, and curiosity filled him.

"I'm not sure where to start," David said, staring back at Andrew.

"Why are you here in my house?" asked Andrew directly.

"I'm here..." David closed his eyes and shook his head slightly. His hand was raised as if the next sentence were on the tip of his tongue, but then decided to not speak it out loud. "I'm here to stop you," David said finally, slouching in his seat a little, looking defeated by what he just said.

"Stop me. Stop me from what?" asked Andrew, perplexed.

"Okay, listen." Again, David raised his hands as if to explain a rehearsed presentation, but again dropped his arms in defeat. "This won't make any sense, but it's the truth. A few years from now something happens, the result of which will make you think that you can...save... your family." David phrased everything almost as a question. He paused after he spoke, holding his breath as he couldn't get any kind of a reaction from his armed audience.

"Just get out," said Andrew after a moment passed. He laid his gun on its side on the arm of the chair. His gaze went to the floor as the answers he was hoping to get never came.

"Look, I know you think I'm crazy, but trust me we don't have time to go back and forth about it." David was sitting on the absolute edge of the couch, pleading with the man to reconsider.

"Why don't we have time?" said Andrew, suddenly cutting him off.

A look of focused bewilderment came over David as if searching the correct way to navigate a difficult maze. "We only have a couple of minutes left before a colleague of mine will be here. I told him I'd be here around five minutes from now, but I showed up early to try something, well, different."

"What are you talking about?" asked Andrew desperately. He had picked up the gun again, waving it loosely in his hand as he spoke. "You're making absolutely no sense. Now get lost before I call the actual cops." He slumped back into his chair, putting a hand over his face. David could tell the man was crying.

The silence was cut as a knock sounded heavy on the door.

"He's early." David stood, looking shocked and confused.

"Who's that?" asked Andrew without raising his head.

"It's my colleague." He spun around to Andrew as he approached him in the chair and knelt down beside him. "Listen to me, okay? That man about to come in here has no interest in talking to you, or me for that matter. His sole purpose is to kill you. You need to get out of here, and I'll come find you later."

Andrew raised his head and had nothing but rage in his eyes. He raised the gun and pointed it at David. "This is my house. I'm not going anywhere, and I don't know who you really are, or who's at the door, but both of you have about ten seconds to leave before I kill both of you. Got me?" His hand was shaking, but this time David knew it was out of anger, not fear.

The door flew open and slammed against the wall with tremendous force. A man entered, dressed identically to David. It was the same tan suit, black tie, and black shoes. He was a blond-haired, clean-shaven, late twenties man with a look on his face of pure contempt. He had a confidant walk about him.

"Hello, David." The man spoke calmly, as if everything were happening exactly as planned. There was an accent Andrew couldn't place, but he knew he had heard it somewhere.

Andrew leapt up and pointed the gun at the man. "Get out of my house!" The man at the door waved his hand in Andrew's direction. Instantly, Andrew felt numb across his whole body, falling to the floor like a rag doll. A moment passed as the man studied Andrew on the floor.

"You didn't kill him?" asked David, confused.

"No, he deserves a chance," said the man, smiling and moving farther into the room.

Andrew regained consciousness, but couldn't open his eyes or move. *Paralyzed?* he thought, yelling in his head. He knew he was still on his floor. No matter how hard he tried he couldn't so much as lift his arm.

"Let's try this again." The man went over to the body of Andrew and waved his hand over him. Andrew slowly started to regain feeling in his arms and legs and flinched at his sudden mobility.

"Have a seat once you can get up. We would like a word."

"Who are you?" asked Andrew, pulling himself into his chair once again. It took effort to form the words as his throat recovered from the effects of what happened.

"Simply put, we are from further along in time," stated the unidentified man. Andrew shot quick looks back and forth between David and the man who stared straight back at him. The two men who addressed him now showed no signs of emotion as they look at him. It was a practiced apathy, thought Andrew. A dog barked from somewhere nearby, and Andrew had to remind himself that all this was happening. It wasn't some hallucination he was in and needed to wake up from. None of it was enough of a distraction from thoughts of his family, of which the quickest thought caused his body to ache.

"From the future?...right," said Andrew, smirking in disbelief. He felt more prepared this time around. His training was starting to come back to him. The last thing anyone would want to give Andrew was time to think and prepare. He knew this unnamed man was the superior and David was of a lower rank or a trainee of some sort. Beyond that there was nothing he could gather from the men before him. Despite the future part he didn't think they were insane. "What do you want from me?"

The unidentified man stepped forward so he was looking down at Andrew. The calmness remained on the man's face. Andrew knew it was an intimidation move; he had seen it before but not from someone looking so calm. The movement seemed rehearsed, like an actor moving on cue.

"An opportunity has come up. One we believe to be mutually beneficial to us all. You agree to help us, and we will help you." A smile came across the man's face as if he had just delivered a presentation.

Andrew remained frozen on the chair, unable to hold a thought in his head.

"Ok....I'll bite. What opportunity?"

"We need your specific set of skills. You studied Al-Shazar for just a few days and you led our boys right to him. The government had been trying to find him for years, and you located him just like that. You can read people. You can look at a place, a person, an event, and predict all the possible outcomes and hone in on what a person will do and how events will unfold. I could use a man like that. It's remarkable, really."

"How did you know about Al-Shazar? That was classified."

"It doesn't matter how I know, but I do know, and I know you're the perfect man for the job." The unidentified man leaned against the wall of the living room. Andrew looked up to see the man was right beneath the welcome home sign. The picture of his wife flashed across his mind and made his eyes hurt.

"You haven't answered my question," snapped Andrew through the headache.

"I need you to sabotage a boat, to be precise."

"What? Why? That's not what I do. I don't do that sort of work."

"After the boat sinks, a set of events will come into play, and I need someone to anticipate moves and countermoves. Ultimately, if things go according to plan a lot of lives will be saved. What I need, Andrew, is a man on the ground, so to speak, someone to call the plays as they happen. "

"Why can't you do it?" asked Andrew, cutting him off.

"There are bigger things at work here, Andrew, that need not concern you," said the man, smiling and shifting his weight. "I'm not good with the details like you are. Plus, what we are offering... I think you will beg me for the chance."

"Well, that sounds great and all, but enough of that for one day. Please leave."

The man pressed off the wall and took a gold watch from his pocket. Before Andrew could say anything all he saw was a flash of blue.

The first thing Andrew noticed when the blue light subsided was that they were outside. He immediately looked around to see that they were outside his house, in the middle of the street. The street was empty, and the air was filled with silence. It was the middle of the day.

"How did we get here, what did you do?"

"I'm sorry about this, Andrew. It's the only way for you to believe me."

A cab appeared, coming up behind them, and Andrew and the man stepped up on the sidewalk. A Japanese man got out and pulled a gun on his fare. They couldn't hear the words being exchanged, but the Japanese man let the fare go off running.

"What is this?" asked Andrew. He started to open his mouth to yell for the Japanese man, but he was stopped.

"You cannot interfere with this," said the unidentified man calmly. "What's done is done."

"What are you talking about?" said Andrew desperately.

The Japanese man walked up the steps of Andrews's house and disappeared through the front door.

"Where does he think he is going?" Andrew tried to walk to his house but was again stopped.

"You don't remember this day, do you?"

"What?"

"This is the day your family was killed, Andrew."

Andrew stopped and faced the man. His body went tense. "How dare you speak of them."

"Look around, Andrew. Doesn't any of this seem familiar? You were racing here in your car, to make it home. Think."

A scream rang out from his home, immediately followed by gunshots. Andrew turned to face the house. He knew that voice that was screaming. "Hannah?"

He took off running toward the home, but the man grabbed him and pulled him behind a corner.

"Wait," said the unidentified man.

The Japanese man came staggering out of the house, seemingly in a daze. He walked out into the middle of the street, put the gun to his head, and pulled the trigger.

"Now you remember?"

Andrew looked down the street to see his own car swerving around the corner.

"I can save them," Andrew said almost whispering. "If we go back again, I can save them."

"If you help me, you won't have to save them because none of this will ever happen."

Andrew was fighting tears as he watched himself check the dead man in the street and then run into his house.

"I want them back so much."

The man put his hand on Andrew's shoulder, and before he could open his eyes they were back in his living room where they started. David sat on the couch, looking patient.

"If I help you, you will take me back so I can save them?"

"If you help me, yes. Then we have a deal?"

"Whatever you want, I'll do it," said Andrew weakly.

"Before I go into detail about what it is I want you to do, I have to tell you about something very important.

"What?" Andrew was still clinging to the thought about how close he had been to them. They were alive, he kept telling himself over and over.

"On the boat, there is a man who will be like me, and he is the man who will try and stop you at every turn. He is very smart, and to beat him, you need to break him." The man's voice sounded more nervous and direct.

"I'm not letting anyone get between me and my family again."

"To break him you must make him feel the pain you have now. That's the only way to outsmart him. If you can't, then nothing can be done for your family."

"I'm not killing anyone. I'm not a monster."

"Evil needs evil to beat it, Andrew. Shall I take you back to that day again?" The man's voice was hoarse now.

"Please don't. All right. Who is this man?"

"The name of this opponent is...Roark. Now listen very very carefully..."

"...and who are you?" asked Andrew nervously

"My name is Adam."

Chapter Seven:

A man with secrets

"You may come in," said Hoover flatly. He stood by his desk firmly planted, almost at attention. He felt the corner of his desk lightly with his right hand. He could tell he was almost sweating from the importance of this moment. He did not wish to see the men who were about to enter. They had forced his hand and had him backed into a corner, and they knew it. It was a meeting he couldn't refuse.

Miss Gandy entered first, looking a little uneasy as the two men followed her inside. They were identically dressed in tan suits. Both looked straight ahead past him as they moved over to the couch. Following closely behind them was a young teenage girl who looked very out of place. His glance remained on the girl, as she was the only one who was looking him right in the eye. Her confidence surprised him.

"Thank you for seeing us on such short notice," said Roark, trying to look Hoover in the eye only to realize he was still staring at Mary. Hoover put up a hand, silencing him before he could finish. His gaze slowly shot to Roark.

"I did not invite you here; you invited yourselves, and I am being forced to oblige. I am in the business of secrets, Mr., eh, whoever you are," said Hoover, half closing his eyes, sounding tired. The clock behind him read nearly midnight.

"You can call me Roark."

"It doesn't matter what your name is. As we speak, I have a team of men investigating all three of you." Hoover sat on the edge of his desk. "By morning I will know everything about you. The business of secrets is always a two-way street, Roark. Now, having said that, why is it your intention to blackmail me?" Hoover spoke smoothly as he addressed the group before him. He had completely forgotten Miss Gandy was still in the room.

"Will there be anything else, Mr. Hoover?" she asked curiously, ignoring the three on the couch.

"That will be all, Miss Gandy, thank you," said Hoover without turning. Mary couldn't help but watch Gandy leave. A mixture of envy and curiosity filled her.

"We need your attention on a serious matter." Kori hurried the words out. His tension returned to him. He leaned forward in his seat, almost as if to stand up once again.

"Did I ask you anything?" snapped Hoover. His glare to Kori was that of a parent scolding a child. He wanted it known that he was in charge of this meeting despite the circumstances. Kori sat back, looking annoyed. Nobody had ever spoken to him in that manner before.

"We do not wish to harm your office or your reputation. Our goal was to be granted an audience with you, and we have done just that. You may have us investigated if you wish, but nothing will come of it. All you will get are dead ends. You will have nothing on us, but we will still have something on you. You're good, Mr. Hoover, but you're not that good." Roark's smoothness matched Hoover's. The two looked at each other, recognizing each other's conviction.

He tried to study both Roark and the other man dressed like him. The one called Roark had a practiced calmness to him, as if all the rage of the world were covered in a fine-looking suit. The man next to him wasn't hiding his agitation as well. His anger poured out of him everywhere except his mouth. The girl still perplexed him the most. She sat the whole time staring right at him, never breaking eye contact. She remained silent, obedient, but he had this feeling that rather than being obedient out of a form of weakness or submission, it was a choice. There was more to her than a child following a leader.

"I don't like being threatened, Roark, and I'm finding I like your company even less. Get to the point, then get out if you would be so kind," said Hoover forcefully.

Kori's glance drifted toward Roark, but Roark hadn't flinched. "We came to make a trade."

"If you expect me to barter to get my secret back, forget it. If I have to fight you in the press, I will. You will not gain anything from me for this."

"That is not our intention. We wish to exchange information with you on an entirely separate matter. One of an even more sensitive nature. One of national security," said Roark carefully, watching any sign of movement on Hoovers face.

"...and then blackmail me if I refuse?" asked Hoover, matching.

"I really wish you would stop referring to it in such a way. That is not what we're trying to infer here."

"It's you who came in here pitching that you have dirt on me and using it as coercion to enter my office. You give me no choice, and you expect me to just get over it—"

"Stop!" said Mary loudly, cutting through the bickering men.

All the men stopped to look at the girl. Roark and Kori looked frightened. They had not intended to hear her speak at all during the meeting. Hoover smiled at the relief her outburst brought to the room.

"Listen to what these men have to say. You value the FBI; it's your creation. Despite the poor execution, these men do have valuable information to give you, Mr. Hoover. What they have would greatly benefit your office." They all listened intently as she spoke. She looked over to Roark and nodded for him to continue. Kori remained speechless. *She broke the rules,* he thought to himself.

"Out with it then," snapped Hoover in a calm but direct voice.

"What we are offering is leverage over the current sitting president, Mr. Roosevelt, as well as his successor, Harry S. Truman, and several more future potential presidential candidates after that." Kori opened a briefcase he had next to the sofa and opened it. He pulled out several files and laid them on the coffee table. Each file had a name written on the tab. Hoover leaned over to read a few of the names. The first ones he saw were Dwight D. Eisenhower, John F. Kennedy, and Lyndon B. Johnson.

"What are these?" said Hoover, flipping some of the folders open. "How did you amass such an amount of information on these men? For what purpose?"

"Call it job security, Mr. Hoover," said Kori with a small smile.

"I don't understand," said Hoover, suddenly sitting back. "You ask to see me and claim to have information to ruin me, now you're offering me a wealth of information of an undetermined value citing it as my job security."

Both Roark and Kori stared at him indifferently. Mary suddenly looked at the floor, feeling guilty for having assisted the men.

"Why twist my arm?" said Hoover pleadingly. "I'm sure there could have been less dramatic ways of getting my attention."

"We didn't have the time," said Roark slowly. "The matter we wish to discuss has some unique time constraints."

"...and the... blackmail?" asked Hoover curiously.

"It was regrettable, the need for it, but it was to ensure a timely compliance."

Hoover urgently sat up straight in his chair. "Who do you work for?" he asked firmly. "You didn't put folders like these together on your own. There's some very privileged information in there. Some of it I already knew, and what I have was obtained by the efforts of this entire building over many months. You expect me to believe that the entire amount here was compiled by you two?"

Mary looked to Roark and Kori furiously, fearing how they would answer the question.

"For now, yes," said Roark simply.

Hoover smiled and let out a sort of laugh. "Whoever you are, you seem to have considerable resources at your disposal. What exactly is the information you need from me in return for all this?"

"We heard a rumor, and we were wondering if you could help us with it?"

"What's the rumor?"

Roark leaned forward and sat on the edge of the couch. "We hear there's talk of a man in Germany assisting the likes of one Adolf Hitler. A man helping him that no one seems to want to talk about. Have you heard of such a man?"

"I have," replied Hoover. "All there is to know is a first name. He goes by the name of Andrew...and I hear he is working on something big for the führer, something to secure the future of the Third Reich." Mary looked off to the window, her face turning white with the fear of what comes next. Her mind drifted to a familiar dream.

\\\\\\\\\\\\\\\\\\\\\\\\\\\\\\\\

"Don't hurt me," said Crantor, doubled over on the ground. The old man clutched at his sides through his robes. He had long, grey hair and a beard that was scraggly. He looked as if he hadn't bathed in some time. He wore the robes of a monk or cleric. "I did what you asked."

Crantor pleadingly looked up at Adam watching him, coming closer to his despair. The man that approached seemed out of place. He was a tall, handsome man in his early thirties. He had blond hair and blue eyes and carried himself with an authoritative poise. He was dressed in an odd outfit. It clung to his body like a second skin that moved all its own. He didn't know what to make of it.

"Are they all secure?" Adam asked calmly, looking at something on his forearm. As the old man watched, the blond man started touching one finger to whatever was on his forearm; each touch made a noise.

"They are."

"All one hundred of them!" Adam snapped to look at the mess on the ground below him. "It is essential there are none left behind."

As he spoke, an explosion could be heard in the distance, and distant sounds of screams started to ring out.

"What's that?" asked Crantor, cringing on the ground, struggling to look up at the sound he heard.

The blond man turned to look over his shoulder in the direction of the sound, but he made no reaction and turned back to what he was doing on his forearm.

"You needn't worry about that. Loose ends. There are none left behind, correct?"

"There are none. There were only one hundred. They said that was all there was. Why do you want to take them from these people?" Crantor asked, almost begging the man for an answer.

"For the greater good, my friend."

Adam checked his watch and 11:45 a.m. could be seen on the face. "Okay, last loose end," he said, squatting down to eye level with the old man on the ground.

"There is one last thing, old man. The journal."

"What?"

"I know you have been keeping a record. A journal of our journey, how we got here, what I have been doing. I can't let you take that back to the world."

"I haven't kept any such thing," said the old man, pleading with him. The old man was sweating, trying to hold himself together enough to speak. "I swear I haven't."

"I'm not much for interrogations." Adam pulled out a revolver and let it hang in front of the old man's face. "Do you have the journal on you?"

Crantor dropped his head, and his tears dropped to the ground. "Why? Why do this? Why do this to these people? What did they do? I never should have brought you here."

"This is not the time to blame yourself. These people are the victims of their own devices. If it weren't you, it would have been someone else. It's as simple as that. Now, do you have it on you?"

The old man, with trembling hands, reached behind his robes and pulled out a broken leather book. He held it out to the blond man.

The blond man stood up and walked away a few steps. "Toss the book over there."

"Please."

"Toss it over there, now."

Crantor tossed the book a few feet away onto the open ground and immediately went back to clutching his side. The exertion stretched his stomach where his injury was.

Adam casually turned to face the journal on the ground and studied it from afar for a moment. He reached into a small pocket on his left arm and pulled out a small capsule. He walked over to the book and broke the capsule over it. A few drops fell over the journal. Next, he pulled a few matches from the same pocket and struck one up. He watched the flame and let it go. As it fell the old man closed his eyes and turned away from the sight. The match hit the cover and the book burst into flames. Within seconds the book started to crinkle up, and the flames caused the book to open, partially revealing pages and pages of dated entries, each written almost in a frantic scribble. As fast as he had lit it on fire the book was nothing more than ash.

"...And now it's done."

"What's left now?"

"Everything. A new era is about to begin. You helped me achieve the first step," said Adam.

"I mean what's left now for me?"

"In ancient Egypt, servants were buried with their pharaohs. Essentially, they were immortalized with the greatness of their past. You will be remembered for what you have done. Immortalized with the greatness you brought here."

Crantor put his forehead on the ground, reaching under his robes where the book was and pulling out something clenched in his fist but hidden from the blonde man.

"No loose ends," he said as he turned around and raised the revolver. He squeezed the trigger and slumped to the ground. Another explosion rang out in the distance as the man checked his watch one more time. The time read 11:55 a.m., and he walked off into the woods, away from the explosion.

A moment of silence passed around the body, until a few steps could be heard. With his last breath the old man saw feet approach him. Covered in tattoos and strange designs, the feet stopped right next to him. The old man reached up and gave the person what was in his hands. As he let go of the item, Crantor fell back to earth. The last bit of life had left him.

The person, a boy, held the item, a crumpled piece of parchment, then unfolded it to see a map with a location circled on it hastily. On the bottom it read, "To undo this lie, find me and send to this address." A set of explosions started in the distance. They got louder and louder, so the person clenched the piece of parchment and disappeared into the trees.

The boy darted into the woods, and once the explosions subsided he re-opened the crumpled parchment. The boy was covered in tattoos of a writing the monk never deciphered. A line of blood ran down his face. His whole body was smeared with the dirt he was lying in. He had to play dead to escape. His whole village was being murdered, and he was powerless to help.

On the reverse side of the parchment he held was a crude map to a location not far from where he was. He recognized the landmark and took off in its direction. The sounds of screams grew fainter as he ran. He wanted to go back, but almost everyone he knew was already gone.

He arrived at the burnt tree as drawn on the paper and began frantically searching the ground. Near the base of the tree some of the soil appeared disturbed. The boy dug into the earth and buried only a few inches down was something covered in cloth. It had clearly been buried in haste. The boy picked up the item and flipped open the cloth to reveal a twisted, beaten journal. The boy had seen the one being burnt from his hiding place. He knew this was, in fact, the real journal of Crantor. *The other was a fake,* he thought as he opened it and read some of the pages.

Voices suddenly were heard in the distance. "He went this way," cried out one of them. The voice sounded like the blond man he had seen earlier. The boy quickly wrapped the journal to start his journey into the woods again. As the cover closed he caught a quick glimpse of the first page of the journal. The line read "This journal of Crantor."

\\\\\\\\\\\\\\\\\\\\\\\\\\\

Mary jolted awake from the dream. She realized they were already in the car en route to see the man whose name she had given to Roark and Kori earlier. They were on their way to see J. Edgar Hoover.

"Where did you go? You've been out since we left," said Kori as he turned around in the front seat to look back at her. They were in an old car she didn't recognize. Roark continued driving, ignoring their conversation.

"It was a dream," she said, looking down. She felt embarrassed. She didn't like talking about her dreams. She remembered being forced to talk about them at the institute. Talking about it made her feel so exposed. It made her feel like a kid. "It's a dream I get sometimes. It's nothing."

"Anything good?" said Kori, forcing a smile. He had promised Roark to try and be nicer to her. He hated that he had to try, but the moment was inescapable.

"It wouldn't make any sense to you; it doesn't to me." She moved her glance from the floor to the window. The buildings glided by, but she stared straight out into nothing.

"Try me," Kori said blankly. His expression was that of forced curiosity.

"There's two men in it. One is this old man on the ground, and he's hurt, and standing over him is a much younger man, and I think he is the one who hurt the old man on the ground. He shot him, I think. They are out in a jungle by themselves." She paused for a moment, trying to remember more detail. She hoped more detail would make her sound less crazy.

"And you're just standing there watching this?" asked Kori, amused.

"I think so. I mean it feels like I am, ya know, but neither seems to be aware that I'm, like, right there. The younger man keeps asking all these questions to the old man, making sure there's a hundred of something."

Kori scrunched his eyebrows, thinking as she spoke.

"I don't know what it means. The old man is a monk or something, that's right, I forgot that part. Then there's something about a journal..."

Suddenly Roark put on his turn signal, moved the car over to the side of the road, and stopped in front of a large stone building. He turned to face Mary in the backseat, looking very serious.

"Was it burned?" asked Roark, suddenly bright.

"What?" said Mary confused. "Why did we stop?"

"Was it burned? Set on fire?" asked Roark again.

"How did you know....?" Mary trailed off. She couldn't put together what it meant.

"Another time... We're here." Roark turned to open the car door. "Remember what I told you." Roark got out of the car and shut the door before Mary could repeat her question.

"How could he know that? How could he know that the journal gets set on fire?" she asked Kori pleadingly. Kori's expression looked as if he had seen a ghost.

"A better question would be, how do you know about that?" Kori quickly turned and shot her another glance, as if to study the girl one last time. She saw that he swallowed hard as he got out.

∖∖∖∖∖∖∖∖∖∖∖∖∖∖∖∖∖∖∖∖∖∖∖∖∖∖∖∖∖∖∖

"Andrew?" said Roark, pretending to ponder the name as if it was new to him.

"You and I both know you have heard the name before. We both deal in secrets. You knew the name before you even walked in here, Roark." Hoover spoke casually now, knowing he was regaining the upper hand on his visitors.

"I had only recently become aware of him, which is why we are even here. What do you know of him?" asked Roark, trying to remain equally cool.

"The man just up and appeared. Suddenly, he had access to the highest offices of the Nazi Party. Instantly, he got up close and personal with Mr. Hitler. Whatever he had to offer the Nazis must have been pretty valuable to achieve that kind of instant popularity.

Roark knew Andrew must have been supplying the Nazis with information on the future; there was no other explanation. *He doesn't know the consequences of his actions.* He knew that Andrew had gone back to the *USS Hornet* to start something, only he didn't know the endgame.

"The odd thing is, no one seemed to have heard of him before 1939. No record of him at all before then." Hoover let out a grunt of laughter to himself at the thought.

Roark tried to contain himself at giving a response as to why there was no record.

"Wait, 1939?" The date almost slipped past him. The year stuck in his mind. "I didn't think any record of him existed before 1941, just his involvement in the Pearl Harbor attacks." Roark knew Hoover had valuable information that could help stop Andrew. It was the puzzle piece he had been waiting for. *If I can learn where Andrew was in 1939, I'll have the exact place to meet him and stop all this from happening,* he thought to himself.

"Involvement in Pearl Harbor? What on earth are you talking about?"

Roark caught himself realizing he spoke about something only he and Kori knew. No one was even aware he was ever on the *USS Hornet* that night. Kori had a look of shock stuck on his face.

"Eh...it's an unconfirmed report. Once I know more I'll be sure to share all I have."

Hoover studied Roark and Kori. He knew they were withholding precious information he could use. He didn't trust them, but he needed them. The mere thought that they were valuable made him sick to his stomach. He loathed the very sight of them.

"What is Andrew offering the Nazis? Intelligence?"

"No, actually. He is building something for them. We believe it to be some kind of rocket," said Hoover skeptically, unsure of whether or not they already knew that piece too. "I have briefed the president on my findings, and a special team will be put together to figure it out and replicate it. If the Nazis are building a weapon, we need to be just as ready."

"Andrew didn't strike me as an engineer."

"Nor did he to me, but he did recommend someone to them. He brought them a scientist by the name of Von Braun."

Mary lit up at the name. She remembered it from her history books. Kori noticed her reaction. "You've heard of him?" asked Kori; Mary quickly gave a small nod.

"He appears to be quite intelligent, this Von Braun. It might be difficult to duplicate his work for us."

Roark leaned forward and plucked a folder from among the pile on the table. "Take a look at this man. I believe he might be up to the task. Maybe even do one better than old Adolf."

Hoover took the folder and flipped through the pages. Immediately, Hoover looked impressed and began flipping the pages faster. "I'll bring this right to the president himself."

The name on the folder read, J. Robert Oppenheimer.

Mary leapt out of the car after Roark. "How did you know what was in my dream?" she demanded.

Roark turned calmly, staring at her with his hands in his pockets. A look of worry crossed his face for a moment. "Mary, this will be hard to accept, but I'm not entirely sure what you believe was a dream was even a dream." Roark stopped to measure her response.

She was filled with a mixture of bewilderment and confusion. His answer merely prompted more questions. Her look prompted him to continue.

"Traveling through time is not without side effects. Going back and forth, creating and closing alternate timelines... it's a lot for the body, and specifically the mind, to handle. It's not just for the traveler either; what we do can affect anyone whose lives we have altered as well. Where things get complicated is that all those experiences, all those memories, can sometimes get scrambled and re-arranged, and the mind can have difficulty discerning one from another. Of course the time when our minds are most susceptible to these occurrences is when we are asleep, and since our minds can't place where a certain memory is from, it gets dismissed as a fantasy. "

"So...you're saying my dream is a memory?" asked Mary carefully.

"Yes."

Kori was ignoring the whole conversation. A thought of Serena came to him. It filled him with a momentary happiness. The thought that after all this he could be with her again filled him with a confidence he couldn't place. He thought about how the meeting would go, and how many times they would have to repeat it to get the answers they need out of him.

"I've been having these dreams since I was little. Although just now was the first time it ever continued."

"Continued?"

"I see the monk get shot, the journal gets set on fire, and then a boy takes a piece of paper from the monk. That's usually where it ends, but this time it didn't."

Kori suddenly returned to the present moment and turned to Mary. "What piece of paper?"

Roark looked equally interested. The two stared at her with a renewed eagerness.

"It was a map to another journal."

"What?" Roark looked surprised. She had never seen him looked so shocked. Kori looked nervous. He suddenly looked around as if to see if anyone else had heard what she said.

"After this meeting you will tell us more about this. First, we have to speak with Hoover. Remember, you do not speak. Anything you say will only make him suspicious. Roark, you ready?"

Roark was still looking at Mary with a weary curiosity. He seemed stuck in a daze.

"Roark?"

"Yes...let's go."

\`\`\`\`\`\`\`\`\`\`\`\`\`\`\`\`\`\`\`\`\`\`\`\`\`\`\`\`\`\`

"Mr. Hoover may I come in?" said the little stiff voice at his door. She was a petite middle-aged woman. Even after a long difficult day, she still appeared as put together, poised, and alert as the moment she first walked in that morning. In her hands was a single piece of paper with barely legible scribbles on it. She had it tightly in her grip as if it were made of the most fragile glass. If it were to fall it would break into a thousand pieces. "Of Course, Miss Gandy, of course—come in." His usual strictness softened a little as he gestured her in with a sweeping motion of his hand. He remained behind his large desk, smiling as she approached. "What can I do for you, Miss Gandy? I was just about to leave for the evening."

"I understand, but I remember what you said about threats to this office or to you personally, and you said if I suspected anyone to come straight to you." She had a slight nervousness to her voice, but steady, as he had come to know her. It was uneasiness, but it was based in confidence.

"Yes, I remember, Please continue." He maintained a dignified control as he listened. He always tried to maintain an air of professionalism. He never broke her stare while she spoke. She maintained an earned respect from him over the years. It was a formal partnership.

"I received a call just now," she said, still standing opposite his desk.

"Please sit, Miss Gandy. I'm sorry, continue," he said stiffly, quickly leaning forward to gesture toward a chair before returning to his upright posture. He fixed his jacket as he sat back.

"Well....there was a man on the phone. He said his name was Roark and that he wanted a meeting with you."

"A meeting. I don't take meetings with strangers—you know that very well, Miss Gandy. The answer is no. Does this Roark have a last name? Who is he?" said Mr. Hoover sternly. There was a callousness to his voice that was practiced, given his distinction in the Bureau. While she spoke, he maintained a look of passing concern.

"He said his name was just Roark." She had relaxed a bit more as she spoke. She never could accurately gauge his temper whenever she came in, which necessitated a hesitant approach. She knew his anger was targeted at most people. After so many years she had become accustomed to his brashness. "He said that Roark would be sufficient."

"Sufficient? What kind of person thinks a first name is sufficient? You see it's these kinds of people I'm talking about with the Bureau. If I can get more phone taps we would already know more about this Roark. Now, what were you talking about in regard to threats? What did he think he could threaten me with?" He cast off the questions as if a tantrum erupted within him. He felt his heartbeat quicken with a jolt of determination. *This is what I've been talking about all along,* he thought to himself. He was already thinking of a new pitch to bring to the president. *I'll revolutionize this country with this Bureau.*

"He said he had pictures, ones that he would send to newspapers if he didn't get a meeting with you. Pictures..." She began to look nervous again.

"Out with it, Miss Gandy." His voice was sharp now. His impatience was showing as his face seemed stuck from making any other expression.

"He said he had pictures of you and Tolson together. You and Mr. Tolson...socially." Her voice trailed off on the last few words.

He sat back in his chair calmly and slowly. He crossed his hands in his lap, staring off and on toward the floor. He had the look of a writer calmly pondering the next line. No anger showed on his face anymore. He was completely relaxed.

"That's all?" he suddenly quipped, lifting only his head to direct his sight at her. She almost flinched at the sudden jerk of a motion. The rest of his body remained completely still, as if his body were still in that relaxed state.

"He said they were pictures of a private nature. He threatened to expose them unless..." She realized how she was sounding and cut herself off before saying more than she meant to. The look she saw indicated she already had gone past that point.

"It doesn't matter what they have; it's nonsense. I'll see this Roark."

"But if they are nothing, why indulge him with...."

"I'd rather hear him out for five minutes than deal with the press for the next three months. Best to just get it over with."

"Yes, Mr. Hoover."

"I will need something set up before they arrive."

"Shall I ready the tape recorder?" she asked, finishing his sentence. A smile came across his face as she prepared the tape recorder under the table. He readied himself, thinking of what he needed them to say for the record in order for the tape to be usable blackmail.

\\\\\\\\\\\\\\\\\\\\\\\\\\\\\\

"You think he will follow through?" asked Kori, pacing the hotel room. They were back in Kori's hotel room number 717. Remnants of their earlier visit were still evident around the space. The adrenaline of the meeting was still in all their veins. Mary sat on the end of one of the beds. She felt the small breath of wind as Kori walked past her over and over. Nothing seemed to hold her attention for more than a few moments. Roark sat on the edge of the next bed, hunched over deep in thought. He had his hands pressed to his forehead as if pressing any harder would make a solution present itself quicker.

"He will," said Roark, almost whispering. There was confidence in his words that did not match his demeanor. The idea was stronger than the man saying it. "But now there is something else we need to discuss." Roark lifted his head and turned to stand, facing Mary from across the room. He backed up against the farthest wall from her. "Tell me more about this dream of yours."

Mary stared at him quizzically. "I've told you all I know. It's the same dream every time. I see someone get shot and that's it. "

"But you said this time there was more."

"Yeah, I saw a boy follow the map and find another journal buried by a tree, but then that's it—dream over."

Kori stopped pacing and faced Mary. He folded his arms, studying the girl.

"And I only saw that part once. It doesn't mean anything." She had frustration in her voice. Her eyes pleaded with Roark to stop, but Roark just stared right back at her.

"I'm going to tell you something, Mary. This is something that has never been said to anyone that isn't like us. I'm breaking a very big rule by telling you this, and I want you to pay attention. Okay?"

"Roark, you can't. Those are not rules you break. It's very clear," said Kori stiffly. "She is just a girl."

"She said she has the same dream every night, but now suddenly it went further. Telling her might trigger another memory that could help us." Roark pushed himself off the wall to face Kori. Kori could feel himself sweating, as the nerves were getting to him.

Mary braced herself for what was to happen next.

"You're playing with fire; I'll still help you but leave me out of this part."

"We're already in the fire, old friend. For this, I'll take the risk," said Roark, moving to sit opposite Mary while Kori went and sat in the chair in the corner.

"Now, Mary, remember when I said that time travel, like any other form of transportation, requires a destination."

"I remember."

"It's only in the past that your destination is known, which is why you can't move forward. Understand?"

Mary nodded her head meekly.

"There was a time when one man may have in fact traveled into the future. We have come to call him 'the traveler.' No one knows how it was possible, but where he went he made a discovery. It was a discovery that changed everything. It reshaped civilization as we know it." Roark paused, lost in thought.

"Why are you telling me this?" Mary demanded. She looked to Kori for help, but he sat still in his chair, unmoved. His eyes were glazed over as if he was drifting off in thoughts of his own. He didn't care for what Roark was telling her.

"It's the reason we do what we do, you understand. After the discovery was made, humanity prospered. Advancements were made beyond our wildest dreams. Think of every issue the world has today. It was all gone. A perfect utopia was created where everyone was happy. Everything was as it should be, and it was all thanks to him. The problem is that no one ever learned when the traveler went to, or how he got there. It was a secret that had to be protected. This is when our organization emerged. Our job was to ensure history played out exactly as it was supposed to. We had to make sure history was not altered or changed. If anything were to change, then that utopia would be lost."

"What does all this have to do with my dream?"

"One cannot travel to a destination that is unknown to him, but if someone else were to tell him the destination or, more importantly, if it were written down somewhere...then..."

"Then it would be possible," Mary finished. Her curiosity was taking over.

"Exactly."

"A fool's venture," snapped Kori from across the room. Mary didn't know when Kori had started to listen to their conversation, but it was clear he'd had enough of it.

"I'm not a fool for searching," snapped Roark right back, standing from the bed.

"Not that, THIS! You're a fool for thinking telling her will accomplish anything." Kori's voice was growing in volume.

"I said it was worth it."

"You've said too much, Roark. You always take these leaps of faith, and every single time I have to pick up the pieces." Kori walked past, heading for the door. "Never again, Roark. I changed my mind; I'm not helping you anymore."

"I'll let things stand when we're done!" Roark yelled to Kori before he reached for the doorknob. He remained frozen at the door, waiting for another excuse to leave. "When this is done, I'll say you died and let you stay in the timeline. I'll do that for you—just stay. That's all I'm asking of you."

Kori didn't move for a few moments, his back still to them. He wrestled with himself trying to convince himself that leaving was the better idea. He wanted away from Roark, but doing so would not let him escape the life. He spun back around, glaring at Roark, tears in his eyes. "Then it's done, and you never find me again."

Roark acted as if he had been slapped across the face. He swallowed hard, realizing the high price for all of this. "All right."

"I'll be downstairs. I can't listen to this anymore. I'll check around to see if anyone may be listening close by." Without waiting for a reply Kori disappeared through the door. A silence fell back over the room.

"We'll be fine." Roark re-adjusted himself in an attempt to assure himself of his confidence.

"I've never felt fine with either of you," said Mary, still staring at the door.

"Now let's continue." Roark motioned for them to return to where they had been sitting before.

\\\\\\\\\\\\\\\\\\\\\\\\\\\\\\

"I hear you have some privileged information regarding the allied forces, and against the United States." Hitler sat coolly in his chair as his interpreter translated. No one else was present except for them three. Those were the conditions laid out over the phone. The room was quiet except for the occasional murmur of voices through the wall.

They were in an apartment building outside Berlin. The only furniture in the room was an old desk and two chairs. No one knew of the meeting except for one other in his office.

"How badly do you want to win the war?" asked the visitor with a sly voice. Quickly the interpreter went into German. Sweat appeared as he translated.

"Do not talk to me like you have any power here. You will never see the light of day if I wish. Now speak. Give me what you have."

"Why do you insist on speaking to me like this? I have given you plenty over the years. I got you where you are, and still you treat me like a prisoner of war?"

Hitler leaned over the table as close as he could get to his visitor. "People may still be listening. You reference that we have met before again, I'll have your head. People must never know who you are," said Hitler in a barely audible whisper. The visitor swallowed hard waiting for the translation.

"No one may know who I am, but there are two men who know I may be here," the visitor said just as quietly. "And this changes things, drastically."

"What do you mean?"

"I must leave here for a while. There are things I need to check on, but in my absence I need something from you, Führer, and I have never asked anything of you before."

"Anything, name it. You have been most helpful to my campaign."

"I need you to build me a hiding place. Someplace fortified. When I return, I will need a place to protect myself."

Hitler turned to his visitor, confused. "What are you expecting to happen?"

"Something might be coming, and we must be ready. I expect to return in two years' time." The visitor never moved the whole time he spoke. He spoke calmly and deliberately. Hitler was amazed at the man's poise.

"Two years?"

"Yes. Until then, I have given you all the tools you need to do with your party as you wish."

"Who are these two men you mentioned?" asked Hitler with a growing concern on his face. "I will have them taken care of immediately."

"No need for that. As much as they know, I do not consider them a threat. It's the girl who is accompanying them. She is of some value, but when I return, that matter will be handled by me personally. I'm afraid this is where I leave you Führer."

"Whenever you return, the Nazi Party welcomes you."

"Thank you." The visitor stood up silently and turned to walk to the door. Hitler walked around the table, pushed pas the interpreter and extended his hand. The man stared at it for a while, then cautiously shook it once and let go.

"I'm so grateful you broke into my house all those years ago, Andrew. I cannot imagine what would have happened in my life if you hadn't."

"It was the start of something, yes. Good day."

As Andrew exited the tiny apartment, he knew he was one step closer to saving his family. He had played this game before in war. An uncertainty lingered in the back of his mind over the consequences of his actions. *I don't like helping this leader, but Adam said this was necessary.* He could see the chess pieces moving in play. All the sacrifices he was making were for the greater good. Already, the guilt of what had transpired before was weighing him down. He took out his Atlas and paused in the alley.

"Ok, Roark. What's your next move?" He took out an old piece of paper and moved the dials forward. He took a deep breath and closed his eyes as he shut the Atlas and was gone in a flash of blue.

Chapter Eight:

The Chaos of Control

"All right, listen up. In five minutes we will be over German airspace." The men sat up in their seats, confident and ready to go. The plane rocked a little as Warren steadied himself against the overhead rail. "This is the day we have been working hard toward, so now is not the time to hesitate. We are the front of the largest, most complex military endeavor in our lifetimes. History will remember this day as D-Day. However, history cannot, and will not, know about our main objective here. Our orders are as follows."

The plane shook again as the master chief spoke to the group. Some of the greener recruits hung on every word, knowing each word learned could save them from what lay ahead. Mary-Ellen gripped her gear, frantically looking around for comfort from anybody who would look back at her. She looked to Roark across from her and saw that he was asleep. Her mind raced, wondering how anyone could sleep in a situation like this. "Hey, don't worry about him," said Kori, staring at her. He had been watching, feeling off about her, since they had boarded the plane. *Something was missed,* he thought to himself.

"What's a Navy guy leading this mission for?" asked one soldier, whispering to another about the master chief. Another man heard the comment and just shrugged. "He's supposed to be one tough son of a bitch, I hear—you see all those tattoos?" said a second soldier, pointing up to the chief still speaking. "Yeah, I saw them back at base. He's got a dragon going up one arm and a bald eagle with a torn Japanese flag hanging from its mouth or something going up the other. He looks like he could punch through a brick wall or something." A few men smirked at the ridiculous-sounding statement. "I wouldn't want to fight him, that's all I'm saying." Another soldier leaned in to catch what was being said. "Hey, isn't he one of those UDT guys? Like they stand out on the end of a boat at night and pick off underwater mines during battles or something. You know, with artillery flying right over their heads," said another soldier. "Jeez, that's what this guy does? You got to be pretty crazy to do that," said one of the soldiers, leaning back against his seat. "He was at the harbor too," said Roark, silencing them all with his eyes still closed. Roark slowly opened his eyes to the men. "That's why I picked him. That's why he's here," said Roark.

"A lot of you may have heard that there are several divisions paratrooping in all over France. This is true, but it is meant as a distraction to give us cover," said the chief as a confused look came over several of the men. "The enemy knows a strike is coming, but they do not know from where. Our strategy is to overwhelm the enemy in order to disguise a small strike team. That team is us." A few men all looked around at each other, more scared than a few minutes prior. "This is our guy." Warren held up a sketch of Andrew drawn in the most meticulous detail. "He is to be taken, alive, back stateside. Do not kill him. If he dies it is mission fail. Let me repeat that—if he goes down, WE lose. Understood?"

Hoo-rah! erupted from the group.

"Grab your gear. Time to take the elevator to hell, gentlemen."

All the men stood. Kori snapped to attention with the rest of the men. Roark looked like he was just waking up from a drunken state. He dragged himself with all his strength to just sit up straight. A strong pain rang through his chest. He grabbed at his chest as if it would alleviate the pain he felt. Mary noticed what he was doing but remained silent. She pitied him in that moment. She was beginning to witness the toll all this was taking on him. All she felt now for him was the pity you would feel for a stray animal on the side of the road. The feeling almost made her feel repulsed by him.

The master chief turned to see Roark dragging himself to his feet. He wanted to react and yell at him, but stopped himself, seeing how much pain the man was in. Roark could feel the outline of the photograph he still carried around with him. The memory it reminded him of crossed his mind but was lost again.

"You going to live through this?" Kori continued to look straight ahead as he spoke.

"It would be easier not to, I think," said Roark. The two smiled briefly.

"Remember what I said to you," said Kori, dropping the smile from his face.

"I know."

"Fix your harness, Roark, or you'll slide out of your parachute gear." Kori headed to the front of the plane to join the master chief.

"What if this is a mistake?" Mary yelled over to Roark. "What if we are not meant to do this?"

"Why would you say something like that now?" said Roark, annoyed at the idea.

"I don't know." Her mind couldn't find the words she wanted. A soldier came up behind her and buckled himself into her. He was yelling over the roar of the wind outside that all she needed to do was hang on and he would do all the work with the parachute.

"ONE MINUTE!" yelled the master chief over everyone.

Kori made his way back to them through the men lining up. "Showtime. Ready?"

Roark stared down at Mary, nervous about what he was putting her through. He needed her by his side. He knew he couldn't do this without her. Kori looked at Roark and immediately knew something was off. The feeling he had before came back to him. Roark turned to Kori, but couldn't find the words so he gave Kori a small nod.

"GO TIME. MOVE MOVE MOVE!"

All the men moved forward, and two by two, jumped out of the back of the plane. The men fell away from the plane disappearing into the skyline. The master chief looked back at Roark and Kori and gestured a half salute, then he turned and leapt off the platform.

Roark went to jump, but Kori put a hand up and stopped him. "For Adele." The words froze Roark with a shiver. For a moment Kori looked as he once did many years ago. It was a hopefulness that he thought was lost in him.

"This one's for Serena, Kori." Roark put a hand on Kori's shoulder, and Kori turned and stepped off the platform. Mary and the soldier she was strapped to moved up next to Roark. He turned and smiled at her. He wanted to reach out and take her hand. He kept the smile on his face as she closed her eyes and stepped off in the blue.

\\\\\\\\\\\\\\\\\\\\\\\\\\\\\\

The wooden chair felt more uncomfortable than the last time he had sat here. He gripped the files in his hands tighter as he realized he was starting to sweat from the nerves.

He looked around the room for something to take his mind off the present. The calendar on the wall read April 1942. He couldn't believe it had been nearly four months since Roark had first arrived at his office. He hadn't seen Kori or the girl since. Every other visit, only Roark attended. He knew the others must have been close by, but Roark never let on.

The meetings were always top secret. No one knew about Hoover's meetings except Miss Gandy. All of the meetings were taped and the transcripts were locked away in Hoover's private store.

"You may come in now, Mr. Hoover." The secretary was a young, pretty girl who most likely recently started. She had an eagerness that only came with youth, Hoover thought to himself.

"Thank you," said Hoover, trying to force kindness.

He stood and tucked the files under his arm as he followed her into the next room. Through the door was one of the most important rooms in the country. He had been in this room before but under different circumstances. *The oval office always looks like it's never been used,* he thought to himself as he crossed in front of the couch in the center of the room.

"Welcome, Mr. Hoover, welcome." President Roosevelt wheeled his chair around his desk. It was rare for him to remain in his wheelchair, as for public appearances he usually preferred to stand, but this was to be an off-the-record meeting with no public around. Hoover found himself quickly moving toward the president to shake his hand. Immediately, he realized how unprofessional he must have looked and quickly regained his composure. "Please sit."

Hoover saw the armchairs facing the desk and swiftly placed himself in one of them. The president turned and wheeled himself back behind his desk. "So, how is the FBI these days?" said Roosevelt as he settled himself up to his desk.

"Making revolutionary advances in forensics, Mr. President." Hoover spoke brightly. The agency was his creation, his baby, and no one could take it from him.

"Do we have our mutual friend to thank for that?"

J. Edgar looked around sharply, as if someone may have been in the corner listening. Roosevelt took notice.

"No one is listening, Edgar, and let's drop the titles. Let us speak normally as just people." Roosevelt smiled warmly, trying to reassure him. "But that's good. I'm glad to hear you're doing well with the agency. I must say I was surprised when I heard your request for a meeting. After our last meeting ended rather unfortunately, I assumed we had an understanding to stay out of each other's way. However, you said you had information regarding the attack on Pearl Harbor. Needless to say, that got my attention. But make no mistake, that is the only reason you are here and that reason alone." Roosevelt leaned back in his chair, staring blankly at Edgar.

"Understood, Frank," Edgar said plainly.

"First, I'd like to know why the FBI is even concerning itself with international matters. Your office oversees domestic issues." Frank had a certain pattern when he spoke. His words told the story of a man who made a career out of choosing his words carefully. He had a directness that Edgar liked as if he was speaking with someone on his intellectual level. As much as he disagreed with Frank over a lot of issues, he was a man worth respect, he thought.

"I'm sure you know the answer to that question, Mr. Presi... Frank." His words caught in his throat, remembering the agreement.

"You mean our friend Roark? If Roark had information regarding Pearl Harbor why would he bring it to your attention, and not mine? Why go the FBI and not the White House?" Frank's face took on a sort of contorted expression as he thought. He leaned forward in his wheelchair to lean on the desk. "Do you trust him?"

"I have not doubted any information he has given me," said Edgar brightly. Having said the words, Edgar had an uneasy feeling come over him. He didn't believe what he had just said, and he felt Frank knew it as well.

"That's not what I asked. His information has proven useful and correct enough that I wouldn't doubt any of his intelligence either, hence why you're even in this office. That being said, do you trust him—his intentions, I mean?" Frank's eyes felt like they were burning Edgar's. "This is between us, Edgar. This man has reached our inner circle. I need to know what you think."

"The short answer is no." Edgar could feel himself sweating in his seat. He readjusted to try and hide his discomfort. "I don't expect anything from anyone, Frank. I don't expect people to hurt me or help me... I simply brace myself for whatever happens; call it mistrust, if you will. The longer answer is that I neither trust nor distrust Roark. I expect nothing of him, but I have taken steps should his usefulness wane. Every conversation I have had with him has been recorded, discreetly. No one knows except myself and now you, Frank." Edgar could feel his heart beating faster, yet despite this he felt relieved at the disclosure. "Enough?"

"I always take whatever I can get from you, Edgar, which will have to suffice for now. As to my original question. Why not come to me with this information himself? Why does he keep going through you with sensitive issues? He is welcome in this office anytime he wishes."

Edgar's discomfort was getting the best of him. "I believe it is a matter of plausible deniability. So should something go wrong, you can claim no knowledge and be telling the truth. "

"I think our friend Roark has been seeing you too long, Edgar. Where you see what he is doing as a favor to me should something not pan out as planned, I see it as a lack of taking responsibility. He is not giving you the full picture, Edgar. As head of the Federal Bureau of Investigation I would have expected you to be more suspicious." Frank paused to study Edgar's expression. He was savoring the power shift.

"The FBI is my creation, and I will not be instructed on how to handle my affairs." Edgar stammered his reply to Frank, fuming from the insult.

"Yet you come in here, no doubt with something in that envelope, ready to blackmail me, with intention to instruct me on foreign policy and acts of war," said Frank, loudly talking down to Edgar. Edgar did not move, for he felt moving would justify Frank's words. "You bully people, Edgar, and now you are forcing compliance upon me."

Frank took off his glasses and dropped them on the desk. Edgar remained still. He felt the moment was inescapable, no matter what he did. Slowly, he could feel his hand moving the folder around to open it. Where his hands were on the envelope the paper of the envelope felt hot, but as they moved he instantly felt the coolness. He swallowed hard, wishing the meeting had already ended—or never had to happen at all.

"Say what you have to contribute, then this meeting is over."

Edgar still remained silent.

"Is there even anything?"

Edgar cleared his throat. "Yes, Frank, there is." He opened the folder that read *Top Secret*. "This is in regard to the mission of the *USS Hornet* on the night of Saturday, December 6th, 1941. Up until now, it was believed that a mechanical failure resulted in the ship's sinking. I am here to tell you that this is a lie."

Edgar stopped and looked up to see what Frank's reaction was. The president no longer appeared as angry as he had been a moment earlier. He had a mixed expression of contempt and intrigue on his face.

"Go on," said Frank, almost in a whisper.

"The mission was a failure due to a saboteur being aboard. As of right now it seems to have been the work of one man. No further evid....."

"You can stop right there, Edgar."

The interruption startled Edgar in his seat. The words continued in his mind as if Frank hadn't stopped him. "Excuse me?"

"I said you can stop there. Did Roark tell you this?"

"Yes, he did—why? He said it was very important I bring this to your attention." Edgar suddenly had a strange feeling wash over him like he was being used. He looked down at the report in the folder, unsure of what to say next.

"That evening, the night of the 6th, Roark came here to speak to me, Edgar. He sat right where you are now and told me he suspected there would be a saboteur aboard that ship. He had overwhelming evidence of who it would be, so I gave him orders to board the *Hornet* and accompany it on the mission. I have been fully briefed on what happened that night, Mr. Hoover. What's curious is why he would send you here to tell me what I already know? Perhaps we need to take a closer look into our mutual friend. I'd like to listen to those tapes you have, Edgar."

"Yes, I think that would be a good idea. I'll bring them immediately."

"I want you to put together a team, Edgar. I am hereby directing the FBI to put all available resources into any and all information relating to this man, Roark. I want to know who this man really is." Frank's voice was growing louder.

"Understood, Mr. President."

"Be careful, Edgar, Whatever Roark is up to, he has proven to be extremely well-informed about us and our dealings. Should he realize what you're doing, come see me immediately." Frank readjusted his glasses, then immediately shifted his attention to something on his desk.

Edgar nodded to the president, as he felt no more should be said between them. He stood from his chair and tucked the folders he carried in with him under his arm and made for the door. He quickly opened and exited the office for fear the president might want more from him. A coolness came over him as he entered the ante-chamber. All he could feel was relief, as what remained in those folders now seemed like such trivial pursuits compared to what Roark may have been planning all along.

\\\\\\\\\\\\\\\\\\\\\\\\\\\\\\

Mary felt a rush of panic as she and the soldier stepped off the platform into nothingness. The feeling of freefall terrified her. She wanted something to hold onto, but the force was too difficult to bring her arms into herself. The sound of rushing wind filled her ears. Everything else seemed to be like a silent movie around her. All around her as far as she could see was a mix of smoke and parachutes amid the clouds and green below. Thousands of troops were all jumping within minutes of each other. The goal of today was to confuse and overwhelm the German forces. Although it was an impressive display of force, she never wanted to be a part of it. But Roark had insisted she come along.

As the ground rushed toward her faster and faster, she could see the dangers below. German forces on the ground were firing cannons into the air, and she realized that soon they would be aiming at her. Suddenly, an explosion burst in midair in the distance, and some of the parachutes near it disappeared in the smoke. Another went off closer, almost simultaneously. Heat from the blast reached her arm, and she felt the burn on her hand. Her breath quickened; she knew how vulnerable she was. *How could Roark leave me alone in this?* she thought, hating him for putting her in this position.

The soldier she was attached to grabbed her arms and crossed them in front of her. She felt her muscles fighting her, as her arms felt stiff. He was trying to yell to her, but between the wind and panic she couldn't make out his words. She gripped her straps as tightly as she could as more shells burst around her.

A shell went off directly beneath her, and all the parachutes below disappeared. A cold shock of fear streamed through her body as the thought that both Roark and Kori could have just been killed. Maybe Roark had kept her by herself in case neither he nor Kori made it to the ground. *I can't think about this,* she thought to herself. *I just want to be away from everything.* She was screaming on the inside, fearing for her life.

As the ground came into sharper focus, she realized that she couldn't let the fear get the best of her. She was in the middle of a war, and no amount of hoping was going to get her out of it. She needed to find any strength that was left in her to make it through this day. *Maybe he knew I could do it,* she thought. *Stick to the soldier,* she remembered Roark saying.

The soldier was yelling something again, but it was again too muffled to make out. As she tried to turn her head to look at the soldier a sudden force jolted her downward. The sudden g-force pulled her straps deep into her shoulders. She felt like they were going to break from the pressure. The soldier had pulled the rip cord. Overhead, she saw the chute open up and block out the sunlight. Suddenly, the rushing wind sound went away, replaced by yells from both the troops in the air and the men on the ground. The shells exploding were deafening.

A harsh reality had set in her mind, looking at the ever-growing field below her feet.

"Keep your knees bent, or they will buckle. You hear me!!!" yelled the soldier.

Mary shook her head up and down frantically, her eyes still glued to the ground.

"One hundred feet!" he yelled, leaning forward to look over her shoulder. Mary strained her head upward to see if there were any other parachutes close by, but the sky was starting to clear of the paratroopers.

"Fifty feet; brace for landing, "the soldier said in a noticeably quieter voice. He was almost whispering. As the ground raced toward her feet she bent her knees and took a deep inhale.

They landed with a rough thud. The shock made her bite her tongue hard. She felt a sudden headache come on. The impact knocked her in a daze for a moment, but when she regained her alertness she noticed the soldier had already detached himself from her, and she was standing on her own.

"Quick get out of those straps," said the soldier before she could even register what was happening. She quickly started grasping at her harness, realizing how cold she was from the freefall. She squeezed her hands into fists to try and keep them from shaking, but she was too cold to focus on the small buckles. The soldier had already gotten out of his harness and raced over to help.

"You picked a hell of a day for a first run, kid. I'll do my best to protect you, but if you get me killed we are going to have words, got it?" Mary managed to nod. It was the first time she had looked him in the eye. He smiled at his own sarcasm, but he also saw the fear coming from her.

"We're going to get out of this, don't you worry. Geez, they didn't even give you a gun or anything," said the soldier, realizing she didn't have much gear with her.

"Don't know how to use it," she said through the cold morning air.

"Here." The soldier pulled out his .45 caliber side arm and handed it to her. He pulled some extra magazines out and pushed them into her pocket. "You hold it like this," he said as he moved her hand into the right position. "Now all you have to do is point and shoot. Exhale when you pull and you will be fine. Got it?"

"And when I run out of bullets?" she said, trying to process the new information.

"Just hit this, catch the mag when it falls out and push another in the same way. It's just you need something out here. Why anyone would send a first-timer out here without a gun is beyond me, but right now we gotta move. Follow me." The soldier snapped up his M1 rifle and motioned for her to follow.

"Stay right behind me, all right? You go where I go."

They moved slowly into the tall grass by the end of the field. Through the trees she could see they were approaching the town she had seen from the air. Every few steps the soldier would twitch his head to peer back at her as if one of these times she may not be there. He felt sorry for her.

"There's SS all over these parts. You never know where some might pop up, so keep it quiet," he said, whispering and keeping his mouth as closed as possible.

As they moved, Mary worried that she was becoming a burden to this soldier. On the plane she had overheard that he specialized in prisoner transport and had experience moving people out of dangerous situations before. *He's never had to bring someone into one before*, *though*, she thought as the soldier suddenly came to a stop at the tree line.

"Step where I step. Nazis may have placed mines all over these woods. One wrong step and, boom, then you would be alone in unfriendly territory." Carefully, he scanned the ground in front of them before placing a foot down. Mary tried as best she could to match her foot to his, but doing so almost threw her off balance.

"Where is everyone else?" asked Mary, whispering to the soldier. "I don't see anyone."

"Wind was a bitch up there. Wouldn't be surprised if a few landed in the next country over. I was aiming to land on the other side of this village, save us some time, but that did not pan out as planned." The soldier had a positive attitude about him. Mary knew he was only doing it to keep her calm, but it only fueled her frustration. We could die at any moment, and he is acting like he is back home.

They arrived at the back of one of the buildings and started to make their way to an alley between them. Some voices could be heard murmuring faintly through an open window. Mary strained to hear the voices better.

"Is that them? Could that be our team waiting for us?" asked Mary, hoping to see anyone she knew so that she would feel less alone.

"Don't really think anyone learned German on the way down. So...no."

"That's not funny," said Mary stiffly, finally having had it with his demeanor.

"Yes, ma'am. Understood," he said brightly. "Just stay close; we are going straight through." They moved up the alley until they were right at the opening to the street.

The place looked abandoned. Most of the buildings' doors were open and the windows broken. It appeared to have been abandoned for some time. *The voices must be a small SS scout team moving from town to town*, the soldier thought. The last things he saw before he turned to go back down the alley were the Jewish markings on all the doors. Immediately, his heart dropped at the thought of the townspeople. He turned to verify that Mary had seen the markings as well.

"Looks like everyone evacuated. I think it's just a scout group in there. Three, maybe four men. They must have a Jeep nearby," he said to Mary as she continued staring out at the village.

"You're lying," she said flatly. "These people didn't evacuate."

"I told you they evacuated, all right? Now come on," he said more urgently.

"They are at the camps. All those people...dear god," she said, holding her hand to her mouth."

"I didn't think you knew. I'm sorry, but we have to go. Now might be our only chance to get across this street."

Mary felt her heart beating in her throat. The soldier grabbed her hand, and they raced across the street. Mary stared at the symbol on the door as they passed. Inside, she was screaming.

"Almost there," said the soldier as they darted between buildings in a full-out sprint to reach the far side of the village. Empty house after empty house came in and out of view as they passed.

Suddenly, a shot rang out. Mary felt the bullet fly by her head and hit the brick wall as they passed it. The soldier turned around to see three men chasing them. "Move," said the soldier as Mary tried desperately to keep up with him. "Through there," he pointed, stopping abruptly. "Down the alley should be the last of it, then you should be in the woods again."

"What are you doing?" she said as she passed him, ducking into the alley.

"What I'm supposed to." He smiled at her as he lifted his rifle and took a position behind a half-demolished wall. Yells came from the alley they had just come from as the soldier opened fire d. Mary recoiled at the noises and was torn whether to stay or leave him. He looked at her and nodded down the alley again, and she knew she had to leave.

An instinct took over her as she gripped the pistol. She stood and ran over to the soldier, joining him behind the wall. The soldier started to scream at her to run, but the German soldiers began firing again and cut him off. She held the pistol out over the wall and began squeezing the trigger. The recoil startled her, but when she fired she could feel her fear slipping further and further away. With each shot she could feel her will to live taking over her body until pulling the trigger felt like a reflex action.

Suddenly, a deafening burst of gunfire broke out all around her. The blast of bullets shocked her so much she dropped her pistol and dropped to the ground in a ball behind the wall. She tucked up as tightly as she could, bracing herself for the end. She thought it was more German troops in an ambush. She had a flash of the orphanage on the earliest day she could remember. One of the people working there was telling her how any day now she would have a family to go home to. Just you wait, the worker would say each day. The next flash was of Roark. Despite all her doubts about him, he has been the only one to care that much for her. The thought saddened her.

The burst of fire was over before she even dropped to the ground. She opened her eyes, realizing she was still alive. A smile came across her face as she checked herself to see that she had not been hit. Immediately, she looked around to see if the soldier was all right.

She looked up to see an outstretched hand. She knew it was not the hand of the soldiers but of someone else. She looked up to see the face of Roark. What surprised her was that instead of a confident man looking down at her, what she saw was his tears of joy.

"I was so worried I lost you," said Roark, using his other hand to wipe the tears from his eyes. Around him were the rest of the members of the team from the plane. The soldier was in the group talking with the chief, who didn't look happy with this detour.

"You're lucky," said Kori, quickly coming to Roark's side. He noticed Roark's tears but looked away, knowing what they were for.

"I thought I was dead," said Mary as Roark helped her up.

"The chief was going to leave you," Kori stated flatly. Mary looked of surprise.

"But I wouldn't let them do that." Roark was still fighting back tears.

"You almost cost us the mission, young lady," the chief interrupted. "Because of you we now have that much more ground to cover, and not to mention almost gave away our location to this whole area."

"I'm sorry," she said instinctively.

"You may be valuable to a lot of people, but what's valuable to me is my men and this mission. So far you are doing more harm than good." Roark stood watching the chief speak as if he were ready to fight him for talking to her that way.

"Let's move it, men—we need to put as much distance between us and this town as we can before the next patrol comes through," he said. All the men quickly turned and started moving back toward the woods. The chief lingered with them for a moment, turning back to Mary. "As for your apology, war has no room for apologies."

Hearing the words, Roark clenched a fist but refused to act on his emotions. Kori put a hand on Roark's shoulder. It was the first sign of compassion Kori had shown him in a long time. As much as he hated doing it, he felt the same obligation to the girl.

`````````````````````````````

"Roark, we have a problem!" Kori said immediately after appearing from the blue flash.

Roark was sitting on the edge of the hotel room bed, sifting through files. Mary was missing from the room. Roark didn't even flinch when Kori arrived. "What is it, Kori?"

"I went ahead like you asked, and there's a problem."

Roark put down the folder and turned to Kori, still looking unimpressed.

"How far ahead did you go?" asked Roark, starting to turn back to his folder.

"Two years from now, 1944. That's how far ahead I got." Kori sounded out of breath.
`````````````````````````````

Roark stood up, dropping the folder back on the bed. He stared off, thinking about what Kori said. "Two years, two years," he kept repeating to himself.

Mary emerged through the door from the hallway. She had some shopping bags that she put down just inside the door. "What did I miss?" she asked, looking quizzically at Kori.

"Two years from now in 1944, what happens?" Roark suddenly fired out at Mary.

"Um...in regards to what, exactly?" she said, putting the rest of her bags down against the wall.

"The war," said Roark with anger mounting in his voice.

Kori started to speak to explain what he saw, but Roark raised a hand, subtly shaking his head. "I want to hear it from her."

"It's D-Day, isn't it? What is Andrew going to do there?" Mary's suspicions were piqued. She thought of what she used to read in history books about that day in June of 1944. It was supposed to be a day that would turn the tide for the Allied Forces, but it amounted to little more than a devastating massacre of them. American and British forces were spread too thin and tried to go straight for Berlin. Instead of the Germans being overwhelmed, it was an ambush.

"So that's his endgame. D-Day."

Roark went to go pick up his jacket that had been draped over the corner chair.

"He means to win the war for the Germans. How would that affect a Japanese attack years later?" asked Kori, stepping in front of Roark.

"The Manhattan Project, right?" said Roark glancing at Mary.

"He would bring the world that close to an absolute end, sacrifice that many people, just to save two." Kori sounded furious as he spoke.

"Wouldn't anyone do the same? What would anyone be willing to do for their family, given the opportunity?" Roark's words sunk deep into Kori. "We need to see Hoover. Let's go."

As Kori and Roark filed out of the room Mary hesitated and lingered by herself for just a moment. She felt a loneliness she had not felt in a long time. She was a part of things happening that she did not want. Her mind went back and forth from clinging to Roark to hating every fiber of his being. The feelings of both screaming in agony and quiet contentment came and went with each passing minute.

As the feeling of agony passed once again, she turned calmly and followed the men toward an uncertain road.

\\\\\\\\\\\\\\\\\\\\\\\\\\\\

An uncomfortable silence came over the room as Roark and Edgar entered the oval office of Franklin Roosevelt. Edgar had gone quiet before they entered the office, and Roark knew something was off about the meeting as he sat opposite the president. Kori stayed out in the anti-chamber with Mary; he was starting to feel like her babysitter. He had agreed to stay outside the office following some blind sense of devotion he had to Roark. It was like a slave's devotion to his master, the shackles being the promise of a reunion with his wife.

Roosevelt appeared confused and lost sitting behind his desk. He gave a smile that did not fit his expression. He smiled at Edgar, who could only manage the briefest of smiles simply to acknowledge that he was there and nothing more.

The three men sat waiting for someone to speak; finally, Edgar realized he was to be the mediator between them.

"Is there something I need to know, Mr. President?" said Roark brightly, an upbeat tone that caught Roosevelt off guard.

"It's Frank, Roark. This is an informal meeting," said Frank, speaking robotically, still unsure of what had happened as Roark walked in the room.

"Forgive me...Is there something you wish to say to me, Frank?" asked Roark again, a little more flatly.

Despite the apparent ease with which the men were talking to each other, Edgar felt a rising tension he couldn't place. He felt as if the two had guns aimed at one another as they spoke. He couldn't shake the feeling that he was the one and only hostage in the room, and he was unsure he'd live through the ordeal.

"Yes, Roark, there is something I recently became aware of, thanks to our mutual friend Mr. Hoover and his unparalleled cooperation with this office. I was hoping to discuss it with you at some point." Frank smiled gaily at Roark as he spoke. He felt he had Roark right where he wanted him.

"Then let's start with that, Frank. I am concerned now that I may not be enjoying your full confidence. I will endeavor to correct that if I can. What is it you wish to discuss?" Roark folded his hands on his crossed knee, patiently waiting. His calmness frustrated Frank.

"This is what I like about you, Roark—you're an upfront man. Isn't that right, Edgar?"

Edgar smiled uneasily. A level of panic had set when Frank made it a special point to mention what he was about to say had been provided to him by his FBI. Edgar considered himself fearless in the eyes of the world; Roark was the only one who ever made him feel as small as his mother once had.

"Tell me what you know of the Manhattan Project. I understand you have taken an interest," said Frank, leaning forward in his seat.

Roark swallowed at the question. He knew that Edgar had leaked the information to Frank. He had only confided in Edgar at Mary's request. It was a small breach in faith, but he also knew that with so much going on and their plan taking longer than anticipated, someone was bound to catch on.

"It's how you will win the war. I had intended to have this remain a secret for a while longer, but my hand was forced in the last few days," said Roark, unsure of how his words would land.

"You meant to bring this to me at some point?" asked Frank, surprised.

Edgar appeared increasingly nervous. He tried desperately to conceal it under a guise of confidence.

"In due time, yes. However, I must state my reason for this visit before we progress any further." Roark cut himself off, switching glances back and forth between Edgar and Frank. Edgar appeared almost frightened, as Roark had not mentioned any agenda of his own prior to the meeting.

"You have come for more information, an exchange as usual?" asked Frank, skeptical about continuing to do business of this nature with a man of such power and secrets.

"No, no exchanges, not anymore."

Edgar straightened up in his seat and quickly looked to see Frank was just as surprised at the statement as he was.

"This has proven to be a great partnership, Roark," pleaded Edgar, turning back in his seat. "Why stop when we have achieved so much?" He knew without Roark he wouldn't have the leverage to position himself where he was. His post as head of the FBI could be in jeopardy if Roark were to leave.

"I must say I'm a little stunned myself. Why the sudden change of heart?" Frank sat back in his chair, crossing his hand in the air in front of him. He wasn't sure if he was relieved or troubled by the abrupt end to their dealings.

"It's for the better," said Roark, returning to his bright tone. "A matter has come up due to unforeseen circumstances, and I must take a leave of absence. I'm leaving, but I will return in two years' time." Roark paused a moment, not knowing how the added news would affect the men.

"You can't be serious," said Edgar, stifling his laughter.

Frank spoke in a candid fashion, pulling a piece of lint off his jacket as he spoke. "You're leaving for two years. What makes you think we will receive you after two years? The war will be over by then, so what use would you be? Your alliance with us has been bound by this war we are stuck in, and without it there will be no need for you."

"I sincerely hope the war is done in the two years I will be gone. I would welcome that end," said Roark with a warm smile.

"Then why render yourself useless before that time?" inquired Frank, once again leaning toward his desk.

"I don't expect you to understand, but know I will return in two years' time, in the spring of '44. There isn't much more I can say of the matter. I hope you will forgive me, but I must be on my way. Thank you for your time these last months. Good-bye." Roark stood as he finished speaking.

Edgar stood in reaction. "Now wait just a minute, Roark." Edgar stuttered as he spoke, trying to put a hand on Roark's shoulder. Frank began quickly trying to wheel around his desk after the men, but Roark had already opened the door into the ante-chamber.

As the door opened, Kori and Mary got to their feet, walking toward the hallway. Kori had an arm under Mary's, half pulling her along with him. She had a somber look about her as she kept her face aimed at the ground so no one could see her.

"Wait, Roark, wait. What just happened in there? Now, you stop there and talk to me," Edgar demanded.

Roark gestured for Kori and Mary to continue toward the front entrance. Roark turned to stop Edgar in the hall.

"Listen, Edgar, you deal in secrets and trust. You just blew both of those in there!" yelled Roark, getting in Edgar's face. "Do not think for one more second that I answer to you in any way. I'm the reason you're standing here right now and not in the gutter. So don't come chasing after me like I'm some kind of lost pup."

Edgar looked as if all the blood had drained from his face. He had never been spoken to that way in his life.

"I'm sorry, Roark." His words sounded insincere and callous.

"I'll see you in two years." The words felt like a knife in the chest to Edgar.

Roark calmly turned and walked to the front entrance and out the front door of the White House.

Once he was clear of the outer gate, he quickened his pace down the street and around the corner. Waiting was Kori and Mary. His anger was all over his face, and Mary could see it.

"What did you say to them? Will they listen to us in two years?" Mary sounded desperate. "This all can't be for nothing. Will they listen?"

"We are not failing. They will listen to me," he said grittily.

"This isn't you, Roark. You are not the man I'm looking at right now," said Kori sympathetically.

"Get your Atlas, and let's go. I just need a minute to calm down." Roark took a deep breath, realizing what he had said to Edgar. He wanted to go back, but he had promised himself he wouldn't, no matter what.

"Okay, then, let's finish this." Kori pulled out his Atlas as Mary raised her hand to Kori's arm. She looked defeated.

Roark turned back to Kori and put his hand on Kori's other arm. It was getting dark out, but Mary could see Roark was holding back tears. Roark raised a hand to his jacket pocket and pressed his hand where she knew the photograph was. *Who was she?* she wondered again as suddenly everything disappeared in a wave of blue.

Edgar returned to Frank's office to find Frank wheeling himself back behind his desk. He was laughing to himself as he noticed Edgar coming back in.

"What could possibly be funny?" asked Edgar, still infuriated from the lecture Roark had just given him.

Frank fell back into his chair lazily. "I told you that the night of December the 6th, Roark came to me about a possible saboteur."

"Yes, I remember," said Edgar, moving toward the armchair.

"And I never saw him since, until today," said Frank, still smiling.

Edgar stared at him, confused.

"The man who introduced himself as Roark back then was not the same man who came in here with you today." Frank folded his arms, waiting for Edgar to respond. Edgar was speechless. He started to speak, but nothing came out. He slumped in the chair, simply staring back at Frank.

"Then, then who was it that came to your office that night? And why was Roark on that ship then, with your orders? That doesn't make sense." Edgar's mind was reeling.

"That, Mr. Hoover, is what I would like to find out."

\\\\\\\\\\\\\\\\\\\\\\\\

"We'll hole up here for the night; get some rest," whispered the chief to the sergeant behind him. The sergeant waved an arm to the group following, letting them know where to go. It was a large abandoned factory complex that had multiple smaller buildings over many acres of overgrown forest. The place looked like no one had been there in years. A good spot, the chief thought to himself as they cleared the first building.

"We're going to sleep here?" asked Mary, looking at the dilapidated buildings.

"If you feel like getting killed there's a hotel in town," said the soldier that she had parachuted in with. He smiled as he passed her. The look she gave him made him walk faster.

After the first few smaller buildings, they came across a large warehouse that stood three stories. As soon as she saw it, she noticed the chief wave his hand toward it. Whispers came down the line that it was where they were to sleep for the night.

Once they got inside the entrance of the warehouse, the sergeant waved everyone in close.

"This warehouse will be our staging area. We are going to hole up here until we get the green light to infiltrate Berlin to our target. Until then, establish a perimeter and sit tight. You know what to do, so get to it."

Master Chief Warren could feel the end was in sight for the mission, and he knew that it would bring him one step closer to returning home to his family. He took off his helmet as he headed to the stairs of the warehouse. Two men caught up with him. "You two on over-watch," he said as they passed him.

"On it, sir." They spoke in unison as they had been trained.

Warren turned and sat a few steps up the stairs to steal the precious few moments he could get to himself. He took the picture out of his helmet and held it in his hands. He had tried to keep the picture in perfect condition for as long as he could, but the war was taking its toll on the delicate image. It was his only picture of the woman he loved. Her warm smile stared up at him in a timeless love. The memory of her always brought a smile to his face. He couldn't remember the last time he had smiled; it had been that long.

"Who is she?" Mary said, standing by Warren's side. She sat down on the steps with an effortless ease. The chance to take her mind off the fear of the moment was too irresistible to pass up.

"What, oh, it's the girl I'm going to marry someday. This is the only thing I have to remember her by. I keep forgetting how long it's been since I have seen her."

The moment surprised Mary. She had only known Warren to be a hardened soldier. Outwardly, he was tough and unyielding, but she was starting to see something else in him, something she couldn't place.

"What's her name?" asked Mary, trying to keep him in that moment a little longer. Seeing someone else at ease made her feel calm.

"Adele, her name is Adele," said Warren, smiling for the first time that she had ever seen.

"Building is clear, sir," said the two men, reappearing at the top of the stairs.

"Thank you," said Warren, standing, placing the picture back into his helmet. "Now, Mary, let's find you a room to yourself," he said, gesturing up the stairs.

On the second floor Warren found one of the only rooms with a door still left on the hinges and motioned for Mary to come down the hallway.

"This one will be yours. Then you can at least have some privacy from the rest of them." Warren pushed open the door for Mary to enter.

"Thank you."

Warren nodded and preceded to close the door to leave.

"Warren? May I call you Warren?"

Warren just nodded and motioned his hand for her to continue.

"Roark is a good man; believe what he says." Her words sounded hollow, and once they were said she wished she could have unspoken them.

His smile that once lit his face slowly drained back to what it was. She felt that the happy man she had seen on the stairs had gone back inside the armor.

"I'm sure you believe that, Mary." Despite his armor returning, his words remained gentle. He gave one last brief smile and closed the door to leave her be.

She saw a backpack that had been left for her with a mat and blanket. She quickly got them out and curled up in the corner. Through the walls she could hear men talking on both sides of her. She knew she was the one to be protected, but despite all their skill and strength she felt as vulnerable as ever.

\\\\\\\\\\\\\\\\\\\\\\\\\\\\\\\\\\\\\

"What do you see?" asked the SS soldier, tapping another soldier on the shoulder who had the binoculars.

He adjusted the binoculars to focus on the three-story warehouse. In the fading light he could see shadows moving around the outside and in the windows.

He put the binoculars down and looked at the other SS soldier. "Americans."

"How many?" asked the younger soldier.

"Maybe a dozen. Hard so say, maybe more. We're losing light."

"What do we do?"

"We go in just before dawn. Catch them off guard."

"Why not just wait until dark?"

"Cause being on watch all night is tiring, especially the last hour before dawn. They will assume they are safe, and their guard will be lowest. Let's go tell the others."

The two men moved back into the alleyway from where they came as the last light was visible in the evening sky.

```
```````````````````````````````````````
```

Warren snapped out of a sound sleep as if jolted awake by some unknown force. He was breathing heavily. The room was silent. The sounds of the men moving around him in their sleep reminded him of where he was. He shook the man next to him, who grunted as he woke up.

"Who's that?' whispered the man.

"It's me."

"Chief? What's going on?"

"Who's on watch? I don't see anyone else awake."

"Jones said he heard something a minute ago and was going to check it out." The man suddenly sat upright, realizing that what he was saying happened some time ago.

"How long ago was that?" said Warren, checking his watch in the moonlight.

"Oh geez, that was half an hour ago."

"Get everyone up quietly. I think we might have company."

Warren threw off his blanket and went for his rifle, but where he went to reach, it wasn't there.

"Did Jones take my rifle?"

"He must have, by mistake."

Warren gritted his teeth at the rookie mistake of grabbing the wrong gun in the night. He searched for Jones's rifle but realized it was going to take too long to find. He went back to his backpack and found his .45 pistol and grabbed his knife. He knew the Germans were nearby and needed to move quickly, so he left the rest of his supplies to retrieve later.

He made for the door, slowly staying crouched as low as he could. Out the windows he could see dawn coming as the sky slowly glowed with the morning light. He made it to the next room where he knew Mary was staying. The door was slightly open per his instructions.
```

Carefully, he crept through the room, trying to see where she was in the darkened room. In the far corner he spotted the backpack and blanket.

"Mary, get up, we have to go," he said as he reached for the bundled-up blanket. He yanked at the blanket to see that she was gone. The blanket was covering the pack and some old debris. *She been taken,* he thought, suddenly worried that she may have already been killed or worse. He threw the blanket down and started back for the door to find that Roark and Kori were already there.

"Where's Mary?" asked Roark, squinting into the room behind Warren.

"She has been taken. I believe a scout team of Germans found us and may be waiting outside to pick us off. "

"Mary," said Roark almost in a whisper. "We have to get her back."

Warren went to leave through the doorway, but Roark blocked his path.

"We have to find her," said Roark defiantly.

"My priority now is to keep us alive so we *can* find her. Now get out of my way, or I'm going through you. I don't care which," said Warren as Roark noticed the knife and pistol he was carrying.

Roark's body betrayed him as he stepped out of the way to let him pass.

Out in the hallway, nine men were waiting for orders. They huddled together so Warren could speak quietly.

"Anyone seen Jones? He left his post about thirty minutes ago."

Everyone shrugged and shook their heads no.

"All right. Here's the situation. I believe a German scout team is outside. I think their plan is to wait for us to come out and pick us off one at a time. Now, scout teams are only about five men strong, so we got them outnumbered. The bad news is we don't know where they are, so they have the drop on us. Now that brings me to another issue. Due to this invasion everyone is in radio blackout. The last thing we want is a firefight, which would bring the whole damn German army down on us and then we will be meeting our maker before we even get to Berlin. So this will have to be done as quiet as possible. Then we have to go find our package, as she appears to have been taken. "

"She probably ran off in the night. She didn't belong here," said one soldier.

"It doesn't matter now. First thing first. Two of you head up to the roof and see what you can see, then report back here double-quick."

The two men quietly raced up the stairs into the darkness, leaving the rest helplessly looking scared of what might happen next.

"Now the rest of you fan out around the perimeter. Avoid gunfire if possible, but if you have to, shoot. One bullet, one kill. Now get to it."

The men fanned out to move out the doors and windows of the building. Kori made his way to the second floor to keep looking for Mary.

Roark was going to join them when Warren stopped him.

"What are you doing?" asked Roark, surprised.

"I have been meaning to get a moment alone with you since we left." Warren's face was difficult to make out in the low light.

"Whatever it is, it can wait," said Roark, trying to leave again. Warren's grip tightened.

"I remember you," said Warren, quietly cutting through the dark.

"What do you mean?" asked Roark.

"From the harbor. I remember you. I found you lying on the ground at Pearl Harbor, and I helped you up. I remember telling you to fight and you turned your back on me..."

"You have me confused with someone else," said Roark, yanking his arm free. He stared at the shine from Warren's eyes, the eyes that were seeing through him.

"No, it was you. What is a coward doing out here? People say I shouldn't be here, but what they should be asking is why you are here." Warren moved closer to him in the dark.

Before Roark could answer, a single shot rang out from behind them.

"That was a .45 shot. We got one then. Four to go. We will finish this later, coward."

Warren left Roark frozen in the larger room, unable to answer with a reply. His guilt crippled him. A tension rose in him, wanting to explain his actions, but how could Warren understand? What use would it be?

Warren was crossing the back room toward the shot when suddenly he was tackled from behind. The force launched him forward, and he dropped his gun and knife as he was pushed into the wall. The dark figure began repeatedly punching at his sides. Each blow felt heavier than the one before it.

Warren was pressed into the wall face-first, struggling to free himself, but his attacker was larger and was holding him in place with all his might. Warren pressed his hands into the wall, bracing himself to push backward, his assailant continuing to deliver punishing blow after punishing blow. The master chief began pushing as hard as he could, feeling every muscle in his arms straining to move. He felt his assailant's punches stop as he heard the attacker reaching for something, and he knew this was his chance—now or never. He pushed back enough to get a foot on the wall and lunged backward with all his weight.

The force was enough to lift him and his attacker off the ground, and the two landed with a heavy thud. Sporadic shots rang out in multiple directions, and Warren knew they had engaged the scout team. The attacker head-butted the chief, knocking him off. For a moment, Warren lost sight of the attacker in the dark, but quickly the man came running straight at him with Warren's knife in hand. The man wildly slashed at the chief, frantic to land a fatal strike. In between a horizontal slash Warren lunged forward, punching the back of the attacker's arm, causing the knife to fly off into the dark. He could hear it hit a wall nearby and remembered where it went.

The attacker swung a haymaker at Warren, but he was able to dodge below it and go after the knife. He caught a glimmer of moonlight off the floor and reached for where it was. No sooner did he feel the knife in his grasp than the attacker grabbed Warren from behind and proceeded to squeeze him in a bear hug, lifting Warren off his feet. It was becoming more and more difficult to breathe as he felt his rib cage tighten. He tried to move his arm, as the attacker didn't seem to notice he had a knife in his hand, but he couldn't raise it more than a few inches. Warren heard a rib crack as he suddenly threw his head back as hard as he could, catching the attacker's forehead. The man didn't let go, but Warren felt himself drop to the floor. He landed and immediately jumped up and back, causing the attacker to trip and fall backward. The chief flipped the knife into reverse grip and rammed it into his attacker as they both fell backward. The impact of the ground only drove the knife deeper into the unknown soldier.

After they fell the room went silent again. Footsteps could be heard outside as Warren pulled the knife from the man and readied himself for the next bout. A man came around the corner and shined a flashlight on Warren.

"Chief?" asked the voice behind the flashlight.

In the light Warren looked down at himself. He was covered in blood and dirt. Looking back up at the man, he could feel the bruises already forming on his body. His chest hurt when he breathed.

"I think I cracked a rib," said Warren, moving to take the flashlight.

"We got four, sir. We couldn't find a fifth. We think maybe he ran off," said the soldier eagerly.

"The fifth is right here." He shined the light on the body on the floor. The large attacker was dressed in an SS officer's uniform. For a moment he expected to see that Roark was the one who attacked him, but he knew the man wouldn't have dared. He told the soldier to make another sweep for the girl, and the soldier went back the way he came, leaving him in the dark once again. It was then that he felt his hands start to shake.

A profound guilt had washed over him that he had killed again. In his career so far, he had shot down planes and even shot a few soldiers, but this was the first man he had killed with his bare hands and a knife. *If it wasn't him, it would have been you*, he kept saying to himself.

"Has Mary turned up yet? Did they take her?" asked Kori, racing around the corner.

Warren clenched a fist to keep his hands from shaking and took a deep breath, turning to face Kori. "I thought you were Roark. The men are out now, looking for her. You're welcome to join them, but I'd be careful. It's still dark enough you might get shot trying to find them."

"Is that supposed to be funny? This is not a joke. We need her," said Kori, stammering.

"The joke is you three. Thanks to the scout team we just alerted every Nazi in this area that we are here, so we should already be off down the road, but thanks to a teenage girl, we have to stay and look for her. She probably ran off, which means she is most likely dead in a ditch somewhere. So I'm leaving for Berlin. If you find her and you don't die in the next day you can meet up with us at the rendezvous."

Warren left Kori to retrieve his stuff from the second floor. Kori knew he couldn't leave Mary to her fate, but he also knew he and Roark were not about to use Atlas to relive this day to stop Mary from leaving. Too much uncertainty happened to guarantee they would survive again.

The team assembled in front of the factory as the beginnings of dawn were on the horizon. Roark and Kori stood in the opening of the door, watching them prepare to leave.

"You're not coming with us?" asked one of the soldiers.

"We must find Mary. She is more needed than the chief believes," said Kori solemnly.

"Without Mary how will you find the bunker? She is the only one with its location," said Roark confidently.

"By going door-to-door until it's done," said the chief, clutching his side that was now bandaged all the way around his chest.

The rest of the men didn't know whether to speak or just remain silent. The chief just turned and walked away, with the men quickening their steps to follow.

The chief had walked only a few steps when the sound of a cracked branch stopped everyone in their tracks. It came from directly in front of Warren, who raised a hand for all of them to get down and train their guns straight ahead.

Roark and Kori dropped as well, knowing they were in dangerous territory.

Warren took a step forward, trying to see into the woods ahead of him, squinting to see through the early light.

"Come out now with your hands raised," said Warren strongly. He knew whoever was out there, it was only one of them.

"It's me, it's me," said the small, shaky voice. Out from the woods came Mary, looking terrified at Warren pointing the gun a few feet from her face.

"MARY!" said Roark, leaping up and running over to her, giving her a hug. The gesture even surprised Kori. Roark let her go, noticing the looks from the men.

"Look at me, girl!" stated Warren, lowering his gun and approaching her.

She turned to face him, telling herself to be confident and strong.

"Where were you? Were you taken by the scouts?"

"What scouts? I was inside all night, I swear," said Mary quizzically.

"Don't lie to me, girl. When we were attacked. Where did you go? How did you get outside?" The chief's voice was growling.

"What are you talking about?" she asked, realizing how her responses were sounding.

"Why is she lying to me?" said Warren, standing to look at Roark.

"I'm not sure, master chief, but I'll find out." He had never had a reason to mistrust Mary, but for the first time he thought maybe she was catching on to him.

"Hard to believe it's been two years," said Hoover, still staring at the wall in front of them.

The hallway was narrow and dimly lit. The walls were solid steel. The silence bothered Roark. *The worst sound in the world is silence,* he thought as he heard what Hoover had said drift back into the stillness of the hall. Next to them was a heavy metal door that looked more like a vault door than anything else. Beyond it lay a hidden room that no one was allowed to enter unless explicitly invited. It was an invitation extended to Roark only.

Roark sat rigidly in his chair, waiting for the knock allowing him to enter. "I'm sorry for what I said to you the last time we spoke. It was not the good-bye I had intended," said Roark. Neither of them reacted when he spoke, and Roark knew the sentiment meant little after a long absence.

"I haven't forgotten. Forgive me if I do not thank you," said Hoover, crossing a leg. The years had made Edgar harder. His paranoia had taken a new hold over him, and he trusted so very few people since they last had met. A fierce ambition to always be one step ahead of everyone was showing through.

"It's me who should be thanking you for getting me in here. I really do...."

"This is the last thing I do for you, Roark," said Edgar, cutting him off mid-sentence.

The warm smile Roark had tried to put on had gone from his face. For a moment he had a look of fear in his eyes at Edgar's words. He knew he had finally worn out his welcome with the man who had helped him so much, and what had he repaid Edgar with? What was his gift for all that loyalty? *Nothing but a sense of betrayal,* he thought, looking at the man. A creeping uncertainty had come back over him. He reached his hand into his jacket just to feel the edge of the photograph there. He felt the edge on his fingers and felt a little better. The picture had become his crutch.

"What will you do from here then?" asked Roark coldly. He immediately regretted his tone, but the way it came out couldn't be stopped.

Edgar snapped his neck to look Roark in the eye. "I know all about you, you know. You think you're smarter than everyone else here, but you're not. When you left, a formal inquiry was launched against you. We found enough to put you away for a hundred lifetimes, but the one thing keeping anyone from doing anything was that you were nowhere to be found." The panic in Edgar's words poured out of him. "After a year, the president decided to stop trying to find you and just wait for you to come in. After the meeting, the plan is to arrest you, Roark. You're wanted for treason. They will bury you by tomorrow. Do you understand what that means? The more you say to me, the more it looks like I'm your accomplice. I spent months in and out of court hearings trying to prove that you coerced me into everything. Every second I sit here undermines that." Edgar caught himself and paused, realizing what he was saying.

Roark was speechless. His mind raced through the implications of what could happen. He wanted to leave, but the hall was too small to use Atlas. He knew he would have to go through the meeting and get out of the building. *If they arrest me, they will take Atlas and I will be stuck here,* he thought to himself.

"Why are you telling me this? Why not just let them arrest me?" was all Roark could say. All hope had gone from his voice.

"Because regardless of how I feel about you, I wouldn't be here if it wasn't for you. You're the reason I've had this career. So I owed you at least for that. But after this, I can't go any further." Edgar's eyes started to water, but no tears came.

"That's why I thank you," said Roark, trying to smile again, but a heaviness kept it from being a true emotion. He became very aware of the tightrope he was on.

A knock came at the door, and it slowly opened. Inside, a man gestured for them to enter a small room with an oval table at the center.

Around the table sat a dozen politicians from around Washington. Roark didn't recognize anyone in the room except for President Roosevelt, who was sitting at the end.

"Good morning, Roark, glad you could join us," said Frank, staring at the folder in front of him. The avoidance of eye contact immediately registered with what Edgar had said in the hall. "Thank you, Edgar. You may wait in the hall until the meeting is over. That shouldn't be long at all. Then you can escort Roark out of the building." Hoover nodded and gave one last look at Roark, who nodded back at him. A look of desperation was on Edgar's face.

Almost as soon as Roark turned back to the group, he heard the door lock behind him. A sense of dread filled the room as he was sure every man seated knew of his fate and were simply waiting patiently for it. He felt like a lamb being led to the slaughter.

"Now, Roark, I have already briefed the group about our saboteur. What we need from you is information regarding his whereabouts, intentions, and what we can do about it?" said Frank, leaning back in his chair and watching Roark from across the room.

Roark wanted to sit but noticed there was no chair for him. The meeting was as much a power play for Frank as it was a search for advice. Frank wanted Roark to not feel in control, and he knew it. *We are the movers of the world,* came across his mind as he braced himself.

Roark took a deep breath and tried to remain calm.

"His name is Andrew," said Roark, only half confident.

"My file doesn't show a last name," said one of the men to his right.

"That's because I don't know what it is," said Roark quickly.

"And that's supposed to encourage my confidence in you, is it?" asked the man, annoyed.

"Last names are not important. What is important is that this man stowed away on the *Hornet* and sabotaged it before it could stop the attack on Pearl Harbor. Afterward, he sought refuge in the one place he was sure to be well guarded and praised for his work. Germany." Roark forced himself to sound confident.

"Why not Japan? Surely they would have granted him asylum," said another man to his right.

"As I believe Japan had no knowledge of his actions, I doubt they would even know who he is, let alone grant him asylum."

"Ah," said the man, flipping through his pages again.

"It was in my search for Andrew that I came upon a mutually beneficial piece of information. Not only are the Nazis guarding Andrew, but Adolf Hitler himself is keeping him in an underground bunker beneath Berlin. An opportunity has presented itself to capture Hitler and at the same time catch our saboteur." Roark could fee all the eyes in the room burning him. They had wanted every reason to doubt him, but the war had dragged on for too many years to neglect a chance like this.

"Where is the bunker, Roark?" asked Frank, smiling. "Then you can go."

Roark knew that the location would be the one thing keeping him out of handcuffs.

"There would be strings attached," said Roark uneasily.

"With you there always is." Frank spoke carefully. He knew Roark might try to run.

"I wish to be a part of the team that goes in Berlin," said Roark, the words almost getting stuck in his throat.

"Absolutely not," said Frank flatly, returning to his pages before him.

"You get me into Berlin, and I'll give you Hitler. It's that simple." Roark's words grew more desperate. He could feel his hand shaking, but he tried to hide it.

Frank sat back, staring at Roark. *I can't let him go,* he thought as he studied the man he had waited two years to apprehend. *If he dies out there, all of it would be for nothing.*

"Here is what I will do, Roark. You may go on your hunt as you like. Your intelligence has proven useful up until this point, so I have no reason to doubt it now and I will not waste it.

However, I must inform you that you are wanted for treason against the United States of America. There are allegations against you from numerous officials, and the FBI is investigating your potential involvement of leaking information regarding the Manhattan Project. Like I said, you may go on your hunt, but should you fail, should Hitler not be there and this turn out to be some kind of stunt, the team that will be sent to escort you will have orders to arrest you immediately. Then you will be brought back here for trial, for which you will face the death penalty. Is that perfectly understood, Mr. Roark?" The words made Roark sweat. He had known this day would come, but hearing the words did not have the effect he thought they would. He expected to feel guilt or shock, but what he felt was a small sense of relief. For so many years he had lived with all the mistakes he had made that he never had to answer for. He had waited ages for someone to sentence him for his actions, but no one ever came.

"I understand," said Roark meekly.

"Good. Now, general, what strategy would you employ to get a team into Berlin?"

The general stood and pulled a map of Europe down on the wall. On it were numerous symbols for troops and tanks and planes strewn all over the continent. It was a massive troop deployment meant to overwhelm the enemy. The men spoke in the room as if Roark were no longer there. It was as if he were a shadow surrounded by light, slowly fading away into the light. He looked at the map again and remembered what Kori had said, and he knew it was not going to work.

"That won't work. That encirclement won't work," said Roark loud enough to silence the room.

"And what do you know of military strategy?" asked the general condescendingly.

"In order to get near this bunker it will take more than force," said Roark, biding his time.

"What would you propose then?" asked the man closest to him curiously.

"Misdirection." Roark felt himself coming back into the room. He knew his days were numbered thinking about how all this might turn out, but how would that be different than any other day? "What this will require is the greatest military distraction in human history."

"And when would this event take place?"

"In June of this year, 1944, on the sixth, the sixth of June."

\\\\\\\\\\\\\\\\\\\\\\\\\\\\\\

They had reached a building just inside the city limits. The city seemed almost empty. Everywhere, people stayed in their homes. A citywide lockdown was in effect.

"Where to now?" Warren asked, peering back over his shoulder to Mary, who was right behind him. She had been instructed to stay within three feet of him ever since she had disappeared a few night earlier. He demanded she stay within sight each night as she could no longer be trusted.

"Two more blocks, then it's the building on the right. It's in there, the bunker," she said nervously. She gripped her gun so tightly her hand was going numb. She was terrified to drop it, but she had held it for so long it felt like a part of her.

"Let's go," said Warren, launching forward.

They quickly moved in single file down the alleyway. They only had a limited window for an incursion. A large number of allied troops were bearing down on the city from the northwest, and every soldier in the city was being drawn away from his post. Only a minimal number of soldiers stayed behind.

They reached the building Mary had pointed out and found it barely guarded. Two men silently sneaked up behind two guards, grabbed them by the neck, and yanked them down the alley. They all moved in through the door to find empty hallways.

This is too easy, Warren thought as they cleared the one-story building. "Downstairs," he said as they all moved down to the basement. Roark and Kori each moved in precision with the other men as they all came to a stop at the bulkhead to something in the floor.

Mary smiled quickly to herself at the achievement.

"Looks like you proved your worth."

Warren gestured to the men to open the door while two others aimed for whatever may be on the other side.

The men swung open the door to find no one was standing on the other side. The team moved down into the tight hallway of the bunker. Warren gave a quick look of disapproval to Mary as he continued down the hallway, going from room to room.

Each room, a soldier kicked in the door only to find it had recently been raided. Furniture and shelves had all been knocked over and stripped.

A muffled voice rang out from the end of the hall, and everyone raced to the last room. Before the men could get in place to cover him Warren kicked in the last door.

The room was emptied out like the others except for a man on his knees, tied up in the corner. Blood trickled down his face, and a gag muffled the man's screams.

"Son of a bitch. Roark, get in here," said Warren, lowering his gun.

Roark came in, looking from Warren to the man tied on the floor.

"Is that your man?"

"No, that's not him," said Roark sullenly.

Warren turned and grabbed Roark by the throat and shoved him into the wall as hard as he could. "You said Hitler himself would be here, along with the man responsible for the attack on Pearl Harbor. Where are they?" said Warren, screaming into Roark face.

"I don't know, they should have been here," said Roark, struggling to speak. He could feel Warren's grip getting tighter.

Mary ran over to the man tied up and pulled off his gag. The man started frantically speaking in German. He spoke so fast he couldn't breathe. After every few words he coughed, trying to regain his breath.

"Last chance—where are they?" asked Warren, turning red as the fury raged in his eyes.

"This isn't helping," stated Kori, who was standing in the corner not offering any help to Roark. Mary stared furiously at Kori for the inaction. Kori just blankly stared back at her. *He is beyond helping,* she thought as she continued to remove the restraints from the man on the floor.

"I don't know," Roark gritted through his teeth. Each time he repeated the words in his mind it felt like a heavier defeat. It had been a long time since he had been truly surprised.

"It doesn't matter," Mary said, quickly interrupting. "Does anyone know what this man is saying?"

Warren let go of Roark's throat and turned away, letting him drop to the floor, choking.

"Corporal Bryan, translate," said Warren sharply as he started pacing back and forth, trying to regain his calm.

The man on the floor continued rambling, moving his hands as he spoke. The corporal was struggling to keep up with what was being said.

"Well?" said Warren irritably.

"He says we only missed them by half an hour," the corporal said between the rambles. "Suddenly, they all packed up and left, taking only what they could carry. No one even noticed I was still there," he said translating for the man.

"That's all. Just that they left thirty minutes ago?"

"Now he's going on about what he was building for them, an engine of some kind. I'm not sure what he is talking about now." The corporal shrugged and turned to Warren, who was just staring at the man. He looked as if he could kill the man, but what the chief really felt was uncertainty.

"What's his name?" asked Mary suddenly. Her expression of curiosity seemed out of place amongst the other men. She appeared much more relaxed than all the others. Roark couldn't help but notice the shift in her behavior. "Ask him his name," Mary repeated boldly to the corporal.

Bryan asked the man to say his name in German, and the man seemed to have finally regained his voice enough to drag himself to his feet.

He attempted to speak in English, enveloped in a heavy accent, but it was enough that the men could make it out. "My name is Werner, Werner Von Braun."

"Am I supposed to know who that is?" asked Warren angrily.

"He is a scientist. Hitler was using him to build next-generation missiles. They were working to counter the Manhattan Project. He was their top scientist," said Mary calmly, helping the man sit back down.

"Let's get him up and treated. He is coming with us. We're leaving." Warren turned to head back out of the bunker. Roark pulled himself up and went after him.

"We can't leave," said Roark, trying to keep up with the chief.

"We can. We are," said Warren without even looking at him.

The men were following him back out. The corporal was helping Mary with Werner, who was limping to keep up. Kori casually walked at the rear as if he were strolling lazily on a summer day. He was growing impatient with Roark, as was everyone.

"He might know which way Hitler went. He might know where Andrew is," said Roark, panicking.

Warren stopped when they reached the entrance to the bunker and looked him in the eye. "Do you even care about how many men we lost on the beaches today? Thousands of men put their lives on the line because of you. All this because you said Hitler would be in this bunker, and he isn't. You said the man behind the sabotage of the *Hornet* would be here; he isn't. This mission is over. At least we got a valuable hostage as a consolation prize. Sergeant Willem."

"Yes, sir," said Willem, rushing to meet the chief.

"Take this man under arrest by order of the president. He is charged with treason and once back stateside, he will answer for his crimes." The sergeant pulled out some ties from his jacket and placed them around Roark's wrists. Roark tried to reach for his Atlas, but the sergeant kept his hands in front of him.

Once outside they made their way back out of the square. They were crossing an enclosed terrace when Kori finally stepped in front of the sergeant, stopping him in his tracks. "That's far enough," he said, refusing the sergeant's attempts to continue walking. Warren heard the command and stopped to see what was going on. "What the hell do you think you're doing, civilian? You have no authority here."

"You're not taking Roark anywhere." Kori appeared to have finally snapped out of the daze he had been in since they air-dropped in days earlier. He looked like himself again.

"He is a prisoner, and we are still in enemy territory. We cannot stay here."

"And you're welcome to leave, but Roark is not going with you," said Kori calmly.

Mary was at the back helping Werner when she heard the commotion ahead of her. Werner felt heavy with his arm around Mary, using her as a crutch. Willem had the other arm.

"No, listen here. I do not care whatsoever for your life as I do not believe you are worthy enough for a soldier's life, but Roark is a traitor and must answer for what he has done. Allowing him a quick death on a battlefield is not justice, so he is coming with me," Warren said as he approached Kori with his hands in fists.

"I'm sorry, chief." Kori pulled out a knife and swung it fiercely to the side, slicing Roark's ties. His hands now free, Roark sidestepped away from the Sergeant and turned to punch him as hard as he could. The sergeant barely knew what was happening as he caught the blow right below the eye.

Warren lunged forward as Kori swiped the knife to punch Kori in the gut with all his force. The blow wasn't so much meant to do much damage as it was to knock him out of the way.

Kori reeled from the hit and stumbled backward, but he managed to stay between the group and Roark.

"I'm not letting you take my prisoner."

An air raid siren went off on a speaker overhead. They all knew a swarm of German troops was sweeping the city. It was unclear if the siren was for them.

"Why would you protect a traitor?" asked Warren desperately.

"I have every reason to hate him, same as you, but he has something I need, and I can't let him go with you.

"He will still be wanted for treason. He is an enemy of the United States. You will be hunted too."

"I know that. I always have," said Kori with tears forming in his eyes. He hated himself for defending Roark. It was a betrayal of his mind.

"You're not a coward anymore, Roark. You're just a fool. Time to go, men. Leave these traitors here," Warren said to the men, who continued along the route out of the courtyard. Mary let go of Werner and walked over to Roark, who looked pathetic at being overtaken so easily. Kori looked down at Roark.

"Don't expect me to save you again," said Kori, walking past Roark.

The men had gone out of sight and only the three of them remained.

"What do we do now?" asked Mary, looking around and hoping to not see German forces coming for them.

For the second time in one day Roark didn't know what to do. "I don't know where to go from here."

\\\\\\\\\\\\\\\\\\\\\\\\\\\\\\\

The heavy door had swung open again as Roark exited the meeting room. All the men at the table watched him leave with curious eyes.

Edgar was waiting in the hall, already standing. An anxious tension was about him as he rushed forward to see

Roark. Once the heavy door was closed again, Edgar knew he had a few moments before a guard would come.

"Roark, I meant to tell you about the investigation that was launched against you. I'm sorry I had to in order to clear my name. If I was investigating you, then all suspicion of us working together would be dropped."

Roark had always known Edgar to be a strong man, but for the first time he saw guilt in his eyes. He had every reason to mistrust Roark, *but then why this rotten feeling,* he thought.

"I know," was all Roark said as he put up a hand to stop Edgar. "You did what you had to. I get it. It's time to go."

"Are they arresting you then?" Edgar asked as if there would be a different answer than what he was thinking.

"Not yet. Frank is allowing me one last request. I have a favor to ask of you, Edgar. Consider it a parting request. If any part of you wishes to still help me, then take this."

Roark pulled something from inside his jacket. It looked old to Edgar. It was an envelope with the paper edges all curled and torn. It looked as if it had been inside his jacket for some time.

"What is this?" asked Edgar, carefully taking the item.

"It's a letter. A very old one."

"What do you want me to do with it?"

"I need you to keep it in a safe place for me. The contents of this letter are... of a level of importance beyond you or even me. I'm heading into Germany to assist with a military strike, and if it fails then that letter will fall into the wrong hands and that is unacceptable." Roark spoke very carefully and was looking around to make sure no one was listening.

"What's in here?" Edgar asked as he went to open the envelope. Roark saw what he was doing and caught his hand before he could touch the lock.

"I wouldn't if I were you. What's in those pages, many men have died to protect. Its contents describe a journal written by an old monk from centuries ago. It's information you do not want to get out. I suggest you lock this away somewhere until I come back for it." Roark's words sounded of fear.

"What if you don't come back?" asked Edgar, intrigued.

"Get it to Kori. However you can, get it to him and no one else. Understand?"

"I do, yes." Edgar seemed dazed, staring at the envelope.

"I expect at some point you may be tempted to read it, but I warn you. Some secrets should stay buried."

Edgar opened his carry bag and placed the envelope inside carefully, then calmly snapped it closed. "May I ask one question about the letter, the monk?"

"Only if you take whatever I say to your grave." Roark smiled, knowing what was coming.

"What was his name?"

"I believe he went by the name of Crantor. It's who he apprenticed for that I believe most would be more familiar with." Roark smiled again at Edgar and began to walk past him toward the elevator.

The name meant nothing to Edgar. He thought about it, but nothing came to mind. He spun to catch up to Roark who was already at the elevator. "Who did he apprentice for?"

"I'm sorry, Edgar, but you had your one question."

\\\\\\\\\\\\\\\\\\\\\\\\\

"All right—everybody off your asses and onto the plane. Time to give one back to Mr. Adolf Hitler." Master Chief Warren approached his team in the hangar as they all scrambled to get their gear together. Roark and Kori were already dressed and waiting when Warren came over. Mary quickly shot up from where she was seated nervously. She was the only one who looked terrified. "Today is D-Day, gentlemen." He stopped in front of Mary, realizing she was there. "And Lady." She thought she saw him smile, but he was off again before it could register.

Roark watched Mary. His eyes were filled with concern. He wished there was some way they didn't have to bring Mary, but despite where they were going he knew she would be safer with him. He needed her, and she would never understand why. Kori saw Roark staring at Mary.

"Why put her through this?" asked Kori sadly.

"It was always her."

"It's only because of you she is even here. If she gets killed, it's on you," said Kori.

"It's all on me. This whole thing, and she is the only thing I have to keep me sane," responded Roark.

"Who is she to you?" asked Kori, his voice growing serious.

"She is everything." Roark walked away as the team got up to head for the plane.

Kori didn't know what to say. He watched Roark walk toward the plane, and he saw him help Mary with her gear and head off with them. He couldn't place what he felt, but he knew Mary was a distraction that would have to be dealt with eventually. She was clouding Roark's judgment, and he couldn't see why.

As they walked to the plane Warren took off his helmet and pulled out the picture of his love, Adele, and looked at it as he walked. *What I wouldn't give to be with her now,* he thought as he kissed the picture and placed it back in his helmet.

Roark, farther back in the crowd, felt a dull chest pain come over him, and he reached his chest to ease the pain. He felt the edges of the photograph through the fabric and took out his picture of Adele and held it in his hands. He remembered her face from the hospital that day when he couldn't bring himself to tell her about James. He was a coward then, but now he wouldn't be.

Chapter Nine:

The Looking Glass

So much is happening so fast, she thought, unable to sleep. Tomorrow, they were about to enter Berlin. *What is happening?* She kept screaming in her head. *How did I get here?* She opened her eyes to the dark room of the abandoned warehouse the team had inhabited for the night. How she longed to see the familiar walls of the asylum. She hated herself for feeling any sort of longing for that place, but what she wouldn't give to be back there. She looked to the door, hoping that somehow, some way, Ian would come through it with breakfast, and that he would secretly bring her things to make her smile. She remembered the bacon he used to sneak her. An almost-smile crept onto her face. The warmth of the thoughts did nothing to ease her mind. She wanted to run, she wanted to scream, but the only one to hear her cries was her own guilt.

"Can't sleep?" said a calm voice, cutting through the dark.

Mary sat up in the corner she was tucked in. The darkness wrapped around her. She tried to look around the room but couldn't see anything except the black of the night.

"Who's there?" Her words echoed in the small room she had to herself.

"I can't remember the last time I slept through the night. I see their faces, looking at me. I miss them," said the voice.

"Tell me who you are, or I'll wake up everyone in this building." Her voice was starting to sound scared.

"Please don't, Mary. I'm not here to do you any harm; I just want to talk," replied the voice.

She heard the movements of someone standing up and footsteps coming toward her. She heard a click, and the room flooded with light. Mary strained her eyes to adjust to the blinding light, but once she could focus she saw the person who had entered her room. It was a face she had hoped not to see. It was the face of her enemy.

"I believe you already know my name, but let me introduce myself. My name is Andrew, and I would be honored to speak with you."

Andrew reached out his hand and put it on her arm as he pulled his chair closer and sat back down facing her. She didn't know whether to scream or stay silent. Part of her wished to get away, to run, to escape and alert Roark or Kori or anyone that Andrew was here. Her body betrayed her by keeping silent. *Why has he come all this way, why has he come here to see me, of all people? How did he know who I was?* Questions kept running through her mind as she stared at him. He looked so calm sitting opposite her. He had a sadness to his face as if he wished to be somewhere far away from there.

"I'll take your silence to mean you won't alert anyone," he said solemnly as relaxed in his chair.

"Why are you here?" was all she could force to come out. She felt her jaw stiffen as if every word spoken to this man was an act against Roark.

"To ask a question. I was curious when I learned that you were traveling with the man they call Roark and his associate Kori. It intrigued me." Andrew attempted a smile, but nothing surfaced.

"What question?" She sat uncomfortably on the floor, but couldn't bring herself to move a muscle.

"Well, two questions I think would be more accurate. One is do you know who you're traveling companions actually are? Second would be to ask why you are with them."

Mary froze for a moment, unsure of how to respond or what to say. "I needed to get away. I didn't want to be in that place anymore."

"Right, the asylum for orphans. Lonely place, but you had the option to walk out the door whenever you wished, didn't you?" Andrew spoke as if he already knew how she would answer each question.

"There was nothing for me out there."

"Of course there was," replied Andrew, cutting her off. "The world is what you make it. You had what very few people ever get in this life, a second chance. You could have walked out that door and done anything you wished, but you chose to stay inside, to hide. You allowed yourself to be trapped in a reality which you created. This made you vulnerable, and then came Roark, right?"

"I think he is a good man. I didn't trust him at first, but he is right. I believe him." She found herself irritated that he was speaking negatively of Roark. She felt loyalty toward him.

"You believe the man who kidnapped you. He took your hand and before you could pull away you were then truly trapped in not just your own creation, but his as well. You're a stupid little girl," said Andrew.

"What do you want from me?" she said pleadingly.

"I want you to wake up. In the asylum you had a chance to walk away from it all. Right now, you have the same choice, but before you make it you need to know who you are so loyal to. You don't have any idea who Roark actually is, or Kori."

A fear was growing in her. She suddenly felt as if she was back to that first conversation with Roark and Kori. She felt something was just as wrong now as it was then.

"How do I know you're not the one who is lying?" asked Mary.

"You don't. I want you to see both sides of the coin, and then you make up your own mind like you should have been doing all along. Roark is a very dangerous man, pretending to be someone he is not. He may act like all he is doing is stopping me, but all he is really doing is protecting his agenda," said Andrew.

"What are you talking about? You're the one who started a war." Mary flung the blanket off of her, starting to stand up, but Andrew gestured for her to stop.

"I'm not here to fight you," said Andrew. Mary stopped herself and re-adjusted on the floor. She realized she had raised her voice, but everything outside remained silent. "You're right, I did. I started a war to prevent one later, and every day I beg for forgiveness for what I have done." The sadness had returned to his voice. "I had a wife, and we were happy. We had a baby girl. I was on my way home when it started. It was a terrorist attack, and my family was killed in our home. Can you imagine what that feels like, knowing someone walked into your home when you weren't there and murdered the two people that meant the most to you?" Andrew had tears beginning to form in his eyes. "I gave up. I shut down. I didn't want to keep going. Then two men came calling one day, and everything changed."

"I'm sorry you lost your wife and daughter, but what you're doing about it is wrong." Mary pushed back, not wanting to be taken advantage of again. "What you're doing is trying to rewrite history in your favor, yes, but at the expense of everyone else. Don't you see that?" Mary struggled to find the right words she meant to say, but the harder she thought the fewer showed themselves.

"Mary you need to open your eyes to what is happening. So much has been kept from you. There are larger things at work than just my personal interests. I am freeing us all from the hold the likes of Roark have over not just you, but everyone else. Yes, I want to save my family, but in doing so I hope to start us over. I want to give people their freedom back to create their own futures. People should be able to live their lives the way they wish, free from being blindly coerced into a predetermined fate. People are not animals to the slaughter, where their futures end according to a schedule. We are individuals who need to create and grow on our own," replied Andrew.

Andrew spoke so effortlessly Mary had a hard time hanging onto her anger. She wanted so badly to find fault in his words, but there was none to find. Her fingers had gripped the blanket so tightly she could feel sweat starting to collect in her hand. A thought of Roark returned, but instead of the surety that she once felt with Roark's ideology she now felt a mark of confusion.

"How is what Roark is doing any different than what I am doing?" asked Andrew. "Have you ever asked him why he is trying to stop me? What cannot be changed that he has to stop me from changing it? Ask him that next time you see him."

Mary was searching for something to say, but no more words came from her mouth. Andrew stood up and walked over to her, holding out his hand. "I would like to show you something that might help you understand," said Andrew.

"Why would I go anywhere with you?" she asked shakily.

"I'm going to give you something that Roark didn't, that Roark never intended for you to have as long as you're with him, and that is a choice. You don't have to come with me; you can stay right here and I'll walk away. However, if you come with me, I'll show why I'm doing what I'm doing and something Roark is so desperate to defend. Some part of you must want to know. Ever wondered who is on the photograph in Roark's jacket pocket?" Andrew continued holding out his hand with a warm smile.

"If I go with you, will you tell me something?"

Andrew nodded slightly, smiling a little wider.

"How many are there, like Roark?"

"Not as many as I had thought. They make it a point to stay as far away from one another as possible. They have been doing this for a long, long time."

"Roark will come looking for me," said Mary quickly, worried about his reaction to all this.

"I'll have you back before dawn." Andrew nodded to his hand for her to take it. She slowly raised her hand and placed it on his. He carefully pulled her up from the floor as he took a step back to bring into the middle of the room. She could hear the trembling in her breathing. "You may want to put on some warmer clothes. Where we are going you will need them."

Mary walked over to her backpack and pulled out a sweater. Andrew waited until she was ready.

"Now one last thing. I need you to prepare yourself." She could see the sadness in him growing as if he had just witnessed a terrible thing and was fighting to hold back his emotion. Where we are going is extremely dangerous, and if you do not do as I say I cannot guarantee your safety."

Mary nodded nervously.

"As soon as we get there, we need to move. Now close your eyes and don't open them until I say." Andrew pulled his Atlas out of his pocket. She was immediately shocked to see how different it was from Roark's. Roark had a worn antique look to his pocket watch, but Andrew's was a vibrant shiny gold, as if it were made that morning. "Close your eyes," he repeated.

The shine went away as she closed her eyes. She felt Andrew hold on to her tightly, and suddenly she felt a rushing sound and she knew they were gone from the room.

"Open your eyes." Andrew had let go of her, and she was anxious to open her eyes even as part of her wished to go back to the room. "Open them," Andrew said louder.

She opened her eyes, and the first things she saw made her legs weak. She tried to look away but anywhere she looked the same scene appeared. She looked down at her feet to realize what she was standing in. Her mind was frozen in horror at the sight. She opened her mouth to speak, but her voice was soundless. A heavy sadness came over her as she struggled to comprehend what was around her. She looked to Andrew, who only looked at her. His eyes never left her eyes.

"I'm sorry I had to do this to you, but it was the only way to get you to understand." Andrews's eyes were red, but he didn't move. He had seen this sight many times now and no longer could bring himself to look. Where they stood was in Fenway Park on the day Andrew's family had been killed.

,,,,,,,,,,,,,,,,,,,,,,,,,,,,

"Why wasn't Andrew there? You said that he knew it was the only place he could be." President Roosevelt was leaning forward in his wheelchair, reprimanding Hoover while pointing at William Leahy.

Edgar sat uncomfortably, trying to avoid eye contact with the president. The general sat rigidly in his chair, staring coldly at Edgar.

"His intelligence has never been incorrect." Edgar tried to put confidence behind each word, but none emerged.

"Until now, you mean," cried Frank.

"I don't believe he would have played us is what I am saying. He is only human too." Edgar felt compelled to defend Roark at least that much.

"Did he say anything to you after he left the council, before June the 6th?" asked Frank skeptically,

"Only that he understood why he was being arrested. Then he left without a word," said Edgar blankly. Leahy continued to stare at Edgar, and Edgar could feel his eyes pulling all the truth from him.

"You're sure he said nothing to you ever, anything that would contradict what he told the council?"

"Nothing."

"And now he has escaped!" Frank raised his hands in surrender. "We use him to help engineer a full-scale invasion and lost countless lives, all in the name of a false hope."

"Despite that, Mr. President, D-Day was a success. We are making immense strides toward Berlin. We have them on the ropes. The fact that your top-secret mission has failed has gone largely unnoticed." William spoke candidly. He barely moved as he spoke, casually crossing his hands on his lap. It was a cool calmness that Frank admired about him. "Who is this Roark anyway—a spy?"

"Of sorts," said Edgar, cutting in.

"For the last several years he had been feeding us intel on numerous activities of both the Japanese and German forces. Up until now he had never been wrong. He stated that he knew the location of Adolf Hitler himself, and a team was put together for the task, but the target was not there and now Roark has evaded arrest." Frank spoke carelessly, seemingly disinterested in the material.

"He is charged with treason, is he not?" asked Leahy.

"I mean to put him on public trial for what he has done to this country. I had Mr. Hoover compile all we have about him."

"As much as America loves a glorified trial, most Americans don't even know who you are talking about. He doesn't exist. Rather than spend any more tax dollars on this manhunt, my suggestion is to bury it."

Edgar turned to open his mouth in protest, but the president waved a hand to silence him.

"Bury it?" asked Frank, concerned. "But what if he comes back?"

"Let him. He is one man. If he thinks we have stopped chasing him, he may come back on his own. Arrest him then." Leahy shrugged, looking between Edgar and Frank.

"Mr. Hoover?" said the president, shifting his attention to Edgar.

"Yes, Mr. President?"

"I hereby order all information pertaining to Roark be locked up. I wish to have the name Roark stricken from all public record. From today going forward the man we know as Roark does not, and will never, exist."

"I will make sure nothing ever gets out. The information will stay safe with me, Mr. President."

The president turned back to Leahy, and they started on again about another issue, and as they spoke Edgar felt a small smile come over his face. *They will go nicely with my other files...*

"We can't stay here. Your promises don't mean anything anymore, Roark. Why put any more faith into you?" Kori said, looking around them at the buildings as they moved across the courtyard. "I see no reason to continue this charade you conned me into. I'll see you in another ten years, maybe."

Kori switched directions and walked away from Roark and Mary down another alleyway. They were too close in to use Atlas; he needed to get out into an open street.

Roark immediately went after Kori. "This can still be salvaged."

The words stopped Kori, but he stayed looking down the alley, wanting to take another step.

"We just enacted an entire war on your promises, Roark. All this was done to find one man, and we couldn't even do that." Roark could hear the tears in his words. Kori turned to look at the man who was once his friend. He pitied the man he once respected. All he wanted was to escape this nightmare that had come back to him after all these years. "How many people have died because of you, Roark? How many more must you sacrifice to get what you want?"

Mary looked on at them from the courtyard. She was hearing Andrew's words through Kori. *Maybe he isn't beyond saving,* she thought, watching him.

"If we don't finish this, then all those people who died would have died for nothing. If we can stop the bleeding and catch Andrew, then all of it would never have happened. We need to win!" said Roark desperately.

"Look at yourself. Are you so blinded by winning that you cannot see what you are? I'm leaving, Roark, before you can do any more damage to my life." Kori turned back around to walk away.

"I spent ten years trying to apologize for that day, a day that I couldn't change no matter how much I tried, and you still can't forgive me," said Roark.

"Forgive you? You just left. Any apologizing you did, you only did for yourself, not me. So don't stand there trying to act noble," said Kori, pointing in Roark's face

Mary knew she had to do something, but a fear of what might happen came over her. She willed herself to step forward. She thought as hard as she could about where Andrew might be going. Years' worth of history scrolled through her mind until something popped out. "I think I might know where he is going."

As soon as she spoke Kori darted his glance over to hers. All she saw in his face was pure disgust. "Speaking of useless," Kori declared flatly.

The insult silenced Roark. The comment surprised him to the point he was speechless. He had known that Kori was growing increasingly annoyed with Mary, as she was a constant reminder of a past long ago. Roark knew he was growing bitter of her, but he had not let it be an issue until now. "You watch your mouth with her. I will take back what I promised if you say anything like that again."

"You think I care anymore what you say, Roark? She is something to you, Roark, and I do not care what that thing is," said Kori softly so only he could hear. "What is it Mary?" Kori suddenly said in a lighter voice.

Roark hated Kori in that moment, but he couldn't let it show.

"There's something I have to tell you," said Mary, watching Kori but directing her words to Roark.

Kori looked as if he was holding back a rage that had been building up this whole time, but he remained silent for a reason she couldn't place.

"Go ahead." Roark spoke softly, giving Kori one last stare as a warning.

"I spoke with Andrew."

The statement didn't immediately register with either of them. Roark looked as if he had just been slapped. It was a betrayal he had not seen coming. *How could she?* Roark thought as he tried to rationalize why she would say such a thing. *Have I shown her any reason to mistrust me that she would do this?*

Kori wanted to smile. He had been waiting for a reason to prove Mary was going to be a problem, and now that he finally had it all he felt was anger. He wanted to doubt Roark every step of the way, but Mary had come through for them. A flash of his wife came across his mind. He closed his eyes briefly, hoping to see her face clearer, but in the same instant she was gone.

"When?" said Kori, gritting through his teeth at her.

"Last night, in the middle of the night he showed up in the room."

All her confidence was gone. She felt as if she were right back at the orphanage, being scolded by the nurses for something. She felt small and weak. *See both sides of the coin,* she told herself in her mind. *Be the voice of reason.*

"So that's where you were during the attack, and why you didn't know anything about it," said Roark apprehensively.

She nodded, looking frightened.

"So, what did he say to you, and why did he not kill you?" Kori's body was rigid. None of them were paying any attention to whether or not any soldiers were going by. The courtyard was filled with silence. It was as if they were the only ones left in the world.

Mary found some confidence. "I haven't made up my mind about it. He said you two were liars."

Kori took a step closer and slapped Mary hard across the face. Her cheek went red from the hit. "Why did you even let him speak? This could have been over with by now. I could have been back with my wife. How dare you take our lives in your hands?" Kori was screaming down at her.

"How dare me?" snapped Mary, putting a hand on her cheek to soothe the pain. "What was all this for then, huh? You asked me to help you. You said what we were doing would save people's lives, but since you asked for my help, look at this. Look at what's happened. An entire war was fought because of you three. You want to know what he said? He showed me how his family was killed. Thousands of people were killed...in a day. It wasn't even the Japanese who did it, like you two thought. It was Russian soldiers. So everything you asked me to help you with was for nothing. I didn't help save anyone, not even a single person. To think that I helped do all of this makes me sick." Mary began hyperventilating and collapsed to the ground, trying to regain her breath. Roark rushed to catch her. He dropped to his knees and held Mary as she tried to slow her breathing. Kori remained frozen where he was, watching her.

"I'm sorry," said Roark, holding her tight. "I'm so so so sorry. I brought you here to remind me of what I once was and stood for. I wanted to fix what I had broken. You're right, we only made it worse. But no matter how awful things are, Andrew is still out there."

Mary pulled herself away from Roark, which made a shot of pain shoot through him. He doubled over, clutching his chest.

"Look what we had to do just to get here, and we are no closer to Andrew than when we started. What will you do now to stop him? How many more lives will have to be ruined for your goals?"

Kori was paying less and less attention to Mary and Roark arguing. Mary's words were replaying over and over in his mind. *Russians*, he thought, saying the word in his mind. "It changed," he whispered to himself.

"I can't do this anymore, Roark. I don't want to be a part of this. How is what you're doing any different than Andrew?" Mary pulled herself to her feet. She felt exhausted all of the sudden.

Roark was still hunched over, reeling from the chest pain that had grown worse and worse.

"He is only out for himself." Roark pushed the words through the pain. He tried to block out the pain and rise up to his feet. He could see the concern in Mary's face, but he knew she would not address it." He is only protecting his family. I am trying to protect everyone's families. I am protecting the greater good."

"People need to make their own choices, Roark. They cannot be pushed into it, cannot be told what to choose. You pushed me into this, and I was stupid enough to follow along, but no more." Mary was backing farther away from him.

"So you're with him, is that it?" The pain in his chest was subsiding, but as the pain left, guilt replaced it.

"No. He is no better than you are. He is standing on the shoulders of others to get his goals, same as you. I realize now that is what he wanted me to see, to see that neither of you is right."

"It's different," said Kori louder, calling out to them both. His eyes were red, but there was a desperate hope in his words. "Andrew did change something." Kori pleaded with Roark, who looked on with an icy stare.

"He took her to where his family was killed. They are still dead, so what did he change? Nothing, nothing is what changed." Roark's words sliced the air, and a hidden rage was showing through that Mary had not seen in him.

"She said Russians were responsible for the massacre. That's what changed. It was the Japanese at first, but because of this...war, it changed to Russians. He is going to shift his strategy now to complete the change."

"The cold war," said Mary softly, which Roark heard. "It starts after World War Two, an arms race to build up nuclear weapons. It never comes to a fight, though. No battles ever occur."

"He means to start one," said Kori, realizing what that would mean. *I'll never see her again,* thought Kori turning to walk off.

"And we gave Oppenheimer and Von Braun to the Americans," said Roark. "What did we do but give them the means to end the world against each other." Roark went silent for what seemed like a long while. Mary saw the change on his face. *I reached him,* she thought as she waited with him.

"The more we change, the more the world pays for it." Mary took a step closer to Roark, who was still staring at the ground.

"Maybe we need to stop too," said Roark calmly. Kori sat up against the wall and looked to Roark when he said it. He could see the defeat in Kori's eyes.

"I won't see my wife again? Is that what you're saying?" Kori strained to speak. It was a question he truly did not want to hear the answer to.

Roark took a deep breath, thinking of what his next words would be to his old friend. The silence around them became deafening. The square they were in was still. It was as if the world was waiting for them to move it.

"If we get Andrew. If we can stop him. Whatever has happened, we will let it go. We will leave the world to its own devices and remove ourselves from the equation."

Mary couldn't help but feel a sense of relief. *It's a step in the right direction*, she thought.

Kori had a severe look of concern on his face, as if he had just been stabbed by some invisible knife. She couldn't place why he had that look. Her mind was so focused on how she got through to Roark she didn't spend another moment on it.

"You would do that?" Kori asked, finally composing himself.

The statement caught Roark off guard. "It's not an easy thing for me to do, you know that."

Kori studied Roark's face, looking for a reason to doubt him. "Thank you."

Roark took another deep breath, fixing his jacket, as if breathing new life into himself.

"If Andrew's next move is to Russia, where would he go?" he asked Mary, attempting to redirect the focus.

Mary was lost in thought. She replayed Andrew's conversation with her over and over. She remembered when he realized things had changed, and he immediately brought her back here to Germany. He had never let on why he brought her back so quickly. Her thoughts changed to what she knew of post-World War Two history. *The cold war covers thirty years,* she thought. It was like thinking of where an imaginary needle would fit best in a haystack the size of a skyscraper. There were infinite possibilities. Then it hit her square in the face.

"1963, Texas. That's where he would go."

"That's not Russia; what's in Texas?" asked Roark sternly.

Kori pulled himself off the ground, lazily fixing his jacket.

Mary stood looking at him. The words were on her tongue, but she refused to say them. She already regretted saying what she had. She didn't want to help them. She wanted to get away.

"Please, Mary. What he is doing won't change his future, he can only change minor aspects of it. What he will do is destroy the present and your future as well. I won't let that happen." Roark tried to take another step toward her, but she backed up a step. She didn't want him any closer.

"Why do you care so much what happens to me? You found me in an orphanage."

"You are important," said Roark.

"Why?"

"I can do a lot of things, Mary, but you can't defend against yourself, can you? That's why I need you, to defend me against myself. Please help me make this right," said Roark, pleading.

Mary wanted to run, but something in her felt it wouldn't be right to leave. She felt she owed him something.

"I'll help you, but I don't trust you. Not anymore."

"I understand."

Roark held out one hand and pulled Atlas from his pocket with the other. Kori already had his Atlas out and had turned the dials and disappeared.

Mary opened her mouth to say something, but Roark shook his head no.

"He has been in a very dark place for a very long time."

"What did you do to him?" asked Mary, staring at his still-outstretched hand.

"He lost the person he loved the most in this world. I took that from him, and I have been unable to get her back for him."

"Why can't you just undo it, like what you are doing to Andrew?"

Roark slowly lowered his hand. "Because there is a difference between moments that just happen and moments that are meant to be. Many moments in a person's life can be altered by even the slightest push one way or another, but some things, once they are done, can never be undone."

"And you promised to get her back to him once all this is done?"

"In 1963, where you want to go, it will be four years before the event that robbed him of her. What would you give to get that much more time with the one you love? I was going to leave him in this time so he could have that second chance, to cherish every moment. If Andrew succeeds, however, then it would have all been for nothing."

Mary reached out and took his hand.

"I'll do what I can."

Roark smiled at her—that was all the response he could muster. "Thank you. I won't forget this."

He closed Atlas, and they were gone from the courtyard in a flash of blue.

Chapter Ten:

The Wild Card

"Welcome."

Kori sat in his chair without looking up at the young man entering the empty room. The young man looked around as he entered, taking in the barren environment. All that existed in the room was a rectangular silver table and two chairs, one on each side. On one wall was a large mirror that covered almost the entire wall. Kori sat at attention, staring carefully at a large folder of documents strewn around the table. The young man recognized a few of them. The door slammed shut behind the young man, which startled him as he quickly looked to the door, then back to Kori. Kori never raised his eyes to look at the man; he didn't care to look.

"Sit down," said Kori sharply. The young man cautiously approached the table and nervously pulled out the chair to sit. He swallowed hard, waiting for the next order. The young man was a sharply dressed twenty-four-year-old in a brown suit. Immediately, the young man felt under-prepared as he brought nothing into the meeting with him. On the table in front of Kori was a large folder with numerous pages splayed out across it.

"It's an honor, sir," said the young man nervously, cautiously unsure of how their interaction would go. Almost before he could finish Kori sluggishly raised a hand, gesturing for the young man to stop speaking. It was not a motion out of anger or discipline, just that Kori no longer cared for the formality of it.

An awkward moment continued between them as Kori glanced from page to page, wondering which to start with. Occasionally, he glanced over to the young man and studied him. A tap was heard from the wall with the mirror that seemed to snap Kori back into reality. A look of concern suddenly appeared on Kori's face.

"What happened there?" Kori leaned forward slightly in his chair and gestured to the young man's wrist. It had a dark scar wrapping almost all the way around it.

"I'd rather not talk about that, sir," said the young man, deflecting. The man folded his hands and tried to make his smile a bit brighter. Kori did not budge; he just stared directly at the man.

"I asked you a question, Marine." Kori almost barked out the statement. The man could instantly feel a bead of sweat on his forehead.

"I...I tried to commit suicide during my time in Russia, sir. I'm sure you must have read that in those pages, sir." The man swallowed hard, brushing the bead of sweat from his head. He tried to do it without it being too noticeable.

"I did read it, Marine, but I wanted to hear it from you instead," said Kori, easing his tone and leaning back to the way he was sitting before.

"...and I'm not a Marine anymore, sir. I was discharged." The man hung his head, a little embarrassed about the confession."

"Dishonorably, correct?" Kori moved a piece of paper to reveal some notes written underneath. He continued reading the notes, preparing for his next question.

The young man could only manage a small nod.

"It wasn't the suicide attempt that got you discharged, was it, though? What got you excused from the military?" Kori lifted the piece of paper with the notes on it so it was nearly at eye level for the young man.

Sweat was forming on the man's palms now. He was worried these things from his past would come up, but he felt like a little kid in the principal's office.

"While I was in Russia I started reading about..."

"Let me rephrase. Are you a communist?" Kori placed the paper down and leaned back to study the boy.

The young man was taken aback by the bluntness of the question. "Sir, I thought this meeting was about a..."

"Just answer the question, son. We will get to that later. These are background questions, standard stuff. If you cannot answer them you are not the one we are looking for," Kori stated flatly.

"No, then, I would not say that I am a communist."

"But your file states here that you proclaimed it, quite publicly, in fact," Kori read from the notes.

"What I stated was that I was a Marxist. There is a difference," stammered the young man, cutting Kori off.

"I stand corrected," said Kori, smiling as he examined the notes to see the young man was in fact correct.

\\\\\\\\\\\\\\\\\\\\\\\\\

The hotel room was hot. The air conditioning wasn't working. All three of them were sweating.

"Don't mean to be nitpicky, but of all the hotels in Dallas we picked this one why?" asked Kori, removing his jacket. Sweat stains had appeared on his shirt.

"Cause this one doesn't keep logs of guests. It's like we were never here," said Roark, walking to the window to look out at the city. Mary was fanning herself, sitting on the end of the bed.

An awkward tension filled the room as each of the three had their thoughts set on something other than the present.

Kori felt an optimistic hope he had not felt in many years. As much as he hated himself for working with Roark, he knew how close he was to seeing Serena again. The feeling of having her next to him again intoxicated every thought. He found himself smiling at his future, but he refused to give Roark the satisfaction of seeing it.

Roark felt a sense of control he had been without for years, almost like how he used to feel. Grief and regret had tormented him ever since the car accident when Serena was killed. It was only now that a sense of redemption was returning to him, and with it came his returning confidence. The only one in the room who felt her world declining was Mary. A feeling of deep regret grew over her as she started to see things in a clearer light. Voices of both Andrew and Roark echoed through her mind back and forth, each explaining why he was in the right and the other was not. Her mind struggled to understand why one goal was more morally correct than the other, or if that was even the issue.

Ever since she met Roark she had been led to believe his actions were justified and Andrew was acting irrationally, but after Andrew's visit neither one seemed as righteous or favorable as she had originally thought. Every fiber of her being didn't want anything to do with either man, as what they were continuing to do was only in the name of a common good that didn't exist yet. She took a deep breath to try to calm her mind, but the more she thought, the less sense she made of it all.

"So Andrew intends to start yet another war? How exactly is he going to accomplish all this from Texas?" A frustration was building in Kori's voice.

"Mary," said Roark, still facing out the window calmly.

Mary was still in a daze and had not heard that she was being included in the conversation.

"Mary?" said Roark a little louder, still facing the window. A stiffness was in his words.

"Oh... sorry. A year ago there was an incident off the Florida coast toward Cuba. A nuclear war nearly broke out between the US and Russia. President Kennedy was able to diffuse the event—barely." Mary spoke on in a drone voice. There was carelessness in her voice that Roark noticed, and he was concerned that he may not have her full support any longer.

"You said that happened a year ago. Why aren't we there?" asked Kori, staring Mary down.

"Because as much as I know Andrew wants to start a war, to tip the scales in his favor, I do not believe he would set out to level the world. I don't think he is an idiot, and I doubt he would interfere with as fragile a situation as that. However..." said Mary, pausing. She didn't want to say her next words.

"However what?" Kori sounded irate.

"In a few days' time an attempt will be made on the president's life by a Russian spy. The attack doesn't even come close to succeeding. So much so that no one ever learns of it until some decades after it's all declassified. But I believe Andrew might use it to his advantage. If he can eliminate Kennedy and pin it on Russia, the country would be certain to go to war."

Kori wanted to find a fault in her thinking. He was desperate for it, but nothing came to mind. "That actually makes sense. So we stop the assassination, catch Andrew in the act and..." Kori paused a moment, having found the flaw he was hoping for. "Who says he would even be there himself? He would just use someone else, a puppet."

"I think he's desperate. That's why he came to me; he is risking more now and wouldn't want to leave anything up to chance." She knew she was lying. She could taste it, but the sooner they made a move the faster this would all end.

"We can't be directly involved either. Last time I was in the White House I was told that if I ever came back to the States I would be branded a traitor and locked in a box for the rest of my life. I'm sure the years have not changed their minds."

"You think they would still arrest you? It's been almost twenty years since D-Day. The day we left, I'm sure they buried you and everything they had on us," Kori said sharply.

"I could try."

"Try. All you do is try. We could use all the help we can get to get this thing done," said Kori, practically yelling.

"But first we will need something. Something to draw off attention. We led the charge ourselves in Germany and nearly got ourselves killed or arrested. We played it too close to the chest and were soundly beaten. That cannot happen again." Roark turned away from the window. He grabbed his jacket off the chair and put it on. "Not just something, but someone."

\\\\\\\\\\\\\\\\\\\\\\\\\

"So you want to be an American citizen again, is that right?" Kori gave the young man a blank stare.

"Yes, yes sir." The young man could feel his shirt sticking to him. The air in the room was growing thicker.

"Then I suggest you stop calling yourself a Marxist. I need a devoted American for this task. Is that you or not?" Kori could see the pride wiped from the man's face.

"It is. I need the money," said the man, swallowing hard.

"The task your country is asking you to perform requires the utmost secrecy. For the next twenty-four hours there will be no contact with anyone until this is over, understood?" Kori paused just long enough to hear what he wanted.

"Yes."

Kori continued without missing a beat.

"Your mark will be right here in Dallas. A parade is taking place tomorrow that you will need to be at." Kori nodded quickly at the one-way mirror as he spoke.

Roark opened the door and entered, causing the young man to sharply turn around. He started to stand to greet him, but Roark waved him off. Kori remained unchanged, continuing to speak as if nothing had occurred. The man sat back in his chair awkwardly.

Roark casually leaned against the wall, listening to Kori.

The man realized he had missed a bulk of what Kori was saying.

"... A rifle has been provided for this assignment, which you can pick up when you leave this property." Kori leaned back, waiting for the man's response.

"There's a presidential parade tomorrow—that's not the one you mean, is it?" asked the man.

"Have you been paying attention, Marine?" asked Kori with a smile.

The man looked to Roark who gave no reaction.

"I choose my words carefully, young man, and I never repeat myself," said Kori folding his arms. "So when I speak, you should choose to listen."

"I'm sorry I was distracted."

"Yes, that is the parade." Roark cut him off before he could ask what he missed.

Kori gave a look of annoyance.

"Your position will be above the parade. We have a spot that we scouted for you. It's in the building where you are currently employed, is it not?"

"I just started there, yes." The young man said as a confused look came over his face. "Are you asking me to kill the president?"

Kori remained silent.

"You want me to shoot the president of the United States?" the man said even louder.

"You are an excellent shot, are you not?" asked Kori, confused by the man's reaction.

"I can't kill the president. I don't like the guy, but I'll go to jail forever if I killed him." The man had a scared look on his face. He had the look of a man wanting to run.

"That not what we are asking of you, Mr. Oswald," said Roark calmly from the wall. "I'm asking you to protect him. We believe there will be a man in the crowd who does mean to kill the president, and I want you in a position to stop it should that man try to do anything."

A moment passed as the man contemplated what was being asked of him. He gave a small nod of approval.

"My name is Lee. Don't call me Mr. Oswald. Call me Lee."

Chapter Eleven:

Convergence

"I've heard a lot of things about you."

Kennedy was leaning back in his chair as he stared over his desk at Roark. There was a tension in the room, and all three men could feel it. Hoover sat on the edge of his seat, unsure of what to say. "I don't know how you know the things you know, but I'd like to first thank you for all the help you have provided to our country. It's a shame that the world will never know your name," said Kennedy, leaning in his chair.

Roark smiled but remained silent.

"But your contract as a consultant ended after the D-Day invasion. All your records ceased to exist after that day. I see Mr. Hoover here was responsible for maintaining the confidentiality of what records did exist, and I thank him for that. Edgar also provided me with a transcript of your last meeting with Mr. Roosevelt immediately preceding the invasion. It says here that President Roosevelt had the utmost respect for you and that he regarded you as a patriot."

Roark turned and gave Edgar a surprised look. Edgar couldn't hide the smile that came across his face.

"It surprises you to hear that?" Kennedy placed the papers back on his desk.

"I find a lot of things to be surprises of late, Mr. President."

"Nobody has seen or heard from you in nineteen years, and yet here you sit, not looking a day older than your last photograph." Roark fidgeted in his seat, forcing himself to remain quiet. "Where have you been?" demanded Kennedy to Roark. "We needed you, and you were gone. You just up and disappeared without a trace." He leaned forward in his seat as he yelled. "Our best men couldn't locate you. Where were you?"

"I don't think I can give you an adequate answer for that question, Mr. President. It's hard to explain." Roark tried to cross one leg over the other to at least appear relaxed. Moving in his seat, he realized he was sweating.

"You are not leaving this room without telling me." Kennedy picked up the receiver to the secretary in the next room. "Yes, hi...right. Please turn them off. Thanks." The click of the phone hitting the receiver echoed through the room. "There, now no one is listening, so no one outside this room will know. You have my word on my life your secrets will be safe with me. Satisfied?"

"Yes...I think so," said Roark.

Hoover sat transfixed. Roark took a deep breath and felt Atlas in his inside jacket pocket, pressing against his chest. "The last time anyone saw me, I was in Berlin," Roark continued.

"Then what?"

"I was under the impression I was no longer welcome, so I wasn't about to risk being in prison for the rest of my days—hence I didn't return." Roark could feel the heat of the room. He looked to the clock to see he was running out of time until the parade.

"And yet here you sit." Kennedy smiled skeptically.

"With this, I couldn't stay away any longer."

"You're not going to give me a straight answer as to where you have been, are you?"

"It would take too long, and you do not have the time, Mr. President. There's something about this parade you need to know."

Kennedy stared at Roark, deciding what to do with him. He looked at the clock to see it was near noon. "Will you tell me the truth after the parade? I need to get down to the motorcade."

"Certainly, Mr. President."

"Then what is it I need to know?"

"An attempt will be made on your life during the parade."

Kennedy's face went blank, then immediately went back to his normal demeanor. "I get attempts and calls about attempts nearly every hour. How is this one any different?"

"It's come to my attention that the person making the threat is a very capable individual." Edgar swallowed hard, feeling the tension of the conversation.

"Who is this person?"

"No one you would know, but I'll know him when I see him."

Kennedy's face changed. "When you see him?"

"I'm requesting to be the fourth man around your car during the parade. Should I see him I'll be in a position to apprehend."

"Has he said all this to you, Edgar?"

Edgar jerked up in his seat slightly. "Yes, he has. He gave me a full background on this man...Andrew was his name. Appears to be a defector from Russia. This could be related to the crisis last year. Former soldier, perhaps unhappy with the result of the incident?"

Kennedy nodded that he understood. "Seen him before, you say?"

"Yes, briefly during the war. He is the one we were after in Berlin. He appears to have resurfaced like I have. Once I heard of this, it was a matter of connecting the dots. If I see him, I can stop him."

Kennedy sat back in his chair and put a hand on his chin. It was as if he were trying to stare through Roark.

Roark knew he had him.

"You can serve as my fourth man, but you will not be armed. Is that understood? You see this Andrew and you point him out to the Secret Service. I'll have one stationed next to you. Those are the conditions; take it or leave it."

"Done," said Roark.

"Head outside and grab a radio. That's all, Roark. Welcome back stateside." Kennedy raised a hand gesturing to the door.

"Thank you, Mr. President." Roark and Edgar stood together and made their way to the door.

Roark opened his mouth to speak, but Edgar stopped him. "You don't have to thank me."

"Why do I get the feeling you are going to use that against me at some point," said Roark, smiling as they exited the office.

A smile came across Edgar's face. "You finally learned..." he said as he closed the door.

\\\\\\\\\\\\\\\\\\\\\\\\\\\

Lee gripped the straps of the duffel bag so tightly he could see the color drain from his hands. He feared letting go of the bag as if he might lose it if he did. He realized his jaw was clenched. He opened it to stretch it, but it clicked every time he did.

The bus jerked to a stop as he looked up to see if it was his destination. He was still several stops away from the parade site, and a growing crowd of people was entering the bus at each stop. It had been empty when he boarded. He knew there would be a large crowd at the event, but he was secretly hoping he wouldn't run into anyone on the way.

A woman was coming down the aisle, and he could see she was eying the empty seat next to him. His mind was focused on the task ahead, and unwelcomed conversation was the last thing he wanted.

"Is this seat taken?" the lady said in a soft, sweet voice. She was an older lady in her sixties, wearing a floral dress. He felt a few people stare, as she was the only black woman on the bus. The eyes of the other passengers traveled from her to him and back. He wanted to be unnoticed, and the looks only fueled his paranoia.

"You can take it," he said gruffly. The lady's smile shrank a bit as she sat.

"You going to the parade? I'm meeting my daughter there with my grandson. I hope there's not too many people there. I told my grandson Billy he would get to meet the president today," she said happily to no one in particular. A smile stayed on her face as if no one on earth could take that from her. She saw the people catching glimpses of her, but she kept looking forward.

He didn't like the president, and he had no love of the United States, either. *I wish the government would have let me stay in Russia. I was happy there, but I was dragged back. Stupid passport.* He would be just as happy shooting the president if he wasn't being paid so well to restrain himself.

"I am going," said Lee solemnly. He gripped the duffel bag straps tighter.

"Something wrong, dear boy? It's a beautiful day, praise the lord."

"I'm fine, thank you."

"Oh, you can tell Aunty Margery. What troubles you?"

She annoyed him. He wanted to just get off the bus, but he had come too far to turn back. He feared what might happen if he didn't do his job. The prospect he might be killed himself crept into his mind. It was a fear that made him want to tell someone. He was told no contact with anyone before the parade, but who would know about this old lady. Nothing would trace back to a stranger.

"I start a job today."

"Good for you. You see, God has a plan for us all. You should rejoice in the gift our Savior has given you," said Margery.

"I don't know if I can do the job I was hired to do."

"It's called faith. You can't know what will happen today, tomorrow, or the next day. As long as you have faith and the courage to move forward, there isn't anything that cannot be overcome. You remember that, and you'll be fine."

He desperately wanted her words to make him feel better, but nothing could shake the dread he still felt.

"Thank you," said Lee as calmly as he could.

"You afraid of dropping that bag?" asked Margery.

"What?" he asked, confused.

"That duffel. Your hands are near white your holding it so tight.

The bus was slowing down at the stop. He could see he was still several streets away, but he had the sudden urge to get out. He quickly stood and shuffled past the lady who sat next to him, knocking her purse off her lap. "I'm sorry," he said over his shoulder as the lady frantically started picking up all her things that fell out of the purse. Lee raced out the bus door before anyone could get on. The air outside hit him, and he instantly felt better. The air was thick, but he took deep breaths, drinking in the day. With each breath a little more confidence came back into him.

A flash of a gunshot echoed in his mind. He pictured looking through his scope at the man, Andrew, lying on the grass. He could feel the metal of the trigger on his finger. He opened his eyes to see the sidewalk ahead of him.

As the bus started to drive off he could see the woman staring at him through the window. *Faith,* he thought as he started to walk. *Faith to move forward. Faith.*

The duffel felt heavy in his hand. The more he walked, the lady's words kept repeating in his mind. He checked his watch to see if it was half-past eleven a.m. already. It was just a few blocks from the book depository building where he was to go.

As he pictured the shot he would take over and over, a creeping thought entered his mind. For years he had wanted a way of getting back at the U.S. for all its lies. It was the reason he fled to Russia in the first place. He pictured the shot again, only instead of Andrew in his scope it was Kennedy. The idea made him smirk as he kept walking. A cool breeze hit him. *Wouldn't that be a switch?* He had only received half of his intended payment from Kori, and he knew if he changed targets he would not get the rest.

How would they stop me if I did it? No one would know until it was too late.

He switched the duffel bag to the other hand to give his right arm a break. As the idea grew in his mind, a slow smile came across his face.

Now that would be an idea that would change the world.

\\\\\\\\\\\\\\\\\\\\\\\\\\\\

Mary and Kori stood near the street where the parade was to take place. People were already gathered, waiting for the president. Mary felt tense, as if she were unable to breathe. The stress on Kori's' face did nothing to ease her tensions. She thought of anything she could to take her mind off the parade and what could happen.

"Tell me about Serena," she blurted out without realizing it.

Kori's' whole demeanor changed in an instant.

She felt as if she had just poked a sleeping bear.

"When did you hear that name?" asked Kori icily.

"You said it to Roark once. She was your wife, right?"

"Is. Is my wife," said Kori, correcting her.

"But she passed away."

"In another life she died, yes. But if today goes the way we want I will see her again." Kori could see the confusion in her eyes. He felt a warmth of happiness blow across him. "You see, it was in this era I met Serena. She is a teacher here, in this time. Once my job is done here, I will give my Atlas to Roark and remain here. I can start over again with her. Make better choices and be the husband I couldn't before. "

Mary saw the change in him. *He isn't beyond saving. Andrew was wrong. There's hope in his eyes.*

"I hope to meet her one day," said Mary.

The warmth that was there drifted away from his face. A pit formed in her throat, fearing she had said something wrong, but his face seemed harder now than before.

"I don't think Roark would allow that. I think he means to take you with him once this is over."

"What...What do you mean, take me with him?" She had not truly considered what would happen after everything was done. She imagined being taken back to the orphanage and left as they found her. No one wanted her. It was a feeling she had known her entire life. *Why would Roark be any different from any other parent who didn't want me back at the orphanage?*

Part of her wanted to stay with Roark. There was a familiarity there that she could never place, but he was also a man she couldn't trust anymore, and that was the part that wanted to escape. She remembered a time when all she wanted was to steal the Atlas away from Kori or Roark and use it to get away. Mary had seen them use it often enough. *Maybe now is the best time,* she thought.

"Where we are now, this place, it's not real. It's a variation of actual reality. Once Pearl Harbor happened an alternate timeline was created. Andrew caused it, and it will end with him. If we all leave after Andrew is stopped and return to the night of December 6th, 1941, this alternate version of history will have never happened. The loop will be closed, as no one would be left to continue it. Roark means to leave me behind so that it will. It will be a violation of our laws to do this, but only Roark will ever know." Kori seemed lost in his own happiness.

"Will Roark take me back to the orphanage?"

The question brought Kori back to reality.

"I'd imagine not. After all you have contributed, I doubt leaving you as we found you would be an appropriate reward."

They continued moving through the crowd gathering for the parade. Near the parade path they found a park bench to sit down. Kori's' face changed as he sat watching the crowd. A worried look showed on his face.

"A reward?"

"What would an appropriate reward be for an orphan girl with nowhere to go?" asked Kori, staring off into space.

Mary was offended by the question. She could feel the tears forming behind her eyes, but they didn't show.

"I want to meet my parents. I want to know why they left me."

"That is something he could do." Kori smiled at her. She had not seen him smile like that before. It was the face of a man filled with hope, but she could see there was something else behind it. Mary had always tried to imagine what her parents might have looked like. When she was younger, she thought up names for them and had imaginary conversations with them. The prospect of getting to meet them brought her a similar hope, but then she felt what she thought Kori must be feeling at that moment as well. They were so close to the finish, but it could still fall apart. She knew they both needed that reassurance.

"I hope so. Where were you before all this? What were you doing?" asked Mary.

The question hit Kori in a way he hadn't expected.

"I was in New York, working. My checkpoint is there."

"What is a checkpoint?" In that moment she remembered that this is what Kori did as a profession. How many others had there been like Andrew? How many more would there be?

Kori realized he had said too much, but he was close to leaving, so what did it matter?

"A checkpoint is how we get work. It's a location where we receive our information with the next runner to catch and so on. Mine was a coffee shop," said Kori.

"Why there?"

"It was where I first saw Serena. I was sitting at a table outside reading the newspaper, and there she was. The most beautiful woman I had ever seen walking right in front of me. I knew it was a chance I had to take so I blurted out, 'Excuse me.' " Mary could see how passionate Kobi was when he spoke of

Serena. It was a side of him she hadn't known was there. "I had nothing to say to her when she turned. I knocked my coffee over as I stood, hitting it with my newspaper. I remember we stood there for a moment, and she was just staring at me. I still had no words and I had coffee sprayed across my leg. Then she just laughed. It wasn't a mocking laugh, but almost like she was laughing at herself. Then she said her first words to me. She said, 'I didn't know I had that kind of power over men.'

We talked for an hour before she had to leave. I called her the next day, and it was history from there. After she died I threw myself into my work, hoping it would keep my mind off everything. I would go back to the coffee shop and sit at that same table. I would hope to see her pass by again and we could start over. Even after all these years later I still find myself at that place, hoping, waiting for an absolution."

"But that is all over now. Tomorrow you can see her and fall in love with her all over again," said Mary.

Kori caught himself. "I hope so. As long as Roark keeps his word."

\\\\\\\\\\\\\\\\\\\\\\\\\\\\

Lee could feel himself sweating as the weight of the bag took its toll. *Just a little farther.*

An uneasy feeling came over him as he thought about what he could do once he reached the nest on the top floor. How easy it would be to change targets. He replayed his actions over and over in his mind. No one would know, especially if there were two shooters. He wouldn't even have to fire; he could just let Andrew go, and Kennedy would be taken care of without him even having to do anything. The notion left him excited and nervous. A chill went up his arms and back, thinking about it.

He reached the Texas School Book Depository Building with half an hour to spare before the parade was to begin. He slung the duffel over his shoulder so he could reach his badge in his back pocket. He heard a quick metal clang in the bag and jolted up straight when he heard it. Lee quickly scanned the crowd to see if anyone else had heard it, but few people in the lobby even noticed he was standing there.

He checked in at the counter and smiled politely at the desk clerk. Carefully, he turned away as to not jostle his bag again and headed off for the stairs.

Walking down the sidewalk with a heavy bag was annoying enough but walking up multiple flights of stairs with it made him aware of how out of shape he was. Flashes of boot camp came back to him, which filled him with disgust. It was one of the many things he hated about the United States.

At the top of the stairs he found the top floor was deserted, as Roark had informed him it would be. Many of the rooms at the end of the hall were unused and filled with boxes. It was a perfect nest to be in.

The corner room was dark, with all the shades drawn. All the windows were low to the floor. He put his bag down against the corner and started sliding boxes around to make a sort of fort. He knew he had to obscure himself from the door so he couldn't be seen should anyone happen to walk by. For a moment he felt like a kid building a fort in his backyard. The boxes were stacked in a random order to look clumsy from a glance. He settled himself down against the window. The room was hotter than outside. All the heat from the building seemed to be trapped in the room. The window was stiff to open. It likely had not been opened in years, but the breeze that hit him felt good.

Below, he could see the forming crowd around the street. Another chill hit him, thinking how the crowd would move once he took his shot. Still staring out the window, he found his duffel and the zipper to open it. He pulled out the pieces to the rifle. The pieces fit together, each with its own click. *Smooth,* he thought to himself as he positioned each one. It was something he was good at in the Marines. His friends used to race him in stripping a gun and reassembling it. Only once did he ever actually win. How long ago it all felt to him.

Once the gun was assembled, he stared at it, thinking about what he was about to do. For a brief second, he thought about just packing it all up and leaving the way he came. He imagined walking back down the street and hearing the shot behind him as he left. A guilt came over him.

The shot needed to be fired, he thought, but who will it be at? He was being paid to protect a man he did not like. It was a conflict of ideals in his mind. He wanted nothing more than an opportunity to seek revenge on the country he felt betrayed by, and yet he was being employed to defend it. *Did they know who they were hiring?* he screamed in his head. Maybe they did.

The prospect hadn't occurred to him until that very moment. *Did they mean for me to kill the president? Was it a cover? Did they only tell me it was about Andrew to cover themselves should it all fall apart? Is there even an Andrew, or was it all a lie to have me be the only shooter? They knew my past. They knew I tried to defect to Russia. What if?*

He took out his binoculars and started looking through the crowd. The faces went by without a second notice until he settled on a sight he recognized. It was the man who interviewed him, Kori. He saw Kori sitting on a park bench with a girl he hadn't seen before. She looked too young to be his wife. His daughter, maybe?

I could shoot him right now and no one could stop me. The power he held invigorated his confidence.

"Who are you?" he said to himself, watching the girl next to Kori.

He drifted away from them to go back to scanning the crowd. He could see Secret Service agents beginning to line the street. Lee placed his rifle in his lap and propped up against the window sill. As soon as he saw his man, he would be ready. The only question that remained was, what man he was looking for?

\\\\\\\\\\\\\\\\\\\\\\\\\\\

"Five minutes till the start of the parade," said the head of the Secret Service to Roark and the other two men.

"Thank you, Roger," said Roark, smiling back at him.

"So you're the last-minute addition?" asked Roger skeptically.

Roark managed a nod.

"We had things pretty under wraps. It didn't need to be changed, but so be it."

"The president is coming now," said Brian, the agent to his right.

"All right, listen up. Mathew and I are up in front of the car. Roark and Brian have the back. Mind the crowd and keep your heads on a swivel. Roark thinks there's a man who may wish the president harm, but he has to get through us for that to happen. Nothing happens without Roark's say-so. If he IDs our man, break off in pursuit. We have several agents behind the vehicle to move up and cover the car. Roark, you want to brief them on our guy?"

Roger had been at this job for many years, and it showed.

"His name is Andrew," said Roark, handing out sketches of the man.

"A sketch, not a picture?" asked Mathew, concerned.

"No picture of him exists. This is all we have. He will be alone. He is dangerous. I do not know how he will come at us, but I am certain he is here and that he will try something."

"Why today? Why not yesterday or tomorrow?" asked Brian studying the sketch.

"I don't know," said Roark, lying. *You can't know.*

"There's hundreds of people in that crowd. This is only a sketch. We could look right at him and not know him," said Mathew, looking over his shoulder at the crowd.

"I'll know him," said Roark bluntly. A mild pain shot through his chest when he said it. It made his face cringe, but none of them seemed to notice. He put a quick hand over his jacket pocket and felt the photograph inside. Immediately, he felt better.

"Let's hope you see him first then."

The president came out with his escort and walked with his wife to the men. Roger commented on what a beautiful day it was, which made Jackie go into her public appearance mode. Some people saw the president and Jackie, and immediately the crowd began to roar.

"Showtime. Roar, good to see you here. Thank you again," said Kennedy, climbing into the car after Jackie.

"You're welcome, Mr. President. We will keep you safe. "

Roark took his position behind the back driver's-side corner of the car. Brian was a few feet to his right behind the other corner of the car. He could see Roger and Mathew up in front of the car, taking their positions.

The motorcade lurched forward as all the men started into a fast walk to keep up with the car.

Here we go. Moves and Counter-moves, he thought as he began scanning the crowd.

,,,,,,,,,,,,,,,,,,,,,,,,,,,,

The crowd suddenly began to roar as Kori stopped mid-sentence to look up.

"Time to move."

They stood from the park bench and moved closer to the street to see the parade. The crowd erupted in a mix of yells and whistle noises as the president could be seen down the street coming toward them.

Kori was fixed on the motorcade, glancing from person to person, trying to look for any suspicious activity.

Mary felt her heartbeat quicken as all the sounds around her seemed muffled. A quietness filled her up inside, and she wanted to close her eyes. A moment passed when she wished she were somewhere else. *I can't be here.* She wanted to scream. These people should know what is about to happen.

Kori was staring at her, knowing something was wrong. She didn't know when he turned to look at her, but she could feel his gaze bearing down on her.

Kori brought his hand to his ear. "Can you hear me?" he said softly to himself.

"What?" she said nervously.

Kori shot an angry look at her. "Not you."

Who else could he be talking to?

"Mr. Zaprudor? Begin filming." He quickly brought his hand down from his ear to avoid bringing more attention to himself.

"What was that?" she demanded. "There isn't enough going on?"

"Roark has his games. I'm introducing one of mine. I wanted assurances, and now I will have them," said Kori coldly.

She started to run to warn Roark, but Kori stopped her and kept her in place.

"What are you doing?" she said, trying to release her arm from his grip.

"This has nothing to do with you."

"Stop it. You're out of control, Kori. Roark said he will handle this. What are you doing?" pleaded Mary.

"Roark can't be trusted. Everything he is doing is out of desperation," said Kori.

"Yes, he can be trusted," she lied. She didn't trust Roark either, not any more than Andrew, for that matter. *He is beyond saving.*

"He is dying, Mary. Can't you see that?" Kori said, gritting through his teeth.

The world stopped in her head. Everything seemed to freeze in place. It couldn't be true. She didn't want to believe the words. Kori realized what he had said and went back to watching the parade motorcade grow closer.

"He's dying?" repeated Mary.

"I shouldn't have said that. He didn't want me to tell you. I'm sorry," he conceded.

"How long does he have?"

"Not long. Days, weeks maybe, if he is lucky. That's why this is so important to him. It's his last chance. That's why he came to me in the first place. I'm the only one that would ever understand."

"What's killing him?" she said as a weight of guilt came over her. As much as she didn't trust Roark she didn't want him to be hurt.

"Time. Roark watched his ancestor die in front of his eyes. A major change to your past like that will slowly change everything. It takes time, but eventually it will catch up to him."

"What will happen when it does?" she said fearfully, seeing Roark down the street coming toward them.

"It will kill him, I expect. If the family that led to you is somehow altered in the past, then you will never have existed. That's what is about to happen to him."

"There isn't anything we can do?"

"No, there isn't. That is why you will never understand why we do this, Mary. Do you have any idea the sacrifice required?" A shiver went through his words. "The lives I have taken...The lives I lost. The lives Roark is responsible for. For what? I lost all the people who ever meant anything to me, and now his family is gone too." He caught himself, realizing what he was about to say. He choked the words back down, but Mary didn't notice. "Roark did an unimaginable evil to me and my family. One that I vowed to never forgive him for, but when he came to me after all these years I knew why he was there. Before my life was shattered, we were like brothers. No matter how much I hate him, I could never deny him a dying wish. He is trying to make amends, I can see that now. I owe him that much," said Kori, wiping a tear away.

She stared off in a daze, wishing she could redo every conversation she had ever had with Roark. *I was so mean to him when I shouldn't have been. Why didn't Andrew say anything?*

As her mind wandered, she found herself looking at the crowd across the street when her eyes fell on a familiar sight. She saw a man crouched on the grass, hidden in the crowd. It was a man with a jacket pulled up over his head. Stretching out from the jacket was a silver piece of metal. The man looked up suddenly to make eye contact with her. Immediately, she knew who it was. *Andrew.*

Her mouth froze with the words. She knew what he was there to do, but she couldn't speak to raise any alarm. Out of the corner of her eye she could see Kori was fixed on the motorcade. *He doesn't know.*

Andrew froze, realizing he had been spotted. The crowd was thick where he was, and any movement would draw attention. She saw something in his eyes that she had not seen the last time they spoke—fear.

Kori had said Roark was doing this out of desperation. She could see Andrew was doing the same thing. She thought of his family that he was trying to save. The crowd grew louder, as the motorcade was almost on them. She thought of their families and how the country would react if the president were to be assassinated. How is anyone more right than another? *See with your own eyes, Andrew said.* Indecision gripped her as she struggled with what to do next. The fate of everything rested on her in that one moment.

Andrew raised a finger to his lips, hoping she would not give him away. Her jaw stiffened watching him. Andrew returned to his rifle and waited. Her heart felt as if it were about to explode through her chest. She wanted to scream for everyone to run. But no words formed. Her mouth betrayed her mind by not moving. All there was to do was wait. *I'm letting this happen.* The thought defeated her. It was too late to start again.

A gunshot rang out that made Mary close her eyes, wincing as the sound deafened the crowd. Her ears hurt as everything went silent for a few moments. A sharp ringing remained. Her mind went to the thought of Andrew. She looked to see if he was there, but he was gone.

``````````````````````````````

Lee breathed heavily as he watched the convertible carrying Kennedy suddenly speed up. He could see one Secret
``````````````````````````````

Service agent leaping onto the back of the car, trying to reach the president. He knew the shot came from the crowd to his right, but he struggled to find where in the panicked crowd. He scanned the mass, going from face to face as if he could recognize the man from sight at that distance. Then he saw something that made his whole body shiver. A man was walking slowly through the crowd as it was dispersing in all directions. The man had a hood over his head, walking away from Lee on the grass. Under the man's jacket was a large object that could be a rifle, but he couldn't be sure. *Turn, turn you bastard! I need to see your face, damn you.* He could feel the anger within him. His moment of glory had been taken from him. A few more seconds and the kill could have been his. Slowly, he saw the man turn, and under his arm was a rifle, just as he thought. The face matched the man he had been looking for.

"Andrew" slipped out from him in a whisper.

Lee placed a finger on the trigger when suddenly, Andrew looked right at him, high up in his window.

Lee moved his eye away from the scope and looked over the top of his gun down at Andrew, surprised at the attention. *He knew I was here?* Andrew put up a hand to wave, but then took off in a run.

Lee scrambled to get him back in his sights and frantically pulled the trigger, ringing out another loud bang through the square.

\\\\\\\\\\\\\\\\\\\\\\\\\

People ran faster after the second shot. The square was in a desperate state. Kori could see the car fleeing the park with Roark climbing over the back toward Kennedy.

"We need to go!" said Mary, finally finding her voice. Her words sounded funny to herself as she said them. Not all of her hearing had returned.

"Not yet," said Kori, too calmly for Mary to hear.

She tried to walk away once more, but Kori grabbed her arm stiffly. "You're not leaving me," said Kori, clearly affected by what was happening. The glint of Atlas could be seen in his other hand. He fumbled at it helplessly.

"We can't stay here!" cried Mary, struggling to free her arm.

"Brace yourself."

"For what?"

"Any minute now. He is running out of time." His hand was turning white from gripping Atlas so hard. "When it happens I have to be holding your arm; if not then you will never see me again."

A moment of panic came over her, scared of what he was talking about.

"What's going to happen?"

"What it is we do."

Mary gripped Kori's' hand as tightly as she could. A mix of fear and adrenaline went through her veins.

\\\\\\\\\\\\\\\\\\\\\\\\\\\

The first gunshot launched Roark into action. Immediately, he saw the president slump over in his seat as Jackie screamed in terror. He felt his legs pick up their pace as he knew the car was about to take off with the president.

He leapt forward with all his strength onto the back end of the car. His hands slipped on the car's edge, but he found his grip.

Before he could even think to react he knew it was too late. The bullet had hit its intended target. The scene unfolding in the backseat turned his stomach to look at. His gaze went to the crowd as he felt the car surge forward to escape the chaos of the parade. Jackie's screams carried over the running crowd.

"Head down!" snapped Roark to the first lady.

She nodded, trying to stifle her cries. She cradled the president's head in her lap, clinging to whatever hope she could that he would be all right.

He strained his neck to look behind him, hoping to catch a glimpse of Andrew anywhere, but all he saw were strangers.

Lee stared through the lens in shock of what he saw.

"I missed," he said out loud, trying to believe it.

He scanned the crowd once more, but he saw nothing. People kept running as the square emptied out, but Andrew was gone. *I failed.*

Every fiber of his being knew he had to leave. A few people had started looking up at the windows after the second shot, and he knew it was only a matter of time before someone looked right at him.

He leaned away from the rifle, staring at it. *All I put into this, and I failed. I didn't get Andrew, and I didn't get the president.*

The sudden realization set in that he might go to prison for the rest of his life for a crime he didn't even commit. Fear gripped him as he backed away from the rifle and went for the door.

"I have to get out of here."

He grabbed a dark sweater with a hood he had brought with him and threw it on and zipped it up. As he left through the upstairs door, he put on the baseball cap he had in his bag.

People passed him on the stairs, trying to take refuge in the building, but Lee deliberately didn't make eye contact with any of them. Even though he couldn't see their eyes, he knew they were all looking at him.

Do they know? They must know.

He made it to the lobby, and a coldness hit him.

Police raced toward him and seized his arms.

"That's him!" someone shouted over the commotion. "I saw him in the window."

He felt the officers handcuff him and pull him to the ground, but the world had gone blurry. Sounds drifted away as all he could think of was how none of it was real anymore.

Roark stared at Kennedy's lifeless body in the car with Jackie's blood-smeared arms around him, and a rage built up in him he hadn't had in a long time. A focus that was lost on him for years came back into startling clarity.

"This is as far as this goes," he said to himself, not wanting any more bloodshed due to his actions. This man had trusted him with his life, and he had failed him.

His hands let go of the back of the car as he leapt off to the ground. He hit the ground hard and rolled as he felt the pavement tear at his clothing. When he came to a stop he felt his forehead where the ground had scraped him.

Without hesitation he ignored the pain and pulled out Atlas. An anxiety came over him, as he was afraid of what he was about to do would cause.

Someone will find out. Adam will come for me.

He opened Atlas and stared at the rings inside. The numerals on the dials were more worn than he remembered the last time he looked at them. He had the rings within memorized and couldn't remember the last time he ever actually just looked at them.

He pressed on the outermost ring as hard as he could and felt it click as he dislodged it from its place.

Three minutes ought to be enough.

The dial clicked three positions over as he pressed it back into position. A low hum came from the device. Atlas was not meant to be tampered with, but he knew how to manipulate it if the time called for it.

His eyes closed as an image of Adele came to him.

I'm doing this all for you.

Atlas clicked shut as he suddenly felt an immense G-force on his body. He felt as if he were being pressed into the ground. His bones creaked, thinking they would break at any moment.

He opened his eyes as the force began to subside.

The end of it will be worse.

The world he saw was different now. He was still standing by the side of the road where he was before, but everything else was changing. Time was moving in reverse. Everything was moving backward in slow motion. The car was coming, driving in reverse back the way it came.

His heart sank again as he saw Jackie once more cradling her husband, calling out for help. The driver was yelling something into his sleeve microphone that Roark couldn't make out.

As the car passed him, he broke into a jog to keep up with the car. Only he would be able to see exactly what really happened in the square, and it would be there that he would find Andrew.

As they approached the square he knew he was close. The crowds were slowly moving back into the spots where they had been. The scene was chaos in reverse. People looked inhuman as they seemingly ran backward to where they had been standing, tripping, and climbing back over each other toward the scene.

Jackie was slowly letting go of her husband as they neared the spot that the shot was taken. It was then he spotted Mary.

"Mary."

He saw her staring off into nothingness, holding Kori's hand. A small sense of relief came over him, knowing that Kori was protecting her. He knew she would be safe, but a sadness remained. He wanted to stop everything and explain so much to her, but there was no time.

Someday...

His attention went back to the president as Kennedy's body started lifting up from Jackie's hold and began moving back to a seated position. He quickened his pace to reach the car.

As Kennedy's body became completely upright he saw what he needed to see the bullet exiting the president, but instead of exiting out of the back of the president it left from the side. He darted his glance up to where Lee was and didn't see any muzzle flash.

It wasn't Lee; it was Andrew after all.

The bullet tracked away from the president as the man was now back to his normal smiling self, waving from the backseat. For that one brief moment the world was the way he wanted it to be, but he knew then that he wouldn't be able to undo everything. *Mary was right,* he admitted to himself.

His gaze followed the bullet away from the car and off into the crowd. He gave one last look at the president as a final good-bye before he turned to go after the origin of the bullet.

It had come from deep within the crowd, and Roark knew only Andrew could have made a shot like that. The crowd was thicker than he remembered, and he knew that he couldn't come into contact with anyone or else he would break the rewind. He was losing sight of the bullet and knew he had to hurry. He weaved in and around the walking people, making every effort not to brush up against anyone. It was then he looked ahead and saw him. Andrew was crouched with a hooded jacket draped over his back to conceal his actions from anyone around him. A rifle was pointing right at him, and Roark knew he had to act quickly.

Right as the bullet entered the gun the muzzle flash blinked brightly. Roark made his move. He lunged and jumped straight at Andrew, picking him up and knocking him flat on his back. As he made contact with Andrew, the rewind broke and a crippling migraine washed over him. Every fiber in his body felt like it was being ripped apart. His body gave out a silent scream of agony as time began to normalize and start to move forward again.

Andrew struggled to get a grip on what happened. He sat up, dazed to find several people looking down at them and seeing the gun.

As one woman went to open her mouth to say something a gunshot broke out from somewhere else, drawing everyone's attention.

As quickly as the pain had hit Roark it started to subside. It had been years since he had put his body through that much strain. *I can't have much time left now,* he thought.

Roark turned himself over to see the crowd fleeing in all directions. *But I stopped the shot from being fired,* he thought, confused. Through the people he saw the convertible racing off down the street with another agent this time climbing onto the back of the car.

Immediately, his attention went to the window Lee was in. The window was empty, but he knew it was Lee who had taken the shot. An anger came over him, but it would have to wait. He turned to find Andrew already on his feet in bewilderment that Roark had found him. He looked across the street to see Mary just as confused. She was still holding Kori's hand, as he had not yet realized what had happened. Mary let go of his hand to run across the street.

Andrew looked up to see Mary coming toward them, his heart dropping at the sight of her. He turned, running. Kori felt Mary let go and looked up to see her running after Andrew. Immediately, he darted through the frantic crowd after them.

Roark pulled himself to his feet as Mary caught up to him.

"Let's go," said Roark, coughing out the words. "We need to chase him, now!"

"He is just going to use Atlas and escape again," stated Mary flatly.

"He can't. This is our chance." Roark coughed again. His throat was on fire.

"I have a car standing by," said Kori, running past the two of them.

Roark and Mary took off after Kori as he led them to a parked car at the edge of the green.

"I'll drive," pronounced Kori.

"No, me," said Roark with a spot of blood running down his nose.

"You're in no shape to do anything, or be of much help to anyone," insisted Kori.

"This ends today, right now. Get out of my way," yelled Roark.

Kori stared for a moment at him. His clothes were torn, and his face looked battered. His dying wish. He stepped aside and let Roark get in the driver's side.

Kori got in the passenger side while Mary got in the back.

"Why won't he use Atlas?" she said as Roark peeled away from the curb. His eyes darted back and forth, trying to figure where Andrew would come out of the crowd.

"He can't," said Roark.

"It's a miracle you lived through it again. After last time I didn't think you had it in you," said Kori, looking out the window.

"What did you do?" asked Mary.

"During the parade when Kori took your hand, did you notice anything?

"It all happened so fast. I don't know," she said, confused.

"Think hard—what did you see?" asked Roark, spotting Andrew with his hood pulled over, disguising himself. Roark hit the gas, but Andrew turned and saw them coming. Andrew broke the window of the closest car and got in. Within seconds he had it started and pulled away from them.

"Don't lose him," yelled Roark to Kori, as the street was still a mob from the parade. The police were sectioning off the area.

Mary tried to focus on the parade. She remembered seeing Andrew in the crowd and Roark behind the car, then suddenly Roark was in the crowd next to him.

"Wait, how did you know Andrew was in the crowd? Did you see him before he shot the president?"

Roark swerved around a group of people, trying to keep up with Andrew.

"He didn't shoot the president; Lee did. I'm sure he has been arrested by now, but that will have to wait for later," said Roark, leaning forward over the wheel to see better.

A grey Studebaker Avanti tore out of a parking lot up ahead, and without a word Roark slammed on the gas of their red Pontiac Grand Prix and the tires screamed to life.

Kori grabbed the seat, the acceleration catching him off guard.

"I thought Andrew fired the shot, the first one," she said.

"He did, but that was before I changed it," said Roark, shifting the car into the next gear. Kori reached under the seat and grabbed a black backpack that was hidden underneath.

"How did you change it? This isn't making sense."

"After the president was shot. I used Atlas to start a rewind, to review what happened. You can only review things as they happen and the longer you're in it, the more unstable the platform." Roark made a sharp swerve to avoid another car.

"Is that why you were almost killed the last time?"

"A rewind requires unprotected time travel. Using Atlas you can go anywhere unharmed, but in a straight rewind, you have nothing. The human body just can't tolerate it," stated Kori flatly.

"If you rewound time to stop Andrew, why did Lee still fire?" asked Mary, raising her voice over the engine.

"That I don't know. He was the least of my concerns, but now is not the time."

They raced to keep up with the fast car Andrew had stolen.

Andrews's car darted in and out of traffic. People ran off the street as they screeched by.

"Damn it."

"What?" said Kori, holding the door.

"The highway. We can't lose him, not today," said Roark, watching Andrew pull onto the on-ramp.

Roark gripped the wheel, bracing for the fast turn. The car fought him as he strained to make the turn at such a high speed. Cars couldn't handle much in these days

"Time to change the rules a bit."

Kori opened the backpack and pulled out some small items and a shoebox-sized rock. Kori turned it over to a display of dials.

"What the heck is that?" asked Mary, thinking it didn't look like it belonged.

"This I borrowed from an old friend," said Kori, smirking.

Roark glanced over at him and immediately recognized the device.

"You get that from Jonis?"

"Yep."

"I'll turn it on when you're ready."

Kori unfastened his seatbelt and started to crawl out the window.

"Wait, why isn't Andrew using his Atlas? Won't he just disappear any second?" asked Mary, trying to stop Kori. "It's useless to chase him."

"The rewind!" yelled Roark over the wind from the window. "It causes a reboot to all the Atlas devices. They won't work for fifteen minutes. He's trying to outrun us for that long. He has four minutes left. That's our window."

Out of instinct, she let Kori go as he continued climbing out the window. He got one foot on the sill of the window and got himself into a crouch in the window frame.

"Steady," Kori yelled back inside at Roark.

Roark pulled the device closer to him and aimed the open side toward the dashboard. "One minute," he yelled back at Kori.

"What is that?" screamed Mary to Roark.

"A gravity well. Creates gravity wherever you aim it. Used in zero-G mining operations. Not meant for use on the ground," said Roark, watching as Andrew slowly pulled away.

"Not for the ground," she said, surprised. "So what will it do?"

"I don't know," shrugged Roark dryly as Kori pulled himself up onto the roof of the car. He knocked on the roof, signaling the go-ahead to turn on the well.

Kori stepped down onto the hood of the car and leapt forward as hard as he could. Mary took a deep inhale and placed her hands over her mouth in shock. Roark flipped the switch on the gravity well, and the whole car lurched upward slightly off the ground, then crashed back down. The tires made a sound as the rubber left and then reconnected with the pavement.

Mary's eyes followed Kori as he continued to leap almost in a glide over to the next car ahead of them to the right in the next lane. She watched his hands reach out and grab ahold of its roof. The force tipped the car he grabbed up onto its two side passenger wheels. The gravity well reduced the gravity in front of them so the cars were nearly weightless.

Kori pulled himself upright as the car continued to tip over to the passenger side, and he knew he had to get off of it as soon as possible. He looked back to Roark, who nodded to the next car in front of them. Kori took a step back and ran off the car's hood again and launched himself toward it. Mary found herself speechless. Roark turned the well to always be facing Kori. As the well turned away from the first car it was already almost on its side in the air. The restoration of gravity caused it to come crashing down on its side, sliding along the road before it went out of sight.

This isn't right, she thought at the callousness of what was happening.

As Roark moved the well across the highway the cars that passed in front of them slowly went up and down almost as if a wave were moving under them.

Mary's thoughts went back to Andrew sitting there in the crowd. Why would he kill the president? His actions didn't match the man she had met back in Germany. "See both sides," he had said to her.

Her eyes went to Roark's jacket pocket, where Atlas was just visible sticking out of the top. A sense of urgency came back to her. She knew she needed to do something. This couldn't go on any longer.

Kori made it to the next car as he got closer to Andrew. She could barely see Andrews's car farther up the highway. All the cars around them were frantically fleeing the scene behind them, and the highway got more and more crowded.

Andrew was trapped from getting any farther away from them, but Roark's window was shrinking.

Roark knew he was drifting too far away from Kori, so he made a desperate move. He turned the wheel sharply to the right and slammed into the adjacent car, forcing it off the road.

"What are you doing?" she screamed, getting as far from that side as she could. Sparks flew up into the window, and the grinding metal hurt her ears. The other driver put up her arms as the car sailed off the road into the guardrail.

Roark gritted his teeth. He knew it was wrong. *It has to be done*. Nothing else mattered.

His foot slammed on the gas pedal to catch up to Kori, who was leaping toward an approaching tractor-trailer. Roark barely got the well aimed at him in time, and Kori hit the side of the truck hard, forcing it up on its right-side wheels. The truck lifted off the ground as it slowly leaned farther and farther over. As the side of the truck turned more, the side surface became almost level. Kori got himself up and made a break toward the front of the truck. He was close enough to make a leap for Andrew's car. Andrew was still trapped by the swerving cars all trying to escape the highway. *Now or never*. It took all his effort to launch himself off the truck to Andrew's Valenti.

Mary knew she had to stop Roark before he hurt anyone else in his madness. She quickly reached into his pocket, grabbed ahold of the Atlas watch, and snatched it from him. Roark grabbed her hand before she could recede from him.

"What are you doing?" said Roark, sounding possessed.

"You need to be stopped!" she cried.

She quickly got the watch with her other hand and leaned back over to the passenger window.

Roark let go of the well and lunged after her. The pain in his chest returned with a vengeance. He didn't have much time left until his past caught up to him.

Kori leapt off the truck but the weightlessness he had been feeling over the last few jumps was not with him anymore. Suddenly, he knew he wouldn't make the jump to the car's roof. He reached with an outstretched arm as Andrew tried to swerve his car away from Kori.

He reached out as far as he could and grabbed three fingers on frame of Andrew's passenger door. His legs hit the ground with a thud as he frantically tried to get a better grip to lift his feet off the ground. The screaming pavement burned at his legs and feet as he scrambled to get inside the passenger window of Andrew's car. Andrew swerved the car back and forth to throw him off of it, but to no avail.

"I need that back," growled Roark to Mary.

"I'm doing what I think is right for everyone." Tears formed in her eyes as her mind reeled from the decision she had to make.

She held the Atlas out the window, feeling the wind on her hand. The Atlas made a series of beeping noises that could barely be heard over the rushing sounds of the highway.

Andrew heard a beeping noise coming from his Atlas as he frantically tried to dig it out from his pocket.

"Finally."

Kori saw his chance and forced himself in through the window as Andrew got his Atlas out. Kori grabbed the watch as it was in his hand.

"You go, we go."

"Can't you see what I'm trying to do? You stop me, and you're betraying Adam and everything he is," said Andrew.

The statement froze Kori in place.

Andrew steered past the cars blocking his way and continued to press down on the gas, going faster and faster.

"How do you know Adam?" asked Kori softly, suddenly calm.

"He is the one who found me and gave me an Atlas. Told me about you and Roark, told me what to do to get my family back. Don't you see? I can't start over, not now."

Kori's mind raced. *Adam couldn't be involved. It was impossible.*

He let go of Andrew's hand out of shock, unsure of what to do next.

Andrew saw his opportunity, flipped open Atlas, and closed the lid just as fast.

"See what I'm trying to do." Andrew was gone before Kori snapped to reality. Kori got into the driver seat just as the car went off the overpass, rocketing off the edge. Kori braced himself as the car went into the air with the hard pavement racing up to meet him.

Mary took a deep breath as she let go of the watch that Roark had coveted so much throughout their journey.

"Nooo!" yelled Roark as he swerved to the shoulder of the road and slammed both feet on the brake. Mary felt her body fly forward as her head hit the windshield and cracked the glass. Roark didn't stop to help her as he got out, leaving the door open. He raced back to see where Atlas had landed.

Mary felt lightheaded as she pulled herself from the car. People were pulling over to see what was happening. She put her hand up to her forehead and when she pulled it away, her fingers were covered in blood.

Roark was running out in the highway, searching for the fallen Atlas. Finally, almost all the other cars on the road stopped, the drivers watching Roark. The unwanted attention made Mary's skin crawl. She wanted to leave, but a churning guilt forced her to stay.

"It's Evil."

The words felt like a release for Mary. She had wanted to say it for what felt like ages, but finally it was out in the open. *How pathetic he looks running around looking for a gold watch.*

Roark looked like a shell of a man. It was all he had left in the world.

Finally, he spotted the glinting watch and scooped it up quickly.

"Do you have any idea what you could have done?" It was as if a bottled-up rage had been unleashed toward her. "If a car hit this, and it broke, everything we had accomplished would have been for NOTHING!" His face turned a dark red. "We would have been stuck here with no way of changing things back to the way they should be. Do you have any idea what that's like?"

A calmness came over Mary as she was reminded of the orphanage where she started.

"Yes, I do."

The realization of what he had said to her washed over him. Suddenly, he straightened up and wished he could take those last words back.

"One less of those things is good," Mary said. Her words were somber. "Andrew showed me what history you and Kori are protecting. Why would you protect something like that? You act like you are doing something so noble and righteous, but you're just like Andrew. You're both murderers."

"The true version of history cannot be changed. Humanity achieves a never-before-seen kind of lasting peace that must be preserved. The series of events that lead to that, along with every horrible, inexcusable mistake that is made, is a necessary evil that has to be endured. We have to accept that. All of us, as a species, have made too many mistakes." Roark was trying to calm himself down, but it was an act.

"You can give us a second chance and end all this. All you have to do is walk away and let people make their own choices." Mary reached out and took his hand. His hand was trembling so much he could barely grip her hand back. *He's so weak,* thought Mary.

"People can't be trusted to make their own choices," said Roark bluntly, pulling his hand away.

"There will come a moment in your life, Mary, when you will realize that all your best days are behind you. What would you give to protect that, to hold on to it? What if they were taken from you and replaced with something else, something cold and empty?"

Roark reached in his jacket pocket and pulled out the photograph of Adele he had been carrying with him since the night before Pearl Harbor. He held it up to Mary. The corners were destroyed and the picture itself was becoming discolored, but it was still clear.

"I've seen you with that. Who is it? You won't tell me."

"That is my mother," said Roark. Mary was stunned. It was as if a switch went off that made it all fit together. "She died the day I was born. I never knew her. When she died my father was never the same. He was a hollow version of himself. So I would visit them sometimes from before I was born. I can remember them the way I want to remember them. I want to see them happy." He carefully put the picture back in his jacket pocket.

"You need to learn to let go. No matter how many times you visit them, the past is still the past," Mary said. "Everything the movers were supposed to be was the idea of helping people let go of their pasts to move on, but now you have become the one thing you swore to stop. You have a chance to stop it now."

"It will stop, but not yet. Now we need to find Kori."

Roark abruptly walked back to the car, leaving Mary alone in the road. People had been listening to their conversation, but no one said anything. She quickly caught back up with Roark as they got in the car without saying another word to each other. The road was filled with people as they slowly meandered their way down the highway.

In the distance they saw smoke billowing from the upcoming overpass. Roark pulled the car over to see a small crowd had stopped as well, and several people were running down the hillside to reach the overturned car below. Mary's heart sank, as she knew it was Kori. Roark stayed in the car in disbelief of what he was seeing.

She almost fell down the hill she was running so fast, but when she reached the bottom the scene made her come to a stop. Kori was the only person pulled from the car. Andrew was nowhere in sight. She forced the thoughts from her mind.

Kori was seated upright against another car as people watched him.

"Did anyone go for help?" asked a bystander.

"Someone went, yes," said a young woman who was visibly shaking.

"Are you okay?" asked Mary. Kori's face was noticeably swollen and red. Lines of blood went down from his forehead over his mouth. His eyes stared off into nothing as if a light had gone out in him. His jacket was torn at the shoulder, and all his clothes were dirty from being dragged by the car. He cradled his right arm.

"I didn't get him. He's gone. I had him, and I let him go." The words looked painful to say.

"Where are you hurt? Kori, listen to me, is anything broken?"

Kori just continued staring off to the horizon.

"I didn't want you to come." Kori managed to turn his face enough to look at her. "I didn't want you to come here. I know what you did for him before. You helped him all those years from now, but you didn't deserve this. I tried, Mary. I tried. Forgive me." A tear ran down his cheek over the blood.

"You're not making any sense. I don't know what you mean." The panic that he was dying grew inside her.

"Promise me, when you see him again that you'll warn him. Warn him. Warn Roark about all of this. Talk him out of it. Maybe there's time."

"Can you stand?" She tried putting an arm around him and helping him to his feet. She pulled him up and stumbled.

Roark came down the hill. Fear filled his eyes again.

"Where is Andrew? Where is he? Is he still in the car?"

Mary brought Kori over to the side of the hill and carefully set him down on the grass. A faint siren could be heard approaching.

Kori seemed to snap wide awake as he hit the ground.

"Mary, you made it."

A smile came across his face as he looked at her.

"I brought you over here, Kori, don't you remember? Roark, he has a concussion. He needs a hospital."

"No, not yet." Roark crouched down in front of Kori. "Where is he?"

"Adam," whispered Kori.

The word hit Roark like a bullet. His expression sank, as if all the happiness in the world had gone away.

"Who is Adam?" asked Mary, putting an arm around Kori, holding him up.

"Adam knows?" asked Roark, fearing the response.

Kori nodded, wincing from his arm.

"Dear God."

"He must want Atlas back and is using Andrew to get it," insisted Kori, struggling to get to his feet. Mary helped him up.

"Who is Adam?" Mary repeated, frustrated.

"He is the best of us. He is the reason we exist," said Roark, thinking. "If I can get to Andrew, I can talk to Adam."

"Have you ever spoken to him before?" asked Mary, confused by their reactions.

"When I was young, Adam recruited me to help him. He gave us our Atlases. When our time ends, he takes them back. He must mean to take mine away from me. Every Atlas must have an owner, he said once. I told you there are only a few left in the world, right?"

"I do. He knows you're going to die?" Roark opened his mouth to speak but stopped himself. An angry look came across his face as he glared at Kori, knowing he had let it slip.

"Not if I can stop Andrew. If I can, then I can still undo what has been done and Adam will let me stay."

Kori stared at him uncertainly. "Adam said the same things to me too, Roark. The rules were clear. When our time is done, it is done. Nothing you say will change his mind. He is the one who found the Atlas devices, and he is the one who decides who the owners are."

"I have to try," stated Roark. "Now, where would Andrew go? Where is he going? What's left to change?" Roark drifted away from them as the sirens grew louder. The police would be here any minute, and when they did, there was no way they would be allowed to leave.

"Adam found the Atlas devices. Where did he find them?" asked Mary, analyzing what Kori had said. Kori flinched, knowing he had said too much.

"It's a place that cannot be found, and only Adam found out how to get there. It is the way he found it that the movers were created to protect. It's what everything we do is for."

Kori stopped himself. "Where was Andrew's family killed?"

Roark stopped pacing as a police car pulled up to the scene that had gathered on the side of the road.

"Boston," said Roark disappointingly. "But I don't know where in the city. Why would he go there?"

"I think he wants us to chase him. He wants this to end just as much as we do," said Kori sharply

"I'll show you, but I have a condition," stated Mary shakily.

"Name it," snapped Roark anxiously.

"If I take you, I want you to take me back to the orphanage and leave me there. I don't want to be a part of whatever this is anymore. This is not what you first told me this would be. I can't go any further." Roark's face was filled with a tension that she knew he was trying to force down.

"I promise, I will leave you where you belong." The words were forced out of him.

"Give me the Atlas. I'll take you," she said reluctantly.

Roark took out the watch. The outside was severely scratched where it had slid on the pavement. As Roark handed her the watch, their hands touched briefly. His hand was shaking. *He really doesn't have much time left.*

Kori put a hand on her shoulder as she flipped open the top and turned the dials where she knew to go. Roark reached out gently and took her hand. As two cops started to walk toward them with their guns drawn, the three of them disappeared in a flash of blue.

When Mary opened her eyes she was at a familiar gruesome scene. A Japanese man lay dead in the middle of the road with a truck stopped in front of him. The scene was exactly as it was when Andrew first brought her there. Roark and Kori studied the street, taking in everything that there was.

"He is inside, in the upstairs bedroom. I'll stay here," she said solemnly.

The two men looked at one another, and neither spoke a word of disagreement.

Kori led the way as the men entered the townhouse, whose door was already open. The living room was destroyed, the furniture tossed over. A banner across the living room reading *Welcome Home* was hanging down to the floor on one side.

The stairs creaked as they went up to the bedrooms. Muffled noises came from the last room as they made their way down the hall. The room was a nursery. Slumped on the floor was the body of a woman, and next to her was the lifeless body of a young toddler. Andrew was crouched in the far corner, tears streaming down his face. *He tortures himself to act*, thought Roark seeing what Andrew is seeing.

"It changed back," said Andrew, mumbling.

"What did you think you were going to change?" fired Kori back at him. Kori stepped over the dead woman to stand closer to the window opposite Andrew.

Roark was frozen in the doorway. The pain in his chest was subsiding. *It's almost time.*

"It was working. Things were changing. I thought what I was doing was working, but now it's back to the way it was. It was all for NOTHING!" screamed Andrew at no one. He hugged his knees, cowering in the corner.

"How did you come to find Adam?" asked Roark, finally forcing himself to speak.

Andrew swallowed hard. He looked up directly in Roark's eyes.

"He. Found. Me," said Andrew.

"Why you?" asked Kori calmly.

"I don't know. He said we had mutual interests, and that by helping me I was helping him. He didn't say how. Once he showed me how to get my family back, I didn't care what else happened, but that's all over now. It didn't work."

Roark could feel a coldness coming over him. *Just a little longer.*

"It's not over. There's always something to do." Roark was surprised at Kori's calmness he spoke. There was a patience he hadn't seen from his old friend in many years.

Andrew looked right into Kori's' eyes with a sudden stiffness. "It isn't my call anymore. It's out of my hands."

Roark became aware of the quietness in the room. "What do you mean it's not your call anymore? You still have the Atlas; you can still make a change, but this time for the better. We can help you." Roark held out his hand, trying to reach across the desolate, cold room.

Andrew withdrew from the two of them as far as he could. "After Texas I came here, and Adam was waiting for me. He said I disappointed him. He said things couldn't continue, and that I had taken too long. My Atlas was taken from me, and he said this alternate timeline must be closed now. I'm sorry for what I have done. I would take it back if I could, but it's too late."

"How does he mean to close it if we are all still here?" said Roark, withdrawing his hand and turning to Kori.

"That's not how loops are closed; Adam knows that," replied Kori.

Roark thought a moment, putting a hand on the wall. His fingertips were starting to feel numb. "Adam can't close loops. That's why we are still here. He means to force us to close it."

"He told me to tell you to remember the *Arizona*, Roark."

Roark turned to face Andrew. His face had gone white. "No," he said under his breath. "What's at the *Arizona*?" he said desperately.

"He said there was a gift for you there, inside the ship. He didn't say what. I think he hid something terrible inside."

A tension rose inside Roark that he struggled to maintain. "I'm going," said Roark turning to leave. "It's time."

"Roark," said Kori, putting out a hand. "This is where we part ways... my friend." Kori's hand was shaking as Roark lifted his hand to shake Kori's. Roark couldn't muster anything to say except for a nod with a half-smile.

"For years I hated you, but it took me a very long time to realize that you were just reacting to what Adam made you do. What happened was an accident," said Kori, holding Roark's handshake a moment longer. "I forgive you. I hope at the end of this you can find some peace of your own. Tell Mary good-bye for me."

"Thank you," said Roark with hope in his eyes.

Roark left the room with Kori still staring at the door brightly for a second.

Roark quickly raced down the stairs and back outside, where Mary sat on the sidewalk calmly staring at the sky.

She heard the footsteps behind her and casually turned her head to look at him.

"Is he dead?" Her tone sounded sad.

"No," he said softly. "I'm afraid we don't have much time. This alternate time is being ended right now, and I don't think we can fix things the way we want. I'm sorry."

"You still don't get it, Roark," she said, standing up. "We aren't meant to."

"Adam has intervened. It's beyond our control now. I have to leave. He left something for me back at Pearl Harbor. There are many things I cannot fix, but first I mean to bring you home."

"To the orphanage. I can't go back there. I came this far with you, Roark. At least let me see this to the end," she said defiantly.

"I can't guarantee what will happen if you come. Adam means to take Atlas back from me. If he does, then however things end is how they will stay."

"And how would that be different than any other day? People have to live with their decisions their whole lives, and accept the outcomes, however they end. I am an orphan who was abandoned by my parents. At least now I can start over and make my own decisions. I'm starting with this one. I'm going with you."

Roark took out his Atlas and stared at it. "I don't know what we will find there. I'm going to put us in the water right next to the ship. We need to see what Andrew put inside the ship. Take a deep breath."

Mary stepped closer to Roark and grabbed his arm. She closed her eyes and took a deep inhale. Roark did the same as he closed Atlas, and they both disappeared in a flash of blue.

Chapter Twelve:

The Road Not Taken

Kori stared out the window, seeing the flash of blue disappear along with both Roark and Mary. He was alone with Andrew in the room. All hope that Roark would succeed and that he could see his wife again faded with the blue light. All reason to live, he thought to himself, was gone.

He turned to face Andrew, who was still staring at him, his eyes filled with fear.

"I still wish you would reconsider," Andrew stated simply.

"I had a wife," said Kori, placing a trembling hand up to his head. He wiped a bead of sweat off his forehead, looking at the floor.

"She was taken from you. Roark killed her in the car accident, I know," said Andrew, finishing the thought. Memories of his own family came back to him in flashes. For a long time he had been thinking he was going too far, but now for the first time he was letting himself believe it. He swallowed hard, reminding himself that this was the only way.

"She meant so much to me. She was the only reason I had to live. Ten years I looked for a way, an opportunity to get her back. Ten years I found nothing." Tears formed in Kori's eyes, but all that filled him was regret. "Roark took everything from me, but it was he who found a way for us to be together again. Once we were done, he was going to let us be together and I could get away from all this."

"She's gone, Kori. Listening to the man who killed her won't bring her back."

"She's alive!" Kori suddenly looked up at Andrew, who seemed surprised at the revelation.

"What do you mean?" Andrew gripped his legs tighter. A slow realization came over him that he was alone without his Atlas. His sense of security had been stripped away.

"She is alive. Here, in this time, she is alive. Roark was going to leave me in this past where I could meet her all over again and have the life I wanted. "

Andrew was putting together what was happening.

"Now, none of that can happen. With what you did, that life cannot happen that way. You took her from me all over again." Kori clenched his fists. "What's in the *Arizona* for Roark?" he asked, suddenly quiet.

"I can't. I'm sorry I ruined your chance at a new life. I truly am, Kori, but I had to try and save my family. It's everything I worked for—don't you see that?" Andrew pleaded, taking another step back.

Kori managed to take a step away from the wall. "What's in the *Arizona*? I won't ask again."

"I'm sorry. Roark can't stop it. He will be too late," said Andrew.

"Too late for what?"

"To stop the missile. Many years ago, Adam hid a nuclear missile inside the *Arizona* and armed it to detonate. It's one of many around the world, some set to just detonate, and others to launch. World powers will think they have been fired upon and will return fire. By the time anyone realizes what has happened the damage will already have been done. He wants Roark to close the loop he had created by visiting his father in the past. He broke a rule, and his punishment is to close the loop, and himself along with it."

"To take my chance at another life with it as well?" asked Kori, defeated

"I'm sorry."

Kori lunged at Andrew, knocking him back into the wall. Andrew barely registered what was happening until he felt himself being pushed backward. His head knocked into the wall. Everything went silent as he tried to shake off the attack. As soon as his awareness came back to him, Kori landed a hard punch across his right cheek, taking him off his feet again. His arm caught his fall as he reeled to try and stand back up. Before he could get a leg up, Kori was on him again. His training kicked in as he landed a quick jab into Kori's' throat before Kori could hit his next punch. The sudden lack of air made Kori stumble off to the side as Andrew found his footing.

On instinct Andrew tackled Kori, knocking him through the door and into the hallway by the stairs. The momentum took Kori off his feet. The force was enough to break through the railing of the stairway. Kori took the brunt of the fall, with Andrew landing on top of them.

Andrew rolled off Kori, sliding down the remaining stairs.

As his eyes came into focus, he caught sight of Kori's Atlas, which had fallen out of his pocket as they tumbled. It landed in the middle of the floor. Andrew lunged for the shiny golden watch, but Kori got a hand on it at the same time.

Andrew put a foot on Kori's arms, pressing down with his full weight as Kori struggled to get out from under him. Kori rose just enough to get his feet under him and let out a painful roar as he launched himself up with all his might to lift Andrew, knocking him off his arm. The force made Andrew lose his grip on the watch.

Kori seized the moment and flipped the watch open, set the dials and was gone in the flash of blue before Andrew could even get off the floor.

A desperate rigidity filled his whole body as his last chance to save his family was lost as quickly as it had appeared.

He looked at the hanging sign near him with the words *Welcome Home* written across it. For the briefest of moments he wanted to call out to them, to say he was finally home. The fleeting feeling almost brought a smile to his face before the moment passed.

He wanted to see his family again. He pulled himself to his feet and made his way back to the staircase. As he placed one step on the first stair, a flash of blue knocked him back to the floor. As soon as he felt the impact a second flash blinded him again.

He opened his eyes and scrambled to his feet. The room he was in was large and empty. The other end of the room was all floor-to-ceiling windows. He walked to the edge and looked out at a city below. *I'm near the top,* he thought, judging the distance to the ground.

He recognized the city below as Boston. *This is the Prudential Tower,* he thought.

"Hey."

Andrew heard the word and spun around to Kori's fist coming at him. An alertness had returned to Andrew since the fight at his house, and this time he was ready. Andrew ducked out of the path of the jab and swung at Kori with his right arm. He landed one hit on Kori's side, then another. The sudden show of skill surprised Kori.

He noticed Kori had a black backpack strapped on over his suit. Kori swung again with his left fist to counter, but Andrew dodged the hit and spun to kick Kori square in the chest. Kori's exhaustion from the earlier fight in the car was wearing on him. A strap broke on his backpack causing it to peel off of his back and almost off his other shoulder. Andrew approached Kori, who was struggling to move on the ground. Blood was smeared on part of his face. *Worn and beaten,* Andrew thought, staring at the pathetic sight beneath him. He reached down and plucked the Atlas from Kori's jacket pocket.

"I appreciate your contribution to my cause," he said, gesturing to the Atlas in his hand.

"You don't know what you're doing." Kori's voice was raspy as he willed himself off the ground once again.

"In a moment, none of that will matter, and we won't ever have had this conversation." Andrew flipped open the Atlas, set the dials, and closed the lid. The click of the lid on the watch echoed in the empty space, but nothing happened.

A moment passed when Andrew didn't register what happened. He looked around, and the realization hit that he was still in the same place. He looked at the watch. It was the same watch Kori had used before. He clicked the watch lid open and checked that the rings were set correctly. He pressed the lid closed until his fingers turned white from clenching it so hard, but again, nothing.

"It won't work, not now."

"Why not? It's never done this before," said Andrew.

"There is so much you don't know, Andrew. You were brought into a world you cannot understand by a man who is unpredictable. You were given a far more extraordinary gift than I have ever seen. Why he picked you is beyond me, but there is a lot more to that device than I could ever explain. "

"What did you do to it? You manipulated this somehow. Fix it." Andrew undid the zipper on the backpack and searched inside. The bag was full of guns, grenades, and a black metallic box. He took out the revolver and pointed it at Kori.

He desperately waved the gun at Kori. "Fix It!"

"I can't."

Andrew opened the bag again. He took out the metal box, which was lighter in his hand than it looked. With his attention on the box Kori lunged forward and twisted all the dials on the box. Suddenly, its weight increased, and it dropped to the floor. With each passing second it pressed into the floor more heavily, cracking the concrete beneath them.

"What is that?" asked Andrew quietly.

"That is a gravity well. In a few seconds it will bring the building down."

All around them the walls and ceiling began making cracking sounds. Kori took a small black square piece of stone from his pocket and held it up to Andrew.

"What's that?"

"This is a jib. It was mankind's sole attempt to replicate the Atlas devices. It was as close as we ever got. Operates on a whole different platform than the watches. You can buy them retail, you know."

Andrew stared at it. It was his only hope of any kind of another chance.

"You can use this to save your family. Take it. I don't want this life anymore. Take it and leave me here."

He held up the jib and stretched out his hand toward Andrew. Without hesitation Andrew reached out to take it. As Andrew took the jib, Kori grabbed Andrew's arm and pulled himself toward him. He gripped the strap of the backpack to lock himself in place. Andrew struggled to get free, but his arms were trapped between them.

"For Serena."

Kori kicked the gravity well and instantly, instead of everything being pulled down, everything above them started moving upward. Kori lifted Andrew off the floor and ran forward into the window, breaking through it out into the open air.

As they fell a massive buckling sound crunched behind them as Andrew saw the top portion of the building lifting off its foundation. The windows around the floor they were on burst outward in every direction. Metal tore apart in a symphony of screeching metal. A thunderous boom echoed out over the city as all the windows on the surrounding buildings cracked and shattered. Glass caught up to them, pushing them down faster and faster. Kori reached his arms around Andrew and smashed the jib between his hands. The sound of rushing wind went silent as they disappeared in a flash of red.

They appeared several feet off the ground on the street below. The force knocked them apart, with the bag being thrown in another direction. Andrew landed on the roof of a taxi, crushing the roof in and shattering the car's windows. Kori landed hard on the sidewalk, rolling toward the wall of a building.

Glass rained on them from all around them. People were running down the street, away from the Prudential Tower. Cars crashed into one another as everyone tried to get clear of the area. Kori managed to twist his head up enough to see what he had done to the building. The top portion still hovered above them, floating effortlessly. Surrounding the floating structure were numerous pieces of twisted metal waiting to come crashing down. The scene was quiet as more and more people stopped to stare. The building was not falling. *As long as the well is on, it will stay.*

``````````````````````````````````````

They appeared in a field and kept holding their breath, unsure of what happened. Mary exhaled, unable to hold her breath any longer. She tasted the salt in the air.

"What happened?" She looked around, not recognizing anything.

Roark let out his breath, staring in confusion.

"Why didn't it work? You said we would appear underwater next to the *Arizona*."

Roark took a step away from her and gently put Atlas back in his pocket. A mild pain lurked in his chest again.

He took out his Atlas again. *Adam.*

"He won't let you go with me."

"What? Who won't?" said Mary desperately.

Roark looked at Mary solemnly. "Listen to me. We aren't far from Pearl Harbor. It's east of here, maybe a mile or so. I'm heading there now, alone. There's a road behind you about a hundred feet. Go there and wait for a car, any car, and go into town. Once I'm done I'll find you there. I have to go alone to the *Arizona*. I know this makes no sense, but you have to listen to me. "
``````````````````````````````````````

Roark reached under his jacket and pulled out a severely worn journal bound in a leather strap. "Here. Take this."

Mary took it carefully." What's this? How long have you carried this?"

"Many years. I'll retrieve it once I'm back."

Mary felt the leather strap that looped around the journal several times.

"Don't open it. You won't like what you find in there if you do. Now go."

Roark turned and ran as fast as he could toward the base. He knew he didn't have much time.

He raced through the tall grass as he heard a truck approaching in the distance. He happened upon a winding road that must loop behind the harbor. It was a military pickup truck with just the one soldier driving.

Roark raced up to the driver door and hopped on the side. Before the driver could even react, Roark had the door open and yanked the driver from his seat. Without a word he got in and slammed on the gas pedal as hard as he could. The truck jolted forward, hitting every bump in the road hard. A tense anger coursed through him. It was the first time he had been separated from the journal in over a decade. Its absence sent a chill down his spine. *It can't be about Atlas. He couldn't be doing all this for that. He wants the journal. He knows I have it.* Through the trees he could see the service gate to Pearl Harbor. He kept the pedal pressed to the floor as the engine screamed to life louder.

Several soldiers near the gate were forming up to block him as the guards in the tower waved him to slow down. Roark gripped the wheel harder as he braced himself for the impact. Roark turned the wheel to aim for the fence gate that stood between him and the *Arizona*. He knew what waited for him at the bottom of the bay. Inside the *Arizona* was something to destroy the base. He had to get there. The *Arizona* was a reminder of a crushing defeat that rested on his shoulders. He couldn't fail it a second time.

Mary stood holding the journal, hands shaking, staring at it. *I know this journal,* she thought, feeling the leather cover. He said not to open it, but somehow she felt she knew what would be inside of it.

Every fiber in her body wanted to run to the road, but a feeling kept her where she stood. In the distance she heard gunshots, and she knew Roark was breaking into the base. She thought about what if Roark was killed, but the thought seemed impossible somehow.

My dream, she thought suddenly, starting to undo the leather strap binding the journal together. The old monk and the strange man. He burned that journal, but there was another. There was a map to another one, a copy. She was moving her fingers faster now to unspool the strap that looped around the journal several times. She took a deep breath as she opened the cover.

The pages were old and frail. Her eyes first drew to the inside cover where a name was etched into the leather. The etching was worn, but she could still read the letters.

"Crantor," she said aloud, hearing the name repeat in her head. "I know that name. From my dream!"

A loud boom sounded through the trees, causing Mary to close the journal and quickly re-wrap the strap.

``````````````````````````````````

*It can't have much left on the charge,* Kori thought, looking up at the floating tower. He knew there was not much time left in the cells. He reached for the backpack, but it was missing. Frantically, he searched around for it, reaching as far as his hands could sweep.

Andrew was nowhere in sight of where he landed. Instead, he was in the middle of the street below the Prudential Tower. All the traffic had stopped as people stared up at the floating structure. The moment of awe froze everything for a minute. Kori searched the crowd until he saw Andrew running in between the cars with the backpack on.
``````````````````````````````````

Kori took off sprinting after him as fast as his legs would carry him. Andrew looked over his shoulder, seeing Kori following, and he picked up his speed to stay ahead. He pulled the single strap of the bag over his shoulder so it was up against his chest as he ran. He undid the zipper and reached inside for anything he could use. His hand gripped a familiar object as Andrew smirked to himself, knowing his next move.

Kori effortlessly slid through the crowd like water over rocks. His legs took on strength of their own as he knew if he slowed down he would miss his chance.

Andrew pulled the first grenade from the bag, struggling to keep a grip on it as he sprinted. He flipped the pin and tossed it blindly behind him.

The explosion pushed him forward, flipping a car up on its side behind him. The jolt almost knocked him off his feet, but he regained his balance enough to continue. A sharp ringing went off in his ears. The world had gone silent to him. The thunderous shock had sent everyone in the street scattering. The frozen moment distracted everyone enough that people didn't know what happened.

Kori watched as the car in front of him was launched into the air, flipping. He ran to the left and jumped up on the nearest car, running across the roof around the blast. He lost sight of Andrew through the smoke. He leapt onto the next car down, trying to get clear of the area. The crowd of people that was once still was now running in all directions in a frenzy of chaos.

The pain in his ears was too much for Andrew. He stopped in the street, clutching his ears. A migraine set in as he doubled over, clutching his head. All he could focus on was the pain until he felt something pressing against his back.

He opened his eyes and turned to see Kori pointing a gun right in his face. People raced past them, seeking shelter as the two stood still.

"This is where it ends," Kori gritted through his teeth, growling.

Andrew's hearing was slowly coming back to him.

"It never ends. Killing me won't bring Serena back. Roark can't save you. What is already the past can't be changed. We both know that," said Andrew, trying to fight through the pain in his head.

"This isn't the past yet; this is the present."

Kori squeezed the trigger slowly. He didn't even hear the gunshot. He watched as Andrew's eyes went blank. His body fell to the ground in front of him, lifeless.

"Put my gun down," said a voice from behind him.

Kori turned to see the policeman he had taken the gun off of earlier as he ran by.

"Put it down!" the officer said again, louder with his backup gun raised.

"That building will fall any second. You should be getting people out of the lower half of it," said Kori sullenly. The color had gone from Kori's face. *Andrew was right.*

"What's happening to it?" said the cop, trying to quickly look back toward the Prudential Tower, still floating over the street. Streams of people were evacuating the bottom entrances.

"The gravity well I turned on is holding it up, but it will give out any second and explode. I'm not sure how big the explosion will be, but I had no choice." Kori looked down at the gun in his hand.

"The what?" asked the cop, confused.

"It doesn't matter. None of it does." Kori raised the gun to his head and looked at the cop with tears in his eyes.

"Hey, hey, hey, you don't want to do that," said the cop, lowering his gun suddenly and putting it away. "There's a lot to live for. Don't throw your life away, sir. Think about your future."

"All I have is my past, what future is there?" said Kori, trembling.

The loud noise of a siren sounded as the top, floating portion of the building began to freefall toward the street below.

The cop turned to the building as people started screaming and running, trying to escape. The screams masked the gunshot as the cop yelled for people to take cover.

The cop turned back to see Kori already on the ground. He quickly went over and picked up his gun, and a feeling of guilt came over him.

He wanted to move the body, but he looked up as the building portion crashed down onto the street in a monstrous boom. An immense cloud of dust kicked up all around the structure. Even a hundred yards away the force of the impact almost took him off his feet.

Immediately, he left to help people trapped under the rubble, leaving Kori abandoned on the ground between the cars next to Andrew's body. The last thing the cop saw before he turned to leave was a blond man in a tan suit crouching down next to the man who'd just shot himself.

\\\\\\\\\\\\\\\\\\\\\\\\\\\\\\\

The guards opened fire in front of the truck to try and get him to slow down, but Roark kept the gas pedal to the floor, racing toward the gate. The guards ultimately abandoned their post on the road to jump off into the grass. Roark braced himself as the truck rocketed through the gate in a thunderous crash. The gate blew off its hinges as it bent and twisted up over the top of the truck.

Hastily, he looked from ship to ship along the dock, looking for the memorial where the *Arizona* resided. Sailors scattered all over the dock as people were unaware of him trying to break in. Men stopped in confusion as the truck passed by.

Roark drove off the road toward the shore near where the *Arizona* sank. The terrain jostled the truck to the point where Roark nearly couldn't hang onto the wheel. The truck hit the muddy shore, which brought it to a sudden stop, throwing Roark through the window and into the water.

Roark reeled in pain, but he pulled himself out of the mud and began wading into the cold waters. A sick feeling of dread came over him as he dove down toward the *Arizona*. Many men were still entombed inside as his guilt of that day came back to him. Disgust filled him as he thought of what Andrew had done to the ship. How could he desecrate something like this?

He swam along the side of the ship. The mangled hull stretched before him in an eerie calm. The devastation that the ship represented sat silently along the bottom of the bay. As he reached the end he turned to swim the opposite side. Finally, he spotted something down in the darkness.

He took a deep breath and dove as deep as his lungs would let him. Concealed under a bent part of the hull was a nuclear bomb bolted to the side of the ship. Roark surfaced once he knew what it was.

It had to be almost ten feet long, he thought, scrambling to think of how to move or diffuse it. He dove again, feeling all along the outer casing. The missile had been there a long time; sea life had started growing along the exterior. The metal felt rough to the touch. Along the side he found the access panel, but the edges were welded shut. There was no way inside of it. Frantically, he grabbed the end and tried lifting with all his might. He let out a scream as he tried and tried to budge the behemoth warhead, but it never moved. It was fastened at both ends to the side of the ship.

He surfaced, gasping for breath, trying to recover from the effort. It would take a team of people with cranes to get it off the ship and out of the water. He knew he had only a few minutes until it went off. The realization came over him as the sound of sirens drew closer and closer. A man on a loudspeaker could be heard, calling for him to get out of the water.

The realization came over him that no matter what he did, the bomb was going to go off. He didn't know when it got there, or how. His jaw tightened, knowing what he had to do. Adam had given him no choice. He took out Atlas and was gone in a flash of blue.

He appeared back in the field where he had left Mary. His heart dropped to find she was still there.

"What are you still doing here?" he screamed in panic. His clothes were drenched. It was the worst she had ever seen him since they met what seemed like ages ago.

"What did you find?" she asked solemnly.

"I told you to go; why didn't you leave?"

"I couldn't."

Roark grabbed her arm forcefully. "I need to find you someplace safe." Roark tried to use the Atlas again, but nothing happened when he closed the lid. The echo of the lid closing sounded as he knew he was about to face the inevitable. Up until that point he hadn't accepted the fact that he might fail, but now it had finally happened. He let go of her arm slowly, staring at the watch. He knew that they had reached the inevitable end of their journey.

"Mary, listen to me. This is important."

"This journal. I saw this before, in a dream I have sometimes. The old monk and the strange man standing over him."

His words caught in his throat. He stared at her curiously. "Did you open the journal?"

"Just the cover. The name, Crantor. Who is that? The man in my dream had a journal just like this, but it was burned by the strange man. At the end of my dream there is a second journal."

The dream frightened Roark. An uneasy feeling came over him as he watched Mary. *She couldn't know that.* He tried to dismiss the notion.

"Mary, you have to listen to me. Everything you said to me, all of it. You were right. For too long I have tried to fix the past, but it wasn't the past that needed fixing, it was me."

Mary broke from her daze staring at the journal. "What are you saying?"

"I'm going to do what you have tried to get me to do ever since you met me—to let go. In order to do that, you have to go, and I have to stay," said Roark.

"What was down in the *Arizona*?" asked Mary, afraid.

"A bomb, and I am sure there are others somewhere else too."

Mary's heart dropped. "We need to warn someone. We need to stop it." Mary started to leave to get help, but Roark held her in place.

"No, we can't. I'm sorry, Mary. It can't be stopped; I tried," said Roark.

"You didn't try hard enough. Do you know what this will do? We can't fail now."

"It won't be worse than what I have already done. I failed, Mary, but you won't."

"What?" said Mary, stunned.

"It's on you now." Roark took Mary's hand in his and placed Atlas upon it. "You need to take it from here."

"I, I don't understand." She stared at the watch in her left hand and felt the journal in her right. A sudden fear gripped her.

"My time is done. I can't go any further. So I am doing this as a parting gift to you. Go back to Texas, during the parade. You saw where Andrew was, right?"

Mary couldn't find the words. All she could manage was a nod.

"Go back there, and alert anyone that he is there. He lost his Atlas here, which means he won't have one at that time anymore. Once he is caught, everything that happened, everything we have done, will stick."

"You would let that happen?" asked Mary.

"You taught me, Mary, that people deserve to make their own futures."

"You can still come with me," she said hopefully.

"This is it for me. I have to remove myself from the equation. That's when my job is done. Once you take the Atlas and leave, this future will be closed, along with me in it. You will create a new future from what we started. "

"I can't do this," said Mary.

Roark looked at her with such warmth that Mary could almost see the man he once was.

"You remind me so much of your mother," said Roark, smiling through his tears.

Suddenly, she knew what she had been feeling all along. All the emotions she couldn't place. *All this time.*

"You knew my mother?" she said, filled with such a hope that her fear had subsided.

"A father recognizes his daughter in any place, in any time," said Roark, fixing her hair.

Mary didn't know what to say. Her body was a conflict of emotions. She had hated him when they met, then all she had for him as pity, but now she realized that through the sympathy was something deeper, something she knew she needed close to her.

"You're my dad? How?"

"In another life, I chose work over family, and it ruined me. In this time, in this place, I tried to get some of that back. Once you stop Andrew in Texas, go back to your time, and go back to the where the orphanage used to be."

"Used to be?"

"Things will be different when you go back. We changed the course of history. Once you go back, it will be as if you never left. The only person who will know something is different will be you." Roark put his hands on her shoulders.

"I don't want to leave. Why didn't you say anything sooner?" asked Mary.

"I didn't know how," said Roark, taking her hands again.

"I have so many questions," said Mary.

"When you get back to your time, you will find your answers there. Now go, leave me here. It's time for me to go home now too. I'm glad I got to see you all grown up and got to know you at least this much. Good-bye, Mary. I love you. At least now I got to say it," said Roark.

"I..." was all she could say as Roark clicked the lid closed in her hand and stepped back. She was gone in a flash of white.

The air felt colder once she was gone. An emptiness filled him. *At least I got to say it,* repeated in his mind as he made his way for the road into town.

Time felt slow as he walked the edge of the road. Buildings were coming into view as he rounded the corner. He thought the bomb would have gone off by now, and the more the seconds ticked by the more he wanted it to.

As he reached the beginnings of town it occurred to him that the bomb might be fake. *What if Adam knew I would close the loop regardless of whether it was real or not?* All around him people went about their day, calm and without worry. All was right with the world, except him.

Suddenly, an air raid siren went off. Everyone on the street stopped and looked up to see what was happening. Roark looked up into the clear blue sky and saw the reason. Toward the horizon he saw a cloud trail behind something coming toward him very quickly. He knew immediately that it was a missile and not a plane.

"This is how he intends to close the loop," he said out loud to himself, watching everyone around him start to head for cover.

Roark remained motionless as he stood in the street, watching people head indoors. Some stayed outside, knowing that no place they could go would be safe enough. Some parents held their children and Roark saw them saying something to them. An elderly couple embraced on the sidewalk as a puppy on a leash circled around their feet. If they only knew that they would be saved, and that soon none of them would ever even know it.

Roark took out the picture of Adele from his jacket pocket. The picture felt flimsy in his hand now. He held the photo, realizing the pains that had been troubling him all these years were completely gone. He let himself go, knowing Mary would have to succeed where he had failed. The image faded away as he closed his eyes. The now-blank picture fell to the ground.

A brilliant flash came from where the *Arizona* was as the missile in the sky landed shortly after creating a second flash. As he saw the destructive wave coming at him, he cradled the photo to his chest as he was enveloped in a flash of white.

Chapter Thirteen:

Where I Belong

The sound of the crowd flooded her ears when she appeared. She raised her hand, frozen, to where Roark's face had been only a moment ago. "I love you too." The words fell out of her mouth in a whisper.

Did he hear me?

She said the words, but a sadness came over her at the thought that she didn't say them fast enough. *All this time?* She thought of everything she had ever said to him. *How?* Her mind reeled with questions as to how she couldn't have known. Roark was her father.

Part of her felt as if she had known it all along, but another part of her didn't want it to be true. *Why did he visit me? How did he know where to find me? Was he even telling the truth?* Questions raced through her mind as the crowd around her surged.

An instant realization came to her that Roark would be here in the parade somewhere.

"He is still alive!" she yelled, not realizing what she had said aloud. People near her stared.

Kori was next to her. He stared at her sudden outburst. "What was that for?"

She opened her hand to show the Atlas.

Immediately he had a look of pure anger. "Where is Andrew?"

"Andrew is across the street in the crowd with a gun." She pointed to where he would be. Kori took off into the street and into the crowd across from them.

Mary struggled to see where he went, but he had already disappeared from view.

A shot rang out from her right as she looked to see the president's car quickly speeding up to escape, except Roark was missing from the car. She only saw three guards around the car and not a fourth where Roark had been.

Panic hit the crowds as everyone scattered. Mary ran across the road as fast as she could to catch up to Kori. She found him standing still in the rushing crowd. By his feet was the dark jacket Andrew had been using to cover himself, but Andrew was nowhere to be found.

"Where is he?"

"Not here."

"Who fired?" asked Mary, confused. "It was Andrew who took the shot. I remember."

"No, it wasn't. Andrew was gone before I got to this spot. It was Lee, I figure. Must have been."

Kori took off toward the building where Lee was. Mary followed closely behind.

The entrance was a mob as people struggled to escape. Police were already coming down the stairs with Lee in handcuffs. A woman was screaming, "That's him, that's the man I saw in the window." Lee was frantically looking around for Roark, hoping someone would come to his aid.

Mary opened her mouth to say something, but Kori shook his head. He gestured for her to follow him away from the scene. As they got around the corner Kori stopped her under a tree.

"That's his Atlas isn't it? Roark's?"

"Yes," said Mary clutching the golden watch as tight as she could.

"What happened from here? He didn't get him?" asked Kori, frustrated.

"I don't know. I just know Andrew doesn't have his Atlas anymore. He loses it, or it was taken or something." Her memory was failing her.

"Remembering the future is difficult. It's like just waking from a dream. Taken? Who took it?"

Why is so difficult to remember? She thought. "Adam. Someone named Adam."

Kori's face went white. "Don't ever repeat that name again, do you understand me? Never." He frantically looked around to see if anyone was listening to their conversation.

"Where's Roark? We need to find him," said Mary.

Kori stared at her silently, studying her. His silence spoke volumes about what she feared not to hear.

"What?' she asked fearfully.

"Roark is, is gone, Mary. I'm sorry." Kori spoke in the gentlest voice Mary had ever heard him speak.

"What are you talking about? He was here just a few hours ago. I came back, so he should be here," she implored. Her voice went shrill with anger.

"Mary," he said still in a soft voice. "At the beginning of all of this, what started us down this road....? Roark watched his father die. That event caused a rift, a ripple through time. We have been skipping forward, staying just ahead of the ripple this whole time. I told him that if it ever caught up to him, his time would be over. Now it finally did. His family tree was disrupted. You don't come back from something like that. I'm sorry, but Roark isn't coming back. When I saw his watch in your hand, I knew what had happened."

Her world stopped. For years she had dreamed of what it would be like to meet her birth parents. She imagined every scenario of how they could meet. In some dreams they would just show up at the orphanage and take her home. In others she would be the one going to them. She pictured going up to the front door of a quaint little house in the woods. She would only have to knock once, and there they would be, smiling at her arrival. *It's what every orphan thinks about,* she thought. The image in her mind went cold, knowing it would never happen. Her mind then drifted to a thought that had eluded her up until that very point.

"Kori?"

He was looking around as if her were waiting to see an old friend. Her question broke his warm smile suddenly.

"Yes?" he said. She noticed his demeanor was only getting brighter.

"If Roark was my father, who was my mother? He never spoke of her. "

"He never spoke of her at all. Work is kept separate from family. That's the rule. Had Roark learned that, I doubt any of this would have happened." Kori went back to gazing through the crowd.

"Are you looking for someone?" asked Mary.

"Yes."

"Who?"

"My wife," said Kori.

"Serena?"

"Yes. She is here somewhere. She won't know me yet, but I have a chance now. Now that this is over, I can have the life I missed."

For the first time since she met him, she didn't pity him.

"There she is."

Through the crowd a dark-haired woman weaved through the calmer crowd. She was taking pictures with a gawky-looking camera. She moved fluidly in and out of the police line that was forming in front of the building Lee was taken from.

"What about Andrew?" asked Mary.

"He lost his Atlas. He is of no further harm to anyone. Let him try if he can, but I'm done running. You can waste your life trying to fix a mistake, but letting go and just living—that's what I intend to do. Go home, Mary. Be done with all this."

"What if I need you?"

"I still have my Atlas. You can always find me here, in this time."

She hugged him as hard as she could. The gesture caught Kori off guard. It was then he noticed that the Atlas wasn't the only thing she was holding.

"What's this, a notebook?" he said, suddenly concerned.

"No."

"You shouldn't have kept a record of what we did. No good would come of it," he said, undoing the leather strap and flipping through the journal. Mary watched his face as it dropped and his skin turned pale. "Where did you get this?"

"Roark gave it to me."

Kori couldn't believe what he heard. *Why didn't he tell me?* he thought. Anger surged in his veins. *The final insult.*

He swallowed his anger, knowing it would never find its revenge. He flipped the pages back to the cover revealing the letters spelling Crantor. He snapped the journal shut and rebound the leather strap. Quickly, he handed it back to Mary. "You must hide that. Someplace no one would ever think to look. Then stay as far away from it as possible and pray it is never found again. I didn't know Roark had that. I don't know why he would. People will know that it was found. They will come looking for it. You don't want to have that when they come."

"Who would come for it?"

"Adam."

Where does he come from?" asked Mary.

"There are many years between now and where he comes from. More than you could ever count. So long as you have that journal, he will find you. Hide it, and be rid of it." Kori looked up to see Serena still clicking away at the building's entrance.

"What's in the journal?"

Kori looked at her sharply. "In this time it's useless information, but in another time, it is the most valuable item in all of human history."

"Who is Crantor? Is it someone's name?"

"Yes. He was an old monk who lived many years ago. Like I said, it's quite useless to anyone else. "

"I dreamt of a monk who gets killed but leaves behind a journal."

Kori studied her curiously. *She remembers*, he thought nervously. *How did we not see?*

"I suggest you head home now, Mary. Back to your own time. It's time for me to go home now too."

Kori reached out and took Mary in his arms. He gave her a gentle hug as she felt his arms squeeze her carefully. She felt disbelief that suddenly all that happened was now over. "We will see each other again. I promise you," he said, feeling a sense of dread, knowing exactly when that would be. He couldn't bring himself to say it to her. *She needs her moment of peace,* he thought, letting her go.

"How things will have changed when I get there?"

"You will know when you look. Good-bye, Mary. It was a pleasure to have met you. You're just like your father when he was your age. If you ever see him again, remember that. Until we meet again." Kori gave a warm smile and turned to walk toward Serena. He didn't wait for a reply.

"Wait, how I am still here if it was my family tree that was broken too?" she said softly to herself. Kori was already nearing his future wife.

She watched him walk up to Serena. She turned and smiled when she saw him. Seeing the two of them together after how many years they had been apart brought calmness to her. For so long she thought things wouldn't work out for him. Andrew was certain that he was beyond saving, but he had misjudged Kori. There was a kindness to him, and she had found it.

Atlas felt heavy in her hands. She opened the watch and stared at the inside rings. Roark had always been the one to use the watch and it was only now she had gotten a real firsthand look inside. Each ring looked to be made of solid gold. Years and years of use had worn the rings' edges. The surface of the metal was speckled with scratches and dents. *If this watch could speak,* she thought, feeling the cold metal beneath her fingers.

Thinking about what she was going to see when she got back frightened her. Slowly, she rotated the dials to the exact day she initially left the orphanage. A pit was in her throat thinking about what if she returned to nothing. What if her future had been erased? *If Roark is my father and he is gone, why am I still here*, she thought. She turned to find Kori, but he was gone. All that remained was Serena continuing to snap pictures. She scanned the crowd, but Kori was nowhere to be found.

She went to walk toward Serena to ask where he went, but the Atlas clicked shut in her hand accidentally, and the crowd disappeared in a flash of white.

\\\\\\\\\\\\\\\\\\\\\\\\\\\\\\\\

"My god," said Edgar, sitting at his desk.

A cold sweat was forming on his forehead. He gripped the chair with his other hand as a tension had taken over his entire body. The voice continued talking on the other end of the line, but most of it was going in one ear and out the other.

"The president is dead." He had to say it aloud. It didn't seem real. He looked at the papers he had been working on strewn across his desk, but the importance of them no longer mattered. He knew that people were sure to come asking about Roark any minute. *No doubt they will pin this on him and connect it to me.* "Oh, yes, thank you for telling me. Good-bye." He hung up the phone with the other voice still talking. Silence returned to his office as he looked down at the phone again. *Was that conversation real?* he thought, wishing he could undo the last five minutes of his life.

His hand moved to the buzzer on its own. "Miss Gandy. Are you there?"

The moment of silence that passed felt like an eternity.

"Yes, Edgar. I'm here," said the delicate voice.

"I need you. Come in here. And bring a pen and paper."

"One moment, Edgar."

The buzzer clicked off, and Edgar could feel the room getting hotter. The more minutes that passed the worse he felt. *It's only a matter of time,* he thought fearfully.

Miss Gandy entered the room swiftly and quietly. An air of purpose filled her every move. Quickly, she set herself in the chair opposite his desk.

"What is it, Mr. Hoover?" she asked calmly.

"Roark is dead. So you know what that means."

She sat frozen in her seat, unable to move. Her mouth started to open to speak but she hastily caught herself and closed it.

"My goodness..." she whispered." Are they coming?"

"Not yet, but they will. We need to get all files with his name on them out of here. Right now."

"Where will you put them?" she asked, concerned.

"You will have to hide them for me, Miss Gandy. I suspect I will be followed from now on. I had the most affiliation with him. You will take the files and hide them for me. Put them with the other files Roark asked you to hold."

"Yes, Edgar."

She began writing furiously on the notepad she had on her lap.

She looked up, expecting more instruction, but Edgar just stared at her coldly.

"That is all, Miss Gandy. Pray those files are never found. From today forward, never mention the name Roark, or Kori, or the girl ever again."

"Yes, Edgar."

Edgar waved his hand for her to go. Quietly, she got up and left just as she had entered. A pit had been forming in her stomach during the whole meeting. Edgar opened a drawer on his desk and pulled out the envelope Roark had given him. The sight of it made him sick to his stomach.

She flopped down in her desk chair, staring at the work that was on her desk. Her notes appeared like scratches on the paper. Her mind went to what Roark had looked like, and the girl. *I wonder what happened to her,* she thought, knowing she had never heard her name.

The phone felt heavy in her hand. Slowly, she flipped through her Rolodex until she found the card she wanted.

Each ring on the other end sent a chill through her. She hoped the spot would be safe enough. Nothing ever seemed so certain. The voice on the other end made her jump, and everything fell back into place. "Good afternoon, this is the Watergate Hotel, isn't it?"

\\\\\\\\\\\\\\\\\\\\\\\\\\\\\\\\\\\\\

"I'd like to speak with my lawyer."

The question offended the sergeant staring at the man in cuffs in the interrogation room. The room was barren save for the metal table and two chairs on opposite sides. The man sat with his hands handcuffed together, resting on the table. The sergeant leaned against the wall casually.

"No lawyer is going to save you." The sergeant clicked his jaw, staring contemptuously at the man. "Courtesy of the one Mr. J Edgar Hoover, your fingerprints are all over the crime scene of Mr. Jack Ruby. That connects you to Ruby, who killed Lee Oswald outside the courthouse, who shot our beloved president. Not to mention Ruby shot Oswald after he already confessed to shooting Kennedy. There is no lawyer on Earth who could save you. "

"There is one who would try. I expect him shortly," said the man quietly.

"We'll be sure to roll out the red carpet. Let's start with why you did it. Why, Lee? Why Ruby? There must have been a simpler way to cover your tracks?" The sergeant pushed himself off the wall and slumped down into the opposing chair. The officer stunk of body odor. The stench made the man across from him lean back in his chair.

"It had to be that way, didn't it? History books won't remember my name. It will say Lee, and it will say Ruby, but not me. I did not engineer all this. I was a pawn just like them," said the man, pulling on his handcuffs. His wrists were red from straining them.

The sergeant looked over his shoulder at the one-way mirror behind him. He gave a look of disapproval and turned back to the man.

"You think I'm crazy?" asked the man.

"Yep, little bit. Listen. Let me tell you how this is going to work. It's over. You're done. We have a truckload of evidence placing you at the scene with Ruby. The DA isn't looking to cut any deals. The government wants this handled so the country can mourn. I am tasked with wrapping up the whole thing and being done with it."

The sergeant leaned forward. "You're going away for a long, long time my friend."

"My name is Andrew."

"If that's even your real name. What's your last name?"

"I can't tell you that."

"Sure you can."

"You wouldn't understand."

"I wouldn't, huh?"

Before the sergeant could continue, a knock pounded on the door and a deputy stuck his head in.

"What?" snapped the sergeant, "I'm in the middle of something here."

"Um, his lawyer is here."

"What? Nobody called anyone for a lawyer."

A man in a tan suit pushed passed the deputy and entered the room, smiling brightly.

"Sergeant, so pleased to finally meet you. My name is Adam, I am Andrew's attorney. Now if I may have a moment to confer with my client it would be much appreciated."

The sergeant stood up, dumbfounded. "Five minutes," he said angrily and rushed out of the room. The deputy smiled meekly and closed the door, leaving them alone in the room.

Andrew opened his mouth to speak, but Adam pressed a finger to his lips. He held up a briefcase he was holding opened it on the table. A slight ringing went off in Andrew's ears.

"There, that's better. Andrew.....what a mess you have made." His tone turned more serious.

Andrew couldn't find the words to speak.

"No reply? My profound disappointment in you cannot be overstated. I saw a great deal of potential in you, Andrew. My hope was that after this test I would offer you a job. However, that path is now closed. A rather large loop has been left open, and there is an active mover still inside it by the name of Kori. Had you not gotten lost, both Atlas devices would be accounted for and the loop closed," said Adam with a neutral expression.

"I'm sorry." said Andrew with tears in his eyes, his body curling over in his chair.

"No, you're not," said Adam quickly.

Andrew pulled himself up to look at him.

"Where is the girl? After the fiasco in the square she disappeared. Can you confirm that she now is in possession of Roark's Atlas?"

The question surprised Andrew. "No."

"Can you confirm if Kori advised the girl regarding your involvement with me?"

"No."

"Why did you approach Mary in Germany?"

"I don't know," said Andrew, broken.

"You don't know?" A tension came over Adam. The room seemed to vibrate in reaction to him.

The statement jarred Andrew back into reality. "Are you going to leave me here?"

Adam adjusted himself in his seat. "You know, in ancient times it was a worse punishment to condemn someone to live forever than to kill them. Did you know that? It was a far worse fate to live indefinitely than to have your life taken from you. You see the guilt as light at first. You carry on with your days only mildly aware of its pressure. However, as the years progress, the burden becomes an immovable anchor that you are powerless to budge. What a hell that would be." Adam stood up to collect his things.

"Is that what you will do with me?" asked Andrew, trembling with fear.

"You created your own hell here; what more could I do to you than leave you here to experience it?"

"I am still useful!" declared Andrew

"You were useful because of Atlas. What are you without it? Your usefulness was defined by its possession. Your fate is not tied to it, nor it to you."

"I know too much; just kill me. You can't leave me here," cried Andrew, desperate for a release from this torment.

"You don't get it, Andrew. This entire reality is just as irrelevant to me as you. What danger does any of it pose?" Adam turned to the door to leave.

"I saw Mary with a book, a journal of some kind. Does that mean anything to you?"

Adam stopped and turned to Andrew. A noticeable change occurred in Adam's face. "That can't be true. Roark betrayed a lot of people, but even he knows the consequences of that. Are you sure?"

"I am. Now get me out of here," said Andrew sternly.

"Thank you, Andrew. It appears you had one useful card left to play. Good-bye."

"Wait!" yelled Andrew as Adam closed the door on him. "Wait!" he yelled again, trying to stand, but his handcuffs kept him in place. His screams echoed through the door.

Out in the hall all time was frozen in place. The sergeant was frozen mid-step, along with every other officer in the hall. All the clocks were silent, their hands motionless. *Crantor made another copy,* he screamed in his mind. A panic came over him as he set his Atlas and disappeared. As the flash of blue went away the world was put back into motion.

\\\\\\\\\\\\\\\\\\\\\\\\\\\\

The flash seemed longer than usual, as her eyes took longer to focus. She found herself in the middle of a street. Quickly, she looked to see if any cars were coming, but the street was empty. Everything seemed strange, but beneath it all was a sense of familiarity.

The thought hit her as she realized she was on the same street the orphanage had been on, but the building she had come to love and hate for so many years wasn't there. Everything was the same—except where the building once stood was a row of houses. It was as if the building never existed.

A car was approaching as she quickly got over to the sidewalk. The driver stared curiously at her as they drove by. A cold feeling came over her as she almost missed the sight of the place she had called home for several years now. *What happened to it all? Where did it go?* she thought fleetingly.

The row of houses stretched down the street on both sides. Immediately, she realized she had nothing to her name anymore. All she had were the clothes on her back, a watch, and the journal. *What am I supposed to do?* she thought as her feet started carrying her down the sidewalk.

The air felt warm on her back as she kept going. Her eyes drifted from house to house, taking in everything new there was to see. Every house looked like it had been there for ages. So much is different. *How did this get here?* As she gazed over each window and every door her eyes fell to the numbers on the side of the mailboxes, and the sight stopped her in her tracks. *I know these numbers,* she thought, suddenly wanting to go back to the houses she had already passed.

"The room numbers," she whispered to herself, looking at the mailbox directly in front of her.

Her room number flashed in her mind. Room 717.

She reached out and felt the numbers on the mailbox in front of her. The numbers 700 felt cool to the touch. *I'm close,* she thought, looking around to see which way the numbers on the street went. She looked up the street to see the side she was on were all even numbers.

Quickly her feet took her across the quiet street again, pulling her to the other side. The number 709 was on the house directly in front of her, and she knew she was close. She turned to see the numbers went up to her right, and she began walking quickly past the next few houses. Then she found the one. 717.

She stared at the mailbox, unable to look up at the house for fear of what she would find. Slowly, she lifted her head and what she saw was a perfect, quaint little home. She had never seen the house before, but somehow she knew it would always look like this. It was a yellow house with a small front porch. It was exactly the way she always pictured it, night after night. A force wanted her to go to the door, but it dawned on her that it was still a stranger's home she was looking at.

Her body willed her forward despite her doubts. She had nowhere else to go.

As she stepped up on the porch a sudden comfort came over her. The boards creaked beneath her feet. A light breeze blew through the wind chime, and it felt like home.

She was lost in the moment as the door suddenly creaked and opened.

"What are you doing standing out here?" the voice said calmly.

The sight made her heart skip a beat.

It was Roark, but it wasn't. The man that stood before her was nearly thirty years older than the Roark she knew. His hair was white and his clothes were different, but she recognized the man inside.

"Roark?" she said, shocked.

The man let out a chuckle. "Is it not cool anymore to call me Dad? I thought you went out with your friends; did something happen?" he said with a look of concern coming over his face.

Words escaped her as she comprehended what he said.

"Dad?" she said awkwardly. "Dad!" She threw herself at Roark and hugged him as tightly as she could. Her heart was bursting with a sudden happiness she couldn't contain.

"You okay? Come on inside and have a seat. Something happen out there?" He stepped toward her and put his arm around her. His touch made her flinch, but she walked with him inside. A chill came over her as they went into the house.

The living room was brighter than she was anticipating, but for the first time in her life she felt like she was right where she was supposed to be.

"You feeling all right, honey?" he said as she sat herself down on the couch. "Your clothes look ragged. What happened to the clothes you went out in?"

Before she could answer, his cell phone rang. He quickly reached into his pocket and pulled it out. Hastily, he swiped the phone to answer. "Hello, this is Roark speaking."

The voice on the other end was barely audible.

"Yes. Yes, she is here. No need to worry, she's home. I don't know why she would leave you all there. You have a ride? Oh, good. I'll tell her. Thanks for calling. Bye, now." He clicked off the screen and put the phone down on the table next to the couch. "You had your friends worried. They said you just up and disappeared on them."

She couldn't make sense of how any of it was happening, but it was. She remembered Roark saying how it would be like I had always been here. *How can that be?* she thought. *It doesn't make sense. How is Roark here? He saw his father killed.*

"I didn't mean to leave them." Her own lie surprised her.

"What made you leave them so suddenly?"

"I wasn't feeling well. I wanted to come home." Saying the word *home* felt different. "I feel better now."

"Well that's good, but don't scare people like that."

"Can I ask you a question?"

"Of course you can."

"Your mom, Adele. She was in Pearl Harbor, right?" she asked slowly.

"Where did that question come from? But yes, she was. Why?"

"She knew a man named James Pilon. He was on the *Arizona*. He died, right?"

"Yes, I think. She did mention him before. She never talked about him much. She remembers that the night before he had asked her to stay the night with him aboard the ship, and

346

she turned him down. That's how she told it," he said, lost in thought.

"Can I talk to her?"

"She passed away some years ago, you know that," he said softly. "You remember that her picture is right there behind you on the sill."

She turned around and, sitting perfectly in its frame was the picture of Adele that Roark always had in his jacket pocket. The sight almost brought tears to her eyes again. *After the journey it went on, there it sits,* she thought, looking at the familiar face staring back at her.

"Is Grandpa still here?" she asked.

"What has gotten into you today? Dad died a few years before Grandma, honey. Why don't you remember that, did you hit your head on something?" he said, sitting up in his chair.

"I just forgot. I'm sorry. I'm not myself today." She noticed a picture of a man in uniform next to Adele. *I know him,* she thought to herself. "Warren," she said aloud.

"Quite the pair, they were."

Roark was standing over Mary, looking at the pictures with her. "Far as I know she never mentioned James to my father. A love lost in time, I suppose. It was a few years after that, they met. The rest is history from there. Well, assuming you remember that far," he said with a smile.

Roark returned to his seat.

"Is mom home?" she asked, afraid of what the answer would be.

"She is out at the store. Should be back soon," he said, pulling out the paper.

She stood from the couch, unsure of what to do.

"You should go lie down. Then you'll feel better," he said, flipping the next page. "Oh, I almost forgot—mail for you. It's on the table," he said casually.

All she could muster was a nod and a smile before she walked through the small hallway into the kitchen. The dining table in front of her made her stop. Three placemats on the table made her stop. She found herself smiling, thinking of how

347

long it had been since she saw three placemats on a table and knew one was for her. Oftentimes, she would think of what a family dinner would feel like. Her heart boosted with excitement, knowing she would finally get to know soon.

The envelope on the table looked worn and old. The edges looked battered, as if the letter had seen a great deal of travel. All that was written on the front was her name. No address.

Picking up the letter she felt the roughness of the paper. A mix of emotions raced through her as she struggled to grasp everything that had happened. *Is this a dream? Will I wake up now?* Questions continued to bombard her mind as she flipped over the letter and ran her finger through the top to open it. Pulling out the letter, the paper was almost like a parchment. She unfolded the paper to see it was a letter addressed to her.

Dear Mary-Ellen,

I hope this letter finds you, and finds you well at the one place you had been hoping to wind up all along—home. The past will always contain your success and your failures as they make you who you are, but let the future be what you make it. Of the many things I am sorry for, there is one thing I owe you the most and that is the truth. The truth is there is something terribly wrong with the world you know. Everything around you is the result of a carefully constructed lie. It is a lie built by one man, Adam.

The Atlas device you now hold is tied to the journal you carry. Each explains the other. The journal is what allowed Adam to create the world you now live in, and his sole purpose is to protect it.

I took the journal to try and undo all that was made in an attempt to give humanity the one thing most coveted by all—freedom. The world deserves a chance to make the future what they make it. You showed me that. I now need you to succeed where I failed.

I want to thank you for helping me find the path I lost, and I hope you find the happiness you deserve in this new life. To you this place is new and different. It will take some getting used to, but to everyone else you never left. Enjoy your new chance at the life you wanted. I'm sorry I can't be there in the way you remember me, but I will be in spirit.

Good-bye Mary-Ellen,

Love,

Dad

"Dad?" she yelled into the living room.

"Yeah," he yelled back over his paper.

"Who delivered this letter? There's no address on the front."

"Uh, it was a courier of some kind. Guy in a tan suit. Didn't ask for a name. Why?" he said, putting his paper down and turning to look at her.

Mary stormed into the living room with a heightened sense of purpose. She could feel her heart beating almost through her chest. She gripped the Atlas in her hand behind her back in the open position. "When did he leave?"

The End

Epilogue:

She found herself in the jungle, alone. The air was thick and hot, choking her all over. The sun pierced her skin as she walked through the thick brush. She was barefoot. The floor of the jungle crunched under each step. She looked down at her legs. They were covered in elaborate patterns of blue lines. The designs went up to her knees.

She realized she was in her dream. She quickened her step through the trees, but a gunshot stopped her. Just through the branches she saw him, the strange man from her dreams. His hair blond, slicked back over his head. His suit, a stone second skin that gripped his body all over. It looked light as a feather, but impenetrable as steel. The stone skin seemed to move on its own as the strange man stood over the monk. The monk doubled over on the ground, dead from the gunshot.

Before she could speak out the strange man suddenly turned and ran off into the jungle to her right. She raced forward into the clearing to help the monk, but it was too late. The monk reached out his hand, and a piece of parchment came tumbling out of it. The wind blew it over to her feet. She picked it up in her hand and saw the map she had seen numerous times before. It led to the journal. And she knew now what it was.

Immediately, she chased after the strange man through the trees. As she got closer to a clearing she started to hear screams and crashing sounds. An intense fear came over her as the dream had never gone on this long.

As she walked, she noticed something moving along the ground. A kind of black dust was swirling along the ground like a cloud drifting over everything. As she moved the cloud grew thicker and thicker, covering the ground. As she reached the edge of the field the cloud at her feet was so thick she couldn't see her feet anymore. The cloud went no higher than her knees, right to the top of the tattoos.

In the field the sight made her heart stop. Strewn across it was an endless display of bodies, mutilated and covered in blood. Farther out she saw vast pyramids and buildings stretching high up in the sky. It was a city, burning. Everywhere she looked was death. In the heart of this city was a wall of swirling black sand standing hundreds of feet tall. At its base was the strange man from her dream. After a moment she realized the cloud was reacting to the strange man's movements. As he moved his arms the dust concentrated into funnels and pulled men from the ground.

Mary inhaled, placing her hands over her mouth from the shock.

The man looked like he was conducting an orchestra, an orchestra of death. Each sway of his hand moved the dust in different ways, leveling the droves of men in front of him. He was singlehandedly exterminating the city.

She tried to take a step, but suddenly the strange man dropped his arms and the cloud instantly dropped to the ground. All the men that were in front of him were dead.

She found herself next to him now, and some time had passed. Suddenly, they were at an entrance to a great pyramid, but not like any structure she had seen before. Behind them lay countless dead bodies of the city's inhabitants. He walked inside without hesitation, deliberately stepping over each body with callous discontent.

She followed, carefully maneuvering between the bodies.

Inside was a great room with torches lit all around. Against the back wall was a golden wall with dozens of golden objects across it. As they approached her stomach turned as she recognized what they were looking at. Arranged on the wall were the Atlas devices, line after line, row after row of them covering the entire wall.

There must be a hundred, she thought, staring at the towering display.

The strange man approached the wall and plucked one of them from its resting place.

"Time to change the world," said the man, smiling at the golden watch.

He flipped over the watch to study it, and Mary saw something she hadn't seen before. The only time she ever saw the back of the watch the letters A-t-l-a-s were etched into the back, along with scrapes and smudges. Roark had taken it back from her before she could get a better look at it. Now she saw that there were more letters on the back.

Suddenly the strange man turned to look right at her. She screamed in fear as the room filled with a black cloud.

She awoke screaming, drenched in sweat. She was out of breath.

"My god," she said, thinking of the dream.

"The letters, it all makes sense. "She reached into her night stand and found the Atlas Roark had given her. She flipped the watch over to see the same five letters she knew were there, but in her dream it was eight letters. "Eight. A-t-l-a-n-t-i-s. Atlantis." She dropped the watch in horror. In the moonlight she saw the journal. *I know what I have to do,* she thought, fearing what would come next.